D1257473

The Last Scroll

A Novel

James Fricton

iUniverse, Inc.
Bloomington

The Last Scroll
A Novel

iUniverse books may be ordered through booksellers or by contacting:

iUniverse
1663 Liberty Drive
Bloomington, IN 47403
www.iuniverse.com
1-800-Authors (1-800-288-4677)

ISBN: 978-1-4759-7515-4 (sc)
ISBN: 978-1-4759-7516-1 (hc)
ISBN: 978-1-4759-7517-8 (e)

Library of Congress Control Number: 2013902163

Printed in the United States of America

iUniverse rev. date: 4/10/2013

Praise from readers...

"★ ★ ★ ★A book for the ages. Wisdom for a lifetime. A must read. It will change your life." Dr. Joseph Barber, Author, Clinical Psychologist, Bush Pilot, University of Washington, Seattle

"This book had me totally enthralled from the first pages. Beautifully written, I could see the story unfold in my mind. The beauty of the country, people, and culture combined with romance and suspense of this thrilling book was inspiring to read." David Wagner, Best selling author of "Life as a Daymaker"

"Beginning with murder, this book will surprise and excite you as it touches the boundaries of suspense, spirituality, love, science, and reality. It's an eye-opening opportunity to view and ponder the depth and breadth of our lives and the world we live in. Grab this book, it's well worth the ride!" Dr. Jeffrey Crandall, Underhill, Vermont

"A rare breed of a book that blends fiction and non-fiction with seamless transition. A masterpiece." Thomas Doyle, Teacher and Author, Boulder, Colorado

"Escape into a world where angels and demons collide with scientific reality. The book is deftly layered with romance, humor, insight, history, and adrenaline." Connie Brothers, University of Iowa, Iowa City, Iowa

"The words and people come to life. Some pages gave me chills and others tears. But all gave me insight." Susie Farquharson, Minneapolis, Minnesota

"A great story that will keep you turning the pages!" Roberto Bandini, Faenza, Italy

"One of those rare books that you sacrifice sleep for, just to get through one more chapter. I couldn't put it down." Kathryn Tagg, St. Paul

Author's Note

It has been a blessing to help many patients who live with chronic pain. Every week, I meet people who find the strength to see beyond the pain, the fear and the suffering to lead a good life filled with the seven Blessings of wisdom, health, happiness, prosperity, beauty, peace, and love. This book is their treasure of knowledge and experience that I share with you. May you embrace your angels and rid yourself of the demons. And, please, be a warrior of the *Last Scroll*, and not a zombie.

The Historical Perspective

The seven plagues described in the *Last Scroll* (ignorance, illness, depression, poverty, drought, hate, and war) have all increased in prevalence since the beginning of this century. The strategies described in each of the seven blessings (to achieve wisdom, health, happiness, prosperity, beauty, love, and peace) are well documented in the scientific literature and are referenced on the book's web site at www.thelastscroll.com.

The origin of the *Dead Sea Scrolls* is well documented. In AD 70, over one million men, women and children lost their lives during the siege of Jerusalem led by the Roman Emperor Vespasian's son and successor, Titus. This bloodshed earned for its triumphal leader a marble monument, the Arch of Titus, which still stands near the Forum in Rome. Following his father as emperor, Titus built the Temple of Peace on the Forum and the Coliseum in Rome to celebrate blessings of peace and happiness, and to remind the people of the sacrifices made in this war. Today, only the Wailing Wall of Jerusalem's Great Temple remains, while in Rome, the Arch of Titus, the Coliseum, and parts of the Temple of Peace still stand.

To protect their divine knowledge from the invading Romans, the spiritual leaders of ancient Jerusalem and the surrounding area hid over eight hundred manuscripts in remote caves off the coast of the Dead Sea. In the spring of 1947, within the disputed territory of the West Bank in the northwest corner of the Dead Sea, the first of these manuscripts were discovered and are now referred to as the *Dead Sea Scrolls*.

The history of their discovery and the surrounding controversy brings even more drama and intrigue to these ancient scrolls. Jum'a, a Bedouin shepherd from a village near Bethlehem, discovered several caves at the top of the Khirbet Qumran cliffs high above the mountain floor and the Dead Sea. With his cousin, Muhammed, they explored the treacherous terrain with its many eroded paths and water channels that traverse through the soft limestone rock cliffs looking for treasure. Instead, they discovered several ancient urns with scrolls rolled up inside. The scrolls were hand written in Hebrew, Aramaic, and Greek, on parchment and papyrus, and were written during the time of Jesus Christ and the Roman invasion.

Over fifty years have passed since the discovery of the *Dead Sea Scrolls*, but only photographs have been taken of them because they are so ancient and fragile that even direct light cannot shine on them. Most of them are in poor condition and survived only as tiny scraps. However, recent examination and translation of the early photographs have allowed teams of scholars from around the world to learn their wisdom.

These scholars have been completing the painstaking work necessary to assemble and translate some of the fragmented pieces of the *Dead Sea Scrolls*. There are over 800 separate manuscripts that date from a period ranging from about 250 BC to 100 AD, the period of the formation of the Old Testament before and during the formation of Christianity and rabbinical Judaism. There are also later documents thought to be an extension of the New Testament of the Bible.

Finally, in this century, nearly all of the manuscripts have been dated, assembled, translated and interpreted, but only a few have been released. As a result, they have been a source of heated political controversy in the Middle East. Even the ownership of the scrolls remains controversial. The Israeli Antiquities Authority currently holds them.

Of the scrolls, the *Copper Scroll*, labeled 3Q15, was unlike any of its companion manuscripts. It was written in a different form of Hebrew and was not made of leather or papyrus, but rather a sheet of almost pure copper. It was discovered in 1952, by an expedition sponsored by the Jordan Department of Antiquities. They found it in two parts because the thin copper sheet snapped into two sections and was found alone in an urn at the back of a cave. After almost two thousand years in the cave, the document was so badly oxidized that it would have crumbled if anyone attempted to open it.

Despite enthusiasm to reveal the contents, no method could be found that would preserve the *Copper Scroll* from harm, until it was decided to send the scroll to Manchester College of Technology in England. There, they opened it by using a precision saw, and cut it into sections to reveal the clay imprint of the text.

When it was deciphered, confusion spread among scholars. The contents were not literary or doctrinal in nature, like all of the other scrolls. The *Copper Scroll* simply listed sixty-four entries that described the locations of a treasure of incalculable value including gold, silver, aromatics, and most importantly, a divine knowledge. The search is on for the missing treasure of this *Last Scroll*.

Chapter 1. The Controversy

Julia Stone bites her lip as she stares out the window of the elegant, old world St. Paul Hotel. It's June, and the first signs of summer are appearing with the tree buds giving way to the light green leaves. The birds are chirping and the sun is warming the cool misty morning. She watches the protestors across the street from the hotel chanting, "RESIST! RESIST! RESIST!" They have gathered in the park for the past few days to protest the newly elected government's efforts to slash the bloated federal budget by shutting down safety net social programs for children and the elderly, the poor, the disabled, and the unemployed.

Julia quickly turns away from the window, pre-occupied with her own mission. She hurries to get dressed, wanting to catch Dr. Jack Killian before his landmark lecture this morning. He will be presenting the remarkable results of research involving the ancient knowledge found in the last of the *Dead Sea Scrolls* in a highly anticipated keynote address before the annual meeting of the International Society for Complementary Medicine Research. She grabs her cell phone, brief case, computer, and black jacket, and then heads for the elevator.

As she steps off the elevator on the ground floor, she sees Dr. Jack Killian in the distance. She hurries toward the lobby of the ballroom, hoping to catch him before his presentation.

Dr. Julia Stone is an attractive petite blonde with intense blue eyes. She is dressed professionally in a black business suit, fitting for the status of her faculty position in Medical Anthropology at Harvard. She likes to add a touch of flare to her wardrobe with a white silk shirt, partially unbuttoned, beneath the jacket, a silk scarf around her neck, and glossy white heels. In any crowd, she stands out as someone who knows what she is doing and where she is going. She smiles as she apologetically squeezes in the buffet line behind Dr. Killian and wastes no time in interrupting his casual conversation with others in the line.

"Excuse me. Dr. Killian!" She extends her hand to shake his, "Julia Stone. Do you remember me? I would like to meet with you after your presentation today? Would you have time?"

Dr. Killian is a distinguished looking older gentleman, with full white hair, an upright posture, a crisp clear voice, and a penetrating stare. He has an unusual level of vitality, clarity, and good looks for his age of sixty-five. As Director of the National Center for Complementary and Alternative Medicine of the National Institutes of Health, the CAM Center, he has been around for some time in academic and administrative positions.

He was one of the forces behind the CAM Center and consistently cites the facts—thirty-eight percent of U.S. adults and twelve percent of children use some form of alternative care. Consumers have spent thirty five billion dollars on visits to these practitioners and purchasing alternative health products and classes. The rising out-of-pocket costs for traditional medical and surgical care for Americans have lead to crippling financial burdens, medical debt, and avoidance of care causing consumers to shift their dollars into more self-directed health care. Because of this, he demands more funding for CAM research, and usually gets what he wants. Julia Stone worked with him this past year on a grant review committee to help determine which research proposals receive funding in this next year.

Dr. Killian steps out of the crowded line for a minute to talk to her. "Dr. Stone. Nobody can forget someone as charming as you. I enjoyed working with you last year. Thanks for your efforts. There were lots of good grants reviewed, and I'll have you know that we funded several of those that you reviewed. I'm glad you're here. You'll like this meeting."

Julia is surprised that he remembered the grants she reviewed and even more surprised they were funded, considering how competitive the process is.

"Dr. Killian, please call me Julia," she says cordially. "I've been following the research involving the last *Dead Sea Scroll* with great interest. The ideas behind this *Prophecy Scroll* are compelling and the controversy can't be ignored."

Dr. Killian does not shy away from controversy, and, in fact, he is known for inviting it into his lectures more than most accomplished scientists. "Then, you know about it," he replies. "The knowledge from the last scroll is surprisingly universal and timeless. The research on it is compelling albeit controversial."

"Yes. I've actually visited the Terme Project in Italy and have seen first hand the power of this knowledge to enhance health and well-being. But this research has stirred up a hornet's nest with the use of sacred religious documents as the basis for research into the human life force. Where are you going with it and how can I help?"

They politely step back into the breakfast line. He picks up some coffee and a whole-wheat muffin while she selects some orange juice and a fresh plate of cut fruit. They carry it over to one of the tall coffee tables in the lobby outside the ballroom to continue their conversation. On their way over, a larger gentleman with short-cropped blond hair accidently bumps into Dr. Killian and spills his coffee. The man apologizes and brings him a new cup. Dr. Killian thanks him, and returns to his conversation with Dr. Stone.

"Julia, and please call me Jack, as much as we know about treating disease, we know correspondingly little about enhancing health. It seems like we're in a losing battle. The *Prophecy Scroll* may wake people up to the advancing plagues in almost every domain of our lives and the slow dramatic decline of our planet. It provides tangible actions for individuals to prevent this demise and usher in a whole new era of promoting health and wellness, as well as, support peace and prosperity. But this will occur only if we prove it with science. I welcome the conversation, and the controversy."

"Dr. Killian, ah, Jack, the research you're funding is radical. You've even had threats. But for what? Measuring the human spirit? Using ancient documents in research? I don't understand what the controversy is. The researchers are simply applying science to test the wisdom of texts from the Biblical era. Yet, some call the research blasphemy. Others say its heresy. Some believe it's a threat to modern religion. Most call it a bunch of hogwash and mumbo-jumbo spirituality. Aren't you afraid of . . ."

He interrupts her with an intense look, "Julia, I welcome skepticism, and the threats are empty attempts at getting publicity for their political cause. Many had the same reaction with advances such as evolution, use of stem cells, and global warming. They're missing the point. Some people fear that science may prove that some of the basic tenets that underlie their faith and beliefs are different than scientific reality. They also fear the political change that may come with these new realities."

"They're fanatics," Julia concludes as she sips her juice. "They have their own political and ideological agendas to push."

"Yes, perhaps. But, it's often that age-old conflict between science, religion, and politics that can stir people the most." Killian drinks his coffee after taking a bite from his muffin. "Galileo, Newton, Darwin, and many other scientists were all persecuted when their science conflicted with the ideology of the day. Religion seeks knowledge through revelation, faith, and beliefs, whereas the scientific method relies on reason and empirical observation. Politics promotes whatever prevailing view is held dear by the power brokers at the time. They often clash, particularly as science advances and either validates or refutes long held practices and beliefs."

"I understand, but death threats?"

"People get their undies in a bundle for many reasons," he laughs. Then, he says more seriously, "You've seen the results at the Terme. The human spirit is a powerful force and the basis underlying most religions. However, when you threaten their religion, you threaten them. People are so volatile these days. Nearly every city has violent protests. Just look outside in the park across the street. People want change and social media spreads the message so fast. Surprisingly little things can trigger widespread unrest. We live in turbulent times. So, I'm not surprised some people take offense at this project."

"But this is about discovery," she says as she takes a bite of the cut peach in the salad. "Most people want a better understanding of the universe. This is the basis for improving life on earth."

"Not if it forces them to change their beliefs or threaten their livelihood," he says as he drinks more coffee. "The project is answering one of the greatest puzzle in all of mankind. What makes life? What makes us, as living beings, different than a collection of chemical reactions? And what exactly leaves us in death and relegates living things to a pile of dirt when they die?"

Julia listens intently with excitement in her eyes. This is exactly the research she wants to dedicate her career to.

He finishes his coffee. "We all recognize the existence of the living spirit, the soul, the life force, the chi, or however you refer to it. We need to know what this quintessential force of energy is that defines life, and as important, how do you measure and enhance it? Nobody has done so until now. I'm not talking about Stars Wars' 'let the force be with us.' This is Nobel Prize type research. The researchers in Italy have shown that our spiritual energy and its daily fluctuations are real and measurable. On top of that, the profound impact that the *Prophecy* principals had in strengthening this energy has been as much a surprise to me as anyone. And we are only at the beginning. But that's why the Terme Project raises such fury in some people. They feel as if their religious foundations are shaking right underneath them. But this is a battle I'm willing to fight. We must move forward."

Other attendees, standing at tables close to the pair, begin to listen in, as the conversation grows more intriguing.

Julia stops eating, listens intently, and says nothing. She feels Killian's frustration at the weight of the criticism against him.

He looks her directly in the eyes and states emphatically, "Listen! I'm the first to debunk these questionable theories without a scientific basis. We need more research to improve our understanding of the human spirit and strategies to enhance our well-being even if it flies in the face of religious dogma and political agendas. Diligent investigators, Paolo Nobili and Vanessa Venetre, have uncovered something special in their study of human energy fields. Maybe, for the first time, this elusive human life force can be measured. The technology they have is revolutionary. The wisdom unveiled in these manuscripts is unparalleled. The results are impressive. I'm excited to present some of it today, and open a few more minds."

"I agree, the research is remarkable," she replies as she finishes her breakfast and dabs her lips with a napkin. "The measurement of spiritual energy and its correlation with the daily actions in our lives is astounding. I found the wisdom in the *Prophecy Scroll* was not only profound but also surprisingly contemporary and universal. And they only touched on four of the ten manuscripts. The *Seven Realms of Life*, the *Seven Beasts*, the *Rules of the Blessings*, and the *Blessing of Health* are each remarkable in their own way. Do you know when they will obtain the others?"

Killian looks at his watch and feels an urgency to put the final touches on his slides and meet with the moderator before his presentation. "I'm sorry, Julia, but I need to go. I relish the opportunity to be the first speaker to wake up the audience and set the tone for the conference."

"Of course," she apologizes. "You must go. Thank you for the conversation."

They gather their things and walk into the ornately decorated grand ballroom as he answers her last question, "The remaining manuscripts are being translated by scholars around Italy who understand the ancient Hebrew languages. When we have all ten, I believe it will provide us with a set of universal truths in enhancing the human spirit and can bring the seven Blessings into all of our lives."

"I'm with you," she responds enthusiastically. "I have a grant in preparation right now, and will need your advice before I send it in."

"We welcome your participation in this research. I'll present some of the results in the next hour. We can talk later about how to improve your grant's funding potential. Does lunch work?"

"Lunch works fine for me."

"Nice talking to you," he shakes her hand before walking through the giant double doors towards the front of the spacious lecture hall. "See you in the lobby at noon."

"Yes! Thank you, Dr. Killian. It will be a pleasure to hear you speak today. Good luck with your presentation."

She watches him walk to the podium stage and considers what a great setting this is for a great man. The ballroom is decorated with three wrought iron and gold leaf crystal chandeliers that span the recessed ceiling and sparkle with color. The walls have black iron wall sconces, red velvet drapes, and gold-trimmed mirrors that reflect the images of the radiant chandeliers and the high energy of the conference.

There is much anticipation for his lecture, as the audience begins to stroll in and find their seats. They have all heard about the controversy involving the research and now want to listen to Dr. Killian directly and make up their own minds about it.

She stands in the middle aisle watching him shake hands with the moderator. She is beyond excited to have finally opened up this conversation with the person at the National Institutes who can be most influential in helping her research get off the ground.

As Killian ends his conversation with the moderator, the man with short-cropped blond hair watches them from the back of the ballroom. He tucks his polo shirt neatly into his jeans, and slowly sips his coffee. Those who commit heresy and oppose the Manifesto will perish, and he will be happy to see it happen. It's been planned perfectly for the morning, in front of a large crowd, when it's least expected. There will be no fingerprints, no blood, no DNA, no links, and no evidence—other than the Manifesto left behind by the Messenger to warn others on the same path. He is just one of hundreds attending the conference. He will find the crime as shocking as everyone. He smiles at the brilliance of the plan.

Chapter 2. The Nightmare

Minneapolis, Minnesota
Sunday Morning

Ryan Laughlin is frozen in fear, with his heart beating like a jungle drum. He peers up the circular marble staircase in panic. He hugs the center support with his back as he maneuvers up the slippery and worn stone steps to escape the unknown assailant chasing him. His fear of heights increases his anxiety with each step. He hears the footsteps close behind him, and he can almost feel the assailant's breath on his legs. But when he looks behind, he only sees flashes of the dark figure chasing him up the stairs. The steps are tilted and awkward, with only a few narrow windows to let light in from the outside.

The claustrophobic staircase causes a panic as if the walls are closing in on him. He feels a nauseating unsteadiness as the building is leaning to one side, ready to fall like a tree cut off at its base. He cannot go back down the stairs for fear of being caught, and he does not want to go up because of his growing fear with each step. He keeps his back to the inside post and moves on. He takes a quick look out the window and realizes that he is nowhere near the top. His head spins.

He notices his shoelaces are untied. Damn it! He backs off and leans against the center of the circular staircase, gasping for breath. He ties the laces in a hurry to avoid tripping. He hears the pursuer continuing after him, faster and faster. His mouth is dry and his heart pounds. He is sweating profusely. He doesn't want to get caught, so he takes two steps at time. He moves up and up. The steps never seem to end. The staircase becomes more narrow and unsteady. He feels it sway back and forth. He is terrified and not thinking clearly. He looks down to see his shoelaces untied again. Damn it! His fear escalates as he hears the pursuer around the corner. He runs like a madman up the remaining stairs.

He steps on the loose shoelace and falls, scraping his knee. He tumbles down the staircase toward the menacing figure. He hurries to get up only to hear the pursuer even closer behind him. He catches a glimpse of the figure. He runs again, up and up the increasingly narrow and never ending staircase. He can hardly fit between the walls, and each step becomes taller and taller, harder to climb as the staircase waves back and forth.

In a wild, fear stricken panic, he leaps up the last few steps, and finds himself at the top of the staircase on an open balcony looking over the rooftops of an old medieval town. The balcony is unstable and waves back and forth from the wind. He gasps for a breath that never comes. He looks back and sees the pursuer arriving at the top of the stairs. He is blinded by the bright sunlight streaming through the opposite side of the balcony and cannot make out who it is.

The pursuer is coming closer and reaches out to grab him. He runs towards the edge of the balcony, but again, steps on his loose laces and trips. Damn these things! The tower sways in the direction he stumbles. The force of gravity knocks him over the cast iron railing as he desperately tries to grab it, only to find that the sweat of his hands makes the railing slippery.

He becomes dizzy with fear as he dangles from the railing high above the ground, desperately trying to pull himself up. He slowly loses his grip on the railing. He screams at the top of his lungs as he falls in slow motion towards the stone surface below. He looks up to see the pursuer looking down on him. The expression on the pursuer's face is one of horror. It's his late wife, Sophia. She is reaching out over the balcony to save him, but he is in free fall. Nobody can save him now.

It is 4 am on Sunday morning, and Ryan Laughlin wakes abruptly from his recurring nightmare, his heart is racing and sweat is pouring from his face. He can't catch his breath. He sits up with a deep fear gripping him. There is no way he can get back to sleep. His guilt over his wife's death is overwhelming. He goes through the same tormenting thoughts every day. For God's sake, he's a physician. He should have known. He should have detected Sophia's breast cancer earlier, but he didn't. He hates the failure. The agony. Damn it. He misses her so dearly.

The nightmares of losing Sophia do not stop. He rationalizes that its rightful punishment. He desperately needs more sleep before the demanding day coming up, but he cannot go back to sleep. He thinks about his patients who use his prescription drugs for sleep, for anxiety, for depression. He's just like them. He lays awake for hours with the same thoughts running through his mind. It's a never-ending tape. He tries to forget, but he keeps waking up to the obvious. He failed.

And now, his guilt and depression dominate much of his thoughts and mood. Caffeine keeps him alert and awake during the day, but causes more sleeplessness at night. He continues as if nothing is wrong, but it's a cycle that's going downhill and gaining speed. He must do something, but what should he do? He's just like his patients. They come to him for help. They're stuck in their lives. All he does for them is give them a few seconds of advice and another pill. He becomes part of their problem. He perpetuates their dependence. The real problem is that they need to deal with their issues and change their lives. But how can he help them do that when he can't even help himself? And he simply doesn't have the time in his packed clinic schedule. Even if he had the time, what would he do? It all seems so hopeless.

Ryan gets out of bed and drags himself to the bathroom. He is tired and alone. It is Sunday, the day of the Lifetime Fitness Triathlon. It is early, 5 am now, and the last thing he wants to do today is a triathlon. He chooses to ignore the fact that he pushes himself to extremes in everything he does, including his remorse.

He has become what he tries so hard to keep his patients from becoming— a distraught, depressed, self-absorbed, insomniac whose life is out of balance. And like most patients, he covers up his depression and stress with cynicism, obsessions, and extreme activities. In his case, its biking, caffeine, patient care, and ruminating about his loss.

Today, though, he just wants to be alone in his misery and prepare for his clinical schedule this week. He has lots of patient records to review. Yet, he is scheduled to bike in the triathlon today with his buddies. He checks the Weather Channel hoping the weather will help him. Sunny, cool, no rain, and no cancellation. It's perfect weather. Damn it. He doesn't want to do this today—not a triathlon. Why the hell did he ever sign up for this punishment? He could pull out, but the hazing from the guys would be too much. It's one of their biggest events of the summer, and he can't let them down. Shit! He just has to buck up and do it.

His heightened sense of rationalization, denial, and self-control takes over. He realizes that he does need to exercise today, and the triathlon, although a bit overkill, will wake him up and give him energy. All he needs to do is the biking part. Ned and Randy will do the rest. They live to compete and have been training for months. He must go down to Lake Nokomis, and just get it done. He begins to put on his gear when the phone rings.

It's Randy. "Hey Buddy. Get your skinny butt out of bed. Are you ready for the big event today?"

"To tell the truth, I'm a bit sluggish this morning. Let me apologize now before I let you down."

"You always say that, and then you go out and bust your butt. I don't expect you'll let us down. Just pour down a few cups of your cappuccino brew and you will be raring to get down here."

"I've had my first cup already. I better have another. See you in a few minutes."

Chapter 3. The Lecture

ST. PAUL, MINNESOTA
SUNDAY MORNING

It's 8:20 am, and the St. Paul Hotel ballroom is buzzing from the excitement of being minutes away from the onset of a landmark meeting on cutting edge international research that integrates modern medicine with ancient knowledge. The protests outside of the hotel make a dramatic backdrop to the conference that was organized to help the very people who are demonstrating.

The organizer of the meeting and President of the Society, Dr. James Jacobs, arrives at the podium. He shuffles his notes and signals to the conference leader and the audio-visual staff to start the recording. He waits a few minutes, and then waves to get the attention of the audience of about eight hundred people. He asks them to be seated.

"Welcome to the tenth annual meeting of the International Society for Complementary Medicine Research. We have an exciting program this year. Not only compelling science, but controversial theories. Our first speaker is sure to generate much lively discussion to kick off the conference."

Dr. Jacobs looks around the room at the eclectic international audience with people from the United States as well as almost every continent of the world.

"It is my pleasure to introduce my distinguished colleague and friend, Dr. Jack Killian. He is Deputy Director of the National Center for Complementary and Alternative Medicine and has been with the National Institutes of Health for the past twenty-five years. He has received multiple national awards including the Merit and Director's Awards, the Public Health Service Special Recognition Award, and the Superior Service Award. He is board-certified in internal medicine, and has pursued additional training in mind-body medicine. His talk today is entitled, *When Science and Religion Clash: The Truth and Consequences of the Dead Sea Prophecy.*"

Jack Killian, dressed in a sharply cut, beige camel hair suit, white shirt, and red tie, walks across the stage with a large collage including a photo of the last *Dead Sea Scroll*, a map of the Mediterranean Region showing Italy and the Dead Sea, an illustration of the scroll's seven-headed beast, and the seven-sided symbol of the Seven Realms.

The collage provides a stunning setting for his presence at the meeting. The recent article in *The New Yorker* about the controversy surrounding the research on the *Prophecy Scroll* has generated strong interest in the conference, and has brought in a diverse group of publicity seekers, true academics, public policy geeks, and religious fundamentalists.

Dr. Killian looks out over the audience. They are buzzing in anticipation. He scans them carefully to see who has angels supporting them and who has demons haunting them. He sees a few beady red demon eyes and smiles. This may be an active group today.

"Good morning, colleagues. It's a real pleasure to be here today and present some of the most cutting-edge research coming out of our Institute. We sponsor research to study alternative strategies to improve our health. These strategies include a group of health care practices that are beyond conventional medicine. Some tap into ancient knowledge. And some are even considered futuristic in nature. But none, to the dismay of our science fiction enthusiasts out there, reach all the way to Star Trek."

There are smiles and a quiet laugher in the room.

"Before I present the research, I have a simple question that I want you to answer that will provide the basis for this presentation."

He pauses, looks around the audience, and then asks, "Tell me how do you define a good life?" He waits for someone to respond. No hands go up. "You mean we have a whole room filled with the brightest minds of our age, and you don't know? Come on! You must either be shy or you've not had your coffee yet."

The crowd sits up and pays closer attention to Killian. He asks again, "For each of you. What factors comprise a good life? Please, tell me." He scans the ballroom for signs of life among the diverse array of people there.

Some younger members of the audience are dressed fashionably in colorful dresses, shirts, and jeans while a broad swath of people have on plain professional suits and ties. There is a hand raised at the back of the room by a young woman wearing a professional, but elegant, women's suit.

He walks from behind the podium and points to the woman who raised her hand. "Thank you, my bold friend."

"Happiness. If I'm happy, my life is good and the opposite is true, too."

"Happiness. Excellent. Anybody else?"

Another hand goes up in the middle of the room, an older man with a full head of grey hair, dressed casually in a contrasting black sweater. Dr. Killian points towards him to acknowledge. All eyes turn to focus on his response.

"Along the same lines, health. When I feel healthy and robust, my life is good."

"Yes, health. I agree. What other aspects?"

Another hand from a young woman with a sporty outfit that includes a beige Sochi sweater and black tights stands up. She's smiling as she says, "If I can get my sweetheart back."

"Where is he?" Dr. Killian asks.

"He's in the military, stationed abroad right now," the woman replies.

"I hope he's safe. Love is an important part of a good life," he replies. "What else?"

The crowd begins to relax as more hands go up. One states the need to have peace in his life, another described prosperity and financial security, and others comment on eating well, having a good job, family and friends, beauty, a healthy environment, and helping others. When he was finished, he had a long list to present back to the group.

"Thank you. We know that we all strive to have a good life. Interestingly, the ancient *Dead Sea Scrolls* manuscript called the *Prophecy*, written two thousands years ago, lists seven Blessings necessary to achieving a good life—and you mentioned them all. These seven Blessings include wisdom, health, happiness, prosperity, beauty, peace, and love. You may think not much has changed in two thousand years. But it does beg the question—is there a universal knowledge that transcends time, place, and humanity? A knowledge, which if discovered, would give all people the capacity to achieve each of these Blessings and a good life?"

The whole audience, both strong believers and skeptics, listens intently to what Dr. Killian has to say. The room is still while Dr. Killian introduces an entirely new era of insight and understanding of the human condition. But he knows that this effort will not go unopposed. There are powerful forces trying to keep this knowledge hidden from the masses for their own reasons. But he ignores the potential threat. For, this is his moment, his time of glory, and he speaks with conviction and confidence. This keynote will blow people's minds.

"The research I'm about to present, if successful, will not only contribute to improving the well-being of the people of the world, but it may shake the very foundations that form the basis of understanding illness and health, and as importantly, our humanity. Why? Let me explain. Historically, most innovation in the diagnosis and treatment of disease has focused on the biochemistry of the body and resultant pharmacological or surgical manipulation of tissues. Now, this research, funded by the Institute, provides a scientific basis for a new approach to understanding ourselves that is based on. . ."

The room of hundreds is silent as he shows a set of slides of a glowing energy field surrounding a smiling boy, an older lady, and a happy dog. "The measurement and manipulation of the electromagnetic energy fields of living things. Let me explain. Ancient civilizations believed the world was made of four core elements—earth, air, fire, and water. However, the heavens, they claim, were made of something very different, and called it the 'fifth essence.' They were right. Recent research in nuclear physics on the Higgs Boson, or the so-called God particle, has now revealed that everything, from the chair you are sitting on here on earth to the space of the farthest galaxy, is made of atoms that are, in essence, energy. Thus, the core of our molecular make-up is all energy. This energy, which perhaps equates to the fifth essence, may be a living being's equivalent to the life force, or the living spirit. With recent sophisticated technology, this energy is measurable with frequencies of different dimensions that reflect different Realms of our lives. The research on this energy, which I will present in the next hour, has demonstrated success with animal studies, and now, human trials are underway. It is nearly ready for wider commercial application."

He lets the audience think about the next slide. It presents one word, synchronicity. "Do you ever wonder why there are certain coincidental events that are beyond chance, or why you connect with some people and not others? Why do some people drain you and others uplift you? Why there is love at first sight? Why do some songs resonate with you perfectly? Or, you may feel so good in certain natural settings? Each of these phenomena is called synchronicity. We have evidence that they are related to the confluence of frequencies of electromagnetic waves that we all emit, and to some extent, can sense. Maybe, it is the elusive sixth sense, that ability to perceive the subtle intuitive dimensions of the unseen world that are not detected by our other five senses."

The audience is watching Killian with an unusual attentiveness for so early in the morning. He turns to direct his pointer to a slide showing a kaleidoscope of monarch butterflies migrating south. "A monarch butterfly can sense the magnetic fields of the earth and are able to travel thousands of miles during the winter to find exactly the same place in Mexico every year. All energy has vibration, a frequency. If two people are vibrating at the same rate, they form a connection, an attraction to each other without realizing the underlying reasons. We connect with other people because our frequencies are literally in tune with that of others. Some people have a more developed sense than others. If we could understand, perceive, measure, control, and enhance our own energy levels, then, perhaps we could gain insights into ourselves that we have never had previously. Whether you want to call it energy, spirit, life force, essence, chi, or soul, we all know deep within us that it exists. And if we broaden our understanding of it, I believe this species called Homo Sapiens has a much better chance of surviving the next few Millenniums."

Dr. Killian turns back to the audience and peers out, pleased at their stirring interest as he presents his next two slides of a *Dead Sea Scroll* and the *Copper Scroll*. They have been impatiently waiting for his first mention the controversial use of these ancient manuscripts and Killian wants to get right into it.

"What is remarkable about this research is that it has foundational elements based in the ancient knowledge from the *Prophecy Scroll*. These manuscripts were discovered after scholars at the Vatican broke the code within the *Copper Scroll* to identify the location of the last scroll discovered. This scroll was hidden securely from the Romans in 70 A.D. alone in a remote cave within the Khirbet Qumran cliffs high above the Dead Sea."

He shows a slide of the caves above the Dead Sea and a photo of a colorfully detailed ancient urn. "Of all the scrolls discovered, the last scroll was the most unique. It was found within the most beautiful of all urns decorated with colorful graphics of a beast with seven heads dueling with angels from heaven and laden with a treasure of jewels, gold, and silver for the ages."

Almost like an entertainer, he walks out in front of the podium and personally directs his next comment to what seems like each member of the audience. "You need to know about the *Prophecy Scroll!* This manuscript not only forecasts the demise of our current world from the Seven Plagues, which they called the Seven Beasts, that have indisputably already begun. But it also leads us down a path of salvation through the divine knowledge of the seven Blessings."

He directs their attention to the next slide of a man lying down within a piece of equipment that resembles an open Magnetic Resonance scanner. "We are validating the wisdom of this manuscript through a new technology that detects the electromagnetic energy fields intimately associated with all living things. We can now measure this energy with a highly innovative technology that resembles a magnetic resonance scanner. Shown here is the spin-exchange relaxation-free, or SERF atomic magnetometer. The SERF measures magnetic fields by using lasers to detect the interaction between alkali metal atoms in a vapor and the magnetic field. This highly sensitive equipment can detect static and fluctuating electromagnetic fields which may become a more accurate and sensitive measure of changes that occur between health and illness."

Killian scans the room to appraise the initial reaction of the audience. He is pleased with their attentiveness and the energy they display. Like most speakers, he picks out a few in the audience to look at directly. He finds Julia and smiles at her. She is embarrassed to be singled out, but smiles back at him. He then scans down the first rows and sees the man with short-cropped blond hair who bumped into him earlier sitting in the second row looking at him with a crooked grin that could easily be mistaken as a sneer. How weird! He is sitting slouched in his chair with his legs stretched out and his arms folded. There is no note taking, no program, no brief case, and no computer. He is just sitting there, yawning and seeming bored. Dr. Killian dismisses him as odd, and continues with his talk.

A woman to his left in the audience, dressed elegantly in a dark burgundy suit with black trim, low cut black blouse, and a matching skirt, raises her hand. "Excuse me for interrupting, but what you are saying is astonishing, if it is true. How do you know that it's the spirit that you are measuring?"

Killian smiles as he appreciates her question. He responds by turning to the next slide showing a graph with multiple parallel colored lines from energy field measurements. "Good question. You decide for yourself. This slide shows the strength, direction, and flow of these energy fields generated using this technology in lab animals. The coils in this scanner are sensitive enough to measure fields as low as 10^{-18} Tesla. For comparison, a typical refrigerator magnet produces 10^{-3} Tesla, and some processes in humans and animals produce fields between 10^{-9} T and 10^{-6} T. The SERF magnetometer can operate at room temperature, allows measurement of the fields, and eliminates interference of the earth's magnetic field. This technology has been applied to animals, and now for the first time, to humans."

He extends his hand towards the woman who asked the question and says with a slow and clear articulation. "So your question is quite relevant, are the energy levels simply a reflection of the biochemical changes in the body? Or, are we measuring something more than chemistry? Are we measuring a human spirit? That is the question that needs an answer."

Dr. Killian takes a drink of water. He pauses to let this sink in as he shows the next slide showing a graph of colored lines with seven peaks. The bright ballroom is buzzing with side conversations. He directs the red laser pointer at each of the seven peaks and tells the story with the excitement of a kid.

"Look at this spectrum of SERF energy scans from a series of animal experiments. Note the seven primary energy concentrations reflected by the different frequencies and colors. These scans measure the level of energy at each center as well as the flow of energy in and out of the center. These fields appear to be an earlier indication of dysfunctional or diseased tissue rather than biochemistry and physiology. Look at this next series of slides."

He puts up a slide with graphs that have three parallel colored lines, and explains in a more serious tone, "On this slide, note the overall mean scores of energy levels in the healthy rats. Now, look at this next slide comparing it to rats with experimentally induced tumors before the tumor shows up, and then, when the tumor appears. The differences between energy levels of these three stages are dramatic and statistically different. The implications of these findings are significant. First, using changes in our energy fields, we can detect conditions such as cancer, heart disease, and even depression earlier in its development, before physical or chemical changes occur. Think about this. Our energy levels, our spirit, can tell us when we will become ill, well before it happens. This will revolutionize prevention strategies and dramatically enhance our perception of what health is. The next series of experiments have focused on the specificity of this energy within each of the Seven Realms of our lives and how our life activities change it."

Killian's lecture is interrupted by another question coming from an older man in the front of the room wearing a jacket and tie. He boldly stands up to speak, "But your results only suggest a correlation exists between the energy and the pathologic condition. They could be generated from biochemical and physiologic changes. But how do you validate that it is in fact energy of the human spirit?"

"Excellent point, Sir!" Dr. Killian smiles as he looks at the man hoping more of these probing questions arise. "The validation process involves time consuming measurements associated with first animal studies, and then, human studies. We measured energy in and energy out, both during life activities and after death in rats. The total energy from body physiology remained relatively constant and did not correlate with the electromagnetic fields we measured. Both the strength and frequency of the energy fluctuated considerably based on many factors including when we simulated behavioral, social, environmental, and pathological states. But after death of the animal, the energy we measured from life force itself disappeared, while the total energy measured from the animal's physical carcass remained constant. There is a life force beyond biochemical changes occurring—and it is measurable."

Dr. Killian finds the glass of water on the podium and sips it to remedy his unusually tight throat. It is getting progressively worse as he speaks. He wonders whether the caffeine level was too high in his coffee. He clears his throat and continues with his lecture. Another man on the left side of the room, with a balding head, directly under the glowing light of the chandelier, raises his hand. Dr. Killian notes to himself that the glow of his head matches that of his energy and smiles to acknowledge him. The man stands up to ask, "Dr. Killian, this does seems a bit like the Star Trek tricorder to me." There is a laugh from the back of the room, and an increase in buzz between members of the audience. "Perhaps, this can be applied to laboratory animals, but it is a far stretch from applying this technology to the complex physiology of humans. Can this be done?"

"Good timing, Sir. Your question brings me to my next set of slides."

He shows the colorful picture of the energy fields from two SERF scans side by side. "See this scan of two subjects. Note how the energy level is different in subject Linda, on the left, compared to subject Ruth. Ruth's scan reflects lower energy in the Emotional Realm. She has clinical depression compared to Linda. This finding has been repeated in a pilot study of a larger sample of people with depression."

He clicks the controller to the next slide. "Watch this video of a patient at the Terme in Brisighella, Italy using a SERF scanner. The ability to detect changes in energy level and flow allows a person to determine what factors will diminish or enhance their energy."

He starts the video and takes another drink of water. The audience is watching intently. "See the pulsation of energy from the body associated with meditative prayer and deep breathing. See the increase in energy, as she gets deeper and deeper into relaxation. Then, see how the energy stops flowing, and in fact, diminishes as the staff person interrupts her. It is such a dramatic shift. The staff was telling her that she was doing it all wrong. This, of course, was not true, but it did illustrate the flow of energy in and out based on the circumstances in this case. They also found that changes in cognitions, behaviors like diet and sleep quality, emotional states, relationships, and even environmental factors could influence this energy up and down. We all know this is intuitively true."

Dr. Killian sees another hand raised from a man at the back of the room. He is dressed in a white shirt, red tie, and black suit. He stands up to ask, "How does this research have anything to do with the *Dead Sea Scrolls* which were written nearly two thousand years ago? It seems like quite a stretch."

Killian loves this question. He stands taller and the enthusiasm in his voice ratchets up. "As I mentioned, the last of the *Dead Sea Scrolls* called, the *Prophecy Scroll was* discovered among the riches of an era. It includes a total of ten manuscripts with the first four having been assembled and translated."

He clicks to the next slide, a circle with a seven-sided heptagon within it.

"The first manuscript is called the *Seven Realms of Life*. This is the symbol of the *Prophecy*. Each point of the heptagon represents one of the *Seven Realms of Life* and the lines represent connections between Realms. With each Realm there is a Plague that reflects lower energy and a Blessing that reflects higher energy within the Realm. These Realms of our lives are well known to us, and include the mind, body, emotion, spirit, lifestyle, and the people and natural environment around us."

Killian watches the diverse reaction of the audience as he shows a slide of the seven-headed beast. Some are startled, others intrigued, and a few shake their head. "The second manuscript, called *The Seven Beasts*, predicts Seven Plagues affecting each Realm in our current world. The seven-headed beast is a metaphor that represents the Seven Plagues that are haunting mankind. To the surprise of everyone involved in the project, the Plagues are noted to begin not during their lifetime but rather a thousand years after the first millennium. That would be year 2000."

Killian notices a couple dozen new arrivals standing in the back of room looking for scarce open seats while listening intently. "The third manuscript includes the *Rules of the Blessings* and presents seven Rules that provide insight into how the human spirit is depleted or enhanced. Then, there are the *seven Blessings of Life* manuscripts. The *Blessing of Health* has been completed. The *Blessings of Wisdom, Happiness, Prosperity, Beauty, Peace, and Love* are currently being translated by scroll scholars in locations around Italy as shown in this slide. Coincidentally, the locations involve ancient cities of Italy that throughout history have been shown to have high energy in each of the respective Realms. Remember the concept of synchronicity. It plays a role in how communities function also."

The audience is silent as they digest this information. Killian looks at the podium clock, and sees that he is right on schedule. He shows a slide of the four sets of seven manuscripts.

"Seven Realms, seven Plagues, seven Blessings, and seven Rules. What are they and what do they really mean? How do they relate to human spiritual energy? We do not fully understand their potential, but if our research confirms our hypothesis, the results are earth shattering. This divine knowledge accurately reflects the changes we see in the human spirit."

Dr. Killian looks down, takes a drink of water, and loosens his tie. He is beginning to feel queasy. The people in the front row do not notice, except for one. The man in the front row with the short-cropped blond hair smiles to himself.

Killian perks up a bit to show a slide of a single number seven in Edwardian script. "The use of the number seven throughout the manuscripts is also interesting. It may have the same religious significance as the seven days of Genesis and the seven seals of Revelation. In much biblical literature, the number seven is symbolic of not only divine insight, but also reflects the concept of integration. Does it mean that we, as individuals, need to bring together and integrate the different Realms of our lives to fully understand ourselves? When we know each aspect of ourselves completely, are we better able to meet our potential and achieve the good life that is available to us all? These are relevant questions for each and every one of us."

Dr. Killian steps back and takes a few deep breaths to settle his increasingly bothersome nausea. "These last manuscripts are unique. Instead of writing about fire and brimstone and vague metaphors about apocalyptical events, here we find a description of real world plagues and real solutions that could prevent them if sufficient people apply them. And they describe the critical role of the human spirit, which they called the light of the stars, as the key to the seven Blessings and the seven Plagues. The researchers at the Terme have focused only on *The Blessing of Health*. They have applied the various strategies suggested in this manuscript and have shown that they will indeed enhance energy. The results have been remarkable."

Dr. Killian notices that even the nerves in his hands and feet are beginning to burn and feel raw. He recognizes the signs of a toxic reaction. But to what, he does not know. He continues to talk, "Before I discuss the Seven Realms, let me tell you about the Seven Plagues."

As he continues his lecture, he is surprised to be interrupted by an abrupt comment from the man in the front row with the short-cropped blond hair, "Sir, I can understand advances in measurement of human energy fields, but when you interject science into questioning the Word of God, are you not at least irreverent, and perhaps, bordering on heresy. Are you willing to take the risk of being considered a false prophet?"

The audience hears what it is waiting for. . . controversy from the fundamentalist religious side. Most of the audience sits up and becomes even more attentive. There is lots of head shaking and conversations between people.

The question gives Dr. Killian more ammunition. He loves to push the boundaries and make people think. He responds directly, "Sir, we're not questioning the words in the *Prophecy*, but rather using science to understand its power. Throughout history, science, religion and politics have often clashed. Galileo was accused of heresy when he discovered, through his sophisticated telescope, that the earth rotated around the Sun. At the time, the church supported Aristotle's belief that the Sun circulated about the earth. The church disliked being wrong, and Galileo paid a heavy price. He was tried and convicted of heresy and spent the remaining years of his life under house arrest. The church and policy experts need to pay attention to the most current advances in science. Likewise, religion has insights that can provide direction to science. They are all important in expanding the understanding of our world. It is not heresy. It's called progress."

The man in the front row nods in understanding as Dr. Killian explains the heresy. He can also sees the effects of the toxin working quite well, as expected. He smirks as he thinks how history repeats itself and can still be dangerous. Killian was warned many times. He should have known better than to continue to pursue this research that conflicts with the Messiah's mission.

Killian's face is strained as he recognizes that he is getting worse, not better. He tries to deal with the increasing nausea, sweating, burning, and dizziness as he presents his lecture. Did he eat something bad? Did he pick up a rapid infectious virus? He tries to gain composure and strains to continue, "*The Seven Beasts* announces the coming of the Seven Plagues. It says the Plagues will destroy a third of the earth. I believe we can learn something here."

He shows a slide that includes the text of the manuscript and a graphical picture of a seven-headed beast. He reads it loud and clear in defiance of his declining status, "Behold, the beast with a leopard body and seven heads of the lion with ten horns on each head and the feet of the bear came from the depths of the seas, the bottomless pit, when the light in the Realms of Life was weak. The Beast brought upon mankind Seven Plagues that destroyed a third of the world and its people."

He is leaning on the podium, pushing himself beyond the ill feelings. "A third of the world was destroyed when the Beast came. They must have been talking about the Siege of Jerusalem in 70 AD. It was a great tragedy, beyond imagination. Millions died. Now, listen to this next part. It tells about hope! Listen."

He reads on. "When people learned about the wisdom of the *Seven Realms of Life*, the Blessings came forth and the people spite the beast, and he was cast back to the bottomless pit and peace returned. And it is said, the beast will come again one thousand years after the first millennium, when the light in the Realms is weak. And with him, the Seven Plagues will come forth again." Feeling angry over his own declining health, Killian responds loudly, "This is ominous!"

The audience is startled by his outburst.

"They write that the Beast will return this century. The Seven Plagues will come forth. What does this mean? Does it literally mean death to a third of us, as it did during their times, or is it just the paranoiac ramblings of a priest about to be sacked by the Romans?"

There is nervous laughter in the room. The audience is staring at him in disbelief as he continues, "But why did the document refer to the Plagues beginning in year two thousand? Why not write about their own time period? Or, even hundreds of years into the future. Why two thousand years? Why this time? It's a stretch of the imagination unless..." He pauses, both for effect and because he's exhausted. "They had a divine insight into the future. We must ask ourselves, are these Plagues for real? Have the end times arrived? Or, is this just a new phase of enlightenment for our population? Can we prevent the Plagues and enter this new phase? These are questions that science, religion, nor even history may be able to address on their own. However, if both science and religion worked together, do we not have more potential to address these predictions?"

Someone yells from the back of the room, "But in doing so, you're questioning the Word of God. Are you a believer or are you not? Applying science to question religious doctrine is still blasphemy and sacrilegious. And it can be dangerous. If the end times are here, you may be one who is left behind."

Usually, Dr. Killian embraces these reactionary comments. But right now, he needs a quick response. He recognizes his need for a break. He is definitely not feeling well. "The disasters described in *The Seven Beasts* are not typical of the time period during which the manuscripts were written two thousands years ago. The predictions appear to be an alarmingly accurate reflection of the world's problems that we recognize today. The predictions are happening now, and most likely, will get worse unless something changes."

He looks down at the floor, and then up. He feels faint, and says abruptly in a weakened voice, "I'm sorry, but for some reason, I'm not feeling well. Let us take a short break of five minutes. Thank you. I will be right back."

Both the discussion of the Plagues and the obvious strain Killian is showing has generated much chatter among attendees. What's wrong? Is he okay? Will he return?

The large man with the blond short-cropped hair walks out of the lecture hall without concern. He knows what can happen when you are in conflict with the Messiah and his Manifesto. It will only lead to Godlessness and tyranny. And he will stop those who do not support the mission. The Manifesto will explain it all. His first mission is complete. He walks back to his room and stands at the window overlooking the St. Paul skyline with a sense of satisfaction and righteousness. Today, he has begun to fulfill his destiny to transform the world in the vision of the Messiah. For he is the Messenger. And it has been done.

Chapter 4. The Revelation

St. Paul Hotel
St. Paul, Minnesota
Sunday Morning

The Messenger leaves the lecture hall knowing Dr. Killian will meet his fate. He slowly walks back to his room with a sense of satisfaction. As he stands in the window of the hotel looking out over the City of St. Paul, the Messenger thinks about the miracles that have happened in the past year, and recalls the turning point in his life. Just a year ago, he was homeless, penniless, and depressed, ready to end the misery he called life once and for all. Of course, he was angry. Anybody would be.

He had many failures until he found his true path in life. He blames the failures on his abusive father, his parent's divorce and the constant shuffling between bickering parents, uncaring relatives, and abusive caregivers. He blames it on his schools, where he fought with other kids who made fun of him and bullied him. And on his employers who never appreciated his work, and his employees who never did what he asked of them.

For God's sake, he was a military veteran with college business courses. He should never have failed in his business ventures. His past life was an endless train of abuse, failure, suffering, and anger until the night that changed it all, before his revelation.

He had a difficult childhood growing up in Idaho. His unemployed father would yell at him incessantly and hit him when he talked back. His mother was withdrawn and depressed much of the time, and did little to comfort him. She eventually left him and his father for the same abuse elsewhere. He learned that the world is a cruel and frightening place for those who were weak.

As a kid, he enjoyed playing outside, away from the turmoil, but had few playmates, and thus, developed his own games. He played executioner to any unsuspecting animal that would wander his way. He enjoyed killing cats in the woods behind his house. He smiled to himself when the neighbors couldn't figure out why their pets disappeared. He used all methods of killing—stabbing, poison, beheading, strangling, blood-letting, and others that he had read about in the gruesome books he checked out at the local library.

When his father passed away of heart failure, he was relieved to live with his mother who had moved to suburban Anoka, in Minnesota, where she worked as a secretary in the community college there. His mother turned to religion as a way to cope and gain forgiveness, but it was not the path for him. The church made an indelible impression on him as a place of power, control, and another source of his deep-seated anger. He had difficulty accepting the church in his life after the abuse he endured as a child at the hands of a priest. But these details were never shared with his mother.

As a result, he had trouble concentrating at school and had even more trouble with his school classmates. His mother would receive regular calls from the teacher and principal about his fights with other students. He'd pick a fight for no other reason than to show his strength and power. He was a large boy, and bullying made him feel stronger, and in control. His mother would yell at him and berate him about these fights and his failure at school. She would send him to bed without dinner and threaten to throw him in a detention center.

He prided himself on his ability to counter whatever punishment God served him. He traveled with his youth group to camping in the North Country, and developed an appreciation of the outdoors. This became his outlet to assuage his repressed anger. He learned as much as he could about the foliage, wildlife, and skills of living off nature. As an older teen, he would go off for days into the Boundary Waters Canoe Area of northern Minnesota with little more than a backpack, a sleeping bag, tent, and food supplies. He would usually go alone, and was an avid hunter and fisherman. In the winter, he went on skis, and learned winter survival skills.

After high school, he spent two years in the military, and as an enlisted grunt, he learned early to keep his mouth shut or be cruelly disciplined. To his enjoyment, the military exposed him to a whole new world of survival and weaponry. Despite his disdain towards authority, he excelled at anti-terrorism and undercover operations using an array of methods, including disguise, infiltration, escape, and killing. He received accolades that provided him some sense of identity and esteem. He was proud to be a dangerous person and was hoping this would be his ticket to success.

After the military, the GI bill gave him an opportunity to try his luck at business by taking courses at the local college. He recognized his need to be his own boss. After his first venture as a camping outfitter fizzled, he tried his hand as a fertilizer distributor, and then a gun shop owner. It wasn't that these ideas were unsound, but his personal skills were sorely lacking. He was demanding, angry, and aggressive in his sales strategies, and defensive if they did not work out. He always knew best, and his employees and customers were wrong.

After a few years of business failures, he found himself back where he started, increasingly alone, anxious, and depressed, with few friends, and even fewer lovers. He was also an unwelcomed regular at the local bars because of his edge. When he got drunk, he'd be aggressive and angry, and often get into fights over the littlest slight. There was an unwritten rule in the bars where they knew him; he was not one to share a beer and conversation with.

He found odd jobs at fast food places to pay his rent, but the jobs never lasted because of his anger issues. After several months of not paying rent, he was kicked out of his apartment and found him penniless, homeless, wandering the streets, and standing on on-ramps holding a sign saying *feed a homeless veteran*. He did not know where to turn. He realized that he was, in fact, a failure and a worthless human being. It was hard to bear the thought, and perhaps, the only solution was to end it all.

He had it all planned out—the location, the weapon, and the date. But first, he felt he needed to take one last trip to the one place he always felt at peace. He spent months raising money from odd jobs and planned his last solo canoe trip to the boundary waters of Minnesota. Nobody would judge him there. He went alone to the Boundary Waters and rented a canoe and supplies in Ely. He had always been an avid hiker and understood the ways of the north woods. He brought a food supply that would only sustain him for several days. He wanted to stay off the larger wind swept lakes and travel the scenic rivers and smaller serene lakes that had good fishing and wildlife sightings. His goal was to reach his favorite lake after several days of canoeing.

He took the North Kawishiwi River triangle because it was the most remote and infrequently used trail at this time of the year due to the unpredictable weather. He wanted to be alone to think about his plight in the world. He pushed off in the river, and then, paddled hard through Objibway and Triangle Lakes. He carried his canoe and backpack through one short and one long portage to circumvent several rapids and falls along the river.

These portages were challenging, but satisfying, as they went through the cool shade and scents of the tall pines. After two days, he reached the tranquility and beauty of Clear Lake and set up camp. He took a hike through the woods to see what natural foods he could scrounge up to supplement his incomplete rations.

In past trips to this lake, he routinely found wild plants and berries and ate them for dinner and snacks. He had a broad knowledge of the local flora and knew what was edible and what was not. He even had taken young scouts on outings and taught them about living in the wild. They collected cattails in the marshes, and ate them raw or saved them for the evening when they baked them over the open fire. They made salads of leaves of dandelion, lambs quarter, wild roses, dock, wild mustard, and watercress and ate them with olive oil and vinegar. He particularly enjoyed thistle flowers, which like artichokes, were boiled and stripped away to get at the tasty heart. He knew where to find wild onions, blackberries, and blueberries. He even found pine needles pleasant to chew on.

On that day, he was fortunate to discover a rich patch of dark berries and ample watercress for a final salad and dessert. As the evening came, the air was cold and brisk, and he started a fire to stay warm and prepare his last meal. The clouds had completely cleared. The sunset lit up the autumn trees on the opposite bank with bright orange, yellow, and red leaves of the maples and oaks between the green walls of tall pines. As the darkness came on, the sky was filled with a million stars. It was a spectacular night, and that proved to be his redemption.

He fried and ate the fresh walleye he caught in the lake. Then, he sat by the fire and settled into thinking about his life, his failures, and the few people left in his life who knew him. He ate the berries he had gathered for dessert. As he sat there, warmed by the fire, he realized that here in the north woods, on a lake, alone, he was at peace with the world.

And this was the best place to end it all. He had the drugs with him that could put him to sleep forever. Should he leave a note to tell the people who disappointed him? How would his mother find out? He figured that they would eventually find his body here, maybe not until spring. It's best to leave nothing and let people wonder. They did not care anyway. This was a fitting resting place—surrounded by nature, yet protected by his tent and sleeping bag.

The bugs came out in force and he retreated to the tent for his finale. As he changed his clothes and arranged his bed, he realized that the berries did not sit well with him. His stomach was cramping and he felt dizzy. He paged though the edible plants guide, but found nothing to indicate what they were, and if they may be toxic. They had looked like blueberries. Perhaps, this would be a surprise ending for him.

He thought it best to lie down, and if he died, so be it. His fitful sleep was interrupted by nausea and stomach pain. He woke in the early part of the night from a terrible dream and increasingly severe stomach cramps. People were yelling insults and complaints at him, "You stole my money. I'll get you one way or another. You're a failure so face it. You're such a worthless scumbag."

He felt dizzy and light headed. His heart was racing and he had crawling sensations all over his skin. He heard voices and saw strange sights. His vision was blurred, and he was shivering cold. He left the tent to vomit. He threw some branches and a large bundle of dried brush on the campfire. The brush crackled as it flamed up towards him. He stepped back. The brightness hurt his eyes. Then, he saw what was to change his life forever.

An old man came out of the smoke and flames, and spoke to him. He rubbed his eyes to clear the smoke, but the old man was still there. The man spoke to him, "You're a failure and a selfish man. Your failure has brought misery to many. It is time now to change your life."

The man not only spoke, but also physically took him and forcibly pressed him so hard against a tree that he could not bear it. He screamed at the top of his lungs. When he released him, the old man asked him to listen carefully.

He was petrified at this very real vision and asked, "I don't understand. Who are you?"

The old man caught him and pressed him against the tree a second time, until he screamed. The man said, "Listen carefully. Do you not understand?"

"No, I don't understand. What do you want?"

He caught him for the third time, and pressed him against the tree again, and then released him. "You will understand, in the name of The Lord, who created you and created man. Listen! This word will bring you bountiful harvest."

His headache and stomach pain were severe, and he thought he was going crazy. He felt that his mind was leaving his body. He could see himself from above standing by the fire, holding his head, staggering about, holding his gut, and moaning in misery.

The old man continued, "Go forth and reap the seeds of faith to the people. Help them see the path of righteousness. Stop those who are on the paths of the heretic, those who bear false words about the divine spirit. Seek out the Messiah. He will lead you down the path of righteousness."

The young man jumped in the frigid lake to wake himself up from this nightmare. The cold water was a shock, but it did nothing to alleviate his pain and rid him of the visions and voice of the old man. Who is he? Is this real? But it can't be real. What's happening?

Then, the young man saw himself falling down in the dirt by the fire. He lay there for a few minutes and everything went black. It was daylight when he woke up, still lying on the ground by the still smoldering fire pit. The nightmare had been so vivid. He remembered that he was naked and people were laughing at him and calling him a fool. They were whipping him, tying his balls so tight with twine that they turned blue. They poked him with sticks, poured burning oil on him, and cut his skin. They were submitting him to every kind of torture imaginable. His head ached. His body ached. He had a deep-seated anguish that could not be quelled. He was not sure where he was or how much time had passed. He was famished and surprised to be alive.

He remembered what the old man in the fire said, "Go forth and reap the seeds of faith to the people. Help them see the path of righteousness. Stop those that are on the paths of the heretic. Stop those who bear false words against the divine spirit. Seek out the Messiah. He will lead you down the path of righteousness. For you are the Messenger."

He felt lucky to have survived this ordeal, but felt drained and fatigued with severe pain. He did not know what to make of this event. How can he be a Messenger? Did he truly hear God speak to him like Moses and his burning bush? Who is the Messiah? How can he find him? The revelation confused him, made him feel anxious and frustrated. He thought long and hard about himself and his life, and knew that he had been drawn to the Boundary Waters for a reason. Was this experience truly the divine word, or was he fooling himself? His life was falling apart. Was this God's answer? Is this his destiny to deliver the message of the Messiah? Who is the Messiah? Instead of ending it all here among the lakes and forests, he needed to find the meaning in all of this. He headed back home in search of his new path.

Chapter 5. The Plagues

St. Paul Hotel
St. Paul, Minnesota
Sunday Midmorning

After Dr. Killian's announcement of his need for a break, Dr. Jacobs, the moderator, rushes to the podium in front of the concerned audience. They all can see that something is wrong with him, very wrong. His face is ashen grey and strained as he leans against the podium.

"Jack, are you okay? Come off the stage and sit down for a few minutes. You look terrible." He hands Killian the glass from the podium. "Here, drink some water." He helps him walk off the stage to find a chair in the front row.

Most people in the audience stand up and a few walk out to the lobby to get more coffee or take a break. There is a large buzz going on in the ballroom.

After sitting down and taking a few deep breaths to gain composure, Killian says weakly, "I don't know what has happened. I was rolling along, enjoying the lecture, and then this wave of nausea and dizziness hit me. I still feel my hands and feet burning. Maybe something I ate. It's like a toxic reaction to something. I'm not sure."

"You look like you've seen a ghost," Dr. Jacobs replies, "We should take you in."

"No, I'll be alright. Just need to rest some. I don't know. I had my usual breakfast this morning. Maybe it was the caffeine, but I doubt it."

A staff member brings him an anti-nausea pill and two pain pills. He takes them and swallows them with the water. He closes his eyes and takes a few more deep breaths. After a few minutes, he begins to feel better. "James, I must continue. This is important stuff."

"It's up to you," he replies. "I think we should bring you in. You're no spring chicken, you know. But if you feel you can go ahead, please do. The audience has been impressed by your presentation. Great discussion."

Dr. Killian stands up and walks slowly back onto the stage and over to the podium. He looks out over the audience as they return to their seats. He smiles as he announces that he will continue the lecture.

There is a raised hand from a well-dressed lady in a professional suit. Dr. Killian turns to her and nods his head.

"Dr. Killian. I hope you're feeling better. What you say seems so dramatic. Are you saying that the plagues in the *Prophecy* are more than just ancient fantasy? What plagues are you talking about? Are they really becoming a reality? Where's the evidence?"

Dr. Killian, feeling better after his break and the medication, brightens up to answer this question, "Let me show you what the *Prophecy* actually says. You be the judge." He shows a slide with white background and the text from the scroll in italics and quotes. A photograph of the scroll is in the upper left corner of the slide while an illustration of the Seven Beasts is in the right corner. "Here is the translation of the Plague of Ignorance." He reads from the slide, "And the seven angels with seven trumpets prepared themselves to sound. The first trumpet sounded and it fell upon the Realm of the Mind, and it is revealed, a third of the people will have ignorance of the ways of the world and speak of ideas that are dishonest and strike down the common good. They rise to become the leaders of the world and gain power through greed, force, and evil."

He looks around the audience before he asks, "Do you know of any leaders who have gained power through greed, force, and evil? Do you know leaders that reject science to support their own ideology? Do some leaders disregard the science of climate change and environmental protection in the name of power and profits?"

He pauses for a moment before showing the next slide of text. "The Second Trumpet predicts the plague of illnesses." He reads from a slide that shows a crowd with mostly obese people in it. "And the second trumpet sounded and fell upon the Realm of the Body, and it is revealed a third of people have affliction with heavy heart, thick blood, slow healing, poor breath, and early death will come.

"There are growing epidemics of heart disease, diabetes, lung disease, cancer, arthritis and other chronic conditions in the world. The rate of obesity has officially hit a third of the U.S. population, and is growing dramatically around the world. The average lifespan, which has been increasing over the past hundred years, will decrease for the first time in recorded history."

He shows the next slide with the text in quotes, clearly centered on the white background and the same pictures in each corner. "The Third Trumpet predicts increasing despair and depression." Again, he shows the next slide with a picture of several alcoholics passed out on the street. He reads the text, as the audience is silent. They recognize that these are sobering but true statistics.

"And the third trumpet sounded and it fell upon the Realm of Emotion, and it is revealed a third of people will feel despair and poor in spirit, and be drunk with wine, and lay down their tools, with sadness that overcomes."

"There is a growing prevalence of depression, alcoholism, and drug abuse around the world. Over twenty percent of people in the United States, including children, are prescribed psychiatric drugs by their doctors for emotional problems. This is expected to rise to over one third in the next decade. Nearly twenty percent of adults are binge drinkers who drink themselves into unconsciousness, and in some cases, to death."

He begins to feel ill again but tries to shake it off. He shows the next slide with alarming pictures of the slums of a city with hungry children standing near garbage. "The Fourth Trumpet predicts the Plague of Poverty.

"And the fourth trumpet sounded, and it fell upon the Realm of the Way of Life, and it is revealed that a third of people will have poverty, and beg for food and drink, with no bed to lay, and no refuge for comfort, and death will come to the children and the frail."

He looks out over the quiet audience and says, shaking his head with disappointment in his voice, "We're already there. The rise in poverty, homelessness, and alienation is growing in the world with almost half the world." He pauses to let this sink in, and repeats, "Half of the world, over three billion people, live in poverty. As a result, thousands of children and elderly around the world die each day due to unsanitary conditions and hunger. Our global economic system is manipulated by a handful of powerful economic players, often for their own profits. They enrich a few at the expense of an ever-growing vast majority of poor people. I fear that this will eventually result in the greatest economic depression that the world has ever seen. The Fifth Trumpet speaks of the Plague of Drought."

He shows the next slide with a picture of a dry farm field with the crops dead from drought, and reads it. "And the fifth trumpet sounded and it fell upon the Realm of Nature and it is revealed that the earth will be dry, and the rivers and seas are made bitter, animals and plants will die, and a third of people have drought and no water, their tongues are parched with thirst, and famine will bring hunger upon them, and death will come.

"The problems of pollution are real. Most environmental scientists agree that climate change, global warming, and environmental degradation are contributing to droughts and famine around the world, and millions of people are without food and water and are at risk of dying. There is evidence that toxins generated by pollutants such as lead, have lead to higher crime rates across the world. Furthermore, global warming has lead to dramatic weather changes with increasing numbers of devastating hurricanes, tornados, tsunamis, and earthquakes. What will happen if these trends continue over the next fifty years?"

He pauses again to let the audience consider this question. "The Sixth Trumpet warns about the rise of the Plague of Hate." He shows the next slide with a picture of graffiti on the wall with hateful, racist words. A wave of nausea comes over him again. He fears that the toxic reaction was only temporarily abated. Regardless, he continues and reads the slide. "And the sixth trumpet sounded, and it fell upon the Realm of the Spirit, and it is revealed a third of the people feel hate and vengeance towards their brother and forsake them for reasons unknown, and bring wrath and violence against them.

"The problems of racism, discrimination, and hate around the world are growing, particularly, against minorities, women and children. Although the United States has had much success in teaching tolerance and acceptance regardless of race, religion, gender, and ethnic background, there are still a growing number of hate crimes and violence in every state. Nearly one in five women has said they had been raped at some point in their lives, and one in four reported having been beaten by an intimate partner. The number of mass murders, particularly of innocent children, increases every year. Hate crimes are flourishing. Gun laws have relaxed, and nearly anybody regardless can wield a weapon today. There are 310 million guns owned by civilians in our country— that's one for every person in our country. Almost fifty percent of all U.S. households have a gun at home. Our gun-crazed society, primarily promulgated by men, is absurd. This excessive number of guns is not about hunting or protection! It's about one thing—hate. For God's sake, what is wrong with our society when we can't even protect our little children at school? Why do we compensate for low energy by buying guns. There are so many positive ways to boost your energy."

There is a quiet seriousness in the room. They all know that the evidence that these plagues are a growing reality is irrefutable.

The next wave of nausea comes and, he pauses in hopes that it passes. He continues, "In the end, *The Seven Beasts* predict that the economic conditions of the world will deteriorate and bring on an expansion of war because the collective energy of the people is low. The seventh, and final, trumpet will sound and the Plague of War is predicted." He clicks to the next slide showing an arsenal of weapons including long-range missiles, tanks, and artillery. He reads the quoted text. "And the seventh trumpet sounded and it fell upon the Realm of the People, and it is revealed that a third of all people will bring war against their neighbors, and through fear and greed, they raise arms against each other, and bring swords to the hand of man, and they will hunt and kill one another. The good life will then be gone for the beast has arrived.

"Right now, there is no world war, but the United Nations reports nearly fifty wars that are being fought in the world, involving over twenty percent of all independent nations. This is not one third of the people of the world, but its pretty damn close. Furthermore, a hidden arms race is heating up among both developed and developing nations. Despite austerity to cut social programs, the military budgets of most nations are increasing. The current conflicts are simmering, and with increasing military capacity, our worst nightmares may come true. Regional crises may escalate. People will become more resistant to being controlled by repressive governments, the wealthy, and the powerful. This will lead to protests, rebellion, and conflict at a scope never seen before in this world."

His next slide shows millions of people protesting, another slide showing picture the planet with red bombs to highlight which countries are currently involved in conflict and war, and then a third slide of a nuclear bomb exploding. "Any number of these major hot spots may lead to a catastrophic world war. The infamous Doomsday Clock, which represents how close mankind is to its annihilation, has recently moved one minute closer to midnight. Right now, it is five minutes to midnight, and may be near a point of no return. With over twenty thousand nuclear weapons in the world, there is enough power to destroy the world's inhabitants several times over. But the devastation may not just come from nuclear threat. There are several other possibilities—changes in the earth's atmosphere, limited resources, biological weapons, you name it."

Another wave of nausea washes over Killian as he puts his hand up to his mouth to keep from vomiting. He is determined to continue. "Many questions arise from these predictions. Why does an ancient manuscript, written thousands of years ago talk about what will happen beginning in the year 2000? How did they know this? How could they predict our future accurately? This is mysterious and ominous. Do we take these predictions seriously and with some urgency? You decide because it is you who has control over our destiny."

The audience is quiet until a man dressed in a grey business suit at the back of the room raises his hand. "Sir, these apocalyptic facts are exaggerations by the media to scare us all, and to achieve certain political goals. Don't you have confidence in our ability to avoid this self destruction?"

Killian perks up at this question. He looks out over the ballroom to appreciate the beauty of this setting with its bright chandeliers, red curtains, and giant mirrors on the wall. It is stark contrast to how bad he feels right now. He responds, "These are catastrophes that we hear about everyday in news sources across the globe. People walk around like zombies, with low energy and little recognition of, or concern about, the Plagues. They are like the walking dead. The science documenting the coming Plagues is clear and undisputed. But I, personally, am an optimist and believe we have the knowledge to avert these changes."

The man continues his questioning, "But, how? How do we avert these changes when there are over seven billion people in the world? Is it impossible or, even, too late?"

Killian loudly snaps back to the surprise of the audience, "It is never too late! This is why the message of the *Prophecy* is so important and timely. This is our time to make a leap in the enlightenment of mankind. Man has evolved through many phases of evolution to our current world. We are in a new phase, a new age and, for whatever reason, the *Prophecy Scroll* seems to have predicted it. We have the knowledge to solve these problems and prevent the Plagues. But, we need to bring positive energy into our own lives to prevent the Plagues and achieve the Blessings. This is the goal of the Terme Project. They are training what they call warriors to teach about the *Prophecy* concepts and spread positive energy to the people around them. Now is the time to stop being zombies and to become warriors to bring on this new era."

Another question comes up from the front of the room from a young man who looks to be a student. He is dressed casually in jeans and a colorful dress shirt with no tie. "Dr. Killian, all this talk about zombies and warriors, you are beginning to sound like a video game producer." The audience laughs as the student continues, "I like the analogy. I agree that the *Prophecy* is compelling. From a scientific perspective, we know the evidence for the Plagues is convincing. But why is this happening now? How can we bring positive energy into our lives and prevent the Plagues?"

Dr. Killian perks up as he answers these questions, "Thank you for those million dollar questions. I do not know why these changes are happening now. Perhaps, it's related to the regular fluctuations of life on our planet, or perhaps, it's driven by the limits of the profit-driven economy for which we have built our society upon, or maybe the Plagues are lessons to humanity to teach us about living in peace and harmony. I don't know. Regardless, the *Prophecy* predicts the possibility of a dire future. But there is so much that can be done by each of us and it's spelled out so beautifully in this last scroll, almost if they knew we will need it now. It brings up the tale of the Tower of Babel. Are you familiar with this tale?"

A few heads nod in silence as the audience listens intently.

He tells the story, "In this old story, the builders sought to create a tower that reached to heaven through their sophisticated technology, political structure, economy, and material wealth to create a perfect world, a utopia. But the higher they built the tower, the more problems they found in their structure and it began to collapse under its own weight and complexity. The higher the building went, the further they strayed from reality, and their foundations, in order to continue the effort. Yet, continue they must, because their whole way of life was built around its construction. Eventually, they found themselves so far divorced from reality that they woke up one day to find themselves speaking different languages—a metaphor for the breakdown in communication, consensus, and collaboration. Sounds familiar doesn't it? Maybe, this is the same finale for our modern world. Are the Plagues a sign that our building is beginning to crumble? Are we zombies walking around dead with little concern for our future? You decide."

He notices himself sweating again and takes a few more deep breaths. The burning in his feet and hands are increasing. There is mumbling among audience as they recognize his energy is weakening and his voice is dragging.

"Maybe, the *Prophecy* points to the great irony of our times, the all-consuming effort to build a tower to the heavens, when heaven is all around us already. Maybe, the utopia is a world filled with blessings that is available to all of us right now, and has always been available. Will people realize this and learn to embrace our own Blessings? Will we learn to live a life that is blessed with wisdom, health, happiness, prosperity, beauty, love, and peace? Will we become warriors and spread positive energy in each Realm to the people around the globe? Is it possible that through the blending of science and religion, we have the political will to embrace this utopian future? Can we discover strategies to prevent our crumbling Tower of Babel and its dismal future?

The audience is looking dumbfounded as Dr. Killian rambles on, like a desperate attempt from a desperate man to finally say what needs to be said before it is too late. They recognize that something is seriously wrong but his message is still so clear.

They listen intently as he continues, "I believe we can create a new vision for the future through the concepts in the *Last Scroll*. Enlightened states of mind, happy, healthy and balanced lifestyles, elimination of poverty, tolerant and inclusive open societies, universal health care, respect for human rights, religious freedom, unlimited renewable energy, shared abundance from nature, protection of the environment, active collaborative governments, international solidarity, peaceful co-existence, and many more ideals. If we can make use of a wise blend of science and technology laden with ample spiritual insight and political will we could lead the way to not only avoid the worst of our past but also build on the best prospects for the future. I believe we can achieve this utopian vision of a good life for all."

He stops for a few seconds, and loses his train of thought. His thinking is becoming cloudy. His thoughts are muddled. He looks out over the audience. They are still with him, watching and listening carefully. You can hear a pin drop in the large ballroom.

"There is hope. Listen!" he reads the next slide of a quote from the manuscript. "The people who seek salvation in the Seven Realms of Life, and follow the truth of the Blessings will escape the carnage. And when a third of the people take up these Blessings in their lives, become skillful in their actions and virtuous in their being, the Beast is cast back into the bottomless pit, to be shut up again, and set a seal upon him, so that he should deceive the nations no more. And the good life returns to the people, and we will have peace for the next one thousand years."

He recognizes that he is going downhill fast and better hurry if he is to finish. He talks more deliberate, straining to continue, "Not surprisingly, the *Prophecy Scroll* suggests a path, a strategy, to a brighter future. It talks about the strength of the light needed to bring the Blessings to the world. A third of the people need to take up the Blessings. Are these our warriors? Is this light the same as the energy we are measuring at the Terme? What are the *Seven Blessings* and the *Rules of the Blessings?* How do we achieve them? The Terme Project research will answer these questions. But it is clear that you, me, and every other person in our world will determine what happens to our future. It reminds me of a modest superhero, Spiderman, who once believed, 'With great power, comes great responsibility.' Each of us has the responsibility, and according to the *Prophecy Scroll*, the power to change things. We all can become warriors in our own worlds."

Dr. Killian's throat is burning. He takes the glass and slowly sips the water as he looks off into the distance. He recognizes that he is deteriorating rapidly and his attention wavers. He was so excited to present this lecture, but his increasing feelings of dizziness, nausea, and confusion are preventing it. He aches all over and is sweating profusely. He cannot speak well and his color is changing. He is laboring to even stand up. Still, he tries goes on. He needs to finish.

"Research has recognized that many lifestyles, attitudes, emotions, and social situations within a person's daily life may act as contributing factors to many chronic conditions including heart disease, obesity, diabetes, and arthritis. When these lifestyles are improved, improvement in health follows. At the Terme Project, the investigators applied the strategies from the *Prophecy Scroll* to each participant to determine the effect on their energy levels and energy flow using a portable SERF magnetometer. What happened next was simply short of amazing."

The audience is on the edge of their seats waiting for his next words. They want to hear it as much as Dr. Killian wants to tell it. His voice is stressed and shaking, "As people followed the Blessings, their energy was stronger, their health and mood was better, they slept better, and they became happier and energetic, and the energy spread to others around them, just as the scroll predicted. Let me show you the scans of these participants. . ."

Suddenly, Dr. Killian gasps, grabs his throat, and falls onto the stage. Dr. Jacobs and several members of the audience rush to his side and open his shirt collar. Dr. Jacob yells to the group surrounding him, "Give him air. Call 911. Get the ambulance here. Start CPR."

A physician from the audience assesses Dr. Killian's condition. His pulse is gone. The doctor recognizes that Killian has classic signs and symptoms of a toxic reaction to some type of poison. They try desperately to resuscitate him, with no success. The paramedics arrive and the defibrillators are not effective.

Everyone in the room stands to watch as the paramedics take Dr. Killian out on a stretcher with a sheet over his head. The audience cannot believe it. Dr. Killian appears to have died in the middle of his finest presentation. The word spreads that the cause of death may have been from a toxic reaction to something, perhaps even a poison. With the threats that he has had in the past, foul play is suspected.

Julia, still sitting in the front of the room, is in shock. She cannot believe what just happened. She will never be able to have lunch with him. She stiffens her face to stifle the emotions and keep from crying. What a terrible tragedy. She goes back to her hotel room and lets the emotions out. She sobs uncontrollably. She needs to talk to somebody about this, but does not want to go back to the conference. She fears for her own life. She calls Dr. Ryan Laughlin, her old friend from med school. To her dismay, he does not answer. She leaves a message. In a few minutes, she calls again. Still no answer, but she leaves a second message asking him to call as soon as possible. She desperately needs someone to talk to, and to get away from here.

Chapter 6. The Call

Ryan needs to get moving with his morning routine of cappuccino, yoga, breakfast and the news if he is to avoid being late for the Lifetime Fitness Triathlon. He puts on his padded black biking shorts and his favorite blue lightweight shirt with a back pocket for his cell phone. He makes himself another cappuccino. He knows that too much caffeine is not good before a triathlon but after his restless night, he needs something to help him stay focused. It may also give him some extra energy for the race. He takes a second to stare out the front window to check on the status of the weather and his lush landscape. He can't keep his mind from thinking about Sophia.

His two story fifty-year-old house, built with stucco, wood from old forests up north, and limestone rock cut from a nearby quarry, is at the end of his cul-de-sac. The ample front yard has several large oaks and flowering pink crabapple trees. The circular raised corner garden in the front yard has a stone statue of a child offering flowers to those who pass by, and a circle of bright red geraniums. The two-foot stone walls that lift the garden up have delicate hanging foliage of yellow nemesia flowers flowing over the edges.

He loves his house, but it reminds him of how much he misses Sophia. She loved the creativity of gardening. They created their private garden utopia together over a few years to enjoy the beauty and serenity of nature. Wherever she went, beauty followed.

He heads to the backyard to stretch before the race. His tile patio overlooks a beautiful hill, filled with colorful perennials including broad-leafed hastas, red echinacea, yellow black-eyed susans, and white daisies. He remembers the times when he and Sophia spent in the garden, designing and building the hill. The beauty of the garden helps him feel more at peace and makes his stretching routine more enjoyable. Right now, he needs to calm his body and mind after the poor sleep. But the caffeine and the impending race is making him jittery. He never learns. He hears the phone ring and runs back in the house, but misses it.

The answering machine is flashing. He hits play, and it starts with last night's message from his mother. "Hi, Ryan. This is your mother calling. I just wanted to see how you're doing. Can't ya pick up the phone and call me sometime? Quit lying around watching sports all night. Get out and meet people. I'm just concerned. Hope you're well. Love you. Call me."

Then, another message from this morning surprises him. "Ryan. This is Julia Stone, from med school. I'm in town for a conference and something terrible has happened. One of the speakers, a colleague of mine, died during his talk. He was talking about research involving an ancient manuscript that predicts seven plagues that may devastate our current world. Some believe the speaker was murdered. I'm at the St. Paul Hotel. I'm afraid. Please call me back as soon as you can. It's urgent."

He is startled by her message as his mind goes back to a vision of an intense Julia Stone, angry at a prank some med school classmates pulled on her. She was so clearly extraordinary. She always sat in the first row and would raise her hand for every question the faculty posed. She always did more than what was expected. She got all A's and was the valedictorian of their med school class. Nothing could keep her down. As a result, she was often a target for pranksters. She headed to a neurosurgery residency, and then, he lost touch with her after she went into a PhD program.

He looks her up on the web and finds that she is now a Professor of Medical Anthropology at Harvard's program on Global Health and Social Medicine. Odd career choice for such a brilliant mind. To her credit, she was always on the cutting edge, and he admits, quite beautiful too. But way out of his league. Really, she was out of everyone's league. It made him nervous just to be around her. Maybe she has changed.

He is flattered that she called him, but the circumstances are not encouraging. What conference and whose death? What did she mean by an extraordinary manuscript that predicted seven Plagues? He looks up the conference on the web. Research on the *Dead Sea Scrolls*? That's a long way from Neurosurgery. Maybe, she's come down to earth, or maybe she has gone off the deep end. The program lists the first speaker as Dr. Jack Killian. He spoke about the measuring the life force and using the *Dead Sea Scrolls* to train warriors. Interesting but weird. Was he the guy who died? This will be an intriguing call.

He looks at his watch to see how much time he has. He sits down again in the kitchen nook looking out over the flower covered the hill. He gathers his thoughts, and is just about ready to make the call, when the phone rings again.

He answers, "Hello? Ryan, here."

"Ryan, this is Julia Stone. Remember? From med school."

"Yes, Julia, hello. Of course. I was just about to call you. It's nice to hear you're in town. What's up? What's so urgent this morning? If it's about the gross anatomy prank, I had nothing to do with that."

His med school buddies were so cruel. She was one of his gross anatomy partners. The other guys somehow rigged the dead cadaver so that when she looked at it, an eye would wink at her. When Julia saw it, she freaked out and screamed. Then, a recording came from inside its mouth and said, "Hello babe. Calm down. I don't mind if you cut into me, but just be careful with those private parts down there. I still hope to get some use from them." It's best to avoid being the gunner in med school.

"Ryan. I completely forgot about that, but now that you remind me, you're right, it wasn't funny. I should be mad at you if you had anything to do with it. Men can be so juvenile. It doesn't matter. I did get back at them."

"What do you mean? I didn't hear about any revenge."

"It was nothing. I have other more important things to talk to you about."

"No, first tell me what you did."

"Ryan, I didn't call to talk about juvenile pranks," she replies anxiously. "I'm scared. I'm here in St. Paul for a meeting on some cutting edge research. Dr. Jack Killian was speaking about research involving measurement of the human spirit and use of concepts in an ancient *Dead Sea Scroll*. Then, as he was telling us about the energy in the seven Realms of our lives, he died in the middle of his talk. It was terrible. They say it could be murder. I know we haven't connected for a couple of years, but I just don't know what I should do! Can you help me?"

"Wait a second, Julia," Ryan replies calmly, "Slow down. What do you mean they believe he was murdered?"

"I don't know. They said it may be murder. Some think he was poisoned. I need somebody I can talk to. I thought about you, since, well, you live in town, and you've always been so nice to me."

"A murder. Here in St. Paul? Why was he murdered?"

"I don't know why," She says with panic in her voice. "He was talking about research that measures the human spirit, the last *Dead Sea Scroll* and its prophecy predicting seven Plagues in this century, and the secrets to seven Blessings for the seven Realms of our lives. I know that sounds like wrath of God stuff, and maybe it is. It is controversial because it flies in the face of religious doctrine. Some people call it anti-Christ science and want to shut it down. Some say they murdered Dr. Killian because of it. If so, I may be at risk, too. I just don't know what to do."

"Who murdered him? And why are you at risk?" He asks.

"They don't know who murdered him. He has had several threats against him. Maybe religious fanatics. He didn't know. I've visited the Terme Project in Brisighella, Italy and have seen the research. It's impressive. I was going to collaborate with Killian. The murderer may have seen us talking. Maybe, I'm at risk too. I'm not sure I'm thinking straight about all of this. I need to get out of here. Are you free today?"

"Not today. I'm in a triathlon this morning, but sure, I'm free this evening. Do you want to meet for dinner?"

"I remember our discussions in med school. I thought about you when I needed someone who could help. Dinner tonight sounds great. Where, and what time?"

"Sounds intriguing. A mystery. Ancient knowledge. Plagues and Blessings. Controversial research. I like it." He nods to himself affirmatively.

"Ryan, this is not fiction. It's a real threat. There are crazy people out there."

"Well, Muffalettas is a nice, quiet, and safe restaurant. Let's meet there, if it is okay with you. It's on Como Avenue. I can call and make a reservation for tonight. About 7 pm? Can I pick you up?"

"Thank you, Ryan. I'll be in my room at the St. Paul Hotel hiding out until then. I'll just take a taxi over."

"Sounds great. Can't wait to hear about it. Be safe."

He sits for a few moments, dumbfounded by the conversation he just had with Julia. He knew her well in medical school. She was so straight-laced. They went on a few platonic dates but no romance. Now, It's eight years later and she calls him with this bombshell. She is so intriguing.

What is she up too? What is this manuscript and prophecy about? What on earth could be so profound that it would cause a murder? This is getting even stranger.

He doesn't have time to ponder these questions. He has to move along this morning if he wants to make to the race on time. But Ryan is a man of habit, and needs a good breakfast every day, especially before a race. He sits for a minute at the kitchen nook to eat in haste. He opens and scans the newspaper for relevant news. He checks the weather and sees it will be a cool 70 degrees with sunny skies and a breeze. Unfortunately, it's a good day for biking. He checks the sports page, and sees that the Twins won again and are moving up in their division. He makes note that there is no mention of the conference. He expects that it will be the headlines on tomorrow's edition. The rest of the news never ceases to disappoint him with an astonishing number of man-made tragedies that are reported in the country and around the globe. Large-scale Ponzi schemes, theft, corruption, terrorism, droughts, and famine, hate crimes, widespread obesity, illness, and wars. You name the tragedy and it will be there.

He knows that it makes good copy and sells papers, but it's depressing and makes people cynical about the direction that the world is going. Who wouldn't be? There are few positive articles about people helping people or new ideas, innovations, and developments that make the world a better place. The old adage, that the only news is bad news, trumps all other news. Maybe, Julia is right. The plagues have begun and are spreading across the globe. He cannot wait for dinner tonight to discuss it.

Chapter 7. The Race

Lake Nokomis
Minneapolis, Minnesota
Sunday Midmorning

R yan shakes himself back to reality, realizing that he will be late for the race if he doesn't get his butt in gear. His buddies will kill him. He retrieves the bike from the garage, and throws it on the rack attached to the back of the Audi Q5 SUV. He rides a Shimano Ultegra out of Osaka, Japan. It is light, fast, comfortable, and relatively inexpensive. He quickly drives over to Lake Nokomis to meet with his co-conspirators in the race today, Randy and Ned, as they wait impatiently for him to show up. As Ryan approaches, he gets the evil eye from both of them as they check their watches.

"Hard time getting it up this morning, old man?" Randy laughs. "The rust sets in easily over a whole night. Better get your butt in gear."

"And don't let your butt drag today, okay?" Ned agrees. "We want to win this. It's been too long between victories. Or, maybe, we're getting too old for this?"

Ryan flashes his typical smile, and is frustrated over their intense competitiveness. "Remember, guys, we talked about it," Ryan says. "This is only for fun. There are too many younger competitors here. We have virtually no chance to win. You're as much of an old man as I am. This is for guys in their twenties. We are officially over the hill!"

Randy responds with a smile, knowing that he's always nudging his buddies to do more, "Perhaps, But I'm giving it a go. I don't want a soft butt like yours. I work hard to stay fit."

"You're fit because you're a hard ass," Ryan says with a laugh. "There's a difference."

"You both have a hard ass," Ned laughs with a grin that's contagious. He needs to get his friends down to business. "Com'on. We're in our thirties. That is not too old to win. Let's go over the details of the race. I agree, this is supposed to be fun. Right? The competition is stiff. Remember the team from Eden Prairie? They're young and back again this year. And what about the group from Duluth? They're tough nuts. We should do okay if the both of you just stay in the pack. That's the most important thing." He looks directly at Ryan, "Don't fall behind. Okay?"

Randy will first do the swim across Lake Nokomis, and then pass the race over to Ryan. Randy is a strong swimmer and a maniac health addict. He swims most summer mornings across Cedar Lake. Then he and his wife, Kerri, run or walk around the lake most evenings. They eat well, sleep well, and exercise well. He seems to have an unlimited energy in almost everything he does. Randy's modus operandi in life is to help people. He does not think about it, he simply does it in every part of his life.

One day last summer, while walking around the lake, Randy heard two girls screaming for help after their canoe tipped. They were struggling to stay above water. He didn't look for help. He simply took his shoes off, dove into the lake from the shore, and swam about fifty yards in record speed. He reached them right before they went under, and pulled them both to safety.

In contrast to Randy's intense swimming, Ned is a patient long distance runner. He runs 5Ks, 10Ks, half marathons, full marathons. He never tires. His legs are solid. His stride is long. His wind seems infinite, and he has great energy and is always there for you. All of their friends love him.

Ryan is happy to be with these guys. They are good friends, friends for life. Ryan needs friends right now. He cannot seem to find his bearings. His sense of self and enjoyment of life continue to decline. It is hard to let go of someone you love deeply. But Sophia is gone. He knows that he has to come to terms with it, but just cannot, on any level. He wants to bury it by staying busy with work and exercise. He will deal with it later.

Ryan is warmed up, but still has not fully recovered from the nightmare and poor sleep. He's tired and irritable. He'd rather just grab a good book, lie down on a lounge chair and veg out for the day. Or, maybe, he can spend the day with Julia. She is new in his life, quite interesting, and needs somebody right now. But, instead, he's here ready to bust his butt in a race. For what? Fitness? Fight aging? Pride? Friendship? He doesn't know and it really doesn't matter. He is here and will compete, like it or not.

Biking is second in the race, and they expect Ryan to at least stay close to the leaders. Ryan understates his competitiveness. Those close to him know that he is a strong biker and is in top shape. He has placed high in nearly every bike race he has entered in the Upper Midwest, but he knows that he's getting older and is competing against a younger crowd. The trio will do well if Ryan can maintain his speed and strength, and stay in the pack. It is hard to catch up if you're behind.

The starter calls the swimmers to the lake. The crowd gathers around the shore to see the swimmers take off. There is a crispness in the air as the sun is breaking through the scattered clouds. The lake is cold, but a perfect temperature for competitive swimming.

The gun goes off. The crowd of athletes runs across the sandy beach and leaps into Lake Nokomis. As usual, Randy starts strong. He is a fish and can swim for hours. He starts in third place then pushes himself to move into second place as he turns the corner. He has a great kick and arrives on shore just behind the leader.

Randy runs over to Ryan for the tag with a big smile. He is not even winded. For him, it's like a quick swim in the morning. Ryan jumps on his bike and takes off down the first leg of the course. The air is flowing across his face and through his hair. He loves to bike on a cool day in the summer, speeding along in the bike lane near the lakes, but today, he's not sure how he can compete. He bikes most days to his clinic. He bikes on weekends for pleasure. He gets energy from biking, and begins to feel it coming back.

He begins to lose the fatigue as the adrenaline pumps through him. Yet, inside, he still feels raw with emotions that are close to the surface. He keeps them under wraps. The years of medical school, residency, and clinical practice have taught him to control his emotions. He can stay as cool as any physician by stuffing his emotions down inside.

As he always does, he starts out steady and cautious checking out the field and, then, tries to picks up speed and position as the race progresses. He falls behind and is in third place after biking around the Nokomis Parkway. He now heads down East 50th Street and takes an immediate left on Woodlawn Boulevard. These are tough stretches, where bikers and cars can crash. As he approaches Minnehaha Park, two bikers try to pass him. Ryan feels his strength slipping and his concentration waning. He pushes to stay on pace but falls behind two more bikers into fifth place. He continues on West River Parkway to the Franklin Avenue Bridge. Two more bikers are moving fast around the dangerously sharp left turn that often leads to spills. Ryan looks behind and is alarmed to find them moving too fast as they approach the turn. They are trying to pass him, one on each side of Ryan. How stupid and dangerous.

They hit the turn, and suddenly, the tire of the biker on the inside track slips out on the loose dirt. His bike tire slides under the front tire of Ryan's bike. Ryan's bike goes down and he flies over his bike taking out the third biker. Ryan and the second biker tumble twenty feet across the pavement. The noise of pain and anguish, metal bending, and bones breaking can be heard across the road as spectators stare in horror. All three bikers are down. Ryan lays there for a few seconds, stunned at what had just happened. The other two bikers are writhing in pain, one holding his leg and the other his head. All are bleeding.

Four more bikers pass them as they swerve to avoid the crash. Ryan feels pain everywhere, but stands up and realizes that he has no broken bones. To the astonishment of the crowd, he grabs his bike and checks it for stability. The bike is fine so he ignores his injuries and hops back on it. The other bikers look at him as if he's out of his mind.

Ryan starts slow, but realizes that his bike is working well. He's back in the race, despite the pain and blood flowing down his shoulder and leg. He realizes that he is now in ninth place after the crash. He returns to cruising speed as he crosses over the Franklin Avenue Bridge. He pumps as hard as he can, and speeds across the Mississippi River on the left side of Ford Parkway. The race masks his pain, and his delirious state of mind drifts to a vision of Sophia.

Sophia loved to stop here for the view on our regular weekend bike rides. The beauty of the downtown Minneapolis skyline rising in the distance has always caught her eye. Ryan shakes his thoughts back into the race and continues to ignore his pain.

He realizes that he has fallen way behind and his buddies are going to be disappointed. The bikers turn onto West Minnehaha Parkway, and find the road is very rough here. He could lose footing again if not focused on his tire position. He barrels down west Minnehaha Parkway, heading towards Lake Harriet, and is beginning to regain his energy and discipline.

He does not want to disappoint his friends so he picks up his speed. He knows the path along the Minnehaha Creek well, and is able to pass two bikers who are tanking out after the first twenty kilometers. Ryan does thirty miles a day and knows that his stamina will sustain him through the morning race, despite the crash.

He loves Lake Harriet. He can see the band shell coming into view. With its multiple white turrets and flags blowing, the city skyline in the distance, the sailboats racing in the middle, it is one of the most beautiful of the ten thousand lakes in Minnesota. It gives him more energy.

The path around the lake is smooth, clean, and safe. The morning air is brisk. The sun is warm on his back. His strength has returned. He feels no pain, even though he looks like he's been in a train wreck with blood streaming down his head, legs and arms.

He is moving fast and gaining on the leaders. This gives him more confidence as he passes two more bikers. He is now in fifth place. He speeds around Lake Harriet and back to the Parkway with his adrenaline pumping and the wind blowing across his face. He clips along on his way past Cedar Avenue to pass another biker.

He arrives to the finish line in fourth place and dismounts at the north-end entrance. He sees Ned in the distance, who is impatiently waiting to kick off the final leg with his 10K. Ryan considers how lucky he was to even finish, as he thinks about the other two bikers who, by now, are in ambulances. He is also fortunate to have Ned running right now.

Ned sees Ryan approach and looks at the blood streaming down his face, arms, and legs in horror. "What the hell happened to you? Did you have to go through a war zone to get here?"

"Go! Go!" Ryan insists, "I'll tell you later."

Ned takes the handoff from Ryan, and is off like a bolt of lightning. He's in fourth place and has a long ways to go to catch up with the leaders. In his mind, Ryan knows it's a lost cause, but in his heart, he knows Ned's strong will. He is a fast runner, and does not just try to win—he simply wills it to happen. He is the secret weapon in finishing a race and pushes beyond his own abilities with any challenge. He makes every race interesting, and is a crowd favorite with his strong kick at the end and amiable personality.

Half way through the race, he has already picked up 100 meters on the leaders, and passed two of the runners. He is moving up fast on the first and second place runners. The runner in second place is in good shape, but not as lanky as Ned. Ned overtakes him at the 7K point, but the lead runner is well ahead. The leader is also almost ten years younger than Ned, and is clipping along at a fast pace—confident of his victory. He does not realize that you never count Ned out of a race.

To the astonishment of the leader, Ned, with his long stride, is gradually catching up. The leader pushes even harder. Ned pumps his stride in the final kilometer, bearing down and continuing to pick up speed. He does not flinch as he passes the leader, running almost as fast as when he started. As he passes, he sees the leader's eyes widen and his mouth drop with astonishment and frustration. In the end, it was no contest. Ned always gets his race.

There are lots of congratulatory comments as they wander over to the tents to replenish their fluids and energy. "Great race. Way to go. What a kick!"

Ryan cleaned off the blood and massaged his headache and aching bones. He has little energy, and prepares to get out of there quickly. He doesn't want to hang around and considers the best way for him to slip away gracefully. He congratulates his teammates, "Great race, you guys. Fantastic finish, Ned. Did you ever think that you might not overtake him?"

"He's just one of those young bucks who underestimates the power of a crusty old fart," Ned replies. "Once he realized that I was coming on fast, he simply wilted away like a limp dick."

They laugh, knowing how true it was.

"Ryan, what happened to you?" Randy asks, "You have a few too many battle scars for a simple triathlon."

"You know that turn off of West River Parkway onto the Franklin Avenue Bridge. An inexperienced biker tried to take it too fast and wiped out me and another biker. I feel lucky to be alive. Thank God for helmets. I didn't break anything, and my bike worked so I hopped back on and tried to catch up with the pack."

"Unbelievable," Ned smiles, "You're one tough nut. I would have called it quits."

"And get a bunch of crap from you guys? No way." Ryan smirks at them.

Randy counters, "You're more a hard ass than either of us. And you are your own worst enemy. You may have a concussion, a broken bone or even two! Your welfare is more important than any stupid race."

Ryan looks at them shaking his head and dismisses the thought, "I don't have any major injuries. But you're right, I should have quit right there, but I didn't. I'll survive. I could use a good soaking in a hot bath. What are you up to today?"

"I'm heading over to the Sharing and Caring Hands to help out this evening," Randy replies.

"How do you have the energy to do more today?" Ryan asks.

"It gives me energy," Randy says as he packs up his gear. "The economy is so bad out there right now. It's sad to see people who had great jobs a couple of years ago lose their jobs and land in the food shelves."

"It's good of you to help out," Ryan says with empathy.

"Just last week, I met an old man who told me he lived alone in his own house. The little money he got from social security went for the house payment. He told me he hadn't eaten for two days. He called his neighbor to help, and she brought him in to get some food. I was shocked when I saw him. He was gaunt, weak, and white as a ghost. He could have died. When you hear people's stories, you get hooked on helping. It's called the helpers high."

"You're a good man, Charlie Brown," Ned teases. "What are you doing, Ryan?"

"Right now, I need to go home and recover. Then, I plan to get together with an old classmate who's in town for a conference. Something about a prophecy and plagues. I haven't seen her in years, but she is freaked because one of the speakers died while giving the lecture. They think it was a murder."

"Intrigue, suspense, and a beautiful damsel in distress. That's right up your alley. Sounds fun." Ned replies with a smile.

"I wish. It's nothing. I haven't seen her for years. Can you pick up our winnings? You know, the fifty cent medals for first place."

They say their goodbyes and congratulations for a winning effort. Ryan fastens his bike to the rack and drives home. On his way, his thoughts drift to Randy's comments about the people at the food shelf and about Julia's comments about the plagues. Things are getting worse, and people are falling through the cracks. He sees it daily in his clinic.

He has a big day of patients on Monday, and he wants to prepare for it this afternoon before dinner with Julia. He also needs to call his mother. He knows what she will say, and recognizes that she is just trying to be helpful. Since his father died, his mother has been alone. She spends a lot of her time doting on Ryan after his younger sister got married and moved out of town. She means well, but has to let go. She needs to move on with her own life. Sounds familiar.

As he drives, he calls his mother on the car phone, "Mom, thanks for calling. What's up?"

She rattles off the multitude of questions and opinions that to her mean that she cares. "Ryan, dear. How was the triathlon? You guys push yourselves too much. Exercising to extremes. I don't get it. Why do you do that? You could get injured. Are you still having difficulty sleeping? Are those bad dreams continuing?"

Ryan rolls his eyes and dares not tell her about the crash, "Mom, I'm fine. I like to exercise. My sleep is okay. I'm good."

"Well, I'm concerned. You're gonna burnout at this pace, don't ya know. Take some time off. Find yourself. Find someone who will love you. We all miss Sophia. She was wonderful, but you need to move on with your life. She will always be with us. Have you met anybody yet?"

"No, Mother. But I do have a Canadian fishing trip scheduled with the boys in a week."

"Ryan, I love you, but those boys are not going to help your social life. Take a cruise. Go to Europe. Meet some nice girls. You're not getting any younger, and I'm not either. What about grandkids?"

He ignores her comment and thinks about the call from Julia this morning. Will that count? His mother continues the one-sided conversation. She tells him about her garden, her volunteering at the church, and his sister. She arranges some time to have him over for dinner and finishes the conversation, always with the last word. She repeats, "You're not getting any younger, ya know. Live a little. I know there is somebody out there who will pop into your life. When it happens, Ryan, just go with the flow, and let life unfold. Don't force it. Remember. I love you very, very much."

Chapter 8. The News

After the race, Ryan comes home and immediately draws a hot bath. Sophia had designed the master bath to be ornately decorated with Italianate columns, arched corbels over the bathtub, a gold trimmed hand painted ceiling, and handcrafted mosaic tiles to create a lavish environment to bath in. He sinks slowly into it to drown his pain and misery. He lies there thinking about the calls from Julia and his mother today. His mother, over the top in doting on him, did say something that stuck in his mind. There is somebody out there for him. Go with the flow when it happens. It's even more interesting that Julia Stone had called him earlier in the day out of nowhere. Are these just coincidences or is there something more happening here?

He discards the thought and gets out of the bath. He examines his wounds and bandages those that warrant it. He is not as damaged as he thought he would be with such a spill. He turns on the television to catch any news about the murder. He expects the reporters are making a sensational story out of it. It's 5pm and he switches channels until he finds a news reporter discussing it. He watches her intently.

"This is Cindy Miles of National News. I am standing in front of the St. Paul Hotel, where Dr. Jack Killian was murdered today. He was attending a meeting of scientists from around the world and speaking on the growing interest in the research on complementary and alternative care. Dr. Killian was poisoned and died as he was giving his presentation. A document was found in his room that implicated both the Vatican and Leonard Kolb, a conservative billionaire, in this tragedy. We break to the news conference with John Steiner, head of the investigation."

The shot changes to an interview with Mr. Steiner from the St. Paul Police by Miles inside the St. Paul Hotel lobby. The perky blonde reporter, fashionably dressed in a black and red dress with an elegant string of pearls around her neck, is standing in the gold trimmed red curtained lobby next to him.

Steiner is a tall, lanky Minnesotan with wispy light brown hair and a thick mustache. He is a no nonsense guy with a calm demeanor and astute street smarts. He says what he thinks. When his grandfather came to the United States from southern Denmark in the early part of the last century, he changed his name from Jenson to his mother's surname, Steiner. He thought it sounded tougher and this toughness had been passed down the generations. The police detective is wearing the same light brown corduroy dress jacket that he wears most days.

Miles probes the straightforward detective about the case, "Mr. Steiner, what is the motivation behind this unfortunate murder of Dr. Killian, the brilliant scientist from NIH? How will the investigation proceed in finding the killer? "

"Cindy, we are saddened by this tragedy and have expressed our condolences to Dr. Killian's family. We have assembled a team to investigate. We have not taken anyone into custody yet, and have no developments to report at this time. We will be interviewing those at the conference to gather what information we can."

"We understand there was a document found in Dr. Killian's hotel room," Miles states. "What did it say?"

"Yes, a Manifesto was left in the room, perhaps by the murderer. We do not know yet and have not identified any fingerprints. The Manifesto spelled out a broad-based conservative agenda including the need to stop scientific research on religious topics. It also implicated both religious and political organizations in the murder. We have yet to contact these organizations so I cannot comment on that right now."

Spectators gather in the lobby to watch the interview.

"Detective, we understand that the Vatican and Leonard Kolb were mentioned in the Manifesto. How will you investigate that?"

Steiner continues his deadpan look, but impatiently shifts his stance as she suggests broader conclusions regarding the murder.

"We do not assume that this is anything more than the ranting of a disturbed mind with misplaced priorities. We have no knowledge that suggests this is a conspiracy. However, we will not leave any stone unturned to find the person or persons responsible for this tragedy. We have our people communicating with the appropriate authorities to investigate. I'll keep you posted. If you'll excuse me, I must go now."

The camera pans back to Miles. After summarizing the interview with John Steiner, she goes on to say, "It is reported that Mr. Kolb and his public policy think-tank, the Freedom Group, has also been working to stop this research. There is no comment from the Kolb Group or the Freedom Group. We'll have more on this story tonight at 7pm. This is Cindy Miles from National News."

Ryan turns the television off and considers the implications of the story. He now understands Julia's concerns. It will be an interesting dinner tonight, indeed.

THE TERME
BRISIGHELLA, ITALY
SUNDAY EVENING

The principal investigator of the *Prophecy* research, Dr. Paolo Nobili, organized an emergency meeting of the staff at the Terme, the ancient Roman Spa in Brisighella, Italy, and the site of the research. As the sun sets in Italy, the twelve staff gather in the Great Hall of the Mind, centrally located in the seven acre Terme complex.

The Great Hall was named after the Mind Realm to remind people of the importance of learning within its walls. It is an ancient two story stone barn that has been converted to a great room with adjacent smaller meeting areas. The large barn doors on the front can be opened in the summer to bring in fresh air. The ceilings have large wooden trusses spanning the width. The doors and window frames are tall and thick, made from dark heartwood that still maintain their natural twelfth century state. The inside lighting is decorated both by natural lighting from the windows above but also a variety of sconces on the side walls made of wrought iron, copper, and ceramics for night use.

The staff primarily consists of educators who each are each gifted in their own right but share one particularly important quality. They have all been trained at the Terme and, thus, have unusually high energy in each Realm. In essence, they are each warriors of the *Prophecy*.

They gather around the center of the hall in a set of wooden chairs. Dr. Nobili is there to tell them the bad news. He is a stunningly handsome sixty-year-old man, who does not look the part of a researcher. Rather, he looks like a country doctor with an understanding face. In this situation, he needs to both comfort and calm the staff as he tells the team about the tragic loss of Dr. Jack Killian, and the affect that it may have on all of their lives.

"Colleagues, I received a call from one of our friends in America. He told me that our Program Officer, Dr. Jack Killian, was killed today. He was half way through his lecture describing our research, and fell unconscious while giving his talk. They tried to resuscitate him, but they could not. They found a Manifesto in his room that is being held as evidence to suggest that it was a murder. He was poisoned, perhaps, because of our research. It is a tragedy. The Manifesto implicated the Vatican and a wealthy American, Leonard Kolb, in the murder. As you know, the Vatican provided the *Prophecy Scroll* to support our research. We are all confused by these developments. There are lots of questions and few answers."

Dr. Vanessa Venetre, co-lead of the research, is in tears, visibly shaken by the news. She is an aspiring investigator who wants to make her mark in science by partnering with Dr. Paolo Nobili on this cutting edge research. But the loss of her close friend and mentor, Dr. Killian, was not only a personal loss, but will also threaten her career.

She trained as a physician at the University of Bologna, the oldest University in the world, and then, moved her PhD and post-doctoral studies in neuroscience to Oxford. She has everything, intelligence, compassion, insight, beauty, but above all, she has an idealism that shines through the most difficult tasks. She asks Paolo, "Who would do such a terrible thing? Do we know if this is a conspiracy or the sole work of a madman?"

Paolo answers, shrugging and raising his hands, "Vanessa, I only just received an email about the circumstances surrounding his death. Other than that, I do not know any more than what I gathered on the Internet. I wish I knew more."

Vanessa continues to explore the implications of this change. "How will the Vatican react? How could they possibly be involved? If they are implicated in the murder, will they shut us down and deny us use of the manuscripts?"

"Good questions," responds Paolo with a sad look on his face, "With no answers, we simply have to wait and pray for the family of Dr. Killian. He was a great man. Let us pray."

The staff bows their heads in prayer as Dr. Nobili says a few kind words about Dr. Killian. Then, the group breaks and some move to one of the side rooms to gather around computers and review the breaking news on the Internet. They watched the interview with Mr. John Steiner. The news report indicated that the autopsy found oleander, a common flowering shrub that if ingested is deadly, in his blood stream. The report stated that the poison was like digitalis, a cardiac stimulator, and causes sweating, vomiting, paresthesias in the extremities, bloody diarrhea and eventually unconsciousness, respiratory paralysis, and relatively quick cardiac death. The poison, after ingestion, reacts immediately, and causes a gradual decline in physiological function.

They stated an unknown assailant, perhaps by tainting his coffee, murdered him. The Manifesto called the research heretical and anti-Christ, demanding that it stop. They are all shocked and saddened. They worry about the future of this research, and more importantly, their own lives. What will this killer do next?"

Chapter 9. The Messenger

The Messenger is standing naked with his arms extended high, at the window of his room near the top of Trump Tower in New York City. He feels the power of his transformation knowing that he successfully completed his first mission in St. Paul and was able to catch a plane to New York to attend the Gala tonight. There, he will speak to the Messiah and expects to gain his support for their mutual goals.

He now realizes that it was all meant to happen—the failures, the redemption, and now, the affirmation by the Messiah. He has become the Messenger of righteousness and freedom on earth. Thoughts of power run through his mind as he reads from his Manifesto. The first mission is to stop the heretical research. Then, he will move on to the Messiah's next mountain to climb, gaining control of the government through his newly elected group of politicians. His journey to this moment is deeply etched in his soul.

The revelation changed it all for him. At first, when he returned from the boundary waters, he was confused. He stayed with his mother and reconnected with the church to find answers to his religious vision. He began attending church services weekly, searching for the meaning to the vision and to life. He went to church most days to pray, but still could not make sense of his experience up north. He did not believe in premonitions, but the frequency of the old man's message replaying over and over again in his mind haunted him.

Every day, he rose early and went straight to church to pray. He would get lost in prayer. The mornings would slip into afternoon, and the afternoons into evening. The ministers would tell him to go home, get some rest, and take care of his mother. When he returned to his mother's house, he would lie in bed, unable to sleep as thoughts of the old man and his punishment repeated in his head like a broken record.

Then, one night, he opened the Bible that his mother had put by his bed and began reading. That's when the Messenger first heard the Voice. Actually, *heard* is the wrong word. He felt it. This vibration was resonating in his chest. It was like his body had become a giant tuning fork receiving energy from above.

He did not consider the sensations unpleasant, but rather odd and they continued for days. He carefully analyzed them, and decided that this was a spirit from the heavens. If the vibrations came from the right side of his chest, it was the voice of an angel communicating with him, and when he felt them near the left side of his chest, it was the voice of a demon. And when he felt the vibration humming inside his head, it was God himself, speaking with him. Soon, the vibrations turned into words, telling him, "Go forth and reap the seeds of freedom to the people," commanding him to fast for forty days and forty nights as punishment for his sins.

After what he has been through, none of this scared him. If anything, he felt a warm, soothing peace wash over him because he finally was being guided. Fasting did not come easily to him at first, but he prayed daily for strength. After a week or so, his mother became concerned. He did not bathe, and his clothes were dirty and falling off of him from losing weight. He had begun to emit a pungent odor, was acting erratically, and singing the same song over and over again.

Although his mother was happy that he found his spiritual side, she was again alarmed at his behavior, and tired of his dependency on her. She told him to get some work. After about two weeks, his mother took him to a doctor, who successfully convinced him to end his fast and move on with his life.

He borrowed his mother's car and went to the cities to look for work with a new attitude. He was still searching, but had a feeling that something big was going to happen to him. As he went to several hotels looking for work, he stumbled into a business convention and heard Leonard Kolb speak for the first time. He listened to Kolb's message of faith and freedom and something clicked in his mind.

Here was a powerful businessman who was professing the importance of faith, and freedom from government power and control. It was a powerful message, one that he could not remove from his mind. Almost immediately, he felt an ecstatic sense of relief, like the weight of the world was taken off his shoulders.

As he sat in the hotel lobby waiting to hear about the cleaning job that he did not get, the message became clearer and he found a renewed sense of purpose and energy. He went back into the meeting and immediately signed up for Mr. Kolb's Freedom Group. He began reading everything he could find about Kolb's message and its Manifesto. He volunteered for every job within the group. Gradually, the dark clouds of confusion and anger that hovered over him went away. The leadership of the group appreciated his enthusiasm and dedication, and offered him a job. He accepted immediately and moved to the cities to work with the group.

However, he would not, and could not, forget about the torturous message from the old man up north. Now, he realized whom the Messiah was and that he must be the Messenger to inform the world of his message. Mr. Kolb helped him step out of the darkness and brought him into his light. His thoughts and actions became increasingly dominated by the need for more strength and power within himself to match that needed to communicate the message to the world.

Anabolic steroids bulked up his physique. His weight training boosted his strength. He even underwent botox injections in his face and forehead to reduce wrinkles and give him the divine look of success. He became a master of himself, and learned every strategy to dominate people and reinforce his self-perceived role as the Messenger. He learned about the power of intimidation, psychological threats, and as needed, physical harm. He became obsessed with the knowledge of change, of persuasion, and if necessary, the use of explosives, chemicals, and poisons.

The thoughts of power were intoxicating. He was transformed into a different person. He had a mission, and it would be communicated to the world through his Manifesto, in the words of the Messiah. After his first mission, he slid the Manifesto under the door of the room so that the world would know. To his delight, his first mission was a great success.

Now, the world knows that the Manifesto is a powerful and insightful message from the Messiah to the free world. It is said in the scriptures, "For I am the Lamb to spread the word of the Messiah. I will come and tell the people about His heaven. For I come to earth in full view of man and bring promises of wealth and power when they live in his place."

As he stands naked at the window, he feels the purity of the divine force on him. His eyes shine with wild power. He laughs out loud at the irony of the situation. His mission is clear, and it will bring him the power that he has craved his entire life. He sits down to read his Manifesto again and again. The world now knows of its truths. Heretical research will all stop for fear of punishment from the heavens. New laws must be passed to bring freedom to the people and to change the fabric of society. The era of big government is over. These are the truths that are held dear to the Messiah and his Freedom Group. And he is the Messenger who will deliver this message.

But he has yet to meet his Messiah and founder of the Freedom Group. Tonight, at the Gala, he hopes to be anointed as the Messenger by the second coming of the Messiah, and then to lead everyone down the path of righteousness. His past efforts were all destined to fail, and now he knows why. He was never on his own path of truth. When he meets Leonard Kolb later, he will finally get the support he needs to further implement the vision. All the pieces are in place. His revelation. His transformation. The Manifesto. The Deliverance. Tonight's Gala. And, finally, the Messiah's affirmation. They all point to his powerful role as the Messenger. He has already begun the cleansing process. This is a war, and there will be more casualties. Now, with God's blessing and the Messiah's support, the Messenger will simply carry out the message. Thank you, Leonard Kolb and the Freedom Group for giving him this glorious purpose.

Chapter 10. The Messiah

LINCOLN CENTER
NEW YORK CITY
SUNDAY EVENING

The shouts of "DIRTY MONEY! DIRTY MONEY! DIRTY MONEY! RESIST! RESIST! RESIST!" are heard from the large unruly crowd surrounding the Metropolitan Opera House in New York City. The building is a monument to the rich and famous, clad in white travertine and graced with a distinctive series of five grand arches and two giant murals by Marc Chagall. Police are in full riot gear and keeping the demonstrators away from the entrance to the theatre. An attractive newscaster with long blond hair, powder-white skin, and full red-glossed lips that contrasts with her stark black suit is speaking for WNEW outside of Lincoln Center.

"This is Sonya Anderson, live at the Metropolitan Opera House. We are here to cover the Benefit for the National Ballet where all of New York's rich and famous are coming to celebrate its success. Its stoic columns, Chagall paintings, and grand arches make it arguably one of the most impressive buildings created for the arts. There is as much excitement outside the event as there is inside tonight as the Occupy protestors gather against billionaire Freedom Group founders, Leonard and Frank Kolb. The Kolbs own oil refineries and multinational corporations across the world and have lead the call for freedom from big government. Let's talk to one of the protesters, "Sir, who are you and why are you here?"

She puts the microphone into the face of a bearded gentleman in jeans standing in front of the screaming crowd. "Good evening, Sonya. Thank you for telling others about our message and our efforts. My name is Jonah Bearings. I'm part of Occupy New York. We're protesting the use of dirty money contributions to buy politicians and change laws that favor profits over people and the environment. We all want a healthy planet for us, for our children, and for our children's children. We are protesting Wall Street, the corporations, and the politicians who throw the elderly and poor out on the streets, shut down education for children, foreclose on our lives and homes, destroy our planet, and send us off to wars for profit. We occupy public spaces for social change to help all the people of our country—not just the wealthy. We must come together and resist this greed. Join us next Friday at 6 pm on Wall Street." He looks around at the crowd listening in and screams at the top of his voice, "RESIST! RESIST!"

The shouts of the large, unruly crowd are heard in the background as Sonya goes back to the camera. "The Kolb's Freedom Group financed the effort that led to the Supreme Court ruling to lift restrictions on corporate funding of political campaigns. This has opened the floodgates to wealthy contributors being accused of buying political candidates who will vote in their direction. This scene makes for an emotionally charged evening tonight. Let's peek into some of these limos to see who we can find."

A limousine pulls over, and a stunning fifty-year-old woman in a sequined blue dress steps out and walks towards the entrance of the Met. Reporters surround Ginger Alistair, wife of Blake Alistair, co-owner of Trump Towers, to get a quote. She ignores them and walks through the double doors and up the stairs to her seat in the third story private balcony of the Met. Her husband follows her.

As they take their seats, they look out over the beautiful Opera House packed with people buzzing with talk of the event and the protests outside. The bright red curtain of the Met remains closed as the audience anticipates the opening ceremonies. The Met, like a Roman theatre, is decorated with a richly detailed gold trim to frame the stage with beauty and grandeur.

Finally the curtains open and the audience stands to applaud as the lanky, handsome, Texas-style oil billionaire, Leonard Kolb takes the stage. Two beautiful young gala hostesses, dressed in different black and white satin dresses, accompany him. Scarlet Andreason, a Texas beauty queen who has starred in several B-movies, and Leni Delici, one of the stars of the ballet, hold tightly to each arm of Mr. Kolb as the walk on stage. The Annual Spring Gala of the National Ballet Theatre is about to begin, and the usual congratulatory introductions were made.

The Messenger is sitting near the front, wearing a black suit and tie, and excited to see the Messiah again. He stands out from the crowd because of his strong physique, neat blond hair, narrow blue eyes, and clean-shaven look. This all makes him look younger than his mid-thirties. He gives the impression of being a successful up and coming star, and to some unsuspecting women, he appears to be quite an eligible bachelor who happens to be here alone. As Leonard Kolb swaggers onto the forefront of the stage, the Messenger stands up alone and applauds his hero.

The trio step up to the microphone, and Scarlet introduces Mr. Kolb with her Texas drawl. "Thank ya'll for coming tonight, and for your warm welcome. It is our pleasure to introduce to you a remarkable man, Mr. Leonard Kolb. We are honoring him this evening for his special generosity, both as a member of the Board of Trustees of the National Ballet and for his substantial donation, which will make this upcoming season one of the best ever. Tonight, we have a very special evening planned for you with a fabulous ten-course dinner by none other than Executive Chef, David Joseph Robinson, from Bezanthine Gables. Then, you will see the wonderful National Ballet's performance of *Le Corsaire*, directed by Delia Francini. Mr. Kolb, would you like to say a few words to begin this beautiful evening?"

Kolb, wearing a light brown suit made by William Fioravanti, the master New York suit maker, stands tall in front of the microphone. He is also wearing a touch of Texas, with his cowboy boots hidden under his dark brown dress pants.

He states loud and clear, "Dear Scarlet, Leni, and friends of the Ballet. You are so kind. When I was just twelve years old, my father brought me to my first ballet performance. At that time, I was into sports and told him, 'what, ballet? That's not exactly football. It's so boring.' But he took me anyway, and I was stunned. The performance was mesmerizing with beauty, elegance, style, and athleticism fused with music and drama. I loved it then, and I love it to this day. It is my pleasure to be a supporter of the National Ballet because they really need my money. I hope you enjoy this evening tonight, and thank you for being here. I will turn it over to Leni to introduce to rest of the evening."

The Gala highlights the societal ascent of Leonard Kolb, who, at the age of sixty-two, is among the city's most prominent and generous philanthropists. He has donated a fortune to renovating several New York City theatres, the Museum of Natural History, and the Metropolitan

Museum of Art. He serves as a trustee of both museums and the Memorial Sloan-Kettering Cancer Center.

The Kolbs, who live in their hometown of Dallas, own virtually all of Kolb Industries, a corporate empire headquartered in Dallas whose annual revenues are estimated to be a hundred billion dollars. The company has had spectacular growth since their father, Edward, died a few years back and the brothers took charge. They now have oil businesses in Texas, Alaska, Minnesota, and Oklahoma. Through a series of leveraged buy-outs, they also control vast amounts of land and major companies in paper, lumber, and, most recently, pharmaceuticals and the weapon's industry. Kolb Industries is one of the world's leading designer, manufacturer and marketer of firearms, ammunition and related products for hunting, sports, law enforcement and military markets. *Forbes* ranks it as the third-largest private company in the world and its consistent profitability has made Leonard and Frank Kolb, who is two years his younger, among the richest men in the world.

Their political and social views also feed into the brothers' corporate interests and their philanthropy. Leonard and Frank are longtime libertarians who believe in no government interference in order to maximize corporate profits. They have lobbied heavily to drastically lower personal and corporate taxes, minimize legislative oversight of corporations, and cut social services. Their Freedom Group has supported recent legislation on campaign financing law, relaxing corporate regulation, cutting research funding, and enhancing tax breaks which represent a political triumph for the Kolbs by turning their private agenda into a mass movement of anti-government sentiment.

They supported passage of recent Texas legislation that allows the state and its corporate partners to be free to release more pollutants than any other state in the nation. In a study released this spring, the University of Massachusetts Environmental Institute named Kolb Industries one of the top five air polluters in the United States. Greenpeace issued a report identifying the company as one of the primary sponsors of quasi research that denies climate science and global warming.

They are brilliant businessmen who put their money where their mouth is.

The Kolbs have money to burn and they spend it freely on broadening their ideology and beliefs to support their view of the world, and of course, their successful businesses. They are truly a unique new brand of businessmen.

Leonard is also a deeply religious man. He became even more devout ten years ago after he survived a plane crash in Texas. He was badly injured, but was the sole passenger in first class to survive. As he was recovering, a routine physical exam led to the discovery of early stage prostate cancer. This early discovery allowed him to be cured with laser surgery. Subsequently, he settled down, started a family, and reconsidered his life. As he was quoted in *Business* magazine, "When you're the only one who survived and everyone else died—yeah, you think, the good Lord has spared me for some greater purpose. I've been busy ever since, doing all of the good work that I can think of, so God will be thankful for saving me."

After introductions and comments by the chairman of the board and a few other dignitaries, dinner is ready to be served. The crowd moves from the theatre to the dining tables. Scarlet links her arm through Kolb's arm, bats her stunning blue eyes at him, and pulls him to a chair next to hers to say in her soft southern accent, "Now, don't go away, y'all. . . I want to sit down right next to you."

He is irritated with her clamoring for his attention. He has a reputation for brazen honesty and many people quietly accuse him of suffering from Asperger syndrome. He can be cruel at times, but does not care. He turns to her, and referencing one of his favorite films, says, "Scarlet, I don't give a damn. Please zip it up, and sit over there. I prefer a conversation with Leni." He turns his back to Scarlett and directs his attention to Leni. Leni is a young ballet dancer who starred in the recent National Ballet, *Giselle*, to rave reviews.

There is several other well-known New York celebrities and politicians who join them for dinner. Among them is his brother, Frank, and his wife, Elizabeth, and Blaine Trumble, co-host of the evening. Other dignitaries included at his table are Senator Roy MacDonald, Designer Diane von Sternberger, Representative Anna Marie Bjorkland, State Senator Kenneth Bailey, Dr. Andrew Lazare of Sloan Kettering, and Ginger and Blake Alistair, Co-owners of Trump Towers. The Kolbs have supported each of these politicians to the tune of millions of dollars through their corporate foundations. They each support Mr. Kolb's view of the world and vote in his direction.

Blaine is excited to tell her guests about the menu, which she personally selected. "I had the very good fortune to be invited to dinner at the elegant Bezanthine Gables in Chatham, owned by Chef David Joseph Robertson. David is a big advocate for local seasonal foods and has created a menu for tonight that is out of this world."

A quick scan of the menu by the guests brought a couple of "oohs," but mostly rolling eyes, and "oh really" from the group. Nothing is ever really good enough for them.

As the wife of Howard Trumble, Blaine owns a large chunk of buildings in New York City. She snaps back, "Come on. Don't be such rich snobs. This menu is creative. It's natural, tasty, and most importantly, healthy. We start with a white wine, the Finger Lakes' Riesling that was highlighted in nearly every wine list this year. The beer service includes the Chatham Brewery Porter. Drink some and loosen up those stuffed shirts."

They each have a glass of wine poured. The conversation begins to roll along as they relax. With the Kolbs present, they need to be cautious about what they say or they may lose their support.

Senator MacDonald makes a toast to special guests, Leonard Kolb and his wife, Caroline, "To a kind and generous man who has been one of the prime movers and shakers of our time. Here's to bringing back freedom, and not to forget, corporate profits. Thank you for all that you have done and will continue to do."

The clinking of the glasses moves the group into conversations about the Ballet and the upcoming election as the hors d'oeuvres are served by the white coated and gloved butlers. They bring out the miniature meat loaf, baked with chunks of diced apples and an apple glaze.

Leni asks Mr. Kolb about his favorite ballet performance, baiting him for a compliment. His response is direct and tactless, "Well, Leni, you were pretty good in *Giselle*, but the set design work, choreography, and music were awful. Who do they have directing that fiasco? My father took me to the *Nutcracker* as a teenager and it was a special show. Things have deteriorated since then. I'm hoping my funding will bring back that same quality. I have some nostalgia for it and would like to see a beautiful show. Can you do something about it?"

Leni is embarrassed. She did not know quite what to say, so she says nothing, smiles politely, and begins to eat. The second course is served, and includes salad puffs filled with nouvelle Waldorf salad with red apples, celery, golden raisins and walnuts with green lettuce and a strawberry dressing on the side. It is served beautifully on ruby colored glass plates. Leni does not eat much. Right now, everything tastes like crap to her.

Representative Bjorkland, a deeply religious woman who always has something to complain about, interrupts the feast, "I was reading the other day in the Daily Beast about this research on measuring the human spirit. I think it is atrocious to try and measure the divine. It is anti-Christian.

On top of that, they are using the research to study the *Dead Sea Scrollsí Prophecy* manuscript written during Christ's time. They are testing whether God is right or not. Hah! What idiots! Of course, the *Prophecy* would predict some terrible times ahead for our world—plagues of illness, drought, poverty, and wars. If most people are as stupid as those researchers, and elect numbskulls as their leaders, we're all done for. It is dreadful stuff right out of the National Enquirer."

Leonard is clear in his response, "If the *Prophecy* is truly the Word of God and not a fake, which I doubt, we need to pay close attention to it. But I agree with you. Any research into the authenticity of God's Word is wrong. Our federal government is going farther astray from the real research that needs to support moral evolution and economic prosperity of our society. Leave religion to the religious. This research is a total waste. I fear they are tampering in areas that are sacred. . . and it's best left to our almighty God. He controls our destiny. What are we doing to get the feds to stop funding this type of research?"

Blake Alistair, who emigrated here from England in his twenties, is almost a twin to Donald Trump. He is an astute businessman who is practical to the bone. As the waiter brings the third course of tomato and carrot pillows with homemade pumpkin ravioli, Blake blurts out, "What we really need is more research that improves our bottom line. We need research that is useful to our companies and to the people who buy our products. The decisions are easy. The Chinese are beating us not only at producing cheaper products but also with superior products as well. The sad part is that most of the products they peddle have been developed right here in the USA with American ingenuity. They keep stealing our intellectual property. Something must be done."

Dr. Andrew Lazare sits quietly, and uncomfortably, listening to the conversation as the fourth course is served. The waiter brings the pheasant potpies with local chanterelles, morels, and vegetables in a miniature casserole dish. Lazare is a sixty-seven-year-old internist and researcher, near the end of a brilliant career at Sloan Kettering. He is a partially balding, wire frame bespectacled gentleman with clear, kind eyes. He speaks from the vast experience and wisdom that comes with seeing much societal changes occur over the years. However, he has never seen the degree of distrust between science and government that exists today.

He is shocked and disturbed by this trend. "I disagree," Lazare says vehemently. "Most people in our country don't understand the significant role that science has had on our economy. Nearly every president, regardless of their party, has embraced the idea that America's success has been founded on innovative research that brings new ideas and new products to the marketplace. They don't just come out of thin air. The U.S. has advanced relative to other countries because of the many innovations that have come from our basic science. And most of this was federally sponsored through our tax dollars. We need to continue this funding."

The table goes silent. The guests are focused on Dr. Lazare as they wait for his next words. They feel a lecture coming on. Out of respect, they are quiet. They do not know his political orientation, but it is apparent to those at the table that he must lean towards being liberal, a dirty word at this table. They invited him because of his prominence at Sloan Kettering and his wonderful care of several people at the table.

Dr. Lazare speaks to deaf ears as the fifth course of carrot and tangerine soup with diced beet garnish served in cosmos glasses is served. "Have any of you ever visited the U.S. Capitol building and looked up at the ceiling of the Rotunda. There is a painting there called *The Apotheosis of George Washington*. It is a fresco painted by Constantino Brumidi in the mid 1800s, at the end of the Civil War. It is designed to be the very center of the American Republic. The fresco has several toga-clad deities surrounding George Washington who is the only president in the painting. A full third of the ceiling is devoted to scientists and inventors. Benjamin Franklin, Robert Fulton and Samuel F.B. Morse are featured with Venus holding a transatlantic telegraph cable, which was the big infrastructure project of the day. The Rotunda makes a clear statement that to be anti-science is to be anti-American. Don't you agree?"

Senator Bailey, always the true politician, responds in a fake, but conciliatory, fashion to Dr. Lazare's comments. He knows where his political future lies, and of course, where his campaign funds come from. "Nobody here denies the importance of science, but there is a need to support the right science. Science that is consistent with the religious founding of this country and the right morality—not research using cells from murdered babies or questioning God's word."

Dr. Lazare is too old to hold back. He just tells it like it is. They can agree with him or be damned. He quickly counters with a challenge, "Federal funding for basic science has transformed the U.S. into a global economic juggernaut. We have fueled giant leaps in areas such as developing transit systems, skyscrapers, genetics, Internet, nanotechnology, computer aided manufacturing, fiber optics, health care, medications, and renewable energy. These are quintessential American inventions that have been used to spur our economy and have lifted the entire world's economy across the globe. We cannot abandon the funding of basic research by strangling the government. This funding is absolutely critical to spur new science and discoveries."

Frank Kolb, who is usually quiet, finds himself irritated by these comments and quickly responds, "Dr. Lazare, we are spending a quarter of our whole economy on health care and patients who are still not healthy. These health care costs take away from our profits when we could reinvest in further growth. And then look at the people of our country. Even the poorest of the poor are fat and unhealthy. They have plenty to eat and usually eat like pigs. If you ask me, they need a kick in the butt!"

There is an awkward silence at the table as the sixth course is served. The rack of lamb roasted with mint pesto on a bed of crimson lentils with herbs de Provence looks delicious to the group as they finally see the meat they wanted badly. It is not that they all disagree with Dr. Lazare, but they have been espousing their anti-government theories so long and are finally getting some traction with the public. They simply want to move on and focus on this fine dining experience, which could be ruined if someone, particularly, Leonard or Frank Kolb, get hot under the collar about Dr. Lazare's comments.

They change the direction of the conversation and small talk ensues about the exquisite menu, congratulating Blaine for it. They finish dinner with a parfait of Old Chatham Sheepherding Company ewe's blue rice pudding layered with a five-apple sauce and crispy gingerbread cookies, all served in Martini glasses. This was accompanied by a champagne service that includes Clinton Vineyards' best peach gala, peche bubbly, or the alcohol free ginger ale, which several partake in due to feeling a bit tipsy from all the wine. It was a satisfying meal for the guests and brought much congratulatory conversation.

At the end of dinner and before the performance, the Messenger stops by the table to express his gratitude, "Mr. Kolb, I'm a huge fan of yours. I work with the Freedom Group to prepare the reports that support your positions. It is such a pleasure to meet you."

Kolb looks confused, wondering if they had ever met before. "Thank you for your work. We are beginning to change the tide of freedom and righteousness in the U.S. and abroad. It takes many young people such as you to make this happen. What was your name again?"

The Messenger, standing tall next to Leonard Kolb replies, "As part of my work, I've completed a research report for your group called *Blasphemy in*

Science: The Fallacy of Challenging God's Word. As you know, recent federally sponsored research on religious documents is sacrilegious and counter to all that the Group and God stands for. It has to be stopped one way or the other, or we will all suffer the consequences. Do I have your support to do what it takes to stop it?"

Kolb nods, "We just had a conversation at dinner about the importance of stopping this research. These are difficult times and we need to prioritize. Money does not grow on trees. You have my support. In fact, I will call the Director of the Freedom Group and tell him that you should be commended for your work. What was your name again?"

The Messenger hands him his card from the Freedom Group as Kolb gets pulled away to speak to the many other people who are lining up to talk to him. He does not hear the Messenger's last comments.

The Messenger bows his head and says, "Thank you, Mr. Kolb. God has spoken to me. I have already begun the cleansing process. This is a war and there will be more casualties. You are the Messiah. God bless you. And thank you for your divine direction."

Chapter 11. The Scholar

St. Paul, Minnesota
Sunday Evening

The evening sun is setting over the horizon in downtown Minneapolis as Ryan drives to Como Avenue in St. Paul to get to the Muffaletta Cafe early, knowing that Monday night is never busy. He planned on meeting Julia at 7:00 pm, but has lots of time to enjoy St. Anthony Park on his way to the Cafe.

Walking to the restaurant, he contemplates the conversation that he had with Julia this morning. Murder in St. Paul, anti-Christ research, measurement of the human spirit, the *Prophecy Scoll*, the Plagues. All interesting stuff. And what sweet revenge did she get on the cadaver pranksters in med school? She is one fascinating lady. He's glad she called him out of the blue and suggested dinner, despite his fatigue from the sleepless night, the triathlon this morning, and his busy clinic day tomorrow.

Muffaletta is situated across the street from the park, and is in an old refurbished mansion on a tree-lined street with a set of outdoor tables on the large front veranda and aqua colored umbrellas to shelter the lunch patrons from the sun. He makes sure the hostess seats him at a private table overlooking the veranda and the park. The waitress quickly stops by to welcome him and asks if he is alone. He says no and that his friend should be here soon.

"Would you like anything before she arrives?" The waitress asks.

"Just the water and bread are fine. Thank you."

He thinks about the few dates he had with her in med school before he met Sophia. There was nothing romantic about them. They were just friends getting together to discuss class-work. But she was knockout beautiful, with long blond hair, a pretty face, a short but trim athletic body, and she was always dressed fashionably. She was pleasant to be with, listened well, and looked directly at you with those clear blue eyes. I enjoyed being with her. Now, she is on the faculty at Harvard Medical School. This is impressive. He heard she got tenure in the minimum six years and published a stack of scientific papers.

He checks her Harvard resume on his iPhone. The papers mention string theory, particle physics in healing, human system theory, energy medicine, and other deep end stuff. Quite interesting. This evening just got even more intriguing. But he also realizes that he needs to keep his cool. He knows how to be charming when he wants to be and will try his best to be the gentleman tonight.

The waitress stops by again. He decides to wait before he orders any wine. He does not even know if she drinks wine.

Julia arrives at the restaurant at 7:10 pm, appropriately late, and sees Ryan patiently waiting at the table. As she walks in, he recognizes her immediately, smiles as they make eye contact, and he immediately gets up to greet her. He gives her a big hug. She is still quite attractive after all these years. Time has treated her well, and in fact, makes her seem a little more human. She also has a worried look about her. Fear shows in her eyes. Understandable, considering what she has just been through.

In his mid thirties, Ryan is still ruggedly handsome with the looks of an intellectual adventurer in the grain of Indiana Jones. His dark tanned face has weathered from regular biking, swimming, and his many other outdoor pursuits. But his eyes are dark and tired from the many sleepless nights during his internal medicine residency, the day in and day out of patient care, and the emotional trauma of losing both his father and his wife within a year.

Still, tonight, his eyes are wide open and bright. When he feels good, he can warm up to anybody, even an anxious, overachieving, academic lady. "Julia, it's nice to see you! Come. I have a table already." They give each other a much-needed hug to help both of them relax. He walks her over to the table and helps her take off her coat and hang it on the nearby coat rack, before he politely holds the chair as she is seated.

She puts her small, faux leopard skin purse on the table as she says, "Ryan. Thank you for taking time out of your schedule to meet with me.

There have been so many things happening that I cannot get my arms around it all. It's nice to be able to talk to someone. First, I just want to say how sorry I was to hear about the death of Sophia and your father. I know how much you loved them both."

Ryan nods in response. "Yeah, it's been a tough couple of years. I'm still having difficulty accepting that they are both gone. It's been over a year and I'm still trying to get over it. But what can I do? Not much." He wants to avoid talking about himself and his own issues so he quickly redirects the conversation. "But tell me. What happened today? It sounded frightful."

Julia needs to get the story off her chest, and Ryan's openness to get right into it is appreciated. She tells him about the meeting and who Dr. Jack Killian was. She tells him about the research, the measurement of the human energy fields, and the use of the SERF equipment. She describes the discovery of the scrolls and a summary of each manuscript, the *Seven Realms of Life*, the *Seven Beasts*, the *Rules of the Blessings*, and *Seven Blessings*. She expresses her concern about the Plagues happening in our current lifetime creating a world of low energy zombies. He laughs at the use of this macabre vision of the walking dead. She describes the process at the Terme to become a high-energy warrior of the *Prophecy*.

As she tells the story of the Terme, he watches her beauty, charm and intellectual precision. He tries to match it while buoying her spirits with interest, intelligent question, and humor when appropriate.

She tells him about the morning meeting with Dr. Killian and the plans for lunch. "Then, half way through his talk, he keels over dead. They say he was poisoned by someone who wanted the research to stop."

"I didn't know academic medicine was so cut throat," he says with his typical cynicism and attempt at humor. "I guess that's one way to cut out your competition." As soon as he said it, he realized that it would have been better left unsaid.

Luckily, in her state of frenzy, Julia missed his awkward attempt at humor. "I can't imagine anybody who would feel so strongly about research to murder someone as wonderful as Dr. Killian," She replies. "But he never shied away from the controversy. Now it came back to haunt him. And who is next? Ryan, I'm worried. Research isn't supposed to be like this."

The waitress returns to ask if they would like to order wine. Ryan reviews the wine list and asks if Julia has a preference. She prefers red wine so Ryan asks about the list of Italian wines. The waitress points out that the Sangiovese is particularly tasty, and they both agree.

He becomes more serious. "Why would someone murder him? Why now?"

"I don't know. I just can't fathom why anyone would kill Dr. Killian. He was a brilliant scientist and an NIH Program Officer. He funded the research that needed to be done in one of the most innovative areas of medicine, complementary and alternative care. Integrating modern medicine and technology with ancient knowledge. It may fit right into your clinic."

Ryan thinks about his patients and how much he cares for them. He turns his head to peer out the window of the cafe to watch the cloak of darkness envelope the trees in the adjacent park. He then turns back to Julia. "I saw the news report this afternoon on TV. They said a Manifesto was left in his room under his door. What did it say?"

"It was twisted," she sits forward on the edge of her chair with her hands on the table held tight and staring at him intently. "Ramblings of extremist religious positions and radical public policy changes that would ruin our country. Cutting research, social programs, eliminating immigration, guns anywhere and everywhere. . . Privatize everything and expand the military. . . Strangle the government beast."

"Sounds like a quasi para-military goon wrote it," he says with a cynical tone.

"It even referred to the second coming of the Messiah."

"I heard," he replies. "Who would ever choose an ultraconservative billionaire to be messiah? Truly strange. Were there any strange people in the audience?"

"Yes, a few," she replies with her eyes opening more. "There was a potpourri of people. A couple of questions were asked about the appropriateness of the research. But who would kill over it? It just doesn't make sense." Julia looks worried, thinking about her own safety. She turns to look out the window at the sparkling lights that decorate the patio and brighten the approaching darkness. She imagines what killers may be out there now.

"Look at the killings in the abortion and euthanasia issues," Ryan leans back in his chair to relax and balance Julia's tension. "There are some people who lose sight of what is humane action. In war, people get confused all the time. They kill their own colleagues. There is no rational explanation. There are a lot of crazies out there. Whoever wrote the Manifesto is way over the edge."

The waitress brings the wine and takes their order. They quickly scan the menus and select their entrees. Julia orders the salmon salad and Ryan the garganelli pasta. The waitress pours each a glass of wine.

Ryan raises his glass and says, "To my favorite lab partner in med school. Here's hoping we both find the good life."

She smiles at Ryan's sweetness. "Yes, to that elusive good life, a laudable goal."

Ryan realizes what most physicians come to know. The more you ask questions and simply listen, the more you learn about a person. And the less you have to reveal of yourself. "So, how did Dr. Killian respond to the negative comments in the audience? Was there anybody that seemed to harass him?"

Julia shakes her head no. "The questions were respectful and his responses made sense. The research involved the use of new scientific methods that measured electromagnetic fields of the human body and referred to them as our human spirit. It demonstrated the power of the strategies in the last scroll to enhance a person's spirit. It did not question their authenticity. It is one of the final frontiers. It links science and religion as a continuum. The known, discovered by science, often follows the unknown revealed by faith. They are not incompatible."

"Bingo!" exclaimed Ryan as he raises his glass and takes a sip. "You just hit the nerve. Some people believe science and religion are mutually exclusive and will use public policy and laws to ensure it. They believe religion and ideology should trump science and politics every time, especially when science proves religion wrong. It can be very threatening to the righteous. That would explain the radical Manifesto."

The panic that Julia felt earlier in the day starts coming back. "I don't know, Ryan. I'm worried about my own safety, particularly since my research overlaps with Dr. Killian's. I've been to the Brisighella Terme. If the killer targets Dr. Killian, where will he stop? I could be next. I'm vulnerable right now. Maybe, I've been followed." She shifts forward in her chair and looks sincerely at Ryan with her big blue eyes and worried face. "I'm glad you're here. Thank you."

Ryan relishes the role of a gallant knight as his caretaker personality takes over. He tries to calm her down by changing the subject. "Tell me about Brisighella?"

Julia sits back as her anxiety lifts slowly. She drinks more wine, and lights up as she talks, "Brisighella is a charming medieval Italian village in the Emilia-Romagna region next to Tuscany. It's nestled in the Lamone

River valley surrounded by rocky outcrops of white selenite cliffs. It's located on the trail from Tuscany to Venice and is quite well maintained. It dates back to the 11th century. They erected a castle on one of the three peaks to protect the people and the village grew up around it. In the 13th century, they built another castle on the second peak over the town, and then a few centuries later, they built a clock tower on the third peak above the village."

"You are making me dream of Italy," Ryan laughs. "When does the next flight go? Are you free?"

Julia smiles as she describes her experiences in Italy, "It gets better. In the summer, you can bike up to the hills and pass through vineyards of lush grapes and flower blossomed orchards. From the crest of the hill, you can see the tall white selenite cliffs above the village surrounded by emerald green forests. The three towers stand tall like soldiers protecting the little village. It's stunning. The Lamone River runs through the town, and steams in the morning from the hot springs draining into it. It's about as romantic as Italy gets."

Ryan lights up as he listens to Julia's stories of Brisighella and the Terme Research Project. His imagination soars as he sees an opportunity to visit Italy again and learn how to use this knowledge to help his patients.

Julia's tension is also beginning to dissipate with the conversation, the wine, and Ryan's charm. It's apparent that she enjoys Ryan's attention.

The waitress returns with their dinner. Their eyes light up with hunger. The waitress serves Julia first and says seriously, "Ma'am, in this entrée, the mustard crusted salmon is the leading character and is nicely supported by a delicious ensemble of roasted lentils, parsnip, carrots, diced beets, butternut squash, and turnip crème with shaved radishes on top."

They smile at her creative description. She, then, serves Ryan's meal. "And, here, sir, the star of the performance is the garganelli pasta tossed in the arena with a number of other food players including a rich butternut squash and a sauce laden with caramelized onions, roasted mushrooms, Swiss chard and toppings of olives, blue cheese and toasted pecans." She, then, says with a smile, "I hope you savor the aroma and tastes of these specialties of the house. Each performer has been working hard to please your culinary tastes."

Ryan smiles as he comments, "Don't eat it yet. We should take a picture. I'm hoping that we'll see your salad actually get up and do a little dance routine? Can't wait!"

Julia counters, "And your garganelli pasta entrée? It looks like it's just about to play an intense game of back street hoops with a group of Italian hoodies in Brooklyn."

The matching satirical comments catch both of them off guard, and they laugh unexpectedly. They know they like each other. Ryan waits for her to begin eating and comments that her salmon salad does look delicious. After Julia takes her first bite, Ryan begins eating and looks up at her, trying to understand his growing attraction for her. He concludes that she is more ravishing than the dinner, which is quite delicious.

As they begin to eat, Ryan beats Julia to the questions, "Julia, please tell me more about the village and the Terme."

"Ryan, I really enjoyed my time there. There was so much history blended into cutting edge science. Two thousand years ago, the Romans set up baths at the site to take advantage of the hot sulfur springs. The baths have now become a modern healing Terme or Spa. Not long ago, the Italian Health Authority would pay people to come to the Terme on a doctor's order to recover from illnesses. What more could you want? Working on your health and wellness in a enchanting idyllic setting."

Ryan says nothing and takes another bite to eat. His eyes encourage her to continue. She says, "The crystal white cliffs, lush forests, vineyards, orchards, the picturesque village, the three towers rising above it, the natural foods and wine of the region, the thermal springs, the Terme, the friendly Italian people. It all makes it sound like a fairy tale."

As she tells the story, Ryan thinks about Julia and the relationship they had in med school. They sat next to each other, dissected cadavers, peered into microscopes, and unraveled biochemistry together. He admits to himself that there were some romantic thoughts, but both of them were totally engrossed in their work, and of course, along came Sophia. This put a serious damper on their relationship. But that was another time, another place. He knows little of her now. Is she still single? Does she have children? What drove her to this new field of research and to Brisighella? Dinner continues to be truly mesmerizing.

"When I visited Brisighella, I saw miracles, literally, miracles occur. They told us that they wanted to save us from being low-energy zombies, you know, the walking dead, who suck energy from others. Instead, they trained us to become high-energy warriors that spread positive energy to those around us."

"Zombies?" He looks at her, puzzled. "I'd hate to be called a zombie. But, I have to admit. I've known too many zombies. When the shoe fits, they have to wear it," he laughs.

"As people practiced the actions and boosted their energy, I saw changes in the health of people that I would have said were hopeless. People who were visibly depressed had re-awakened during a couple of weeks. No anti-depressant could have done that. Another patient, who had severe asthma, went into remission and breathed freely. Another patient had rheumatism pain, and every movement hurt. After two weeks, she was dancing all evening. People were transformed."

She pauses to eat her dinner and drink more of the wine. "I saw myself awakened to a new knowledge of how to be healthy, happy, and at peace with myself and the world. I felt I didn't need to prove to myself that I was a good person over and over again. I wanted to be a warrior and help others achieve the same."

"What strategies did they use?" Ryan asks, thinking about how it could help his own patients, as well as himself.

"The *Prophecy Scroll* described simple routines of exercise, meditation, eating and sleeping well, creative pursuits, staying clean and organized, learning, helping others to boost the energy in the seven Realms of our lives. We practiced them every day, maintaining a balance between each of our Realms. They could measure our energy in each Realm and show us what was happening."

"What are our seven Realms?" He asks, not wanting to show his ignorance. "I don't remember them in med school."

"Think about it. They are part of all of our lives. Our mind, body, emotions, spirit, way of life, and the people and natural environment that surround us."

"Yes, that makes sense," he agrees. "How did the actions change you?"

She sits forward, closer to Ryan, and takes a sip of wine. Her voice elevates as she enthusiastically describes her transformation, "Within a week, I became aware of things around me, and inside me, that I had never felt before. It was almost like my antenna was broadened to include many more stations. I could feel energy from all directions. I had insight and wisdom that was new. I opened up to joy and happiness. I noted synchronistic events that were imperceptible to me previously. I could feel my own energy go up and down. Sometimes, it would rush in and out quickly, sometimes increase slowly or dwindle slowly. I could feel it. When I met someone who acted like a zombie, who was mean, with low energy, I could feel the energy being drained. I became more cautious around people with low energy. When I met someone who was positive, insightful, and caring, my energy would zoom. It was kind of scary at first, but seemed so natural as I learned and practiced more. That's why I called you. I remember you nearly always had such positive energy. I knew I could talk to you about anything, and you would not drain my energy."

Ryan smiles as he thinks about his growing attraction to Julia. "Thank you," he replies. "I appreciate your kind words. I listen because I want to know."

She smiles back, appreciating his interest. "For example, certain food and drinks can increase or decrease your energy. Take this glass of wine." She held up the glass with Sangiovese and looks at it through the light in the room. "I thought most wines were similar. I knew that they had different tastes, aromas, colors, and qualities, but I drank it to loosen me up and relax. I wasn't too discriminating. Now, I'm aware of the energy in different wines like never before. When I bring a glass of wine to my lips, I can tell if the wine will enhance my energy or deplete it. Does it fit with my own energy? I can do this now with many foods and drinks. It's no longer about taste only, but its effect on my energy. Some foods make me feel good and some don't. After a week of paying attention to my energy levels, my headaches and neck pain went away. I slept like a baby. I made friends who enhanced my energy. I had fun. I was creative. I connected with certain music and songs that had more meaning and boosted my energy. I went on walks and bike rides in the hills above Brisighella. I organized my life. I became connected to my past and could see my future. It all flowed so easily." She catches her breath and watches Ryan's reaction. She takes a few more morsels of food, and finishes her first glass of wine.

Ryan smiles and lets her talk. He pours her another glass from the bottle wrapped in the stand next to the table. He continues to eat, not wanting her to stop the intriguing dialogue.

Julia takes a sip from her replenished glass of wine, and continues, "It was only for two weeks, but it seemed like an eternity of learning about the good life. And the best part about it was the realization that this life energy and the feelings it created are available to me anytime. And these actions have a foundation in science. There is clear and irrefutable research evidence that these actions can dramatically help people improve their health and happiness." She smiles and pauses to see his reaction. "They can help anybody, especially zombies."

"What do you mean—anybody?" He sits up straighter, and leans forward. "Are you implying I'm a zombie?"

"No, of course not," she says with a coyish smile. "But this knowledge can help anybody who is willing to work at it to enhance their energy. They can achieve a good life regardless of their family background, their personality, their genes or other seemingly permanent situations. Whether they are rich or poor, a lawyer or a plumber, tall or short—any person can achieve high energy. It's so liberating and gratifying to recognize that you have control. No one is stuck where they are."

"But how did you get from Neurosurgery to here?" He asks, "It's quite a revolutionary change."

"Well, how much time do you have?" Julia takes a deep breath and takes a bite of her meal. "It's a long story, and I don't want to bore you with it." She looks at him for approval.

"Julia, your story is not boring," he insists. "This knowledge, the research, the Terme project, the Italian setting. It's all very interesting and relevant to my own life. Go ahead. Try to bore me."

"Well, okay," she acquiesces with a smile. "If you insist. I'm different now than I was in med school. I've gone through some remarkable changes. I suppose you could say a reawakening. I finally realized that I didn't have to be the best at everything, beat everybody, and always win the game. As you know, I went into Neurosurgery residency as a graduating doctor ready to make my mark in the most intense residency available. Everything has always been so easy for me and every door was open. It seemed natural to go into the most intense specialty of medicine. Boy, was I wrong."

Ryan nods, understanding. "I've heard this from other neurosurg residents. It's pretty macho, very intense."

"That's an understatement. It was hell. You're a slave to every whim of the neurosurgery faculty and the patients. There is no life outside of the program. Literally, I felt like a zombie walking around, dead to the world. The inside joke is that they call the six years *the ordeal*. Others call it *the gauntlet*. We had an intense schedule of studying, patient care, scutwork, and grabbing sleep whenever we could. They belittle you. They criticize you. Take the worst of the Socratic method, sprinkle in a steady stream of verbal abuse, then add sleepless nights, and voila, you have very unhappy campers. Frankly, I believe it borders on abuse. You feel diminished every day. Then, you go home and study more. They make you hate it. You dream of having a normal life doing normal things like exercising, sitting down for a good meal, going for a brisk walk, watching a movie. Don't get me wrong. The faculty were good people trying to make the best of a demanding specialty. It is a life and death job where the littlest mistake will kill someone. They want someone who is extremely disciplined. You need to rise to the occasion, or move on."

"But it doesn't matter who you are," Ryan rationalizes. "Everyone needs balance, or there are consequences."

"Yes, I had to learn from the Terme what many people know intuitively," Julia continues. "There are consequences if you get out of balance. You lose your edge, your energy, and your spirit. And for me, my answer to the multiple-choice question was always—all of the above. For three straight years, I buried myself in the work. I was stressed out. I lost my mental edge and my motivation. I drank tons of caffeine. Coffee, the dew, and energy drinks sustained me. I was an insomniac. I had headaches and back pain. I was agitated and snapped at people. I had no life, few friends, and no lovers. Every night, I went to bed alone. I needed a change."

She stops and looks down embarrassed that she felt like a failure. "I didn't need someone to tell me what was wrong. I knew what was wrong. I was losing my energy with the slow grind. I had to give up too much. I wanted more in life. I wanted friends, a family, and a social life. I wanted someone who would love me, someone I could love. I wanted a rich full life. But I was missing the boat. I hated this more than anything else. The boat to a good life was sailing right by me." She is surprised that tears well up in her eyes. She knows that they are as much from the release of her anxiety and fear tonight as they are from the remorse she still feels about her failure. She takes a tissue out of her purse to dry her eyes.

Ryan is surprised and pleased to see this vulnerability. He puts his hand on hers and looks directly into her eyes. "Listen to me. You don't need me to tell you how smart, kind, and giving a person you are. You have so many gifts that I cannot begin to describe them. It is clear that Neurosurgery was too limiting. You need a broad palette that will bring you the world. The world is a better place because of what you're doing now. Neurosurgery would have been a waste of your talents."

"Thank you, Ryan. I'm sorry for getting so emotional. It's not like me. It's been a long haul. And now, with this murder, I'm just on the edge." She dabs her tears with the tissue. "You're a sweetheart to listen and feel such empathy for me, considering I called you out of nowhere." She sighs as she continues her story, "I finally decided that I didn't want to be a Neurosurgeon."

"You just quit?" Ryan widens his eyes. "Do they allow that?"

"Well, I didn't exactly quit. I met this resident at a meeting who told me about the research going on in Brisighella—about energy medicine, ancient scrolls, Plagues and Blessings. It just clicked. Then, I did what was the only acceptable thing to do when you're in Neurosurgery. I started a PhD. I selected the field of Medical Anthropology because I found the research at Brisighella fascinating. It gave me energy. I did my thesis on their research. I visited for weeks at a time. Italy was unbelievably beautiful and enriching."

She pauses, takes a few more bites to finish her meal. She empties her second glass of wine. She knows that she may be rambling, but what the hell, he seems quite interested. She is so glad to have called him. He is the right man at the right time.

Likewise, Ryan continues his questions, deflecting any conversation about his own miserable life. He is genuinely interested in what she is saying. It's obvious that they have much in common. The fact that she is also quite attractive makes it all that much easier simply to watch her and listen.

She carefully dabs her full lips with the napkin and continues, "What I discovered about myself and about health and healing seemed revolutionary to me. The *Seven Realms* manuscript makes so much sense. It reinforced concepts that are universal truths for man. I found ageless knowledge that was both ancient and futuristic at the same time. This is all deep stuff, highly relevant and accessible to anyone."

Ryan smiles and replies, "I understand. I often have the same thoughts when I'm in clinic. We have a long way to go before we fully understand the healing process. The biomedical model and reductionist thinking does not cut it. Why try to improve a blueberry pie by changing one berry? Why not look at the whole pie. There's a much better chance of improving its look, aroma, and flavor. Likewise, we need to look at the whole patient. Tell me about Medical Anthropology. I've never heard of it, but it sounds fascinating."

"To me, this field was the most intriguing. Its focus is the study and development of new systems of medical knowledge that involve the integration of innovative contemporary science with ancient or alternative medical systems and approaches to care. It recognizes that ancient healers and healing practices have much to offer modern medicine. The research focuses on the interaction of medical knowledge with social, emotional, cognitive, behavioral, and spiritual factors within diverse cultural and physical environments. The seven Realms again! We all know these influence health and illness, both for the individual as well as the community as a whole. The field also focuses on understanding the roots of violence, hate, physical and psychological harm and suffering."

As he listens into the night, Ryan's fascination with not only the conversation, but with Julia, is obvious. He not only wants to learn more about the Terme Project in Italy, but more about Julia. He likes this new Julia now that she has had some wine and the panic she had initially has passed. It is the same Julia he knew in med school, but wiser and gentler— and more attractive. He could see himself being drawn to her at so many levels. He wants to spend the night listening to her. "Tell me about the *Prophecy Scroll?*"

"Each of the *Seven Realms of Life* mentioned in the scroll has a different activity that can boost the energy. Take the Spiritual Realm. The manuscript suggests that boosting energy can be done through prayer and meditation. The research at the Terme is quite consistent with other research. For example, in studies of chronic pain, they found that after only a few days of meditation training, teaching people to focus their attention, concentrating on soothing imagery, and relaxing their muscles, two-thirds had a reduction in their pain—roughly equivalent to taking morphine. Other studies found meditation to increase pain thresholds and moods, reduce anxiety, heart rates, stomach acid, and boost the immune system. And this action focuses only on one realm, the spiritual. What happens if you enhance every Realm in a person? And what happens if many people together in a group take action? The results can be dramatic!" She pauses to gauge his reaction. She wonders if she has shifted too much into lecture mode and might lose Ryan's interest. But he's obviously interested. She holds up her glass and realizes that she's emptied two glasses already.

"Do you want some more wine?" he says as he tilts the empty bottle.

"No, no. I've had enough already," she says with a half smile. "I don't want to embarrass myself in front of a near stranger."

"Okay, but do you mind if I have another?" Ryan asks discarding the principle of moderation in drinking. "It's amazing that they had this insight two thousand years ago."

"Go ahead and have another glass," she insists. "You can tolerate more wine than I can. Have I reached your threshold of boredom yet?"

He orders another glass from the waitress. "You're not boring me. It's relevant to my own life too. Please continue."

"Okay, whatever you say," she brightens her blue eyes as she continues. "What was quite interesting was that the principles not only applied to the individual but also to the group. When a critical mass of people, it says a third, follow the actions, an enlightened state of the people will be achieved because of a higher collective energy of the group. Groups of people, whether it's a family, a neighborhood, or a nation, feed on the positive energy of the group and everybody gains. This can and will prevent the Plagues in each realm. People will adopt healthier lifestyles. They will protect the natural environment and provide abundant food and water. They will spread love, tolerance, and open societies that respect human rights. We could avoid the worst of our past, and build on the best prospects for the future, simply by boosting our own energies. This provides hope for the future."

"Now, you're beginning to sound like an idealistic tree hugger," he jokes. "You know that's frowned upon by the current political realities. With the right intervention, maybe you can be cured."

"I'm serious, Ryan," she snaps back, "The good life that you, I, and everybody else want is achievable through the actions in each Realm. And it's not about money. It's about your energy. No one should ever feel stuck where they're at."

"Well, I for one feel like I'm stuck," he says discouragingly with his cynicism on full display. "It's hard to do these things routinely. And if it's hard for me, a physician with a high degree of education and training, then, it's hard for most people. We all have so many self defeating behaviors that we fall into during our daily routines. It's no wonder that over twenty percent of teens and adults are depressed."

He tells Julia about the loss of his father, then his wife, and how he got stuck in a routine of excess work and exercise with poor sleep and minimal socializing. "I feel like I'm practically a shut-in. Until today, I haven't had a date with a woman in over a year, and I'm not even sure you can call this a date. It seems more of a plea for help then a date. Don't you agree?"

"Maybe, but let's call it a date for both of us. I'm in the same boat. Overworked and under-funned."

"Under-funned? Is 'funned' even a word?" He laughs.

"You know. Little time for fun, not doing enough things you enjoy. Funned up is the opposite of being fucked up. Sorry for the expletive. If you over do the fun, it's called funned out."

"So true," he laughs. "I don't think it's a word though, but I can go with it."

"Sometimes you need to be silly," she replies. "I would not have said that ten years ago. The point is that following the *Prophecy* actions will change your life if you give it a chance. You can become a better version of yourself. I also believe that if we do not make these changes collectively, our generation will leave behind a population of unhappy, depressed, and largely unproductive people who hate each other, are constantly at war, are starving, and live in desecrated environments. It is not a happy future. I think we need to do something about it. Don't you agree?"

Her obvious passion and conviction does not surprise Ryan. She has always been intense. Her mission right now is to be a warrior to spread the word of the *Prophecy* to the unsuspecting millions of zombies out there. She wants to do what she can to prevent the Plagues. But it's not a mission that Ryan shares right now. He doesn't consider himself a free thinker, much less a warrior. In fact, he wants a simple life with a family and a job that help people every day deal with their health issues. He begins to realize that hers and his are very different paths. He also recognizes that it is late. He is fatigued, and has a full day of patients tomorrow. He looks up and is surprised to find the restaurant has cleared.

He finishes his third glass of wine, pays the bill, and then answers her question. "Julia, as Mahatma Gandhi said, 'be the change that you wish to see in the world.' I agree, but this seems like a pretty overwhelming task at this time on a Sunday night. As they say, you can only change one person at a time. Your positive energy has convinced this zombie in spirit, and I hope that suffices for tonight. Can we leave the rest of the seven billion people in the world for another day? I have a full day of patients at 8 am."

They both laugh. She sees the fatigue in his eyes, and decides to wrap up their dinner. "I'm so sorry to keep you here so long. And as reluctant as I am to go there, I guess I'll need to get back to the hotel. Can you drive me?"

"Of course," he considers the situation here. A damsel in distress. Intriguing information. No romance in his life. An intense day tomorrow. They're both emotionally fragile. Should he offer her to stay at his house? He weighs each side, and realizes that he has no clue. Damn it. Life can be so cruel and delightful at the same time. Go with the flow or go for it. He needs to decide.

Chapter 12. The Dilemma

As they walk out of the Muffaletta Café, the St. Paul night is clear with a three quarter moon over the eastern horizon and a few of the brightest stars shining through the city lights. Ryan's SUV is parked on the street down from the Café. As they walk slowly to his car making idle conversation, Ryan thinks about his misconception of Julia and feels empathy for her situation. He is not surprised at her radical change in direction and he likes it. He also recognizes that, after all these years, he is still attracted to her.

As they approach the car, the obvious question on both of their minds is—how do they end the night? Neither wants to bring it up.

Julia avoids the question first by noticing the bike rack on the car. "Oh, I forgot to ask!" she says. "How did the race go today?"

"It was surprising that we won," he replies quietly. "I took a spill and almost killed myself. My compadres are maniacs and made up for my accident to pull out a victory. Do you bike?"

"I enjoy it, but not competitively. Cape Cod is a beautiful place to bike." She looks at him for injuries from the accident and now notices the several cuts and bruises that she did not see earlier. "You do look a little ragged. Are you okay?"

"I'm starting to feel every little bruise," he says with agony on his face. "But you, the fine meal, and the wine helped me forget about it."

Small talk continues until they arrive at the hotel. They walk together into the lobby to say good night. The lobby of the St. Paul hotel is a quiet place on a Sunday night, with few people checking in or out. The adjacent restaurant is teaming with people from the conference. Julia is hoping that she doesn't run into anyone she knows. She simply wants to forget about the tragedy this morning.

They stand in the middle of the lobby and face each other. Ryan looks up at the lavish chandelier behind her to find some clever words that don't come. Finally, he says, "Thank you for calling me today. I enjoyed the evening. I learned a lot." He smiles.

She lowers her head and raises her eyes to connect with his. She has an apologetic expression. "I'm sorry I did all the talking. It helped me calm down. I still don't know what you think about all this. The Terme Project has helped transform my life, but I want to know how it fits into other people's worlds like yours. How would you apply this knowledge?"

Ryan stands opposite her quietly considering the question. Most doctors learn to say just enough to be clear, but not too much to reveal personal feelings. However, right now honesty is a virtue. "I wish I could apply it to my patients tomorrow," he says. "Nearly everything you've talked about is something that I have thought about for years. It makes sense. Personally, I don't have the good life stuff figured out, particularly since Sophia's death. I have a lot of sadness and guilt. You know, bad dreams, restless nights, morning fatigue. I bury my feelings in my work and escape into the lives of my patients. But as you say, I need more balance too. I need a life. I will be thinking about our conversation for a long time. But I'm not sure I'm ready to jump on the warrior bandwagon, but I definitely want to learn more."

"I'm sorry that Sophia isn't with us," she says with sincerity. "And thank you for sharing your thoughts. I respect your opinions. I get excited, almost possessed about this new knowledge and how it applies to the world. It takes me off into many different directions. It's helpful to gain perspective from someone as practical as you are. I've had relationships, but have never been married. I'm working on balance, too. It doesn't come naturally to me."

"Will you be staying the rest of the week for the conference?"

"No, I've arranged to leave tomorrow and skip the conference. I still have some fear. I'll feel safer back in Boston. My parents are there and I've got a lot of work to do now that Dr. Killian is gone. I need to rethink my efforts."

Ryan knows he must leave, but they stand awkwardly silent in the lobby, not knowing what to do next. He gives her a big hug, and she holds the embrace for longer than usual. Neither seems to want to let go. She looks up into his sun-bathed face. He wants to kiss her and make it better, to reduce her fear and insecurity, and see where it leads. But it's just too bold. It's not like him. And he doesn't know her well enough. There are always too many 'buts' in his life. He might as well just go ahead and ask. Go with the flow. It won't hurt.

"Julia, are you going to be okay?"

"I'll be okay," she looks him in the eyes waiting for him to say more. Nothing comes. "But thank you for your concern."

After the pause, he finally says, "I normally do not do this, but would you feel safer if you stayed at my place tonight? I don't want to be presumptive, but it may be better to have someone close to you. You know. To give you company. It's a just an idea. No big deal. Don't feel obligated." Ryan believes that he just completely blew it. Doubt fills his mind. What is he doing here? He realizes that he just put her in an awkward situation.

Julia is thinking along the same line. Did he really invite her to his place? What does that mean? Is he making a move? She really does not know him that well. But then, she has known him for nearly ten years. He has always been someone she could trust. She stifles a smile and decides to go with the flow on this one.

"You're so kind, Ryan. It's nice of you to offer. I doubt that I would be able sleep much at the hotel here. Too close to the crime scene. But, I don't want to put you out. Are you sure?"

"Oh, no. No problem," he stutters, surprised at her response. "I've got an extra room. Private and comfortable. I live in nice house in south Minneapolis. It's just a quick twenty-minute drive from here. But I apologize for it's condition. I may need to clean it up bit since I wasn't expecting guests. You know how sloppy guys can be." He laughs uncomfortably.

"Great. Thank you. Let me get my things."

"But you can only stay there on one condition." He ventures into unknown territory.

"What is that?" She says hesitantly wondering about his intentions.

"You must tell me what you did to get revenge on those jokesters back in med school."

Surprised, she smiles at Ryan with a mischievous expression. "Come on, do I really have to? Are you sure you want to know? It was a stupid thing. I'm glad nobody found out. If I tell you, you must promise not to say anything to anybody. Okay?"

"I promise. You can tell me on the ride over to my house."

"It's a deal. You open your house, and I open my wicked past." She laughs and she leaves to retrieve her luggage.

As he sits in the lobby alone thinking about the situation, he has second thoughts about the wisdom of having her stay with him. He is so busy on Monday, is exhausted and bruised from the Triathlon, and really needs to get a good night's sleep. The situation may not only prove to be awkward, but could turn a spectacular evening date into a disaster, if either of us decides to pursue a more intimate relationship. On the other hand, it could lead to something even more special between the two. Either way, it will not cater to him waking up refreshed and ready to provide the best care for his patients on Monday.

Julia has the same thoughts and wonders whether this is the right thing to do. She really doesn't want to stay in this creepy hotel but her options are limited. She could stay at another hotel or head to the airport and hope there is a red eye to Boston. From a practical point of view, it makes more sense just to take up Ryan's suggestion and head to his place. But she wonders if he has any ulterior motives. He's a nice guy—respectful and kind. She's always liked him and she will feel safer at his house. But if she has to stymie his advances, it will be more than awkward. It could ruin the wonderful evening. Then, on the other hand, this may be the start of a special relationship between the two. Either way, the decision has been made and she will have to go with it.

She returns with her things, and Ryan greets her with a reluctant smile. As she checks out, he takes her luggage and puts it into the trunk of the Audi. He opens the door for her, and helps her get into the car while Ryan walks briskly over to the driver's side.

Julia is initially quiet not wanting to bring up her foolish past unless she is forced to.

Finally, Ryan says, "Well, I'm waiting. A deal's a deal. Tell me about the revenge. I am really quite intrigued. You don't seem the type."

"You're right. I'm not the type, now. But I was so angry at their stupid joke. So I mixed up a batch of iodine crystals and clear ammonia, dried it, and put it all over their bench in biochemistry."

"What does that do, stain their hands? That's not so bad."

"You must not have paid attention in Chemistry 101. This chemical combination creates an unstable compound that releases energy rapidly when touched. It simply explodes. No damage. . . but a lot of loud bangs. It doesn't hurt."

"You put a contact explosive on their benches that went off when they touched it?" He says, astonished.

"Those juveniles deserved it. When the explosives went off, they panicked. Not only did they run like scared chickens, the professor cleared the entire building into the street on a cold winter day. Of course, I wasn't anywhere near the building that day, but heard about it later. They were blamed for making the explosives, and spent a day explaining it to the dean and the police. Just retribution for being jerks."

"Did they ever find out?"

"No. In fact, right now, you're the only person who knows about it," she moves her fingers across her lips. "So, keep your lips sealed." She laughs out loud, "I have my academic reputation to uphold now."

Ryan laughs with her. "Okay. I just learned not to mess with you!"

As they get closer to his house, the conversation tapers off. Both are trying to figure out what will transpire in this scenario, but neither really knows nor has any expectations. As soon as they arrive, he takes her things out of the trunk and walks them directly upstairs to the guest room. Luckily, he finds the bed is already made since his mother sleeps there on occasion. She always tidies up and makes sure clean sheets are on before she leaves.

He yells to her from upstairs to make herself at home. Julia sits down on the overstuffed couch in the living room and looks around with approval. It's not as bad as she would have expected from a busy single guy.

As he comes back down the stairs, he says apologetically, "Sorry for the mess here. As I said, I didn't expect to have a guest tonight." He quickly runs around the house picking up clothes, an empty bag of chips, dirty dishes, and the miscellaneous newspapers and magazines that have been lying around the house for weeks.

"You have such a nice house here," she comments politely. "How long have you had it?'

"Six Years," he yells from the kitchen. "Sophia and I bought this house soon after we got married. It was a run down old house and we remodeled it. We loved the stonework and the old European feel of the house. The patio and backyard garden were big attractions for us."

She looks out the back and the accent lighting displays the richness of the perennial garden, annual flowers, waterfalls, and statues. She is impressed. "Ryan. I know it's late, and I'm sorry to impose on you like this. You're sweet to let me stay here, but you need to get to bed. You said you have full day of patients tomorrow."

"Yes, I do have to get up early. However, I want to make sure you're settled in and comfortable." He walks her up the stairs and he shows her to the guest bedroom. "Here's the spare bedroom. The sheets are clean. My mother makes sure of that. Here's the bathroom. I'll let you be now."

As Ryan prepares for bed, he thinks about his evening and his natural attraction for Julia. He decides to simply say good night to her, without fanfare or long discussions. He knocks on the door of the guest bedroom to say good night. She answers in her nightgown, a soft silk gown with narrow straps on bare shoulders. The embroidered lace luxuriously conforms to her athletic body. She has let her hair down and her face radiates like a teenager. She is a beautiful woman, and it hits Ryan like a brick. He stands there looking at her like a dufus.

Finally, his mind and mouth come back to reality. "Ah, I just wanted to say good night. If you need anything, please don't hesitate to knock on my door. I hope you sleep well."

She stands at the door of the room and looks at him in his pajamas. He wears a clean white t-shirt to bed with shorts. She was surprised to notice how muscular and firm he is from his years of working out and biking.

She looks up with her soft blue eyes, and says, "Thank you, Ryan, I'm just fine. I'm just happy to be out of the hotel. I'll sleep much better here. You're very kind."

With that, Ryan returns to his bedroom and closes his door. There was no good night kiss, no hug, and no small talk. He gets into bed and turns his light on to read a few pages of the Maeve Binchy novel, *Minding Frankie*. He is exhausted and cannot stay focused on the book. After a few minutes, he turns the light off and falls asleep.

He sleeps soundly until about 3 am when he is awakened by the sound of a creaky wood floor from footsteps walking towards his room. He lies there, his eyes closed, wondering who it is. Then, he remembers that Julia is here. He hears her walk closer to his room, and then opens the door. He wonders what she is doing. The wood floor creaks as she walks softly toward the bed. She lifts his covers and quietly slips into bed with him. Ryan says nothing and stays still. But he is clearly not still as his heart begins to beat faster and he becomes aroused.

She gets close to him and puts her arm around him. "I'm sorry. I just can't sleep," she says quietly. "I'm still worried. Do you mind?"

"No problem," he replies. He turns to hold her tight in his arms and, then, kisses her head. He has not slept with another woman since Sophia. He loves Julia's scent, the softness of her gown, and the warmth of her touch.

Her body is snuggled warmly close to his. He desperately wants to kiss her, but he does nothing. He'll let her take the lead, if she is interested. He waits for her touch, a gentle embrace, a sensuous kiss, but none comes.

His thoughts wander to what should he do next. As much as he needs love, he will let her sleep rather than meet his romantic needs. His responsibility tonight is to help her feel secure and safe. He has a natural tendency to be overly protective of the people he cares about. He holds her securely and she falls quietly to sleep in his arms. He sleeps on and off for a few hours thinking about his future and what role Julia may play in it. It was a special night with a special person. He drifts off to a sound sleep. When the morning comes, he is still in need of love but he is quite content.

Ryan sneaks out of bed while Julia is still sleeping. He goes to make the strongest coffee he can. He thinks that he slept maybe four hours last night. Yet, he doesn't feel tired, and in fact, he is excited. He is happy that he showed surprising restraint in bed with her last night. He still maintains a few traditional values including that men should know a woman well before he commits to loving her.

Julia wakes up a half hour later and comes walking into the kitchen stretching her arms and yawning. She is wearing the tattered bathrobe that Sophia bought him when they first married, "Ryan, I'm sorry I woke you last night. I wasn't sleeping, and was afraid that. . ."

He stops her by gently putting his finger to her lips, "Don't even think about it. I enjoyed your warmth and softness. I've not had the pleasure of having someone next to me in bed for a long time. It was special. No need to apologize. Are you hungry? Want some coffee?"

"Thank you, Ryan. I did have a nice sleep thanks to you. You were a gentleman, too." She smiles at him in appreciation for containing his testosterone.

He prepares a cup of coffee for her and offers her some breakfast. She defers. Both are in a hurry to get out the door this morning. She already called a taxi since her plane leaves this morning. As the taxi arrives, Julia gets her things from the guest room. Ryan hustles to prepare for his clinic day. He had wanted to spend more time with her this morning, but will have to leave it to another day. He walks her to the door to say goodbye.

Standing under the front foyer, she turns towards Ryan and looks up at him with affection. "Ryan. Thank you. You're a kind person. I would like to spend more time with you. I hope you can come to Boston sometime."

"It is I who needs to thank you," he says. "You brought a whole new world to me last night. I'll be thinking long and hard about our conversation.

I agree, we need to get together again soon. I have no trips planned right now, but there are a lot of meetings held in Boston."

They hug each other and want it to last, but the taxi is waiting. She breaks away and walks to the car. She looks out the window to watch him standing in the door. Their eyes lock and she smiles at him as the taxi drives away. He hopes and prays that she is safe. She brings a wonderful energy, insight, and enlightenment to the people around her.

He scrambles to find his cell phone, Macbook Pro, backpack, wallet, and keys. He glances in the mirror as he heads into the garage and gets into his Audi to drives to the clinic, fifteen minutes away. On his way to the clinic, his thoughts continue to focus on the conversation with her.

He knows their dinner will transform his life, but is not sure how. He also knows intuitively that Julia's appearance was not a coincidence. Perhaps, in some level of spiritual fantasy, she could be viewed as an angel looking after him, perhaps facilitated by Sophia. He still loves Sophia deeply and the thought of loving someone else rattles him. He thinks about the research at the Terme and his situation. Is Julia's visit a wake up call for him? Is she an answer to help solve his own problems? He has no time to think about that. He has to see his first patient in minutes. There is always something.

Chapter 13. The Vatican

Cardinal Martinelli walks swiftly down the hall to the Pope's private quarters. He carefully, but urgently, knocks on the Pontiff's door. It opens slowly, and the Vicar of Christ peeks out with a stern look on his face. "What can be so significant as to wake up an old man having wonderful dreams of the afterlife?"

The Cardinal, pale and panting after the quick climb up five floors to the Pontiff's private quarters, tells the Pope of the situation, "Sir, I'm very sorry to bother you, but there has been a tragedy that you need to be aware of. Dr. Jack Killian, a doctor and program officer at the National Institute of Health, was murdered on Saturday night. A religious Manifesto was found implicating the Vatican and you, Your Excellency, in the murder.

The Pope, shaken out of his sleepiness, responds patiently,

"There must be some mistake. What are the circumstances surrounding this?"

"Dr. Killian was presenting research on the *Prophecy Scroll* to determine the effects of the divine word. Remember, that is the last of the Dead Sea scrolls discovered. We are assembling and translating it here at the Academy. Dr. Killian was poisoned to death and died while he was giving a presentation about it. They found the Manifesto under the door of Dr. Killian's room at his hotel. The Manifesto mentions that any research using the manuscript is anti-Christ and heretical. It states that God and the

Vatican do not support this research. The Manifesto quotes you as stating that this type of religious research must be stopped one way or another. It will hit the news today. Perhaps, we need to convene your inner circle to know how to respond. Reporters will be at our doorstep this morning."

"Cardinal Martinelli. Thank you for waking me. This is alarming and will continue to fuel reports of conflicts within the Vatican. I do not remember saying anything about the *Prophecy* research to anyone. Please bring together those of my Council who are here. Also, please include those who have helped translate the *Prophecy Scroll*. Tell them it's urgent."

As the President of the Pontifical Council for Justice and Peace, and one of his secretaries, Cardinal Martinelli is one of the most influential members of the Pope's inner circle. He quickly assembles the members of the inner circle who are at the Vatican. This includes one of the Pope's secretaries, Monsignor Grandscheid, a Bavarian priest from Germany. Monsignor Grandsheid is conservative and literal about his interpretations of biblical writings and frequently accuses Catholics of crossing the boundary between science and religion. The position of the rest of Vatican's innermost circle on the conflict is unknown.

The Council is almost exclusively made up of Italian men in their seventies including Monsignors Vittorio Dall'Arancio, Antonio Vaselli, Francisco Termeni, Luigi Guissani from Malta and Paolo Ricci from Bologna. They are each part of the Pontifical Academy of Sciences and scholars in their own right, having translated many biblical texts from the ancient Hebrew and Greek languages.

The Academy also includes several scroll scholars, who after years of study, are respected by the Pope and his inner circle for translating and interpreting the holy word. Vatican scholar, Gabriela Gaetti, and Notre Dame Theology Professors and visiting scroll scholars, Eugene Unico and James Monsein, made the landmark discovery of the *Prophecy Scroll* using the locations cited by the *Copper Scroll*. Since the discovery, the Vatican has been collaborating with the Antiquities Authority of Israel, who has possession of the *Dead Sea Scrolls*, to assemble and translate them with help from scholars throughout Italy. The Vatican's support in providing the manuscripts to researchers has been viewed as a greater willingness on the part of the Vatican to be more open and collaborative in scientific issues.

They do not want the world to think they are anti-science and still believe the sun revolves around the earth. This informal position is consistent with other recent Vatican activities, which include hosting an

AIDS conference, releasing a report on bioethics issues in stem cell research, and the announcement of a new stance on supporting condom use.

However, the Vatican will not endorse or explore anything that contradicts the church's teaching on the belief in a creator who existed before any big bang theory could set the universe in motion. This is also why the Vatican supports the Brisighella research, which involves interpreting the power of the holy word and not abdicating it. Unfortunately, with the murder of Dr. Killian, the Vatican's discussions on the role of science in religion will become even more heated and polarized.

The group gathers in the Pope's meeting room, off from his central chambers. After the Pope arrives, Cardinal Martinelli opens with remarks about the circumstances prompting this dramatic gathering including the murder implicating the Vatican and the Pope, "The media reports will come out today, and reporters will undoubtedly be at our doorstep. We need to have a plan to respond."

Monsignor Grandscheid immediately speaks up, "Do you remember our heated discussions on this topic? I stated emphatically that we should not release the *Prophecy Scroll*, and that we should not support this research. It professes to measure the human spirit. This is ridiculous and heretical. Now, it's coming back to haunt us. Are we not questioning the Word of God with this research? Is it not inconsistent with the Church's teachings and beliefs? What are we doing here, gentlemen?"

The group looks troubled, avoiding direct eye contact with Monsignor Grandscheid. Monsignor Martinelli turns to Gabriela Gaetti and says, "I appreciate your position, Monsignor, but we need to look at the broader picture here before we make judgments. Dr. Gaetti is the lead scholar involved in the assembly and translation of the *Prophecy Scroll*. She is under the advisement of our Pontifical Academy of Sciences. Dr. Gaetti, would you please update us on the status of the manuscript and the research?"

Gabriela Gaetti sits with a straight upright posture in her chair. Her original passion was to join the Sisters of St. Andrew's to become a nun. However, her academic interest in ancient manuscripts and biblical writings trumped her dedication to a life in the sisterhood.

The puritanical and austere lifestyle of one of few women scholars at the Vatican cannot subdue her natural beauty. She has short-cropped brown hair, big brown eyes, a soft face, and a complexion that most Italian cosmetic companies would pay millions for. However, she has little interest in worldly pursuits, and spends her time devoted to translating and interpreting the Holy Word. She has been a good friend and an avid supporter of the work of Drs. Paolo Nobili and Vanessa Venetre. She has developed a close friendship with Dr. Venetre through this project that will last a lifetime. Both women are unique, knowledgeable, and successful in their own right, and well respected in circles traditionally dominated by men.

"Thank you Monsignor, I'm happy to," Gabriela says in a quiet and respectful voice. "Let me give you some background. Last year, we assembled and translated several of the recently discovered *Dead Sea Scrolls* to support Operation Scroll led by the Israel Antiquities Authority in Jerusalem. One particularly important finding was the *Prophecy Scroll*. This manuscript was discovered as part of our work here at the Academy. As you know, it is the Academy's responsibility to advise the Church on scientific matters and their policies. Let me introduce you to Drs. Unico and Monsein. They are visiting here from Notre Dame University to help us assemble and translate the *Prophecy Scroll*. They are also advising the Academy on its implications for the Church."

A few of the Pope's inner circle are not even listening. They've already made up their minds and know what needs to be done. However, they are respectful and patiently wait until Dr. Gaetti finishes.

"This *Prophecy Scroll* was found just last year using the locations noted in the *Copper Scroll*," she continues. "This scroll included underground hiding places for a vast treasure of gold, silver, and aromatics from the Temple of Jerusalem before it was sacked and burned by the Romans in 70 A.D. We solved the encrypted code within the scroll to find the twelfth cave. In this cave, an urn was found that contained the *Prophecy Scroll* on a fragmented metal scroll not unlike the *Copper Scroll*. The scroll is shown here in these pictures."

She passes around a picture of both the *Copper Scroll* and the *Prophecy Scroll* as she continues, "We have collaborated with the Israel Antiquities Authority to reconstruct some of these scrolls here at the Vatican. Under direction of the Academy, we began the painstaking process of assembling the fragments and then translating the initial text. We discovered the first of these manuscripts contained a prophecy that had significant implications for the broader religious community and the people of the world. As each additional manuscript was assembled, we sent copies to our scholars around Italy for translation. The translations are going on right now. In addition, on approval of the Academy, we supplied the manuscripts to researchers in Brisighella. They evaluated how the strategies described in the manuscripts affect human electromagnetic energy fields that may reflect the human spirit. Here are pictures of the energy fields. This is where the controversy lies."

Monsignor Grandscheid carefully studies the information provided by Dr. Gaetti. He tilts his bifocals down and looks at them sternly. Then, he looks up at the group, and with an argumentative and cynical tone, he states, "We appreciate your work in translating these important historical manuscripts. But why did we give them to a group of researchers to test the Word of God? This research borders on heresy and has put the Church in an unfavorable light. We need to heed this murder as a message to stop all connection to this sacrilegious research."

Dr. Gaetti is taken aback, and is embarrassed by his criticism. She knows her role at the Vatican is always on shaky ground. She drops her head and avoids looking at the group.

Monsignor Ricci responds quickly to the comment, "I'm from Basilica of San Domenico in Bologna, and have visited the Brisighella Terme many times. The research is not only progressing well, but also showing remarkable results. I met with Drs. Nobili and Venetre. I can tell you that the early results are very promising. It provides revolutionary knowledge that what we do every day in each realm of our lives affects our human spirit and our health, happiness, and peace. It confirms that a person's spiritual health is an integral part of our overall health, even if you are non-believer. This is a groundbreaking project! I emphatically and enthusiastically support it."

Gaining some confidence with Monsignor Ricci's comments, Dr. Gaetti looks up, and with a quiet hesitation, tries to explain, "What Monsignor says is true. Let me explain further what's going on at the Brisighella Terme, and what they have found. We realized that research funded by the U.S. National Institute of Health was being done to measure the human spirit. As word of the *Prophecy Scroll* came to light, Dr. Venetre contacted us to use the content of the manuscript in a series of natural experiments to demonstrate the truth of its power. The manuscript has some alarming predictions of plagues, but it also presents strategies to achieve Blessings. The overall goal is to show the power of these Blessings in hopes of preventing the apocalyptic vision and to lead people to the principles of a good life filled with Blessings. Both the group in Brisighella and the Vatican's Academy believe that by enhancing a person's spirit, it can influence the health and well being of a person. This research may scientifically document the effects of the Blessings on the human spirit and confirm the power of these Holy Words."

Monsignor Martinelli speaks up to support Dr. Gaetti, "Is this research controversial? To some, yes. However, the Academy has determined that the Vatican should only make the manuscripts available and stay quietly neutral on the research. Although this position is somewhat risky, the Academy felt that it may hold promise in sustaining a larger interest in the church and the people of the world when the results come to light. It could be viewed as expanding the importance of religion in society and in our daily lives. This is something we have needed for many years. We all know that less and less people see religion as relevant to their lives. However, the controversy involves conducting research on these divine words. Measuring that which is spiritual in nature may be viewed as sacrilegious. So we decided to approach this patiently while monitoring the research closely."

Monsignor Dall'Arancio interjects with a puzzled look, "How does the research play into the death of the American doctor?"

They turn to look at Dr. Gaetti as she responds, "We do not know why Dr. Killian was murdered. The Manifesto mentions the Vatican as disapproving of this research. We do not yet have a copy. We need to know more before we can make any judgments. We know the Manifesto specifically references the need to stop research that involves religious content. It also mentions stopping research on global warming, abortion, stem cells, evolution, and new life forms and what seems like any research that conflicts with the author's ideological stance. It mentioned the need to return to the traditional teachings of the Church."

Monsignor Ricci adds in a carefully worded cynical voice, "And it says we should reject science to favor historical religious doctrine. Does that mean we should go back to believing the earth revolves around the sun?"

Despite his cynicism, Gabriela appreciates Monsignor Ricci's supportive comments, and hopes it helps the group become more sympathetic to her position. With her head down, Dr. Gaetti turns towards the Pontiff, and she looks up with her eyes to ask him for guidance.

The Pope has listened carefully to what is being said. Dr. Gaetti keeps her head bowed in respect as she says, "It specifically mentions you, Your Holiness, as the inspirational leader of this teaching. However, it is important to note that the *Prophecy Scroll* is a document of great significance to the world and not only because of its apocalyptic predictions, but because of its Blessings. These call on the people of the world to enhance their spiritual energy. We need to pay attention to it. Thus, I have been quietly supportive of not only assembling and translating the manuscript, but also making it available to others to study. We hope this is consistent with the intent of this Academy and your directives. If not, we can change our position and retract the manuscripts."

Monsignor Termeni interrupts, "The latter is exactly what we should do. This research is wrong, and should not be taking place. Science should not be performed to test God's authenticity. We need to denounce this heretical work and ensure that any implication of our connection to the murder is non-existent."

Monsignor Dall'Arancio calmly counters the Monsignors' opinions and says with confidence, "After hearing both sides and reading extensively about the manuscripts and the research, I believe the opposite is true. If we stay supportive of this research, it will demonstrate that we do not agree with the Manifesto and do not feed into the motives of a killer. We do not give power to evil. Let me recall the words of the *Prophecy Scroll* 'When a third of the people take up these Blessings in their lives, become skillful in their actions and virtuous in their being, the Beast is cast back into the bottomless pit, to be shut up again, and set a seal upon him, so that he should deceive the nations no more, and he shall be tormented day and night for one thousand years.'

We need to spread the word of these Blessings. This is what the research is doing. We are on the right track here."

Monsignor Dall'Arancio's knowledge of the manuscript surprises the group. Dr. Gaetti is relieved by his comments, and smiles quietly to herself. The Holy Father is listening intently to the discussion. He is a staunch conservative and defender of the historical traditions and teachings of the Church. Yet, he has also been a firm believer of living in the present and seeing into the future. The world knows that the Vatican's official position on topics of science has been historically sketchy. It took the Vatican more than 350 years to admit it was wrong about Galileo and his theory that the earth revolves around the sun, finally cementing its contrition by erecting a statue of him in 2009. Its pronouncements over the years on life issues such as birth control, stem cells, new life forms, and its historical vacillation over the theory of evolution is at odds with the scientific community.

The fact that the Vatican's stand on this research has been neutral suggests that its position may be interpreted as boldly going where no Catholic Pope has ever gone before. Some believe this would stir excitement among followers.

The Holy Father looks down in thought and prayer. All eyes are on him as he looks up. His eyes are old, but warm and understanding. He patiently and calmly talks to his inner circle, "This is a very important discussion where each side is right. If we change our stance and oppose the research, we play into the hands of evil and those who have accused the Vatican of involvement in the murder. If we support the research, we are criticized for testing the authenticity of these divine words. We need to be cautious before proceeding."

He looks out the window to contemplate this dilemma. He eyes look into the distance, as he appears to be in dialogue with God. He then says, "Above all, we have a responsibility to help the people of the world understand the knowledge in this manuscript. If it is as important as you believe, it is something that the church needs to bring to world. The church has much to offer the world, and, the *Prophecy Scroll* can help. Thank you, doctors, for your help in bringing this masterpiece to the world. I will deliberate for the rest of the day, and with each of you, before making a final decision."

Chapter 14. The Vacation

MINNEAPOLIS/ST. PAUL AIRPORT
SATURDAY EVENING

Ryan is sitting alone in the waiting area of Gate forty-three at the Minneapolis/St. Paul Airport excited to be traveling to visit the Terme Project in Brisighella, Italy. He is still shocked that he made the decision to skip fishing with the boys during his week off, and instead, travel halfway across the world to take a much-needed vacation and relax at the Italian spa. He expressed his apologies to his buddies for the last minute change in plans. They understood, and were able to pull in another friend to replace him.

He was hoping that Julia would come with him, but alas, her teaching schedule was overwhelming. But he appreciated her help in arranging the visit through Dr. Vanessa Venetre, one of the principal investigators of the Terme Project. As he waits, he responds to a few last minute messages on his cell before he hears the boarding announcement.

He walks slowly down the ramp and onto the plane to find his window seat in cattle class for the flight to Amsterdam. The Saturday overnight flight is oversold and packed. He will stop for two hours in Amsterdam, and then, take a smaller plane to Bologna, the closest airport to Brisighella. He wonders who else is on this plane and carefully scrutinizes each passenger. He is a bit spooked by the murder a week ago in St. Paul, and wonders if his destination may also be that of the killer. He sees nobody that he knows, and nobody who looks even the least bit suspicious. The crew helps passengers get to their seats and lift carry-ons to the compartments above.

As he settles in for the six-hour flight, he wonders what knowledge and experiences await him at the Terme.

Needless to say, he is excited to have changed his plans. Although any vacation at this point is a good vacation, he is proud of his choice to pursue a health-related venue. Even his mother was happy to see him go. This spontaneous adventure to Italy is surprising for someone who appreciates a life that is predictable and routine. But he was driven to do something to change his life that is more dramatic than his previous attempts. Thus, this opportunity came at just the right time, and easily trumped fishing with his friends.

Sophia would also have been proud that he is sitting here right now. Not only did she love to travel, particularly to Italy, but she also prodded him to step out of the box and live a little. She would say, "Life is short, Ryan. It isn't always about work." Her prophetic words keep coming back to haunt him. Tears well up in his eyes as he wishes she could be with him right now. Had she survived, they would have children and be going to Italy together for this vacation. She was his portal to the world, and life outside of his clinic.

What a coincidence that Julia called last week because of the unfortunate circumstance at the conference and now here he is on his way to Italy. He is relieved that she is safely in Boston. When they talked yesterday, she was enthusiastic about him going to see a place that she loves. She is a remarkable woman. Unlike himself, she was able to make a major paradigm shift in her life. How did she do that? It must have taken a lot of courage to drop out of Neurosurgery. He will call her again when he arrives.

Before he left, he printed an online article about the research in Brisighella Terme by Drs. Paolo Nobili and Vanessa Venetre. As he reads it, he thinks about the content of the *Prophecy Scroll*. Enhancing your spirit. Casting away demons. Finding your angels. Achieving Blessings. Return of the beast. It does sound more religion than science. But that is to be expected. Priests at the Temple of Jerusalem whom, as some would say, were connected to a divine source of knowledge, wrote it two thousand years ago. His B.S. detectors go way up.

It's all strange and brings up many questions. How did they happen to predict plagues that would occur two thousand years into the future? And how did they know that the Plagues would actually become reality? And why would they predict a third of the earth would die? This is just not possible.

But if the Plagues are beginning, should we not be able to prevent it with our modern technology? We live in an intellectually advanced and enlightened society. If a large number of people boost their energy in the seven Realms, will it prevent the Plagues? Or, are we in a slow decline due to our inability to live in peace. Will our advancing war technology and selfish thinking lead to our eventual decline and self-destruction? What does it mean to be a doctor in a dying world? Will I be able to apply this knowledge to help my patients achieve health, healing, and the blessings of life in this world scenario? Will my efforts help prevent the Plagues? Lots of questions, but more doubt than anything else fills his mind. This manuscript is simply the paranoid musings of a priest who is about to be sacked by the Romans. His cynicism often gets the best of him.

Yet, here he is on the plane flying to Italy to check it out and find that elusive good life. If this journey to the Terme turns out to be a mistake, he can always travel around the beautiful country of Italy. He ponders his own destiny. His life is a winding path right now. He has no expectations. As his mother keeps telling him, "Just go with the flow." Right now, it is his modus operandi.

At least he is taking a vacation. He laughs to himself. If the world is going to end, he might as well be at a magical Italian spa. The fact that the Romans have enjoyed it for hundreds of years makes it good enough for him. He cannot think of a better place to go right now. Pleasant thoughts of Sophia and Julia gradually lull him to sleep. It is a sleep that has been needed for several weeks now. It is a quiet restful sleep.

The plane arrives in Amsterdam in the afternoon on Sunday, but it is still early morning for Ryan due to the seven-hour time difference. The lights go on, and he hears the announcement from the flight attendant to wake up and get ready to depart the plane. He needs to get his butt in gear, but is sluggish from the deep sleep and the early morning hour. He gets his things and stumbles off the plane to find his next flight.

He is alone among thousands of people scurrying in the corridors of the Schiphol Airport. He has to walk about fifteen minutes to his next gate. On his way, he stops at one of the terminal's magazine shops. He sees a recent issue of Europa Health. He notes the cover mentions the Terme Project at Brisighella. He purchases it, and is excited to read everything he can about this unique project.

He stops to pick up a cappuccino to help him wake up before he is able to find his gate. He sits down, drinks the warm coffee, and settles into the article. A well-dressed younger gentleman, sitting next to him, looks over Ryan's shoulder and says, "Excuse me. I couldn't help notice that you're reading the article about the Terme research. What a coincidence. I happen to be going there myself. Is it a good article?"

Ryan looks up from the magazine and smiles at the gentleman. "Yes, it's quite interesting. I'm also heading there for a well-deserved vacation, and perhaps, learn a thing or two about the research and myself. They welcome visitors. What brings you there?"

"Well, I found out about the research at a recent conference in Minneapolis, and thought I would also visit to find out more. It sounded intriguing. Evaluating religious documents with scientific research on the human spirit? What could be next on the horizon for science? Determining if God exists or not, I suppose."

The comment piques Ryan's interest in this gentleman. The cynicism in the man's voice is eerie, and if he was at the conference, he must know about the horrific murder. Ryan feels a need to defend the research as he thinks about Julia's passion for it. "I'm Ryan Laughlin," he extends his hand.

The man responds by shaking Ryan's hand, more firmly than expected. "Hi, I'm Brian Johnson."

Ryan continues, "I understand that the science is not to evaluate whether the manuscript is valid or not, but rather to determine the extent of their insight and effects on people. It sounds relevant. There is a need to validate the measurements of the human energy field. I'm a physician and it's pretty ground-breaking to me. It could change how we view our lives."

"Yes, I suppose," Johnson replies. "I'm here to evaluate the value of it for my religious study group. It seems pretty radical and innovative. We wanted to see what's going on there for ourselves."

Ryan turns back to his reading, but then thinks about the gentleman's comments. Was he one of those at the conference who was questioning the relevance of the research? The Manifesto left in Dr. Killian's room had the same questions. He does not want to jump to conclusions, but this is odd. The guy looks pretty innocent and friendly but he should probe further.

"Sad about the loss of Dr. Killian at the conference," Ryan turns to the gentleman to see his reaction.

"Yes, dreadful," he shakes his head. "I understand his death was tied to the research. So unnecessary."

"Yes, some people are crazy," Ryan replies as he looks at Johnson and acknowledges his innocent response. Not everybody with skepticism is a serial killer.

The small plane begins to board and Johnson tells Ryan that he looks forward to seeing him in Brisighella. He finds his seat a distance away from Ryan's.

After the two-hour flight, the plane touches down at the Bologna airport. The passengers walk down the steps to the bright sun outside since there are no direct jet bridges to the single story airport building. The passengers hop on a bus with their carry-ons, and ride to the airport terminal gate. Ryan is surprised that the passengers are bussed to the terminal since it is literally a few seconds walk to the gate twenty meters away. Some regulations are as impractical in Europe as they are in the U.S. He steps off the bus, waits to find his luggage in the baggage claim area, and then pulls it through the arrival gate to the main terminal.

The Bologna terminal is a small, but surprisingly elegant, building with colorful ceramic art tiles on the floor and walls, a prosciutto deli, and an espresso bar filled with Italians getting their kicks. He looks around for Brian Johnson, but does not see him. Perhaps, he took a taxi straight to Brisighella.

Ryan finds a taxi outside the terminal to take him to the train station in Bologna. At the Bologna station, Ryan finds the forty-five minute train that travels to Faenza. He switches trains in Faenza to take an old steam-powered locomotive the final few kilometers to Brisighella. As the train passes over a deep ravine overlooking the Lamone River, he sees the groves of old pina trees with their broad pine boughs, a row of majestic country homes set back from the road, and a long trail of yellow roses that line the path to Brisighella.

He steps off the train and walks into the ancient but well-restored single room train station. He feels as if he is stepping back fifty years in time. He walks out of the station pulling his luggage. He can see the park across the street with a row of chestnut trees, a stone park bench with several older ladies sitting and chatting about the local gossip, and an ancient fountain of mermaids with water flowing from their urns situated in the center of the park. He can see the three towers of Brisighella on the cliffs in the distance. A row of centuries old pastel colored stone buildings is just beyond the park with a gelateria and an outdoor café at the ground floor. There are a dozen or so chairs at the cafe filled with older men having conversations and watching people walk by.

He decides to stop at the gelateria. As his first action on this glorious vacation, he indulges in one of his favorite vices—ice cream. He scans the dozens or so varieties and is confused about what he should order. They have such a delicious variety of *gelato*. His stomach growls at the conflict. The young girl, with a nametag saying Marta, is dressed formally with a uniform comprised of a white shirt, a yellow fancy apron, black dress pants, and a white hat. She is serving espresso with a shot of grappa called *caffè corretto* to the smiling older gentleman dressed in a jacket and bow tie.

When she is done, she turns to Ryan and says, "*Buon Giorno. Vuoli Gelato? Cono oicialda?*"

Ryan smiles and peers at her with a puzzled look.

She smiles back at him, and says, "*Sei englesa?*"

"*Si,*" he replies.

With a flip of her hand, she says, "*No problema*. Would you like a sugar cone or waffle cone?"

"Thank you," he says, relieved. "Waffle cone, please. I'll have the *gelato la torre speciale* with *fragola*, *nutella*, and *pistaccio*. *Si?*"

Her eyes widen as she turns to prepare the largest of their sweet treats. She hands him a giant *gelato* cone with ice cream balls that teeter like the Leaning Tower of Pisa above his hand. Nine Euros later, he sits down to eat this full meal masterpiece on the park bench. He sits next to the two older Italian women with old flowered dresses and colorful scarves over their heads. They smile and look at Ryan. They enjoy a laugh together at his obvious immaturity in buying, and trying to eat, the giant gelato tower before it melts all over his clothes.

Ten minutes later, his stomach is hurting with the satisfaction of eating the whole Italian indulgence. He is no longer hungry. He walks around the small village of Brisighella. It has a charming *piazza* with narrow mid-level stone streets lined with quiet shops that fan out in four directions from *il centro*. He stares in awe at the three towers that Julia talked about. He walks the five blocks from the train station to the Terme. With the exception of pulling his rolling luggage behind him as it thuds across the cobblestone way, it's an easy walk to the Terme.

Ryan arrives at the Terme and checks in at the reception desk. The light of the day is still present on this Sunday afternoon. The reception room seems to have its original features with warm terracotta floor, ornate dark wood paneled ceilings, and frescoes on the wall that may date back to the Renaissance. There is a small, but bright, chandelier with minimalist, modern furniture in the room. There is a large door with a window that looks out into the courtyard. The front desk, characteristic of older and elegant small hotels in Italy, is a raised counter of dark wood and a hidden counter behind. Two large paintings of the local countryside and the town grace the wall behind it. Two young, attractive Italian women are standing and greeting new arrivals. They both have dark hair with big brown eyes, and are wearing comfortable Fila running outfits. One has her hair pulled into a ponytail and the other lets her hair flow across her shoulders.

As Ryan approaches the desk, one of the ladies looks up at him. She has a warm welcoming smile and extends her hand to greet him. As he takes her hand gently in his, he feels a warm energy that travels up his arm and spreads to his body. He immediately feels more relaxed. *"Buon giorno, signore, la posso aiutarti?* May I help you?" She only says a few Italian words to Ryan, but it is how she interacts with him that gets his attention.

Ryan begins to feel the excitement of being here at the Terme, as if he has discovered a hidden treasure. He tries not to show it, but feels warmly welcomed by the brief encounter with this kind lady. He has a sense that he may be in the right place. "Ah, si, ah, *bone giorno,*" He says in broken Italian learned on tape this past week. *"Eeo sono* Ryan Laughlin. I check in. . . *a le* Terme?"

"Si. Si. Dr. Laughlin. Sorry. I thought you were one of our handsome Italiano guests. It is such a pleasure to have you here. I'm Christiana Rava and this is my associate, Isabella Tosi." The second girl with her hair pulled back extends her hand to shake his, and he feels a similar sensation. He immediately feels cared for by these two women, and loves it. Maybe, it is more about how he feels. It seems such an insignificant transaction, to be welcomed warmly, yet he feels so good about it.

"Let me get your registration information." Christiana looks down at the computer, and then quickly rifles through the file of materials on the desk. "Si, Dr. Laughlin. You're one of our special guests here. We're so happy to have you. Thank you for coming. It's an honor. Wait a moment while I call Dr. Venetre, one of our lead investigators. Despite being Sunday, she wanted to personally welcome you and give you a special tour of the facilities. Please have a seat, and I will arrange your room keys for you. May we take your luggage to your room?"

Ryan looks up at her, trying to stifle the smile on his face, but cannot. "Oh, *Grazie. Si,* please take my luggage to the room. *Grazie.*"

She takes his luggage and walks away. He notices her Superga Italian designer athletic shoes—the ones which Sophia always envied. He sits down in the non-descript reception room. It's nice, but not elaborate. They obviously do not have a major sponsor to bankroll their research. Yet, it has a relaxed, comfortable feel about it.

As he sits down on the red, modern sofa, he studies the paintings on the wall behind the desk that dramatically illustrate the classic Italian countryside that surrounds this medieval town. One shows the rolling fields of flowering red poppies lining the winding hillside road with tall cypress trees at attention on each side of the road blowing in the wind. Another is a painting of an old stone church on top of a hill with cascading silhouettes of hills in the distant sunset. The third painting on the adjacent wall is of Brisighella with its three rocky pinnacles topped by the ancient stone castle, the unusual clock tower, and the brick sanctuary tower. He also notices the lemon water, cappuccino, fruit, bread, and cheese available on the side table. The people going in and out of the reception room are of all ages, from young and beautiful students to middle aged mothers with their children, to an older couple from America.

Ryan sees a stunning Italian woman walk in. She is trim with flowing light brown hair and the elegance of a model. She is wearing dark blue Benetton pants and a white, loose fitting, silk blouse with yellow and blue flowers that is unbuttoned at the top to reveal her distinctly feminine curves. She strolls in with grace, elegance and authority, and walks directly to Christiana, who points towards Ryan sitting in the chair.

The woman walks over to Ryan and extends her hand with a bright smile, beautifully aligned white teeth, and an intelligent gaze. She has a face that would melt soldiers and generals alike.

"Dr. Laughlin. I'm Vanessa Venetre. I'm one of the principal investigators here at the Brisighella Terme. It is such a pleasure to finally meet you. Julia Stone told me all about you. Thank you for coming all this way to visit us. It's very special to have you here."

She extends her hand to shake Ryan's. He looks in her big brown eyes and sees the entire world in them. Her long light brown hair frames her soft olive skinned face and radiant broad smile. He takes her hand, and like Christiana, he feels a gentle warmth and energy travel up his arm. He hesitates in letting go for a few more seconds. He's never had a simple handshake feel so good. What is it about this place?

Then, his traditional skepticism, learned from many years as a wary physician, kicks in. What are they trying to sell me here? Do I feel a timeshare sales pitch coming on? Then, he shakes his head and laughs at his own ridiculous cynicism and realizes that he needs to get over his bad attitude. Just relax a little and enjoy the experience. Vanessa seems nice. It is even surprising that she came here especially to welcome him to the Terme on a Sunday.

"Dr. Venetre, it's a pleasure to be here," Ryan smiles. "I've been in need of a vacation, and your research sounds fascinating. It seemed like a natural trip for me. Thank you for coming to greet me. I hope I'm not taking you away from your family."

Vanessa charms him with her melodic Italian accent. Her unique style and beautiful features make it hard not to enjoy listening to her. "Please call me Vanessa. I'm sure you are tired after your long flight. Let me take you to your room? I can accompany you, and show you around at the same time."

"Thank you. That would be delightful."

Vanessa leads the way into the courtyard. It is a beautiful setting with multiple old buildings that surround a generous outdoor pool with mist clouding the surface. He can see the trees surrounding the Lamone River that flows through the west of the property. She mentions how unique it is because of the clear clean aqua colored water that flows over the white Selenite rocky bottom. He can see the hills in the distance speckled with sheep and cattle grazing. It's a scene out of an Italian love story.

Vanessa explains as they walk briskly past several stone buildings, "At the Terme, we have several residential buildings as well as a nice pool, a warm spa with naturally healing sulfur springs, several gathering rooms, and craft, recreational, and exercise facilities. We are particularly proud of our traditional dining facilities complete with natural Italian cuisine that enhances your energy."

Above all, Ryan simply wants to eat great food and wine as the cornerstone of a relaxing Italian vacation this week. "Wonderful. The food is one of my major reasons for coming here."

"Tell me more about the restaurants here and in town."

"We have a four-star restaurant on the Terme as well a great deli for more efficient eating. Both the restaurant and the deli focus on locally produced natural produce and meats including a special local wine selection. And yes, as our guests expect, the food here is high quality. I can recommend some nice restaurants in town also if you would like. She points to the castle above the village buildings. "Look up there above the village. L'Infinito Restorante is in a particularly beautiful setting with a terrazzo overlooking the castle and the old clock tower. A friend of mine owns it. However, we don't want you to gain weight and deplete the energy of your Body Realm. Thus, all indulgences in food must correspond to an equally indulgent effort in exercise. They go hand and hand."

"I have a weakness for pasta and wine," Ryan admits. "And this is exactly what I had in mind for dinner tonight."

"We don't encourage over-eating, nor excessive alcoholic beverages," she continues, "but we make sure it is abundantly available at reasonable prices. We recognize that wine can act to relax people, enhance their energy, and act as a social lubricant. We want people to interact here, and we have several opportunities to do that. To enhance the People Realm, we help you get to know each other through group meetings to discuss where you are in life and how to maintain your energy levels in each Realm. We also have opportunities to help others in town at the senior, childcare, and cultural centers. We have creative outlets for the emotional energy including a craft room with both pottery and painting, and a game room for cards and other games. In the Body Realm, we have great exercise facilities and, of course, lots of room for nature walks and biking. As you'll find out, it's all important to achieve a good life filled with positive energy that will spread to others."

"Do they allow video games here?" He asks, and then cringes as he realizes that it was a dumb American question. He's in Italy now, and he'd be damned if he's going to play stupid video games. He has to get his American lifestyle out of his mind. He's here for relaxation, health, and growth—not fun, games, and romance. "Sorry to ask," he quips. "I doubt I'll have much time for video games."

"I'm glad you asked," Vanessa replies. "We do have lots of interactive video, card, and board games because they can enhance your energy in the Emotion and People Realms. Some focus on social interactions, others enhance positive emotions, and some are quite educational, focusing on the Mind Realm. They can enhance your energy if they are not shoot 'em up games."

They continue to walk beyond the courtyard and towards the residential buildings on the edge of a rock face. He notices how enthusiastic she is about the facilities and opportunities to boost your energy at the Terme. He also notices how positive and warm her energy is. He feels good just being around her.

"We also have a choir who performs regularly in town. You must hear them while you're here. We have exercise and meditation rooms with coaches in each room. We encourage you to take walks, be outside surrounding yourself with the natural beauty and energy of the area. We want you to work on your Nature Realm by working in the vineyards, gardens, orchards, and help nurture the environment so that it remains clean, organized and beautiful. This applies to organizing your own life too."

They walk past a large, old stone, three story barn with large wooden doors on the front. "That's the Great Hall of the Mind. We do all of our group session here. You will meet there tomorrow morning at 8am sharp. We want you to learn about each of the techniques cited in the *Prophecy Scroll* to boost your energy and see what best applies to you personally. This is what we consider the most important currency here. Although money is needed to keep this place operating, our focus here is about boosting your energy." She hesitates, and then states seriously, "Please don't let us fail in this one goal." She smiles sweetly, and then with her sensual Italian accent, she says, "Just to let you know, if you fail this goal, the demons will inhabit you, you'll become a zombie, develop vices, become unpopular, hate everybody, and lead us down the path of destruction and widespread plagues. But don't sweat it too much. You're here on vacation, right?"

Ryan laughs nervously, not sure if she was joking or not. Ryan's curiosity and interest in technology prompts his next question, "But this is research right? You measure people's energy level, both individually and collectively?"

"Yes, we measure everybody's energy level in each Realm daily using special equipment while you're here."

"Can you truly measure a person's spirit? How do people react to knowing their level of energy? Do they freak out?"

"Nobody freaks out," she responds quickly and emphatically. "We are measuring a person's electromagnetic energy. If you want to call it your spirit or soul, that's up to you. The measurements do correlate with the daily activities and how you approach your day and the people around you. Although some people start with high energy and others with low energy, nearly everyone learns to boost their energy. It's wonderful when this happens. We find a growing harmony, happiness, good feelings, and enhanced health and productivity. People just laugh and feel good. We love it because everybody gains energy. It spreads. The group effect is quite remarkable. We'll show it to you in the next few days. Everyone helps everybody else. The community benefits from each person's individual efforts if they are successful. I won't mention what happens with the demons if you are not successful. It's nasty." Ryan gives her a look that she ignores as she walks up the stairs to Ryan's room.

When they arrive, she uses an old fashioned, large bronze key to open the door. She walks in and opens the red curtains and the double doors to the balcony to get some fresh air in it. She hands Ryan the key and says, "We have you in room 334, third floor with a balcony overlooking the courtyard.

I hope you like it. It's one of our suites, since you're our special guest. We don't have many physicians attending so we welcome you with open arms and high energy. When they come, we help them understand the principals of our research in order to apply it to their patients. You're opinions are important to us. We thank you for coming."

"Well, I'm happy to be here," Ryan says with a smile, and not a bit of jet lag. He finds her quite charming and attractive. "I was introduced to your work by Dr. Julia Stone, from Harvard. She was here last year and was very impressed. It was unfortunate that Dr. Killian died at the meeting last week. I know he helped arrange funding for much of your work."

Vanessa cringes and looks away, surprised by his comments. She wonders why he would come here if he knew about Dr. Killian. He must know that the murder brings fear to the Terme. "Yes. We're all so sad. We blame ourselves for his murder. We are working hard trying to do the right thing for people, but some people misinterpret our research. They think we are testing the Word of God, but actually, we are evaluating its power and impact. It's the first step in bringing science and religion closer together. They truly are not separate concepts, you know."

"I agree. I've talked to Dr. Stone, and have read about your work." Ryan comments, "It's unfortunate that some people do not view it favorably."

"We are scientists. We test hypotheses. We want to know if the knowledge in the *Prophecy Scroll* does actually influence a person's electromagnetic fields. It's straightforward science. Nothing more, nothing less."

Ryan is still surprised at the boldness of this research. He can understand why it steps on a few toes. "Then, people shouldn't be getting their undies in a bundle about your research."

"What do you mean—undies in a bundle?" She asks with a puzzled look on her face.

"Never mind," he says, "just a stupid American phrase for being upset. I would love to hear more about the intricacies of the research. I certainly do not want to impose, but would you be kind enough to have dinner with me tonight? I do not want to take you away from your family. I need to stay awake to change my time zone and your presence at dinner would be infinitely more interesting than falling asleep early in my room. Are you available?"

Vanessa is a bit surprised to be invited, but likes Dr. Laughlin. He is positive, interested, and well, does lean towards being a sensitive male. He's also quite charming. She recognizes the need to be cautious in getting too close to visitors, since they are technically subjects. But she rationalizes by considering him more of a physician observer than a participant.

"Ah, thank you for the invitation. Let me see, Dr. Laughlin."

She checks her cell phone as a formality to give her some time to think before acting. She knows she has nothing planned for tonight, especially since she and her husband split up after his affair with a colleague over a year ago. Since then, her social life has been missing in action and she has devoted herself to the research and her own seven Realms. However, this is not information she wants to share with Dr. Laughlin.

He interrupts, "Please, call me Ryan."

"I happen to be free, Dr. Ryan, I accept," she says with a smile. "I can give you a little tour of our precious Brisighella and update you more on our research. What time should I stop by your room?"

"Well, let me check my schedule," he says facetiously. He looks at his watch. "Seven pm fits nicely into my packed schedule. That will be noon, my time, so I'll be famished. My *gelato la torre especiale* from the local *gelateria* will be wearing off by then."

"You had one of those?" She laughs heartily. "Nobody, but American children, buy those."

He says goodbye to Vanessa, and gets excited, almost giddy, about having dinner with her. He will not only get all the inside scoop on the Terme and the research, but her energy and beauty, have solidly hooked him. He unpacks his luggage and checks out the beautiful view of the orchards and vineyards in the surrounding countryside.

He would like to rent a bike to explore the hillsides, vineyards, and the Borgos that populate the surrounding hills. He finds an information brochure about renting bikes in his room and biking to the Borgos, the ancient stone villages that were inhabited by small communities of farmers over a century ago. Now, they have been converted into grand bed and breakfasts and private estates. Brisighella has a famous Borgo just a few kilometers up the hill from the Terme. He finds that the Terme has several bikes to rent at the exercise facility, and calls to reserve their best for the upcoming week. He is eager to take his first ride through the gorgeous Italian countryside. He puts away his things and gets dressed, and prepares the bike. What a magnificent start to his vacation.

When he arrives at the bike rental facility, he is surprised to find an Impulso Coast to Coast Bianchi twelve-speed bike available. Bianchi has been manufacturing racing bikes for the top Italian bikers since the 1800s. Like the French, the Italians are also fanatical about biking. He adjusts the bike to feel comfortable, completes the paperwork, and rides out of the shop for a spin.

He heads up Valle Baccagnano as it winds like a serpent to the top of the hill. The hill has so many turns, curves, and steep banks near the road's edge that, as the bike staff repeatedly said, it is very dangerous. They also said that Italian drivers do not slow down for bikers. To alert oncoming cars, most drivers honk their horn as they approach the hairpin turns to avoid hitting the opposing car or bike driving against the traffic. However, since most Italians drive as if they are in a *Formula Uno* race, anybody riding bikes in the countryside needs to be overly cautious, or have a suicide wish. As he approaches each bend in the road on his way up the hill, he is cautious to stay in the traffic lanes and keep up with cars to avoid problems.

He gains energy as he bikes at a steady pace up the hill taking in the incredible view of vineyards, castagni chestnut trees, and tall cypress pines in the foreground. The afternoon sun is an intense yellow as he watches it set over the distant hills lighting up the sky and horizon equally. The scene is identical to the painting hanging in the Terme reception area. The air is brisk, and he smells the scent of the olive trees. Sheep and cattle are grazing along the road. It all creates a magical setting for his vacation. He loves it.

Ryan rides by the *Corte Dei Familgia* Farmhouse on his way up the hill. It is a beautiful old stone house with small brass lamps that run along the winding stone entry path to the house. The vineyards of the famous Sangiovese wine spread leisurely across the rolling hills. He reaches the Borgo at the top of the closest hill overlooking Brisighella. He gets off his bike to walk around the historic grounds to enjoy its old stone houses, the large open stone barn, two stone silos, and an outdoor amphitheatre nestled in the crest of the hill. He can imagine that it does not look too much different now than it did two hundred years ago when the farm families were busy preparing dinner for the evening.

He sits on the crest of the hill and stares down at the small commune of Brisighella. He is excited and happy to be here and wonders what will be in store for him this week. He thinks about Julia, and how appreciative he is for connecting him to this place. He will e-mail her as soon as he gets back to his room.

He leaves his contemplation, gets back on the bike, and speeds back down the hill listening for car horns to sound. He arrives safely back at the Terme and heads up to his room to get ready for an interesting evening with Dr. Venetre. He e-mails Julia about his experiences so far. Everything is perfect right now. He thanks her profusely.

Among those checking into the Terme on Sunday, is the Messenger. He will take his time this week to find the best opportunity to send his message of righteousness and freedom to the world, by ending their research any way necessary. He is standing on the balcony of his room looking out over the courtyard of the Terme. He considers that this place would have been better left as a relaxing health spa than a setting for heretical research. He is repulsed by the thought of it and how it opposes everything that the God has intended for our world. It is blasphemy. And, he knows that it is his responsibility to punish those who defile the Words of God. Thoughts of this enormous responsibility run through his mind. He believes that the Messiah has anointed him with their meeting in New York.

For it is said in the scriptures: "For those who are heretics, the unbelievers, and the sinners, are you ready to see your sins? The cross is offered to all. Are you ready to suffer the shame, the pain, and the blood of the cross—or do you cry out with indifference? He who is not on the cross is not worthy of me."

He sits down to read his Manifesto again. The world will know again its truth. The Messiah will be pleased. The Messenger has begun the cleansing process. This is a war, and there will be casualties.

Chapter 15. The Investigator

Ryan is surprised that Vanessa arrives early to go to dinner, a bit before seven. As he opens the door, he is startled by her elegance. How can she be a researcher! She does not even come close to looking the part.

Vanessa is dressed in an elegant, low cut Kenzo dinner dress of silk printed with delicate green and red flowers. She wears a beige knit cashmere shawl over the dress. It's a cool June evening, and she knows that they will sit outside. He feels a bit down-dressed with his blue jeans and white button down shirt. Nevertheless, he is who he is, and wears what he feels most comfortable for the occasion. With jet lag beginning to set in, he needs to be comfortable.

They walk from the Terme to the Piazza of Brisighella. Ryan is compensating for his jet lag by throttling up his thirst for knowledge. He wants to learn everything about Brisighella, the Terme, the research, the *Prophecy Scroll*, and of course, Vanessa. He has a special talent, honed from years as a physician, in expressing his genuine interest in another person. And he is quite sincere in his interest in Vanessa. "Tell me about the history of the village," Ryan asks. "I'd expect that it has had its colorful moments."

"We all know about our history here," Vanessa says as she launches into a treatise on Brisighella. "And we are proud that the village goes back to the earliest of Roman days. The Romans would head north to Brisighella whenever they were ill and needed to recover by relaxing in the healing waters here."

"That explains the development of the Terme. What about the castles?"

"The first castle dates back to medieval times toward the end of the eleventh century. Maghinardo Pagani built the castle and called it, La Rocca, for one of the three white selenite rock cliffs that overlook the village."

"What is selenite?" Ryan asks earnestly.

"The ancient residents called it the stone of the moon. They had a belief that these transparent white crystals, which are a type of gypsum, were from the moon and waxed and waned as it moved across the sky. It has natural thermal insulating properties and feels warm to the touch. The rocks in the cliffs are warmed from the deep thermal hot springs that run through the rocks below. The caves weave their way through the cliffs as a result of erosion from underwater rivers. The remains found here suggest they were inhabited by the earliest of humans. In 1300, Francesco Manfredi, Lord of Faenza built another fortress on the second cliff overlooking Brisighella. Then, a clock tower was built on the third peak a few years later."

"The three towers give it such a picturesque image," Ryan says. "They're beautiful."

"I love living here. Brisighella has been awarded a prestigious certification every year for being one of the most beautiful villages in Italy. It carries its ancient heritage quite well."

They walk to the center of the village and the piazza. They pass next to a beautiful green park with chestnut trees, playground equipment for the kids, the large fountain, and the many statues by the local artists.

"I stopped here after I arrived on the train," says Ryan. "I saturated my sweet tooth with a giant gelato right there." He points out the shop. "I had the leaning tower in ice cream. It filled my stomach and more."

She laughs, "As I said, that's for the children of American tourists. Have you not grown up yet, Dr. Ryan?"

"Ah, well. I'm working on it," they both laugh. "It gave me lots of energy to overcome the jet lag."

"I bet it did. And a few kilos also," Vanessa laughs. She points to the second story arches above the storefronts. "See the illuminated arches on the second story of this street? This is known as *via degli Asini*, or the donkey trail, to remind us of the animals' hard work when they carried the stone material for the buildings from the nearby quarries. Let's walk to Il Centro, where the piazza is."

They pass by several bars that serve cappuccino and vino with the local sweet *piadina* bread. At least a half dozen older gentlemen, dressed formally in nice jackets and hats, are sitting at the small tables outside the open double doors to the bar laughing up a storm. As they see Dr. Venetre approach, they watch every step that she makes as she walks by. You could see their heads turn in a perfectly synchronized movement as they gaze at all of her body parts move by—her head, hair, arms, legs, bottom, and of course, her bosom. They all shake their head in approval.

Ryan glares at them, and she notices his concern. "Ryan, it's customary to do this to any younger woman who walks by," Vanessa says. "In general, they do not mean to intimidate or harass women, but rather display the traditional Italian male ritual of paying homage and respect to the beauty of women. Most women consider the practice flattering, and perhaps, are even slightly insulted if they do not get the men's attention."

Ryan feels remorse as he remembers that he did not complement Vanessa when she arrived tonight. In an effort to recover from that possible indiscretion, he says, "I don't blame them, Vanessa. You look absolutely stunning this evening."

"Of course, the older men pass this custom down to the younger men, who sometimes take it to a higher level, with inappropriate whistles and cat calls. It's all a matter of tolerance and respect. Some women like it. Some don't."

Ryan quietly agrees. He could watch her all night long if he let her. He shakes himself back into reality, recognizing that he is just an observer here among professional colleagues.

She walks them over to the entry of the Collegiate Church of San Michele Archangel. "The Church was completed in 1697," she continues. "This beautiful bronze doorway is typical of the churches in the area."

Ryan's head tips back as looks toward the top of the doorframe. "They're gigantic. Did you have a fair number of medieval goliaths who lived here?"

His attempt at humor went unrecognized. They walk inside. The church has an exquisitely preserved sixteenth century wooden crucifix, a multi-colored neo-Baroque altar, and a painting of the local town by the artist Marco Palmezzano.

As they walk, Vanessa hooks her arm to Ryan's. "It's also traditional for people, particularly women, to hold another's arm as they go on walks, whether it be a man or a woman. Do you mind?"

"I like this tradition," he smiles. "It shows respect and support." He thinks about the times walking with Sophia in the evening around their neighborhood holding hands, particularly when she was having cancer treatment. They both loved it.

"Italians are proud of their traditions and history. We take time to learn them. Some of the young ones have less interest in it. Many want to be just like Americans with their movies and video games."

"Sorry for that," he says. "I agree it's important to keep these traditions alive. It can help the connection between the young and old. In our country, some people simply discard the old people as useless. If they take the time, as I do in my practice, they will find that they are more interesting than any movie or video game is and can fill you with energy."

"You're already understanding that life is all about your energy, Dr. Ryan Laughlin! Let me show you *la via degli Asini*, the donkey's street. It's on the way to the restaurant," Vanessa says as she holds Ryan's arm tight as they walk to the street above the piazza, and then up the stairs to the covered passage. "It's a special street because it's the only example of an elevated, covered deck above a stone street in any medieval town in the world."

As they navigate the uneven cobblestone path of the covered street, they can see the shops on the street below through the broad half moon arches. Vanessa points out the view. "During the day, light from the sun penetrates through the arches and brightens the street, while at night, the path is illuminated by burning twilight candles. Very romantic!"

"It is surprising that this walkway has lasted for over five hundred years," Ryan says.

"They made things to last then," she replies. "Not so much now, unfortunately. We are such a throw away world."

Vanessa continues to hold Ryan's arm as they walk up the hill to the restaurant. He can tell that she's sizing him up.

"L'infinito is often called the *locale incantevole* because it is beautifully set on a hill overlooking the town of Brisighella, half way up to La Rocca. The restaurant has three levels built on the side of the hill. It's one of the most picturesque settings in Brisighella."

"You said a friend owns it?" Ryan asks.

"Si. Maria Theresa Cortina. She runs a very efficient, festive, and tasteful restaurant. Even by Italian standards, the food and presentation is to die for. *Spectaculare e molto romantico!* Come this way." She smiles, as she obviously enjoys showing him the town.

Vanessa pulls Ryan closer to her as she points out the illuminated La Rocca looming above. "Hundreds of years ago, it was built to protect the town and make the residents feel secure." It's surprising, but Vanessa feels an elevated sense of security right now with Ryan at her side. And she could use more security with the threat of a killer on the loose at the Terme. With the controversy, the death of Dr. Killian and, even their funding in question, it could only help for people to learn more about the research in the states. She wants to make sure he has a wonderful experience.

They reach the top of the hill and stand at the stone wall outside the restaurant door. They look out across the clay rooftops and pastel row houses of Brisighella. The dark shade moves across the green rolling hills and the cliffs above the Lamone valley. Vanessa tells him about the old stone farmhouses, the growth of vineyards and orchards, and the history of the tall cypress trees that line the roads.

Ryan stares at the sun as it sends strings of light radiating between the clouds over the west horizon. It lights up the sky like an orange and purple blanket that has been laid out for their comfort and pleasure. Maybe, it's the jet lag, but he is beginning to realize this may be his version of heaven on earth. "Look at the view," he says excitedly. "You can see the whole valley in the distance. It is such a romantic view."

Vanessa excuses herself to check on their reservation for the restaurant. As Ryan stares over the stone wall into the distant sunset, contemplating his place in life, Vanessa yells, "*Vieni qui!*" and waves for him to come to the base of a selenite cliff behind them. She shows him a door at the base of the cliff that is small enough to fit a dwarf but nobody taller. They both bend down to go through it. It opens into a quaint three-story restaurant that winds it way up the side of the cliff.

"*Buona sera.*" The hostess greets them warmly.

"*Buona sera, come stai?*" Vanessa responds, "*Dove Maria Theresa?*" She explains that Maria will be here in a half hour and will come up to the *terrazzo di jardin* to say hello when she arrives. "*Vouoi sederti fuori enlla terrazzo?*"

"*Si, signora.* It is beautiful on *la terrazzo.*" She adds in English, acknowledging that an American is present.

They walk up the three flights of steep, narrow stone stairs that wind up to the terrazzo at the base of la Rocca. The sun has set and they stand beneath the dark maroon sky as the brightest of stars try to peek through. They can see the old castle on the left and the clock tower on the right while the evening lights of Brisighella are shining brightly to create a stunning panorama. Ryan would not trade places with anyone in the world right now. Thank you, Julia, he says to himself.

The waitress, dressed in an elegant evening dress, walks over to present the menu. "Welcome to L'Infinito. *Mi chiamo* Miria Vanelli. Would you have interest in appetizers *oi vino di Emilia-Romagna?*"

They both nod affirmatively. Ryan smiles to himself. He would like to learn more about the wines of the region by drinking each of them.

The waitress continues, "Sir, *tu viene dall*, America?"

Ryan nods affirmatively, and says, "*Si, si.*"

"We 'ave special English menu for you, if it pleases you."

"*Si, grazie. No problema,*" Ryan says while trying out his newly learned Italian.

"Emilia Romagna ees one of the largest producers of wine in Italy," the waitress continues with her accent. "Most wines 'ere are different from rest of the country. They more sparkling, frothy, and fruity. Lambrusco ees the king of sparkling wines 'ere, and Sangiovese ees king of still wines. Both good with local pasta and formaggio."

She smiles proudly at her effort to speak English. "Our neighbors in Tuscany use our sangiovese grapes. They make Chianti with it. Emilia-Romagna also grows grapes for *tutto il mondo*, you know, for the whole world. They include cabernet sauvignon, chardonnay, pinot grigio, and merlot. You want to try our local vino, maybe, *sangiovese di Romagna?*"

Ryan explains that although he has been to Florence, Venice, and Rome before, this is his first visit to this area of Italy.

Vanessa studies the wine list carefully. "Si, *mi piace il Brunello di Montalcino, il mio vino preferito,*" she says.

Then, the waitress turns to Ryan. He smiles and says, "I'd like a glass of the sangiovese, *per favore*. And a glass of water with ice also. *Grazie.*"

"I'm happy to bring a glass of wine. But if ees okay with you, we'll just leave the whole bottle here. You can take as much as you'd like. We don't like to go back and forth since most people empty the bottle. Also, we don't have ice. Most people just order bottled water, which ees chilled. Okay for you?"

"Ah, si, please, that would fine. What the hell, bring the whole bottle!" He says with a tone of reckless abandon and embarrassment due to his naivety about the local customs.

Vanessa laughs as she sees an honest charm in Ryan that is unusual among Italian men.

Miria brings the wine immediately, and pours each a glass. She reviews the entrees and tonight's special meal, "We have a special tortellini that is a work of art on a plate. The fresh pasta parcels are filled with local ingredients such as prosciutto, mortadella, Parmigiano, and ground pork depending on who prepares it. We also have a larger version of tortellini with a filling of ricotta, spinach and herbs. We can serve it with tomato sauce, ragu', or butter and sage each with a sprinkle of Parmigiano on top. On other nights, we also have a variation filled with pumpkin and amaretti stuffing. Eet's quite tasty. Hope you come back and try."

"The special tortellini sounds like the perfect meal for me right now." replies Ryan. "*Con ragui per favore.*"

"You need to be warned, Ryan," Vanessa says with a smile. "According to our local legend, this pasta was inspired by the navel of Venus. It drives men crazy with passion when eaten."

"Wonderful. I could use more passion in my life right now," Ryan responds with a laugh.

Vanessa turns to Miria, "I'll take my usual *insalata traditionale con pollo e vinaigrette con olio díoliva e aceto balsamico.*"

Vanessa then turns to Ryan and says, "With *ensalata* as my meal, I always leave dinner with more energy than when I arrived. To me, that's the best measure of a great meal."

She then raises her glass and says, "*Salute.* Here's to a great week for you, my friend from America. I hope you enjoy it and your energies soar here."

"*Grazie*, Vanessa. And to a great hostess also."

They both drink from their first glass of wine. Ryan watches her out of the corner of his eye and appreciates her radiating beauty. He continues the conversation, "Julia said Emilia-Romagna is the breadbasket of Italy. And we all know that Italy is the cooking capital of the world. It can't get better than that. I'd love to hear more about the food here. But I warn you. I do follow the old saying, 'The secret to a man's heart is through their stomach.'"

"Well, that makes it more interesting, doesn't it?" She smiles. "We are particularly proud of our foods. It's the main reason people love Italy so much. Take, for example, our olive oil. We use it on everything. The olive trees that you see on every hill have been growing since the Roman times. They used it as a topical rub after a Roman bath. It is still used that way at our Terme."

Ryan laughs out loud at the thought. "I can just see a fat Roman senator coming to the Terme and getting rubbed down by the beautiful local maidens with olive oil after they've had a huge meal of pasta and vino. The whole Roman army would be at your doorstep looking for help."

Vanessa laughs. "I'll tell you more. We're also known for our *aceto balsamico tradizionale*. It's a dark balsamic gourmet vinegar used on salads. It's produced right here by our artisans in the province of Modena. Only local grapes are used, and the minimum aging is twelve years, with up to twenty-four years for the extra old. It has a rich flavor that's sweet and intense and goes well with Parmigiano cheese."

"That explains the popularity of salads here and the slender waist lines," Ryan replies.

Maria Theresa arrives on the terrace and gives Vanessa a big hug, and a kiss on each cheek. She is dressed in a Dolce Cabana low cut animal print dress that attractively displays her cleavage and is well matched to her Jimmy Choo shoes. She has that look that announces she is the no-nonsense boss of her restaurant. Maria smiles at Ryan as she whispers close to Vanessa, "*Chi ei quell belliuomo? Ei il tuo?* The handsome gentleman. Is he yours?"

"No, no. *Lui ei un medico Americano che sta visitando leTerme.*

"*Bello! ei un single?*"

"*Maria! Non lo so e non lo chiedo!* She exclaims under her breath.

Ryan missed most of the Italian conversation, but did hear the comment with the word single in it. His eyes brighten as he smiles at Maria.

She reaches out to shake his hand. "Welcome to L'Infinito. We hope you enjoy it."

"I like the ambience very much. The setting is gorgeous. The company is divine."

"*Grazie.* I hope you enjoy the food and wine as much."

"I can't wait," Ryan eyes continue to shine brightly. "Vanessa has been telling me about Italian food, the wine, and love, not necessarily in that order."

"Si, one does feed on the other. Oh, I must go," she says in haste as she sees other guests coming. "But I'll check back later. Enjoy the food, setting, and, of course, the love, but not necessarily in that order." They all laugh.

Chapter 16. The Conversation

The waitress brings their dinner of insalata and tortellini and fills their wine glasses again. Ryan follows her lead before he starts to eat. "Do you mind if I ask some questions about your research while we eat?"

"*Si, per favore.* Go ahead. You're here for learning, right?"

"Well, yes, but this is a vacation. The food, the countryside, the people, the culture, the history and everything else about Italy are all pretty attractive." He laughs, "But I'll start with the research. How did you get started here in Brisighella?"

"This village has a long history of healing and health," she explains. "As I mentioned, it was home to healing waters during Roman times where treatments were performed with the natural hot springs. The spring included both sulphurous and sodium chloride bromide and iodide waters. In our early studies, we studied the health effects of the spa through the University of Bologna. Since Brisighella was in close proximity, and we knew the owner, we decided to work with the participants here."

"What were your early findings?" Ryan asks as he consumes his pasta.

"We were measuring negative and positive ions," she explains. "The spa brings negative ions to the body that can enhance the immune system by removing positive ions in the body that contribute to inflammation and illnesses such as auto-immune disorders and cancer. Negative ions are odorless, tasteless, and invisible molecules that we inhale in certain environments like the Terme. You also find them in abundance in typical tourist places like mountains, waterfalls, and beaches. They make you feel good. When negative ions accumulate in our bloodstream, they lead to biochemical reactions that increase levels of the mood chemical called serotonin. This helps alleviate depression, relieve stress, and boost our daytime energy as much as any anti-depressant would do. They can also increase the flow of oxygen to the brain and improve alertness, decrease drowsiness, and enhance mental energy."

"How does this connect with your research?" Ryan tips his wine glass to his lips one more time.

"Out of the blue, we decided to apply for funds from the U.S. National Institute of Health and the Italian Research Fund to fund our research on the negative and positive ions here. To our surprise, we were awarded two grants. Then, our research moved into another area that is parallel to the work on ions. We wanted to validate the new SERF technology to measure human energy fields and how ions affected it. It's the next new imaging technology beyond MR scans. It's truly a remarkable technology. Measuring a person's energy or if you want to call it, the human spirit. Think of the implications."

"How did the *Dead Sea Scrolls* come into play?" asks Ryan.

"That decision may be our downfall," she says in exasperation. "Dr. Gabriela Gaetti is a Vatican scholar and a close friend of mine. She told me about them. The content was amazing and so consistent with our current research. We wanted to determine what specific lifestyle actions mentioned in the *Prophecy Scroll* impacts human energy levels, and subsequently, improves our health."

"I heard about these manuscripts from Julia," he says. "She did talk about the Plagues beginning in the year 2000. Kind of alarming."

"They not only predict disastrous consequences for the world, but also solutions to avoid it. It is eerie because both the seven Plagues and the seven Realms are well documented in our current scientific literature. It was almost as if they had a true connection to a universal divine knowledge thousands of years before science confirmed it."

He notices that Vanessa is as intense as Julia was in describing the manuscripts. They seem to become quite precious to anybody who reads them. Bizarre. It's as if they have an energy of their own. He asks, "Where are the manuscripts now?"

"The manuscripts that have been assembled are currently stored at the Israel Antiquities Authority in Jerusalem. Israel took control of the Qumran region after the 1967 Six-Day War, but was supposed to turn the land back over to the Palestinians as part of a peace settlement. This is doubtful too. As a result, ownership and control of the Scrolls are regularly debated. Our research will make this even more complicated."

"It sounds like a political nightmare," Ryan responds with concern.

Vanessa's intensity heightens as she describes the controversy surrounding the use of the manuscripts. "It's a mess. Now, with the death of Dr. Killian, we may lose these startling discoveries forever unless we move quickly. I fear that the other six Blessings manuscripts will be taken away, or worse yet, be stolen by the people behind the murder of Dr. Killian. We're all tense about this situation. And we're afraid for our own safety."

Ryan quietly listens as he finishes his tortellini. He recognizes the seriousness of the situation and avoids any attempt at humor, despite downing several glasses of wine. "The fact that the Plagues are actually unfolding before our very eyes is alarming."

Vanessa takes a drink of wine, and has hardly made a dent in the salad as a result of Ryan's continued barrage of questions. Then, she looks up at the glowing clock tower above them. She fidgets with her fork, and unintentionally points it at Ryan, as she emphasizes her next point. "I don't want to be too dramatic, but these are alarming apocalyptical predictions that may determine the ultimate destiny of the human race and the end of our ordinary reality. If our research is true, these predictions may also come true. I'm concerned."

"Now you're confusing me." Ryan's cynicism never stays away too long. "Can we seriously believe that a document written two thousand years ago would be considered an accurate prediction of our current state of the world?"

"Well, at first, I was skeptical too." She replies, "But, then, I realized that nearly every religion teaches this. A future apocalypse has been prophesized in many ancient manuscripts since recorded history. Even, the Bible suggests this. This does not necessarily mean a brash single destructive event but may only reflect a new phase with different realities. We just don't know."

"Vanessa, what does the *Prophecy Scroll* actually say?"

"The *Prophecy* is short and succinct. Let me show it to you. I keep it with me to remind me of the seriousness of the predictions." She reaches into her purse and pulls out a wrinkled and worn document. She unfolds the single page. "You carry a copy in your purse?"

"Yes, you should also. Sit for a minute and read this. You'll get your copy in your materials tomorrow."

Ryan reads the document aloud, occasionally looking up at Vanessa. "And it is said, the beast with seven heads and ten horns will come again each thousand years when light from the angels in the Realms is weak. And with him, the seven Plagues will again come forth. And seven angels are sent to the earth, and they are given seven trumpets to warn of the coming beast with seven heads and ten horns. And the seven angels, with the seven trumpets, have prepared themselves to sound."

Ryan shifts uncomfortably in his seat. "The beast is a powerful image. I expect it was created to shake people into reality. That's not too different than what they do today in the media. Who are the seven angels?"

"Perhaps, they represent individuals or, even organizations," Vanessa shrugs. "I like to think they represent the seven international organizations that work on collaboration to improve peace, prosperity, and health in the world."

"What are those?" He quickly replies.

"They include the United Nations, World Health Organization, World Bank, International Monetary Fund, UNESCO, UNICEF, and Greenpeace. Then, it talks about the Plagues. Read them."

He reads the rest of the document. It foretells of seven Plagues including war among at least a third of the countries in the world. Vanessa states with concern, "The last trumpet of warning, about war, is very scary. All of the others seem to be coming true. The research is pretty convincing. Will this one also come true? Eerie, isn't it?"

Ryan takes another drink of wine. He notices a sinking feeling as he reads the manuscript. He is surprised at his uneasiness given his usual skepticism. He quells his feelings with first denial and, then, by dismissing the predictions. "I expect people will ignore the manuscript and the Prophecy," he rationalizes.

"That's exactly what the manuscript says. People will ignore this warning," she counters. "Listen to the next part. It's particularly graphic with the arrival of a second beast, which appears to represent evil leadership in the world."

Ryan reads from the document, "And a second Beast comes with the body of a lamb and the tongue of a dragon. He speaks for the first beast and tells the people about his heaven. For he comes to earth in full view of man, and brings promises of wealth and power when they live in his place. But the Beast is given power to rule, and deceives the people of the earth. He takes their light and sends his demons with their eyes of fire and deceiving spirit to act as false servants of righteousness and live in the people. And they bring the seven Plagues upon the people and they have ignorance, afflictions, despair, poverty, drought, hate, and war."

He stops reading and looks around the restaurant. Nobody is paying attention to him, but there is an unusual silence in the entire restaurant. He is surprised since he did not read it loud enough for others to hear. "Who are these two Beasts?" He laughs nervously and takes another sip of wine. "One has seven heads and the other the tongue of a dragon."

"You tell me. Who do you think they represent?" Vanessa asks. "An evil leader? The super-wealthy? The political elite? A secret society? I'm not sure."

Ryan pauses for a few moments. "It's a lot to digest. And cause indigestion," Ryan adds, in an attempt to ease his own queasiness. He takes another drink.

"Want to hear a way out of this mess?" She says sipping her wine. They've gone through two bottles already. "The next phrase tells us that a third of the people take up the Blessings that will send the Beast back into the bottomless pit."

Ryan starts laughing and cannot stop. The wine has finally gone to his head.

Vanessa looks at him, puzzled. "Why are you laughing?"

"Whoever wrote this didn't paint a very rosy future for us. It doesn't miss much. It hits nearly every evil ever subjected on mankind. I suppose this is someone's way to scare the hell out of us. But to his credit, he does give us an escape route. The Blessings. But is this an easy way out or not? People don't like to work too hard."

Vanessa looks at Ryan disappointedly. "Ryan, you're not taking this seriously. It's the end of the world! Come on, isn't that important?"

He shifts into his inebriated, but somber voice, "This is fire and brimstone stuff. As you said, lots of doomsayers have predicted the apocalypse. Bible Revelations. Mayan Prophecy. Nostradamus. We can't interpret it literally. It never really happens. It's a metaphor. It must be considered in the context of our own modern lives. And it depends what's in the Blessings. Are they easy to do or not? Do they make sense to people or not? Are they consistent with science or not? If it suggests that we all need to rub our tummies and pat our heads at the same time to save the world, then, we're doomed."

"You're right. People don't like change, especially if it's work," she shrugs her shoulder. "Okay. I admit I'm a bit of a drama queen."

They both start laughing and cannot stop. The tension is too great. The emotions, the wine, and the jet lag are too close to the surface. There is also an attraction between them that is at least apparent to the others on the terrace, if not to them. Their laughter eases and they become more relaxed.

When they finally settle down, Ryan says, "Vanessa. You're a remarkable woman." He raises a wine glass and says, "*Salute*. This toast is to your idealism and desire to save the world. All I can say is that I cannot agree with you more. I'm here to be your messenger. I vow to help bring your message to the world, as ambitious as that sounds."

Chapter 17. The Attraction

While Vanessa excuses herself from the table to talk to Maria about family matters, Ryan looks up at the stars above him, and then stares at the castle and the clock tower above him on each side. He takes a deep breath to appreciate the romantic setting. He knows that between the jet lag and the ample wine, a comfortable fatigue is beginning to sink in. He is delighted and honored to be able to spend so much time with Vanessa. Maybe it's the wine, but he is also surprised to feel such a strong attraction to her. There is no doubt that she is beautiful, but the attraction goes beyond that. But he must not be presumptuous. For all he knows, her husband is checking his watch right now wondering why she is so late. The last thing he needs on this trip is misdirected affection.

Vanessa returns and sits down, "I love Maria. She's a good friend and is always there when needed. I told her about the threat to the Terme, and she has some friends that can help if needed."

"What does she mean by friends?" He asks as a matter of fact.

"Just friends. No explanation necessary," she responds succinctly.

Ryan takes that as a "don't ask" response, and thinks about the many Italian mafia movies he's seen. He decides to let it go and asks, "What about music and creative energy? How do they fit in?" As the fatigue and wine sets in, Ryan simply wants to gaze into her expressive eyes and listen to her talk about anything and everything.

Vanessa, on the other hand, still has lots of energy right now and is happy to be with someone who has growing enthusiasm for their work at the Terme. "Music is so compelling and personal because the frequency of the energy behind music can resonate on several Realms at once. It can elevate the emotions, teach the mind with lyrics, and affect the body with the rhythm. It resonates with each person individually. We found that people's energy rises with a particular song or band that synchronizes with their energy, while the same song will reduce energy in others. You've seen people go nuts at many live concerts in response to the power of music energy. And it's not just for young people. Studies have shown that when older adults become engaged in music and dance, it can improve both cognitive and physical decline. It generates powerful energy."

"Interesting," he replies. "These concepts have relevance to every part of our lives. So, how does this apply to my patient care? I would like to improve my care to address the whole person, but changing the system is impossible."

Vanessa smiles in agreement. "I know I'm preaching to the choir, but we all know there are limits to the current biomedical model of disease and our current health care system. If we change each Realm as noted in the Blessings, will it change the actual physiology or biochemistry of the body and cure an illness? We are careful not to promise that here at the Terme. Or, perhaps, the actions in the Realms are too subtle or delayed, and thus, will not improve the condition."

Ryan nods in agreement. "My experience tells me that when care is only focused on the physical, like with medication or surgery, the outcomes are limited because all of the Realms of a person's life are not addressed,"

"There is a mountain of research that supports these conclusions," she emphasizes. "Specific lifestyle changes such as exercise and meditation can have as much of an impact on many conditions such as cancer, heart disease, musculoskeletal pain, and even aging."

"Do you believe you can delay the aging process with the techniques in the *Seven Realms?*" Ryan smiles. "With jet lag coming on, I'm beginning to feel ten years older right now."

"You do look tired. Do you want to go?" She asks kindly.

"No, this is too interesting," he insists. "I need to know. If I have high energy in each Realm, will it slow down the process that leads to arthritis, Alzheimer's, heart disease, cancer, and other chronic illnesses? Is it a youth serum?"

"I don't know, but the Blue Zone studies on people who live to be over a hundred years suggest this is true," she replies.

As much as Ryan denies it, his judgment is increasingly impaired as he opens the door to a topic even more emotionally charged than saving us from the end of the world, discovering the fountain of youth, and fixing the health care system. What the hell, he thinks to himself. "What about the energy of love? How does it work?"

Vanessa smiles. She sits back in her chair, and looks beyond Ryan to the lighted castle above her. She contemplates on how best to respond to this question. She knows he's on vacation and romance is often in the air, particularly after a night of wine and engaging conversation. He is a bright caring physician who wants to discover something more important about his life and is most likely not here to fall in love. She doesn't even know whether he's in a committed relationship or not. Yet, she recognizes there is an attraction between them. It is more than his rugged handsome face, warm compassionate eyes, and charm. There is a synergy between their energy.

Regardless of his status, she believes their relationship should be viewed as one of a working relationship and is cautious about stepping beyond professional boundaries that should not be crossed.

She responds with a cool pre-recorded response, "We've not studied the energy changes seen with love or sexual relationships in our research, for obvious reasons."

"What are those reasons?" Ryan pushes the envelope, smiling, with his arms on the table and his hands propping up his head.

"Well for one, I expect our human subjects committee would not be too happy if we acted as a matchmaker and moved into sexual oriented research. There is just no way. We are not Masters and Johnson, and we're not running a brothel. We will leave that to other researchers. But things sometimes happen here beyond our control. There is a romantic aspect to our research in the pursuit of higher energy. We cannot control everything. Romance sometimes just happens."

Ryan looks directly into her eyes, showing an obvious attraction to her, if not out-right flirting. "Tell me how it just happens."

The wine, and her own attraction to Ryan, leaves her open to being a bit more risqué response, "We have found some interesting results. A few months back we had two people here who developed a relationship. Of course, we frown upon that and take all precautions to prevent this from happening. But we cannot control the energy of love." She laughs as she remembers the participants.

Ryan is staring at her with an attentiveness that makes her a bit self-conscious. He is again thinking about her sense of humor and intellect. She has an energy that matches his own. He can feel it. He says nothing.

"What are you looking at, Ryan?"

"Nothing. I'm just interested in hearing the story. Please go on."

"This fellow, a shy guy from Sweden, was infatuated by a young female participant from Siena, Italy. He was not too handsome, but was rather a rough rugged type. The girl was here for a week at the spa, but also signed up for the research thinking it would be fun. Well, she was quite attractive and always wore these delicate bikinis to the pool. When he first met her, he kept coming to the pool and staring at her day after day. It was kind of embarrassing, since we all noticed it, including the girl. But she completely ignored him. The staff was privately cheering him on, but we needed to keep our distance."

"What happened? Did they get together?"

"We do not know the full details," she says with an air of propriety. "We don't snoop on the private lives of individuals here. However, as part of our routine protocol, we measured energy levels in each of their Realms every day. Their energy level in multiple Realms was weak initially, perhaps, due to problems they both were having back home. Then, something must have happened. I'm not sure what. Perhaps they were diligent in boosting their energy through daily actions. But the next time we measured, their energy in multiple Realms went sky high. Once, she came into the room while we were doing his reading. The flow of spiritual energy between them was, well, what can I say, off the charts. It was supercharged. We think he finally boosted her energy right into the sack."

They both laugh while trying to control it without success. Vanessa makes a devilish smile. "Then, for fun, and don't tell Dr. Nobili about this, we compared their baseline energy frequencies and found that they both had a close match from the beginning—in both frequencies and amplitudes in multiple Realms. Maybe it was true love that happened."

"Tell me about true love," Ryan stares with a stupid look on his face.

"Ryan, perhaps the jet lag and vino are catching up with you. Maybe, we should go."

"No, I'm fine," he protested knowing full well he was in the can. "I just wanted to hear your perspective on true love. You brought it up. I didn't."

She huffs, shuffles in her chair, and shifts back to her academic tone, "Okay, you asked! I believe a full romantic relationship between two people needs synergistic energy at multiple, or perhaps even all Realms, for it to develop into lasting love. I expect that a relationship that is focused on only one realm such as. . ." She hesitates and wonders if she should go on, not wanting to get into discussing sexuality with Ryan. It only leads men on.

It is late and Ryan can smell the sultry air of the night. The wine, fatigue, and deep personal conversations in this romantic setting have stirred his attraction to her. He is becoming aroused. The restaurant has cleared, and the silence between them tells all, as Ryan just stares at her with every word she speaks. He knows he is moving into dangerous territory but has lost control.

Mama mia! She says to herself. She might as well lose another guy. Maybe American men are different than Italian men, but she doubts it. Men are men, anywhere in the world. She expects her complex response will shut the door to yet another man. She knows that she over-analyzes everything, but that's just the way she is.

She takes a deep breath and continues her train of thought, "...the physical realm. It feels good. It makes you want to come back and do it again. However, if there is no consideration to the other Realms early on in the relationship, common sense and experience leads us to conclude that the relationship will fall apart. Since the energy of sexuality is so powerful, it is easy to miss paying attention to low energy in other Realms."

Ryan sits back in his seat and puts his arms behind his head. "That's a no brainer," he smiles thinking about himself right now. "And I mean literally. The mind just goes blank when sex is involved. Tell me more."

She can feel her emotions flowing and her attraction to him growing. "We all know that sexual relationships that go beyond the physical, including at least the Social Realm with caring, the Emotional Realm with happiness, and the Nature Realm with beauty will evolve into a lasting love. I suppose there are those that can fall in love at first sight due to closely synchronized energy, but that is a rare breed. High energy in the Spiritual Realm of love appears to be, at least in our research, the most difficult to achieve since you must feel good in all Realms to love fully."

Ryan leans forward. "That's hard to achieve with most people. Love is complex. When you have it, you know it. When you lose it, it can drain all of your Realms."

This topic energizes both of them as they continue to talk about the ingredients of love. They are both surprised to find they agree on most points. Ryan sees this as an opening for a more personal conversation. He must find out more about her. "So, Vanessa, tell me more about you. What moves you?"

"You know the rules about the Terme. I don't like to get too personal with participants. I suppose we have broken that rule a few conversations ago."

"It's okay," he tries to rationalize. "I'm here to observe and learn from you. I'm a special guest. Right?"

"Then, you tell me first," she insists. "What brings your energy up?"

Ryan knows this is a loaded question that can blow up in so many ways. So, he believes its best to take the direct and honest approach. "Well, I feel best when I'm biking around Lake Harriet, in Minneapolis, with the fresh morning wind blowing across my face." Then, he bites his lip to maintain his composure as he continues, "I feel worst when I wake up from a nightmare about losing my wife to breast cancer a couple of years ago. Now, what about you?"

Vanessa frowns and touches his hand to shows understanding and empathy, "I'm sorry about your loss. I'm sure it was very difficult."

His openness encourages Vanessa to open up also, "I like many things. I feel best when I'm preparing a special meal of pasta, ragu, and insalata to serve my friends and family. I felt worst when I knocked on the door of a girlfriend's house, and my husband answered the door in his underwear."

Ryan's face drops and his energy sinks. How terrible that must have been. "I'm sorry to hear about that. What's happened since then?"

"Well, I'm happily divorced, and overly cautious about men. I simply will never trust them," she says with a sad smile.

"That's a pretty blanket statement. Is there any wiggle room in that?"

Vanessa starts laughing again. Ryan laughs with her. Their secret traumas are out in the open. They relax and continue to talk about the challenges they face in relationships and their road to recovery. Both are still fragile from deep wounds. Recovery does not come easy.

Ryan pays the bill, and they say their goodbyes to Maria. They walk back to the Terme along the stone walks and over the Lamone River Bridge. They stop and watch the water glisten in the moonlight. She holds his arm as they walk.

When they arrive at her apartment, he hugs her and then kisses both of her cheeks in the Italian tradition. They are both happy to have found a new friend in each other, but respect the caution that both have about deeper relationships.

Ryan walks back to his room recognizing that the jet lag has finally set in. Although his eyes and body are tired, his mind and emotions are running at warp speed. He slept some on the plane coming over, but not enough. He is ready for bed, but not ready to sleep. It is 11:00 pm in Italy, but only 5:00 pm in Minneapolis.

As he lies in bed, he thinks about his conversations with Vanessa. It was a dreamy evening filled with the excitement of deep conversations about the essence of life and the discovery of new knowledge, and a new relationship. He is not surprised to feel a hint, and in fact, an avalanche of romantic fantasies towards her. He wonders about its potential. Then, his mind drifts to Julia. She is also an amazing woman. His mother was right. Just go with the flow and you never know what will happen. For Ryan, life is getting a little more interesting, but a lot more complicated.

Chapter 18. The Terme

Ryan wakes up early and is surprised to find how well rested he feels, despite the travel, dinner, and wine. The first gathering of participants is at 8:00 am, and he is eager to begin his first day at the Terme. He walks out onto the balcony of his third floor suite to view the brilliant summer morning. The overnight mist is still hanging over the Lamone River and the base of the distant hills. The sun is rising behind them. It causes the hilltops to glow and the hillside vineyards to glisten in the distance.

He decides that he has time for a brisk bike ride through the countryside so he dresses in his biking pants and shirt. He consumes the piadina sweet bread, formaggio cheese, and juice the he picked up on his way to the Terme. He fills his water bottle, heads downstairs, unlocks and hops on the rented Bianchi bike. He heads up the hill on the Valle Baccagnano.

The air is brisk with a scent of lemon and orange from the orchards nearby. The morning sun warms the vineyards, herds of grazing sheep and cattle in the fields, and cypress trees lining the top of the hills. He rides by the Corte Dei Familgia Farmhouse that he saw yesterday. He reaches the same borgo at the top of the hill overlooking Brisighella that he walked around yesterday.

He does not have much time this morning so he heads back. He speeds down the hill hoping nobody is coming up this early in the morning. He listens for the horns of oncoming traffic. The fresh wind blowing in his face awakens him. It's clear sailing the entire strip of the winding road. It's exhilarating.

When he returns, he showers, dresses in casual khaki pants with a white button down shirt and a brown sport coat, and heads over to the morning gathering. He is excited to meet the people here, and finally see the research for himself. He is also looking forward to seeing Vanessa again. He cannot stop thinking of her. He checked his e-mail, but no word from Julia. He'll check again later.

The purpose of the morning gathering of staff and participants is to welcome the new group of participants. Each week, the Terme has a new set of participants who often come from a distance. Current participants have the option to stay for a second week to allow for continuity and re-validation of the research. Nearly half of the participants stay for another week, making the retention rate and social mixing of participants quite high. Experienced participants mix with the new participants, and the transfer of knowledge occurs quite effectively. Many participants develop friendships for life here. The Terme has several large meeting rooms for group sessions, each named after a different Realm.

Today, they are all gathering in the Great Hall of the Mind, the ancient three story stone barn where the larger Terme meetings are held. As Ryan walks in one of the two large wooden doors, he sees dozens of folding chairs, in several rows, throughout the center Great Hall facing a podium and large slide projection behind it to the left. Ryan grabs one and sits down, as the information session is about to begin. He gazes around the room to see about fifty men and women of all ages and racial backgrounds. Some appear as if they are from America, wearing tourist apparel, while most are well dressed Europeans and a few Middle Easterners and Africans. This is quite an eclectic group. The room is decorated with ancient beams, hand-crafted iron-work, tapestries, terra cotta tiles, and stained glass in some windows. The ambiance and beauty of the large room is stunning.

The Director of the Terme Research Center, Dr. Paolo Nobili, comes into the room. He is wearing a casual dress shirt and a Gucci jacket with comfortable loafers and a loose fitting tie. He sees Ryan and walks up to him to shake his hand. "Dr. Laughlin. I'm Paolo Nobili. It is a pleasure to have you here at the Terme. Julia Stone and Vanessa have said some pretty flattering things about you. Did you have a nice trip?'

"Yes, I did, thank you. I'm quite happy to be here also. Your research is fascinating. The integration of the *Prophecy Scroll* is not only ground breaking, but has generated interest from people around the world. Congratulations."

"It is a bold move," he admits. "But because we have such humble beginnings with little research funding, we needed to be creative to get the attention needed for funding. We are so appreciative of the funding from NIH. We just hope we don't step on too many feet by doing so."

"I understand. I'm sorry to hear of Dr. Killian's death. I even met a fellow on the plane to Bologna who was coming here. He seemed to be more interested in the controversy than the science but he will learn."

Dr. Nobili nods sadly and says, "We get all types here. But I'm pleased that the people who follow the strategies to enhance their energy almost always have a positive experience. We have a high rate of satisfaction. Anyway, it is nice to meet you. We need to get started with the first session."

Dr. Nobili turns to walk to the front of the group participants and smiles. *"Buon Giorno a tutti di miei amici,"* Dr. Nobili begins. "I'll speak in English since I believe all of you speak this international language to some extent. Tell me if you don't."

The participants in the room are quiet and attentive to Dr. Nobili. No hands are raised. He continues with his introductions, "It is such a pleasure to have each of you here. I see many familiar faces. Welcome back. And I also see a lot of new faces. To all of you, we hope this week will be one that you will never forget, forever etched into your hearts and minds to help you begin a new era in your life. In this research, there is a lot that we want you to accomplish while here. But the most important is to help each of you find the good life with high energy in each of your *Seven Realms of Life*."

Ryan is sitting in the third row taking in this whole scene. Sitting in the large, stone barn with the sun streaming in, are international participants of all types, women and men, young and old, with nearly all races represented. It is truly as inclusive a group as possible.

Dr. Nobili looks at Ryan and smiles. "Before we start, I would like to introduce Dr. Ryan Laughlin. He is a physician visiting from Minnesota. We are pleased to have him here with us."

The group looks at Ryan, and then turns back to Dr. Nobili to hear more. "Now, let's get started. As much as we appreciate your interest in our research, I must caution you. The Terme is a spa and may be a great Italian vacation, but you will not find money, romance, or adventure here. We're not a matchmaking service, nor a tourist bureau. You have a more important role in the world. We are all worried about the Plagues cited in the *Prophecy Scroll*. We believe they are becoming a reality because the collective energy of the people in the world is low. With the knowledge and skills you will learn here, we need you to spread this knowledge to the people around you when you return to your lives."

He looks around the room at each participant, and then raises his voice to say, "For if you do, each of you will become our *Prophecy* warriors, fighting to save our world from low energy zombies, demons, and the Beast of the Plagues."

The group looks at each other in surprise. They're not sure what they've gotten themselves into here. Finally, an older gentleman in khaki dress pants and an Italian soccer shirt raises his hand and asks with honesty and directness, "Sorry to interrupt, but can you tell us what a warrior, demon, and zombie is? Halloween is not until October."

There is a laughter among the participants that begins to break the ice.

"Thank you. I was hoping someone would ask that question. What's your name?"

"My name is Bob Baker, from Nebraska." He places his hand on his wife's shoulder. "This is my wife Beatrice." She smiles, hesitantly.

"You've come a long way to get here," Dr. Nobili continues. "We're glad you're here. Let me tell you about warriors and zombies. We use these terms in a playful way to illustrate certain points. First, we want you to become a warrior by enhancing your own personal energy through learning about the actions that will boost or deplete your energy levels in your *Seven Realms of Life*. A warrior is someone who works to achieve high energy in each Realm and spreads this positive energy to others to bring virtues, blessings, and a good life to all of us."

"What about zombies?" Bob asks. "In the movies, they're dead people who look alive."

"Exactly!" Nobili says with smile, "A zombie is someone with low energy in many Realms who sucks energy from the people around them. They have lots of vices, problems, and are part of the Plagues. They are like the walking dead, and bring misery to the world. You don't want to be a zombie."

"How do I know if I'm a zombie or not?" Beatrice asks sheepishly.

"Each of you must ask yourself that question. Do you make people around you feel bad or miserable? Do you take more than you give and suck their energy? Do people avoid you? Now, you may not be a zombie, but most people are somewhere in the middle, between a warrior and a zombie, and you can go in either direction. Right now, few people are warriors with high energy in each Realm. We want to help you become a warrior."

"What are the *Seven Realms of Life*, then? We need to know what they are first." Beatrice asks with determination.

"Si! The seven Realms represent each facet of your life including the mind, body, spirit, emotions, way of life, and the people and nature around you. Each of these Realms emanates a different frequency and can be measured as distinct energy fields. We will teach you how to enhance your energy in each area, and then measure the changes in the energy before and after your documented daily activities. But before I explain more about the research, are there any other questions?"

A man in the back of the room, dressed in a sport coat, bowtie and dress slacks, raises his hand. "Doctor, I was been diagnosed with cancer last year, and have gone through surgery, radiation, and chemotherapy. I'm currently in remission, but I fear it will come back. I'm hopeful we have cured it. However, they say it may come back within the next two years, and will be more aggressive next time around. When I heard this, it made me cry inside. Then, I read about this project, it seemed so promising. If I become a warrior, will it prevent the return of cancer?"

"Good question," Dr. Nobili is careful in how he handles it. "What's your name and where are you from?"

"Henry Williams. Birmingham, England. I'm here to see what I can learn. I'm happy to be one of your warriors. But will this help me keep the cancer away?"

"Henry. Thank you for being here. We all have empathy for your situation. There are others here that, perhaps, are in similar situations. We have found that the knowledge you learn will help your overall health and well-being. However, this research is in its infancy and we are not a treatment facility. This study is about understanding your energy fields, and not treatment of disease. However, if improving your energy improves your overall health and a specific condition is improved, we would be delighted and want to know about it. However, we want you to follow-up as usual with your doctors. Does that make sense to you, Henry?"

"Yes, it does. Thank you. I'll remain optimistic, and am excited to be here."

Another hand is raised in the back. "Doctor, I'm Brian Johnson from New York. I'm here representing a religious group. We understand that you're using the *Dead Sea Scrolls* to determine if the strategies can lift a person's spirit. There are people opposed to this type of religious research and consider it sacrilegious. Has this research been vetted by the Church?"

Drs. Nobili and Venetre look at each other with concern, knowing that these are the same comments found in the killer's Manifesto. The man is tall, with short dark hair and a short beard. He is dressed like an odd American tourist, wearing a short-sleeved plaid shirt, dark dress pants, and running shoes.

Dr. Nobili tries to respond diplomatically, "Thank you for the question, Brian. We are using several manuscripts from the *Dead Sea Scrolls*. They have been provided by scholars at the Vatican to evaluate the power of the holy word in these documents. We are not testing the validity of the divine word, but rather their influence and power to help people. I'm happy to talk to you more about this personally. Now, I would like to introduce you to Dr. Vanessa Venetre. She is my esteemed co-principal investigator on this project."

Vanessa steps up to the front of the Great Hall looking both professional and elegant. She is wearing a simple champagne colored Armani pants suit. She accents the outfit with a thin necklace of gold and pearls.

"Welcome, warriors of the *Prophecy*. Grazie. Grazie. Grazie. It is truly a pleasure to have you here. You're the lifeblood of this project. You will be its success. Without you, we are nothing. As Henry noted, we expect that each of you are here for a specific reason. We feel your pain. We see your angels and your demons. We want you to gain as much by being here as we will. As Dr. Nobili mentioned, this research is all about your life energy, the spirit that surrounds you. These energies are your angels. They encompass you, protect you, and guide you. The energy is you and you are your energy. Your life is all about your energy."

Ryan recognizes her special gift for connecting with the participants, not only because of her sincerity and knowledge, but also her idealism and generosity. And she does it with style and grace.

"To be alive is to manifest this life energy," she continues. "It flows in and out like the air we breathe. You use this energy in your daily life, and so we need it replenished every day. You receive energy from the universal source, which manifests in our natural environment, in the people around you, and from all living things. Nearly every culture describes the energy that exists in living beings. Christians call it spirit. Taoists call it chi. Hindus call it prana. Muslims call it qudra. Every day you are giving and receiving energy to and from others. We grow to understand this instinctively and most of us are intuitive about sensing the shift when someone gives us or takes away our energy."

As she lets the group think about this for a moment. She walks to the left of the room to connect more personally with them. "Every cell, whether of muscle, brain, stomach, or skin tissue, has its own furnace and burns fuel for the cells to function. The fields from this energy can be measured at the cellular level. Likewise, our spiritual energy also generates electromagnetic fields. We have a sixth sense like an aerial antenna built into our bodies to detect these electromagnetic fields. And, like a radio receiver, we can receive and transmit this energy from the living environment around us. This research is about detecting, understanding, and enhancing our life's spiritual energy."

An attractive young lady from the front of the room raises her hand. She is dressed in tight blue jeans and a white sheer blouse with a visible red bra underneath. Her long brown hair falls in loose waves around her face. She says with a proper English accent, "Dr. Venetre, my name is Lily Bonnet. I'm a graduate student in Kinesiology from Paris. I'm interested in the measurement of energy fields, but how do we detect them? Can we see the energy fields or only feel them?"

"Good question, Lily. Most people cannot see the energy fields around your body. It's a different frequency range than your usual visual sense can detect. However, recent research in monarch butterflies suggests that a cellular protein found in both human and animals, called cryptochromes, is sensitive to magnetic fields, and are involved in the circadian rhythms of some plants and animals. Monarch butterflies can sense the magnetic fields of the earth and are able to travel thousands of miles during the winter to find exactly the same place in Mexico every year. The genes in butterflies are similar to the human cryptochrome gene. Thus, these cells can be active in human eyes."

"We have the same equipment as butterflies?" Lily comments with astonishment.

"Yes, but unfortunately, not all of their equipment. Most of us are not able to flutter about like a butterfly following people's auras. However, it does raise the possibility that detection of electromagnetic fields may be a sixth sense that can be developed to allow one to feel or even see a person's energy fields. We believe that with practice in enhancing your own energy, most people can learn to feel the energy of others intuitively. When someone around you has low energy, you will recognize it. Not only will it drain your own energy—you can actually feel it—but these people have many negative qualities, vices, which are obvious to those around them. Everybody knows these people. We call them zombies. Likewise, it's nice to be around people who give you energy. They attract people by their wonderful virtues, and make people feel happy to be around them. You know who these people are also. We call them warriors."

Lily continues with her questions, "So, if we can't see these energy fields directly, how are you measuring them?"

The participants are paying close attention to her response. "We'll measure your energy levels with a new technology called a SERF meter. This stands for spin-exchange relaxation-free atomic magnetometer. We will use this technology to measure both the level of energy in each Realm and the flow of energy going in and out of each participant using the SERF transmitter on your wrist. This allows us to get real time measurements of your energy levels."

Bob, the older gentleman in the Italian soccer shirt asks, "What do you do with the data?"

"The data is stored and analyzed to see how your energy level correlates with your daily actions. You may find your results to be quite revealing. As participants practiced their own selected energy boosting strategies and documented this deliberately, their scans showed higher energy in the Realms where the activity took place."

"When we do these things, our energy becomes stronger." Bob asks. "We'll feel better, and not so old, right?"

Vanessa walks to the right side of the room to be closer to Bob and Beatrice. "Yes, Bob. You'll find yourself in a better mood, sleeping better, more comfortable, feeling happier, and more energetic. These actions work quite well," she says with a smile. "And, maybe, you'll feel a bit more youthful."

Bob turns to his wife and says with a smile, "Did you hear that Beatrice. I told you coming here would be like a fountain of youth."

"Bob, she didn't say that," Beatrice says in a quiet, deadpan voice, shaking her head. "You're always exaggerating. You know there's no magic bullets. We're all just getting older. Face it."

Vanessa smiles with a compassionate look of understanding. "She's right. We have no youth serum here. But with high energy, we believe you will become healthier, feel better, and maybe, live longer."

Brian, the dark haired gentleman with a beard from New York, looks frustrated. He asks again, "But how is the *Prophecy Scroll* used for this study. I'm still concerned about its use in this science. Many people believe it is sacrilegious to do so and will take us down a path of destruction."

"Brian, let me first note that the *Prophecy Scroll* is, first and foremost, a powerful message to humanity. The scroll has been provided by the Israeli Antiquities Authority to a group of Vatican Scholars for assembly and translation. They and the Pope have given their blessing for this research."

"We know that it's powerful!" Brian states emphatically. "That's exactly what I'm talking about. You're evaluating it. Testing the Holy Word to see if it's true or not. We think that's wrong. It's not needed. We're worried about the repercussions of doing so."

She looks at Dr. Nobili, and hides her emerging fear from the group. "Thank you for your concern, Brian. We feel quite confident that this project is respectful in the use of the manuscripts. Now, let me tell you about them before we get too far off track. Here are your information booklets about them."

Brian shows a face of disdain for dismissing him.

The staff passes out folders to each participant. They eagerly open them up for review to see what all the fuss is about. "If you look through your folder, you will find four manuscripts that have been translated by Vatican scholars. They include the *Seven Realms of Life*, the *Seven Beasts*, the *Seven Rules of the Blessings*, and the *Blessing of Health*. The other six manuscripts, the *Blessings of Wisdom, Happiness, Prosperity, Beauty, Peace,* and *Love*, are still being assembled and translated."

"When will they all be available for us?" Bob asks.

"They are being translated right now, and I was told the *Blessing of Prosperity* and *Love* will be available soon," Vanessa explains. "This is exciting news. Each manuscript will provide us with a knowledge and insight into an aspect of our humanity that transcends history and different cultures. The others need much more reconstruction. We are hoping that when we have all of these manuscripts, it will lead us into an era of peace and prosperity that the earth has yet to see. Study them carefully, for as Dr. Nobili mentioned, you will be the warriors that will bring this knowledge to the world."

Chapter 19. The Seven Realms

At the break, participants are buzzing about the manuscripts and their unique role as *Prophecy* warriors in the world. Some are enthusiastic, some have doubts, but most are questioning how they, as common people, can become warriors. Right now, it just doesn't make much sense to them. However, they are here to listen, to learn, and to at least apply this research to their own lives. If they can do more, so be it.

Vanessa returns from the break and stands in the front of the Great Hall of the Mind to lead the continued discussion with the participants. There is a large screen behind her that shows the same collage of pictures that were shown at the start of Dr. Killian's last lecture.

There is one person in the room who is quite familiar with this slide. The Messenger. He saw it in St. Paul, and now, he is sitting at the Terme, taking it all in. He will be patient and deliberate. He will make sure that this Italian fashion queen is the first to go. Meanwhile, he will help all participants understand the fallacy and danger of this research.

Vanessa begins the next session despite her anxiety about Brian Johnson and his comments. Is he a threat or just a concerned participant? She tries to be upbeat, "Now, the fun starts. The rest of today, we will review each of the four manuscripts, and teach you the actions that will boost your energy here at the Terme. We have great facilities to help you, and of course, you must indulge in the Terme spa. Are you ready?"

There are enthusiastic nods from nearly every person in the group. Then, she holds up the document folders that were passed out earlier in the day and shows the participants which one to refer to. There is a rustling of papers as the group hurries to find the first one.

"The first manuscript is entitled the *Seven Realms of Life* and talks about how to maintain high energy in each Realm of your life," she explains. "This is what the Terme project is about. Please read it. If you follow the Blessings, you will bring energy into each Realm of your life. When you do these actions, the good life will come and you will escape the demons and the plagues. This knowledge has enormous implications for the people of the world."

Bob raises his hand again from the back of the room. He is not shy about asking questions. After all, he paid a lot to get here and wants to get his money's worth. He has always been a regular at church, and has been told about judgment day since his childhood. He never thought any of it would become a reality when he was still alive. He asks, "We know what zombies and warriors are now, but how do the demons, the Beast, and the Plagues fit in. When did you say the Plagues would come? Is this the same as judgment day? Should we be preparing for this?"

Vanessa walks down the aisle closer to Bob and smiles in appreciation for his steady stream of questions. "Like zombies and warriors, we believe the Beast and demons are metaphors meant to add impact to the lessons," Vanessa explains. "They're symbolic of the problems that we confront in our daily lives. However, the Plagues are described in quite realistic terms." Then, she says in a serious tone, "To everyone's surprise, they reflect real conditions that are present in our world today. There is evidence that the Plagues are here and getting worse."

The participants in the room stare in disbelief, some look worried, some look confused, but all look intrigued. Vanessa continues the mesmerizing presentation about the seven Realms and the seven Plagues. She uses every strategy to keep them riveted. She uses her hands to illustrate points. She walks back and forth or up and down the aisles. She uses her charm and attractiveness to make them smile. She talks directly to individuals to make them think and, in this case, Bob is getting her attention.

"Before we get too far ahead of ourselves, let's review our path to boost our energy in each Realm and become the warriors that you can be. I assume we all want to avoid the Beast and its Plagues."

She puts a slide on the screen behind her of the seven Realms. The group confirms with their full attention. Bob's steady stream of questions cease, at least for now.

"The *Seven Realms of Life* is an impressive manuscript that describes each dimension of a person's daily life. Surprisingly, these dimensions are recognized both in religion and science and apply as much today as it did two thousands years ago. As we mentioned, they include the mind, body, emotion, and spiritual dimensions, our way of life, and the people and nature that surround us. Let's review each of them."

She pauses to give the group an opportunity to read with her. "You will note that each is associated with actions that can bring the light of angels into your life. The angel is symbolic of a divine messenger who brings universal knowledge to the people. When you take the actions it suggests, it will bring energy into that Realm. Every time you do these actions, it will boost your energy. The more you do, the more energy you will have, and the better you'll feel. This information is as good a guide to living a good life, as you will ever find. Let's review the actions for each Realm. You will find them quite familiar to each of you."

She puts up the next slide with a picture of Albert Einstein in the corner. The slide reads, "When light from the angel shines in the Realm of the Mind, it will bring the Blessing of Wisdom and insight into the past, the present, and the future by understanding of the knowledge of man and the ways of the world by reading, studying, listening, and learning of the truth each day and by being honest with yourself and others."

She continues, "We all know that reading, studying, learning and listening will strengthen our knowledge as well as the energy in this Realm. This is obvious but often neglected. We need to learn daily, especially the listening part. We have lots of opportunities to learn here. However, the last line of this is the most important. We need to be honest with ourselves and to others. Truth, honesty, and wisdom all go together. Next is the Body Realm."

She puts up the next slide with a front view of a row of naked human male and female bodies standing next to each other. She reads, "When light from the angel shines on the Realm of the Body, it will bring the Blessing of Health to the flesh and take away affliction and crippling by being active, walking, running, stretching, and using the body well each day.

"If you exercise routinely and stay active, your energy here will be enhanced and your health will improve. You will literally feel stronger, with less pain, more energy, and be more able to do a better job at your daily activities. We will help you get into a regular exercise routine that will supply you with energy every day of your life."

Lily raises her hand to ask, "Does exercise change your energy only in the Body Realm, or other Realms too?"

Vanessa walks over to her and smiles. "Good question! We found the energy level improves in the Body Realm, but then spreads to other key Realms including the Way of Life and Nature Realms. The opposite is true too. There are many studies that show exercise will improve or prevent most chronic conditions including heart disease, arthritis, asthma, obesity, and cancer. Interestingly, this ancient knowledge, written thousands of years before the concept of science was even conceived, is consistent with the scientific literature on how to best promote health and well being. Their insight was divine. Next is the Emotional Realm."

She shows a slide of a baby with a broad, toothless smile on his face, and then reads the slide, "When light from the angel shines in the Realm of Emotion, it will bring the Blessing of Happiness and a life of contentment that lifts you to the heavens by bringing the creative spirit with smiles and laughter, music and art, sport and games to your life each day."

She walks back and forth in front of the room. "Happiness, elation, enthusiasm, sadness, depression, despair, anger. There are so many emotions we exhibit. Research shows that positive emotions such as joy, happiness, and optimism, which are all part of being content, are enhanced by creative actions. The opposite is true too. Positive emotional states will facilitate creative pursuits. They are linked. Whether it is music, art, writing, cooking, gardening, sports, playing games, or whatever creative pursuit you enjoy, they can all boost your energy in the Emotional Realm. They can free you from restrictive thoughts and improving your problem solving skills. Thus, we will help you express your creativity on a daily basis. We have many activities here at the Terme to help you. Our Italian cooking class is particularly popular. Whenever you need an emotional energy boost, take a creative break. You will be surprised how good it makes you feel. Next, the Spiritual Realm is a bit of a surprise."

She looks at her next slide of a mother hugging her little daughter with expressions of love on both their faces, "When the light shines in the Realm of the Spiritual, it will bring the Blessing of Love for yourself and those around you by learning to seek help through prayer, to be calm and seek insight through meditation, to understand the meaning of your life and see your past and future and to live a life that is merciful each day."

She turns back to the group and says, "It is not surprising that boosting your energy here is done through prayer and meditation. These are core teachings of nearly every religion. But the fact that they mention them both as different actions is surprising to some people."

"What's different about prayer and meditation?" Beatrice asks. "I pray at church, but I thought meditation was something practiced by secluded monks."

"They are different, and both can help us in different ways. Prayer is asking for help and guidance from God, while meditation is the practice of calming yourself inside to see life more clearly. There is much scientific evidence to support the efficacy of both prayer and meditation in improving our mood, health, learning, and relationships. In fact, it can help each Realm achieve the Blessings. It's quite simple and insightful. Most people know how to pray, but you also need to learn to meditate daily. We have some wonderful instructors to teach meditation. The next Realm, the Way of Life, also makes sense."

She shows a slide with a colorful basket of lettuce, peppers, apples, oranges, and other vegetables and fruits. "When light from the angel shines in the Realm of the Way of Life, it will bring the Blessing of Prosperity and success in life by working hard and steady, by having good sleep and breathing clean air, by being modest in eating and drinking the purity of nature's food and water, for these will bring light to all Realms."

She points to the tapestry, hanging on the stone wall to her right. It shows a cornucopia of natural foods flowing out of the basket. "See that old tapestry on the wall. From the earliest times, people understood the importance of natural foods. So, it's interesting, indeed, that they believe the path to success is not money, but rather a healthy lifestyle. Wealth is one of many by-products of a healthy lifestyle. By working hard, eating, drinking, sleeping, and breathing well, success will come. We all know they're each important, but it's how you do them that is the key. We will work with each of you to understand these components and follow a healthy lifestyle."

"This is my downfall," Bob laughs, as he grabs his oversized belly. "I work hard, but it's difficult to stay away from all that unhealthy junk food. If you're a lifestyle zombie, what do you do?"

Vanessa laughs with the rest of the group. "I know it's tough, Bob. With all the advertising and temptations out there, it is easy to fall into an unhealthy lifestyle. This action may be the hardest to follow, particularly for young people and men since they have the greatest tendency to live life in excess. It takes discipline and positive peer pressure. We can teach you much about eating and sleeping well, but you have to find your own path to high energy. Then, there is the Nature Realm."

She shows a slide of a serene lake with a mist coming off the mirror-like water and a green canopy of trees lining the shore. A red canoe is parked on the bank of the lake. She reads, "When light from the angel shines in the Realm of Nature, it will bring the Blessing of Beauty and abundance will come by living in and being part of the harmony with the earth, and its land, seas, and skies, and by being organized, clean, and not wasteful and taking care of that which surrounds you."

She points to the giant framed photograph of the earth from space that is on the wall to the side of the doors to the Great Hall. "As it says, this is about living in harmony with the earth, by spending time outside in nature, by being organized, clean, and by avoiding pollution and waste. Each of these actions is well supported by the scientific evidence to improve public health. Advances in sanitation are the major reasons that the average lifespan of modern man has increased by at least twenty years. You will also find the main attraction of the Terme is its natural healing springs. These naturally healing springs, which have been used since the Roman days, bring you close to nature's healing touch, the negative ions that emanate from the natural earth. You will find by simply meditating in these natural springs you will feel great. It's magical. Then, if you also allow yourself the pleasure of one of our cleansing body rubs, followed by a deep muscle massage, and spending just a little time in our warm soothing sun each day, you will find heaven is right here on earth. Each of these activities will also boost your health by enhancing vitamin and mineral levels in your body. They also help prevent many conditions such as weak bones, arthritis, and senility. The seventh and last Realm is the Realm of the People. It's the most complex Realm."

She shows a slide of men and women helping others at a food shelf. "When light from the angel shines in the Realm of the People, it will bring the Blessing of Peace and a life of harmony and goodness by sharing and helping others, being generous and giving of yourself, and supporting those around you and the communities you live in."

She walks to the back of the large room and asks the Terme staff to hold hands with those standing next to them in a line. She raises their hands in the air. "We are so lucky to work here. We boost our energy every day in this Realm by helping you. And when we have high energy in this Realm, it brings harmony, peace, and goodness to us all. Think about these actions. They make sense. Sharing and helping others. Being generous in your service to others. We need to support and help those in our families and the communities we live in. We have many service opportunities here to help others, including childcare and the senior centers. And you can simply help each other learn."

She puts up the slide of the *Seven Realms of Life* symbol again. "Remember, maintaining high energy in all Realms will have the most powerful effect in achieving a good life and becoming a warrior. Do all of them every day, and you will see a difference in your life. Remember, it's all about your energy."

"These actions seem pretty simple and obvious," Henry from England comments. "Exercising, learning, prayer, meditation, eating and sleeping well, being creative, staying clean and organized, helping others. If this is all it is, I can do that."

Lily adds her two cents, "I agree. We all know this stuff. Our parents taught us these lessons. We should be doing them anyways."

"Si, they are simple," Vanessa agrees. "But, surprisingly, they're often neglected in our daily routines. Because they are simple, each person has the capacity to apply them regularly as part of our daily lives. This is part of being a warrior. When you do these things, they will naturally and magically spread to others. You don't even have to convince anybody. The energy just spreads through the *Rule of Gatherings*. We will discuss this set of lessons later. The are called *Rules of the Blessings* and quite relevant to understanding how your energy can change each day."

"Before we move on, tell me again how the *Seven Realms of Life* relate to the research you are doing here?" Henry asks.

"We are applying science and technology to this universal knowledge by measuring the strength of energy in each of these Realms," Vanessa explains. "The so-called *light from the stars* is measured by the SERF technology that you wear on your wrist. Look at these slides of energy readings from participants. Each of the seven Realms is distinguished by different frequencies and colors."

She presents a slide showing the energy fields of an individual and the different colors for different Realms. "Can you see this person's strong and weak Realms? We found that the dominant Realm is one that people maintain easily through their own natural talents and daily activities. For example, most athletes have high energy in their Body Realm. Doctors and scientists focus on their Mind Realm. Sales people and social workers in the People Realm. You see the pattern. You need to know what Realms are your strongest to understand how you bring in energy naturally as part of your daily routines. You also need to identify your weakest Realms and learn to boost them in order to maintain balance and overall health and well-being. Ultimately, if enough people do this, we will prevent the plagues."

"I just want a good life," Bob concludes. "I'm not much of a warrior type. And I'm not really cut out to be a zombie, either. But if we prevent the Plagues in the process of finding the good life, I'm all for that too."

"Thanks Bob," Vanessa smiles. "Those are appropriate closing comments to end this session. Now, let's take a short break. Please enjoy our natural refreshments designed to boost your energy in the Way of Life Realm. Back in ten minutes."

Chapter 20. The Seven Beasts

At the Terme Project, completing the research is the primary goal. Yet the participants are only beginning to understand the importance of being trained as a *Prophecy* warrior. Each of them will be sent back to their small corner of the world to counter the declining state of the world, bring zombies back to life by spreading their high energy, and fight the return of the Beasts and its seven Plagues.

The participants have also been told that these altruistic goals are controversial, and some people will oppose it for their own reasons, whether it be infringing on religious dogma or threatening the status quo. The murder of Dr. Killian is an ominous sign, and there is fear among the staff that the Terme is the next target. The staff must be prepared, but more importantly, they must continue this mission despite the impending threat. They hope the threat will take care of itself by doing so.

At the break, the group hovers over the refreshment table to the left of the chairs that includes bottled spring water, natural fruit and vegetable juices, cappuccino, almond-flavored bruttiboni biscuits, and a wide variety of whole wheat, banana, walnut, and blueberry mini-muffins that cater to western tastes. The participants mingle casually with each other and then return to their seats from the brief break. Although many in the group are quietly considering the material that was covered, there are strong feelings of interest and excitement among the conversations in different groups. Vanessa returns to the front of the three-story large open stone barn. The large screen is behind her and she stands with her legs crossed beside the podium with her left elbow resting on it. She is waiting for the group to take their seats. The fifty or so participants are slowly returning to the cushioned folding chairs in the center of the room.

Vanessa continues, "I hope you had a nice break. Now that you understand the *Seven Realms of Life*, we can answer Bob's original question," "What's this Beast, and its demons, and plagues? In contrast to *The Seven Realms*, the manuscript called *The Seven Beasts* is darker and more ominous. It worries people the most. The manuscript predicts Seven Plagues will result from low collective energy of the people in each of the seven Realms. It has motivated us to work harder and train more warriors to prevent this from happening.

She shows the next slide and reads the introduction, "And it is said, the beast with seven heads and ten horns will come again one thousand years after the first millennium when light from the angels in the Realms is weak. And with him, the seven Plagues will again come forth."

A young man with short dark hair, wearing a white western shirt and boots, sitting in the front row, stands up and raises his hand. "Hello, y'awl." He turns and waves to the group.

All eyes shift to the tall gentleman with an American accent from the south.

"My name is Wayne Smith, from the great state of Texas, in the good ole' U.S. of A. This is my first trip to eetalia. I've been sittin' back and listening to all this talk about warriors and zombies and I kinda like it. It's a lot like my video games back home. But to tell the truth, this Beast and the Plagues gives me the willies. Video games are fantasy, but this sounds too real. What's the carnage that's predicted? And when is this suppose to happen?"

"Well, according to our calendar," Vanessa replies. "One thousand years after the first millennium, which makes it beginning this century. It's likely already begun. Thus, if we take these predictions seriously, each of us, the people of the world, need to work harder to prevent these disasters from unfolding in our current lifetime. If we learn to follow the actions in each Realm, and boost our collective spirit, it says we can prevent these Plagues. This is what we do here. We hope that is why you're here also."

"Well, if it is true, this prophecy does not bode well for our future," Wayne complains. "But let us have it anyways. And don't sugar-coat it, sweetheart."

Vanessa smiles to herself as she continues in a serious tone, "We understand that the *Prophecy* predictions can generate a sense of pessimism and paranoia. But, remember, it is balanced with the rays of hope and optimism in the *Seven Realms of Life* and the *Blessings* manuscripts."

"Well, fine," Wayne says. "Let's hear about the fire and brimstone!"

Vanessa raises her eyebrows and looks at Dr. Nobili in the back of the room. She is thinking Wayne is a real piece of work and may be hard to deal with. Is he also a threat?

Dr. Nobili smiles back and shakes his head. He does not believe Wayne is the killer and doubts that he is a threat to the staff or the research.

Vanessa turns her attention back to the larger audience. "The Plagues reflect low collective energy of the people in each Realm. For each Realm, there is a corresponding plague. In the Mind Realm, it is widespread ignorance. In the Body Realm, it is rampant chronic illness. In the Emotional Realm, it is depression and despair. In the Way of Life Realm, it is poverty. In the Nature Realm, it is drought. In the Spiritual Realm, it is hate. And in the People Realm, it is war. Just like a virus, low energy spreads. More and more people lose energy and become zombies. When there are a sufficient number of zombies in a group, whether it is a family, a community, or a nation, the plague will come to that group.

"The worst part is that the scientific evidence suggests these Plagues are already here. The Beasts and demons are symbolic of the low energy in our lives and the vices we have. It was written to scare the hell out of people with a gruesome vision of reality, just like Hollywood does."

"So you're saying that Hollywood is going to make a movie of this?" Wayne cracks. "I can see the Beast with seven heads flying out of the seas to wreak havoc upon the world. Are you the heroine, Dr. Venetre? You've got the looks."

"I don't underestimate movie-makers, but I'm not the Hollywood type," she smiles and says sarcastically. "I suppose they'll make a movie called *The Seven Beasts* starring Arnold Swarzenegger as the warrior who kills all of the zombies. As usual, they would only focus on the death and destruction part, and skip the solution."

"Maybe, I should I just wait for the movie to come out!" Wayne replies.

Laughter breaks the tension and lightens the mood.

"I wouldn't wait for the movie," Vanessa laughs. "There are zombies all over the place right now sucking the energy right out of you. One day, you may wake up to become one of them!" She laughs as she looks at Wayne.

Then, Vanessa shifts into a simulated newscaster's voice, "Sir, the seven Plagues have arrived and turning millions into zombies. There is widespread ignorance, poverty, sickness, despair, drought, hate and war in every corner of the planet. You have a mission impossible here. If you choose to accept it, your mission is to save the world from death and destruction. To do so, you need to become a warrior with high energy in each Realm. Sir, do you accept your mission?"

Wayne, with his big, full toothed grin says, "Now, I know why my mamma sent me here. You guys are a bunch of bad-asses. Last week, I was a drug-dazed zombie and, this week, I'll become a warrior. Life never ceases to surprise me." The group laughs as Wayne continues, "If I accept this mission, Dr. Venetre, what do I need to do? Is there a shoot'em up video game we could play?"

Vanessa re-evaluates her opinion of Wayne. He brings humor and playfulness into the group, and clearly boosts their Emotional Realm. "No video games, Wayne," she replies. "But you're doing exactly what you need to do right now. You're here, you're listening, and, I believe, you understand. Our mission at the Terme Project is to teach you to spite the Beast, transform yourself from an emerging zombie into a warrior, and make up a good life for yourselves, a life of Blessings. You do not need to become a celibate monk, but you do need to be drug free. Are you?"

"Yes, Ma'am," he says emphatically. "I promised my mamma that I would give up the drug life, and I intend to keep my promise."

"Excellent. And you'll find that the more you learn, the more you will want to learn," Vanessa replies. "It feels good and becomes self-motivating. It creates a snowball effect designed to make you, and the people around you, happier and healthier. Not such a bad deal for your first trip to eetalia, Si?"

"Let's do it!" Wayne exclaims.

"I love your attitude. First, you need to understand how your life energy works and how our daily routines can boost or deplete our energy in each Realm. There are many ways to do this. You simply have to do them."

Ryan is amazed at how talented she is in working with the participants. There is an excitement in the room, as they are eager to learn, to help themselves, and, hopefully, to help the world.

"Are there any other questions?" She looks around the room at starry-eyed participants who are trying to grapple with the enormity of their responsibilities.

Then, a slight, pale young woman with delicate features, and blond streaked hair, carefully raises her hand. She is dressed in ripped jeans and a loose white embroidered shirt. She speaks with an eastern European accent, "Hello. I am Eliza Arcos from Romania. You say the actions in each Realm will prevent the Plagues. How does that happen?"

"Good question, Eliza," Vanessa recognizes her shyness. "It leads us right into the next manuscripts called *The Rules of the Blessings*. We will discuss the Rules this afternoon, but let me tell you about the most important one right now. It's called *The Rule of Gatherings*. I mentioned it earlier. It deals with group energy."

Vanessa, with a steady stream of positive energy, walks down the aisle to speak closer to where Eliza is sitting. "You need to know that your individual energy will affect all of us whether you want it to or not. When high energy exists among individuals in a group, this collective energy will spread and transform all of the people in the group. For example, if most of the people in a group are happy, the rest of the group will absorb the positive energy and their mood improves also. The problem is that the opposite is true also. When a majority of people in a group has low energy, it depletes the energy of others in the group and the zombies take over. The low energy of small groups then affects larger groups, which leads to plagues within the community, state, and eventually, national and international levels. It's a cascading decline of the world from collective low energy. The world becomes filled with zombies. We need to stop this downward spiral and it can only begin with each and everyone of us."

Brian then raises his hand with scowl on his face. He has been stewing quietly during the last sessions. Finally, he decides he has to say something, "I don't agree with your assessment," He says defensively. "The reason for the Plagues is that the people of our world are ignoring Christ, our savior. The predictions are coming true because you and so many others in the world are questioning the Word of God. We need to simply accept His word and follow it. Why do you need to do this research to test his word? God is the final word, and it's a sin to question Him. This will open the door to the demons and lead us down a path to hell."

Most participants listen carefully to Brian's words of warning and then look at each other in surprise. The attention is brought back to Vanessa to see how she'll handle Brian's comments.

Vanessa, trying to diffuse his negativity, responds with honesty. "Could you be a bit more dramatic, Brian?" Laughter follows, which incenses Brian even more. She continues in a more serious tone, "It is fine to disagree,

Brian. But as we said before, our goal is not to question the Word of God, or to test if the Blessings work or not, but rather to learn how to best use them to help people. We are spreading the knowledge, not testing it. Eventually, we hope that all people will see the Blessings for what they are, simple, practical advice."

Brian's energy sinks deeper as if he feels he has just been dismissed. He glares at Vanessa and then looks away. He considers his options, which most likely will not include hanging around here too long.

To Vanessa, it was not what Brian said but how she felt when he was saying it. She could feel the pull of his low energy. They get all types of people and opinions at the Terme, but Brian's demons were out in full force and his continued negative comments were too close to the killer's Manifesto. Vanessa and Paolo recognize the need to check in with him later to see where he is coming from. He's not in a good place and, in fact, may be the threat they feared would come.

Then, a well dressed pretty Italian woman in her thirties, with a low cut blouse, ample breasts, elegant make-up, and a flowing hairstyle stands up to ask a question. All heads turn her way and quickly forget about Brian's comments. "My name is Cicci Beretta, like the gun. I'm from the town of Faenza. Before we head too far down the path to hell, I think our group wants to hear about the Rules and the Blessings. Can you share that information with us?"

This is Cicci's third time here this year. She can be irritating to the staff because she takes the research as a social opportunity and not too seriously. She wants to meet the good-looking men who come to the Terme, after her third husband left her. However, right now she is saying the right thing at the right time—and Vanessa is relieved. She welcomes Cicci's effort at trying to defuse the situation with Brian.

"Thank you, Cicci," Vanessa replies. "We just reviewed the *Seven Realms of Life* and the *Seven Beasts*. Next, we will discuss *The Seven Rules of the Blessings* and *The Blessing of Health*."

"What's with the number seven?" Lily asks. "Why did they choose seven, why not five, or my favorite number, four?"

"Seven has special significance in the historical religious documents just like it does in nature," She explains. "There are seven days in the week, seven notes on the musical scale, seven colors of the rainbow, seven directions—left, right, up, down, forward, backward and center. The list goes on and on. It makes it easy to remember."

The group nods in understanding and appreciate the simplicity of it.

Vanessa continues, "With the *Rules of the Blessings*, our focus is to help you understand and enhance your energies. Thus, for the rest of the morning, we will break into small groups. Each group will be lead by one of our trained staff."

Cicci asks casually without a hint of sarcasm, "Dr. Venetre, could you just tell us what we need to know to save our souls, and move on, so we have some time to get to know each other?"

Vanessa's brief support of Cicci's contributions quickly ends. She knows that this is typical Cicci trying her best to bring attention to her. Her soul does need saving, but it'll take more than this research to get through to her.

"Enhancing your energy takes more than reading a brief summary," Vanessa replies patiently, trying to maintain the energy. "It takes understanding, time, and effort. However, you're correct in suggesting that we need to get to know each other better. So, after the break, our facilitators will meet with your small groups, and you will have a chance to introduce yourselves to each other, and more importantly, learn how to help each other. Here are your small group assignments, and the area in which you'll meet. Let's be back in about thirty minutes."

Vanessa passes out the group assignments, and then looks around the room for Brian. He has already disappeared. She goes to talk to Paolo at the back of the room. "Paolo, that participant," she says with dread in her voice. "He was strange and had such low energy. The look of demons was in his eyes. It was dreadful. Do you think he could be the murderer? I'm worried. Should we call the *polizia?*"

Paolo is very protective of Vanessa. He has been her mentor and father figure for years. He originally developed this research and brought Vanessa into it as one of his glowing post-doctoral students. He is protective, not only because she and her parents have been close to his family for years, but also because she will be the one who will take over the research in the future.

He looks at Vanessa with eyes that will calm a swarm of bees. "I agree. He's definitely a strange one. But we've had these strict religious types before. Let's talk to him to find out why he's here and what he's up to. The last thing we need is a conflict. Remember what happened last year when that male stalker came for one of the participants. Everybody's energy dropped."

"Our participants are so sensitive to negative energy," Vanessa agrees. "Any disruption can bring their learning to a stop. And he was such a zombie. If we don't call the *polizia,* we at least need to connect with him sooner than later."

Paolo looks out at the group and says, "As soon as the session is over, we should find him and have a friendly talk. We can see what his motives are and ask him to leave if he's not interested in learning and participating in the research."

"Well, we do need to find out who he is and why he is here," Vanessa replies. "But I favor getting the *polizia* involved sooner rather than later."

"Let's not jump to conclusions," he repeats. "We need to focus on our energy here. Mr. Johnson will show his face sooner or later."

Chapter 21. The Gathering

All participants have their own motivation and needs for coming to the Terme, and Cicci Beretta knows her own quite well. At the break, she makes a beeline for Ryan, like a predator finding her prey. She has had her eyes on Ryan all morning and finds her way to stand right next to him. When she arrives by his side, she looks up at Ryan with her big brown eyes, like a puppy dog wanting to please, and says, with a thick Italian accent, "Ciao, me ees Cicci Beretta. It's a good place 'ere, is it not?"

Ryan looks down at the diminutive, five foot two inch Cicci. He is startled by her radiant smile, physical allure, and forthright approach. He loses his train of thought for a few moments, and then says, "Oh, yes, it's so stimulating," He cringes at his choice of words. "It seems relevant to everybody."

When Cicci first meets a man, she makes a quick appraisal of whether the man could be the love of her life or not. She decides that Ryan is handsome enough to meet her basic criteria. She wonders if he has the *passione* for her. She does not want to wait too long to find out so she moves fast before someone else does. She refocuses her charm to a more intimate level. "I no understand the energy. You understand how to get more energy? You from America, Si?"

"Ah, yes. Excuse me for not introducing myself. I'm Ryan Laughlin from Minnesota. That's near Chicago."

Cicci likes what she hears. He is an American who is articulate and polite. Good qualities. She knows that American men, in general, are easy targets in the hands of attractive and sophisticated Italian women. They either melt fast with just a little bit of attention, or they have no clue. But they never turn away.

"It's a pleasure to meet you. I'm here alone. And you?"

"Ahh, si, maybe," he says with ambivalence.

"I know I just met you, and dees is crazy," she says and hands him her card. "Here's my number. So call me, maybe?"

Ryan looks dumbfounded. Is this how Italian women act? What has he been missing?

"Or, are you free for lunch today?" Cicci persists.

He sees Vanessa in the distance and wants to tell her how much he enjoyed dinner last night. He doesn't want to miss catching her. "I'm so sorry, Miss Beretta, but I already have plans today. Perhaps later would work."

"Oh, dat's too bad. Then, call me. Okay?" She frowns, and wrinkles form in the middle of her brow. He may be more difficult than she thought. "I like to get to know you more. Do you have phone number? Maybe later, we go for walk. I show you Brisighella and have some good Italian vino?"

"Ah, yes. Sure." Ryan responds more confidently. He writes down his cell phone number. "Perhaps, after we know more about today's schedule. I need to talk to Dr. Venetre now, but I'll see you this afternoon. Right?"

Cicci stares at Ryan with an exaggerated sad look. Ryan, then, heads over to greet Vanessa. He waves to get her attention at the other end of the Great Hall.

"Vanessa! Vanessa! *Buon giorno!*" He raises his voice.

Vanessa looks up and sees Ryan coming towards her. She makes eye contact, and a business smile comes across her face.

"Good morning, Dr. Ryan," she says formally. "It's nice to see you, today. What do you think about the morning session?"

He gives her a smile, and pauses to find the right words before responding, "You were truly engaging, and I agree, it's ground-breaking research. The measurement of energy fields coupled with use of the *Prophecy* wisdom will have a major impact on our understanding of health and healing around the world. I hope that it will also bring science and religion closer together. Both have so much to offer the world. Are you having lunch right now? Can we discuss it more?"

"Oh. I'm sorry, but I have to go back to my office and make some calls before this afternoon. Please come to the reception this evening, and we can talk more then. By the way, have you seen a gentleman by the name of Brian Johnson, from New York? He was here most of the morning, and made those strange comments. We're worried about him."

Ryan looks around the room. "No, I don't see him now, and didn't see him slip away. He was pretty weird. Interestingly, I also met him briefly on the plane from Amsterdam to Bologna. He made some strange comments then also, but I didn't think anything of it. There's a lot of insecurity among extreme religious types these days. They are critical of anything that may infringe on their rigid religious beliefs."

"If you see him, please tell me," she says. "I'll see you later."

Vanessa begins to walk away with a worried, distant look on her face. Then, she turns to tell Ryan one more thing in a sharp tone, "Also, just for your own safety, you might want to stay clear of Cicci Beretta. She is what we call a *pirania* in the form of a man-eating divorcee. She'd love to sink her teeth into you."

Then, she turns her back on Ryan and walks away. Ryan immediately feels his energy sink. What just happened? Was he just snubbed? What a strange comment about Cicci. There must be some history that he didn't see coming. Anyway, he recognizes the need to focus his efforts on learning the program and avoiding any romantic entanglements that would drain his energy. He decides to stick with a collegial relationship with Vanessa, despite the natural attraction he thought they had for each other last night. He will simply blame the wine for being to upfront.

He decides to head back to his room to avoid the whole Cicci scene. He stops at the deli to pick up some natural foods to eat for lunch. As he walks back, his mind drifts away from the complex world of women's emotions to his experiences at the Terme so far. The charming medieval town of Brisighella. The invigorating bike trip this morning. The classic Italian scenery. The concept of spiritual energy. The ominous Plagues. The food, and, of course, the attractive, but challenging, female company. He's definitely going to enjoy this week.

After he arrives at his room, he sends an email to Julia, his mother, and his buddies. He tells them that it's been a good trip so far. He takes out the light snack of fresh carrots, cheese, bread, and spring water and eats it slowly. He thinks of the intense dinners he had with Julia and Vanessa. Both are amazing women. He wonders what he would do if Julia was here. She would be a major, but pleasant, distraction.

After lunch, he casually wanders back to the Great Hall and stops to watch the gentle flow of the River Lamone, to see who's laying around the expansive swimming pool, and take in the views of the rolling countryside with its vineyards and fruit trees trailing off into the distance. For the first time in months, he is right where he wants to be.

Back in the Great Hall, he finds his small group in the corner with chairs sitting around a circle. He sits next to Bob Baker and his wife, Beatrice, from Nebraska. He introduces himself to both of them. They are eager to hear more about who is here. They hope to meet some famous people on their first trip to Italy. To them, nearly every Italian is famous, so it should not be too difficult.

An Italian woman in her early thirties with long dark hair and a trim athletic body sits down to lead his group. She is dressed casually, in one of Roberto Cavalli's splashy green and red print blouses with matching pants. Her face is bright and sunny with a sincerity that makes you simply want to please her.

"*Boun giorno!*" She starts with a radiating smile. "My name is Linda Lo Bianco, from the University of Bologna. It is my pleasure to be with you this week, and facilitate our small group discussions. I'm happy to see those of you who returned from last week, and I'm especially happy to meet those of you who are new participants. Warriors, welcome. We want the Terme to be a special place for you. It is our job to facilitate achieving this for each of you. But first, we must get to know each other."

Ryan looks at the people sitting in the chairs around him. He is familiar with some of them, because they spoke this morning. Cicci, Wayne, Bob and his wife, Beatrice, and Eliza are there, but several others are new to him. He does not see Brian Johnson in his group, or in any other group around the Great Hall.

"Now, we would like you to share your stories with each other," Linda explains. "When you do, you will see one of the *Rules of the Blessings* in action. The *Rule of Gatherings* tells us that our energy is influenced by the energy of those around us. As people tell their stories, you will feel your energy grow stronger, or in some cases, weaken. You will see how one person can affect the collective energy of the group. Be sensitive to your energy. Don't worry if you can't feel it right away. Sometimes, it takes time to feel your own energy. You will like being able to recognize it when it happens."

Ryan is excited to see how this works. He decides to be the first to speak up and encourage positive energy exchange. "I'm Ryan Laughlin. It is a pleasure to be here. This is my first week. What would you like us to focus on?"

"Just tell us some things about yourself and why you're here," Linda replies. "Being honest and sincere will generate the most positive energy."

Ryan looks around and speaks to the group. As he does with his own patients, he chooses not to reveal too much of himself. "I'm a physician from Minnesota. That's near Chicago. This is my first day here and I felt the morning presented some remarkable ideas. I hope to use them to improve the care of my patients. Most of them have conditions that are affected by their lifestyles. If they recognize how their daily activities affect their energy, perhaps it will help them change and develop healthier lifestyles. I also want to learn more about myself. I want to know what actions boost my energy and what depletes it."

Linda nods in appreciation. Then, a man in jeans and a white dress shirt with rolled up sleeves stands up tall and speaks to the group, "My name is Jack Kriesberg. I'm visiting from Utah and this is my first week. I ended my military tour two years ago, and I'm working for a group focused on freedom. I read an article about the use of the *Dead Sea Scrolls* in the research here. I want to learn about strategies that bring peace and not war."

"Thank you, Jack. Please go ahead."

"Well, I don't mean to lower your energy, but I was injured in Iraq a few years back. I was a weapons expert, and diffused bombs. We were on patrol outside of Baghdad and drove across a roadside bomb that exploded. I was unconscious and didn't know what hit me. I was covered with so much blood and debris that my buddies thought I was dead. So, they put me in a body bag and zipped me up."

Jack shuffles uncomfortably in his chair. His eyes are intense, and anger rises in him every time he thinks about it. The memory of being left for dead plays over and over in his mind, and drives him a bit crazy.

"When they came back to get my dog tags, the paramedic said, 'Hey guys, there's some movement here. This one might still be alive.' They took me out of the bag and put me in a hospital. I had wounds on seventy five percent of my body. Only my head was intact. I lost two of my buddies. No one expected me to survive. There were a lot of miracles taking place during those few days. I was in and out of consciousness. When I was awake, I prayed to God every day. I was sent to four hospitals, had a dozen surgeries, and took two years of recovery. I died three times on the operating table. They put my body back together, but I believe it was God at every step of the way that breathed life back into my shattered body. He had a mission for me. I'm hoping this place will tell me what that's about. I still feel the demons of war are still haunting me. I have nightmares and panic attacks. War is so unnecessary. I guess I'm here to find my way and learn about the *Blessing of Peace.* I want to bring peace to myself and to spread peace to the world."

"Thank you for sharing that with us. Very dramatic," Linda says with a surprised expression on her face. She turns to address the group, "As Jack told his story, I saw lots of anguish on your faces and tears in your eyes. It is truly one of God's miracles that he is here. By showing empathy for him, you boost your own energy, and that of others, in the room. This is called the *Rule of Gatherings.* Did you feel the change in your own energy as he told his story? Anyone else want to share their story?"

Wayne, the tall lanky Texan, stands up to tell his story with a bashful look and a sideways grin, "I'm Wayne. Again. This is a long ways from Paint Creek, Texas, which is close to nowhere. My mamma wanted me to come here. She figured I could use a place like this to get myself on track. This is my first day here. I fell off the track so many times with drugs that they figured I'd be better off anywhere but home. She heard about this place from our church. Says you'd use a lotta Bible talk to cure me of my vices and my stupidity."

He looks down at his cowboy boots and shuffles around. Then, he tells of his daddy dying, his failure in the army, his problems at work, the bad group of friends he hung with, and his drug problem. "I had some problems in the Army. I couldn't take the stress. They said I had somethin' called PTSD. Ya know, post-traumatic stress on the brain? I worked several jobs, but then this winter, I got fired from my latest job and had to move back in with my mamma. Some buddies from the war kept comin' round the house, eating our food, drinking our beer, and bringing drugs."

The participants in Ryan's group are glued to his story. It's difficult to see a happy ending in this. They already feel energy being drained.

Wayne continues, "My mamma got so upset that she called my older brother, Robert, to come over and straighten me out. It all came to a head when Robert did something that I call stupid, but mamma says it saved my life. He's a cowboy kind of kid who rolls his own cigarettes and plays the tough guy. When mamma gets home after working late, she's always tired as a hound dog. She don't like my buddies hangin' out like leeches and gettin' into all kinds of trouble. Well, Robert decided enough is enough and took some badass action."

Wayne stops in the middle of telling the story for a few seconds leaving everyone in suspense. "Sorry, I still lose my train of thought due to the PTSD and the drugs. Where was I?"

Finally, Linda offers, "You were talking about your brother. What happened? What did Robert do?"

He looks up at Linda and continues with a shaky voice, "It still scares me to think about. My brother's certifiable. Ya know crazy. He found a six-shooter gun hidden in a box of fun things my daddy left, and he came running out with fire in his eyes and shooting the gun in the air. He yelled at my friends that he was going to kill them all. We were fuckin' scared outta our minds. I yelled, 'He's coming for ya. He's coming for ya. Get the hell out of here.' They ran off in all directions as fast as they could. They haven't been back since. I still don't know what I'm doing here. I wanna cure my PTSD, get my life back on track, and find that *Blessing of Wisdom* so I don't screw up again. Have y'all reviewed it yet?"

There are lots of quiet whispers about Wayne's low energy. They all want to avoid lowering their own energy by hanging out with him.

Then, Eliza, the pale woman from Romania, speaks up. She talks slowly and softly, with sadness in her voice, "'Ello, my name is Eliza. This is my second week. I'm only nineteen-years-old, but I feel like I'm all used up. This place has helped me reclaim the whole of me, and help people judge me not for what I was, but for what I can become. I'm just like any teenage girl, except I have been a prostitute since I was fifteen." She tells about her poor family and the fear they had about becoming homeless. She told a story about how she and her girlfriends dream about having fancy new clothes. A few summers ago, an older man named Marcos told her she was very pretty and offered to buy her some of the new clothes that she had been staring at in the shop windows every day. As first, she said she was shy and ignored him. But he persisted, and eventually, she accepted the clothes.

After that, she said they met regularly at the shops and he bought beautiful clothes for her. Then, one day Marcos asked her to come home with him. He gave her a couple of drinks and made her laugh. Eventually, he took those nice clothes off of her, and she had sex with him, to please him. It was her first time. She pleased him regularly after that. Then, he told her that he would buy her even more new clothes and give her some spending money if she would please some of his friends. Her mother and father had lost their jobs, and their family desperately needed the money or they will be thrown out of their home. At first, she said no, but he kept pressuring her. Finally, she consented to meet this man at a hotel. They had sex and she's been working as a prostitute ever since. They sent her to Amsterdam where the money was good and, she worked every day, almost like a slave.

"I sent most of the money back home to my family," she rationalizes. "I could not take it anymore so one day, I just ran away. But I had no place to go."

She puts her hand in her face and starts to cry as she tells the story. The group is frozen in empathy for the sadness in her story. Most know how common her story is for girls from Eastern Europe.

"I was a smart girl, but poor," Eliza continues. "I ended up being what I feared the most, a penniless homeless girl working the streets." She pauses and looks up at the sky through the windows in the large doors. "Someone told me about a shelter for abused girls. There I learned that I was a victim, like all the girls there, whether they're rich or poor. They let me stay there, helped me finished high school and gave me a job."

She looks back at the participants in the group and sees the understanding and compassion in their eyes. She feels the energy coming from them and begins to gain her composure and says, "I still feel so worthless but it helps to talk about it. The shelter recommended that I come here. Everybody's nice. I've learned much about my energy and gained so much energy from the group last week. I want to continue to boost my energy in all Realms, find the Blessings, and learn to be a kid again."

"Thanks, Eliza," Linda replies. "I know how difficult it is, but we're here for you."

Bob, the gentlemen from Nebraska, speaks up. He is not quite sure what to say, but starts in a low, slow voice. "Hi. My name is Bob Baker. This is my wife, Beatrice. Eliza, we want you to know that you're with friends here. Whatever we can do, don't hesitate to ask. Our story's pretty ordinary compared to yours. This is our first week, and we're just happy to be visiting Italy."

Bob and Beatrice talk about their little mom and pop café that was a cornerstone of their small community for the past thirty years. They knew everybody by their first name, and brought the community together. Then, one of those national restaurant chains moved in and took away their business. They went bankrupt.

"I guess people these days prefer an impersonal anonymous café experience," Bob says dejectedly. "They have these disinterested kids working there. They take orders without even lookin' at ya. I just don't know what's happening out there. The community just stopped supporting us," he shakes his head. "We're not bad people."

Then, he says with more optimism, "So, when our business went down the tubes, we decided to take our first vacation in twenty years. We always dreamed of visiting Italy, and seeing the Leaning Tower of Pizza. So, we scheduled this trip. But this spring when I was baking buns in the back room, I got these severe chest and back pains. I got really tired."

He holds his hand over his chest. "I was afraid, so I drank a few more cups of coffee 'cause I couldn't take a break. I'm usually pretty friendly, but the pain and caffeine made me damn irritable. Later, when I went to the doctor, he told me that I had a silent heart attack from a blocked artery. He also said I have a pinched nerve in my back, and diabetes. The years of sleeping poorly, getting up too early, eating sugar, and standing all day running the café took its toll on me. He said I needed a heart roto-router to open the heart vessels and to lose weight, change my diet, exercise, and take some medication. We thought, 'Gosh darn it!' That's the end of our dream trip, and maybe, the end of my life. Then, that very same day, I was listening to this radio show. It was like some kind of divine intervention. I heard about the Terme here in Italy doing this health research. And it wasn't far from the Leaning Tower."

He stops to catch his breath. "Well, I went home and talked with Beatrice. We decided to sell our café, swear off the caffeine, start exercising, eat better, get healthier, and see the world. I didn't want to sit there and wait to die. It's just not me. So, here we are ready to find the *Blessing of Health*. Tell us what we need to do. We're all ears."

"Thank you, Bob," Linda says sincerely. "It is nice to have friends like you here. Anybody else want to share their stories?"

After a few seconds, a gentleman with a square jaw, a week's growth of beard and short dark hair in his early thirties, looks at Linda, who's sitting next to him, and raises his hand slightly. He's wearing jeans and a button down short sleeve shirt that is open at the top. He has an intense look about him. "Hi. My name is Trent Reed. I'm from Chicago. This is my first week here, too. I've never told anybody what I'm about to tell you."

The group holds their breaths, waiting for his next words. They could feel his uneasiness in determining whether he should tell his story or not.

He appears both defensive and apologetic. "I was only fourteen when it first happened," he stutters. "The priest wanted me to help him in his private room." He tells the story about being sexually abused at the hands of his priest. It had gone on for two years, and as a result he became angry and depressed, which drove him to have fights at school. He became one of the school bullies and took out his anger on others. In high school, he did poorly in school and blamed it on others. He went into the army to get straightened out, but only learned more about violence. When he left the army, he continued with one failure after another in business and in love. He was sad, alone, and hateful of the world.

"One day, I hit rock bottom. I hated everybody including myself for my failures," he says. "I felt like I was not worth shit. I drove into the country and took a semi-automatic revolver with me. I put one bullet in it, and thought—let God decide if I was to live or die. I played Russian roulette with myself, and God as my witness, I put the gun up to my head and pulled the trigger once. It didn't fire. I pulled the trigger again and nothing happened. Then, I pulled the trigger four more times, quickly, and it still did not fire. I thought to myself that the stupid gun was broken. A car drove by so I stopped. I drove back to the house and tried it again. The next round went off in the air. The gun was not broken."

The group sits, stunned into silence. They feel for this man's struggle. "Through divine intervention, I'm still alive today. I had a vision from God that gave me hope, and helped me find direction. Now, with support from my group back home, I'm following this path. It has brought me here to the Terme to learn about God's righteousness."

"Thank you, Trent. We're glad you're here," Linda pats him warmly on the shoulder. "Is anyone else interested in sharing your experiences? As I mentioned, sharing your honest thoughts helps in two ways. It will boost your energy in the Mind Realm by being honest and in the People Realm by sharing with others. We are happy to listen."

A young overweight woman in the back of the room, with large dark glasses, and dressed in jeans waves her hand. A distinguishing feature about her was the red heart tattoos on the back of her neck.

She speaks with a strong British accent, "'ello. My name is Mona Watson. I work for a book publisher in London. I guess you can say I'm a bibliophile. I read all the time. This is my first time to Italy. Londoners love Italy, so I thought it was time for me to come 'ere, and see what all the rave's about. I heard about the research through the *London Daily*. It's just what I needed to spruce up my life. I thought a little R&R in Tuscany, and maybe, some L&L at the Terme would be good for me. Si?"

"Welcome, Mona," says Linda. "I know what R&R is. Rest and relaxation. But what is L&L?"

"It's a lot of a lot," she laughs. "I love words and I'm open to them all. Maybe it's lessons and learning or, perhaps, living and laughing, but it would be nice if there is a little love and lust also." She laughs again. "But I just don't want to be a loser and lamenting. I already feel like that."

The group laughs.

"I try my best to be a good girl," Mona says with sincerity. "But I keep falling off the wagon. I 'ave a lot of friends, and we go out a lot to the clubs. Too much stress in my life. Guys are dogs. I'm not popular. I deal with it by eating. I know I'm overweight and ugly so I thought this place would be a good for me. I need to get some R&R and maybe some L&L too. I want to lose weight and change my entire look. It's so stagnant. The *Blessing of Beauty* sounds so good."

"Welcome, Mona. There are a lot of lessons and learning as well as living and laughing here." Linda says, "But if you want to find lust and love, you may want to try Venice or Florence after we help you with the Blessings. The Italian men will love you. Anybody else want to share?"

She looks at Cicci, the only one left who has not told her story. She usually has much to say, but this week, she is holding back to appear shy. She wants to be more attractive than usual for a special reason. Dr. Ryan Laughlin is in the group.

"Cicci, would you like to say something?"

She gets up and says apologetically, "Well, I've been here before, and I will be here again. Each of your stories touches my heart, but I'm sorry if my story won't touch your hearts. It's easy for me to come here because I live in Faenza, the town next door. I used to come to the Terme as a child. In the spring and summer, we could bike here along the road lined with the blooming yellow roses and white cherry trees. We could smell the vineyards and the flowers of the blossoming apple and peach orchards. As kids, we explored the white cliffs, the green forests, the dark caves that go deep into the hills, the warm river, and the castle. I saw it all as a fairy tale land. We would climb to the ancient buildings of the Terme and the Borgos in the hills. We would play kings and queens with knights of honor saving us from the cruel conquering tyrants. Sorry, sometimes, I get carried away talking about my fantasies. I'm nostalgic for the past because my adult reality is not so good. I should say no more."

"No, Cicci, don't stop," Eliza speaks up. "It is interesting to hear about this place. Please go on."

Others nod their heads in agreement. Linda looks up impatiently and rolls her eyes. Like most staff at the Terme, she knows that Cicci is more interested in romance than helping others, and is simply working her charm on some unsuspecting man here. Despite this, she feels sorry for her and wants to maintain the energy of the group. There is someone out there for Cicci Beretta. Unfortunately, the Terme with all of the challenges, fears, illnesses, and insecurities among the participants, is the wrong place. She has yet to realize this.

"Okay. Are you sure?" She looks at Linda, who smiles and signals with her hand to go on. Ryan is entranced by her story. For most men, she is as pleasant to listen to as she is to look at.

She looks at him, smiles, and continues, "Mio babo, my father, ran a clothing shop in Faenza. We always met many nice men. When I was eighteen, I met a man who swept me off my feet. I was married in a couple of months. I had a baby right away, and suddenly, no more fairy tale life. I had to take care of her and work while my husband was away traveling. Unfortunately, I found out that he had other wives in other towns that he did business in. I was so *ero distrutta*, heart-broken. I hated him. I got a divorce and was alone with my daughter. But I was young and beautiful."

She pauses to see if Ryan is still watching her and listening. He is, and she continues, "One of the young men in town. He always played with me as a child. He loved me for a long time and proposed marriage to me. I 'ave no good judgment in men. I do not like to be alone. So we got married. At first, it was good, but then he became a very jealous husband. I had lots of friends. Both men and women. He didn't like that. Then one day, he hit me. From that point, the romance stopped. After my second divorce, single men stayed away from me. I needed someone so I made the mistake of secretly seeing an older married man. He loved me so much and brought me gifts and money to help raise my daughter. Eventually, he left his wife and proposed to me. I had my own little boutique fur shop and was doing well. My reputation in town was already ruined with two divorces, but he was a good man and he loved me. I kept saying no, but eventually I say *si*. However, I was not in love with him. Then one day, I met another man who was visiting from France. We fell madly in love. He was a sports player and was handsome, athletic, and adventurous. He traveled the world and told me about all of the beautiful places that he would take me. It was true love."

The group holds their breath, cringing at what would likely happen next.

She puts her head down and says with remorse, "*Mio* husband found out. Eet broke 'ees heart. A few months later, he died of a heart attack. The man I loved moved here from France to be with me. After a while, he stopped loving me too. I don't know. I don't have *fortuna di amore*. So, I come here to learn about the *Blessing of Love*. I still want to meet my knight in shining armor who will sweep me off my feet and live 'appily ever after. I know this is fairy tale, but can I still dream, *si*? I like it here because I meet new people who give me energy. I learn about me. Some day, I learn what I need to know to be happy, but I am slow learner. I'm sad about the men who left me, and 'ave much fear about love. I need your help to stop the fear. I feel little hope for the future."

She looks at Ryan. He looks back at her and smiles. She has worked her charm, and he seems to be responding. It is difficult to say no to Cicci Beretta.

Linda, trying to keep the group from being swept away with Cicci's emotional stories, abruptly states, "Thank you, Cicci. Sadness and fear are big things to overcome. It is a major reason people fail when they leave the Terme. There's fear of failure, fear of relationships, fear of feeling emotions fully, fear of criticism, fear of illness, fear of hurting others, fear of the truth. So many fears and so little time to confront them. They can immobilize you, freeze you in your steps, and make you depressed and desperate. They can stop your learning, your growth, and your ability to change and adapt. You need to face your fears straight on."

"But it ees so hard to do," Cicci says apologetically. "What can I do to overcome my fears?"

"I know it seems difficult," Linda says, "But it's the one thing we are all here to do. We need to strengthen our energy in each Realm. The *Prophecy Scroll* has laid out the path for us. We need to simply follow it. You will then gain the confidence and insight in overcoming your fears and bring love and happiness to your life."

Linda turns to the whole group and says, "Thank you for so eloquently sharing your stories. They were filled with honesty and emotion, with sorrows and dreams. I hope you were able to feel your energy change as the stories were told. It was also clear that each of you have been a victim of the Plagues that are affecting the world. If the collective energy of the people in the world is dwindling, only we as warriors, spreading positive energy, can change this. Let's take a break."

The group including Cicci disperses towards the refreshment table. Ryan continues to sit to contemplate what Linda just said. It hits him like a hammer that she is correct, each of the participants have been a victim of the coming Plagues. Jack was a victim of war and Wayne, a victim of ignorance. Trent is a victim of the hateful crime of abuse while Mona suffered from hate for herself. Eliza is a victim of poverty while Bob suffers from the chronic illness. Cicci, in some ways due to her own makings, has succumbed to the plague of despair. In each case, the Plagues are real and personal when you hear about them first hand.

Cicci walks back toward Ryan with two glasses in her hands. As she approaches, she looks up at him with a smile, "I brought you some peach juice. It ees from the local orchard. You like it?" She hands him one of the glasses and says coyishly, "I hope I didn't bore you with *mio picolo* story. It seems so hopeless."

"No, Cicci," he takes the glass and says with a conciliatory tone." I understand, you've been through a lot." Ryan recognizes that it is easy for men to fall in love with Cicci Beretta, but not so easy to stay in love. He can feel a natural male attraction to her. But she may look like an angel, but she is a mess. He takes a sip from the glass. "Thank you for the juice. It is very tasty."

"*Prego.* Let's go for walk during the break. Get some fresh air," she says, looking up at Ryan with her aqua blue eyes.

"Ah, yes. Good idea. It's a beautiful day out." As he accepts her invitation, a feeling of dread creeps through him. He hopes that he does not come to regret saying those words.

Chapter 22. The Investigation

The effervescent reporter is standing in front of the entrance to the Science Museum overlooking the Mississippi River. Her voice is clear and bright as she introduces herself, "This is Cindy Miles of National News reporting on the murder of Dr. Jack Killian, the renowned scientist from the National Institute of Health, right here in St. Paul."

"We are talking with John Steiner, head of the St. Paul police department's investigation of the murder."

The camera pans to Detective Steiner. She is standing next to the perfectly coiffed blonde reporter, dressed in her fashionable, but subdued, burgundy suit. A small crowd has gathered around them, listening intently to the interview.

Miles turns toward Steiner and asks her first question, "It has been two weeks now. What developments have you made in this sensational murder and how is the investigation proceeding? Have you identified any suspects?"

Steiner, in his tan herringbone blazer, thinks about his response before answering, "Our team of investigators has conducted extensive interviews with those at the conference, with Mr. Kolb, as well as friends and family members of Dr. Killian. We have not taken anyone into custody yet, but we have identified a possible suspect. Apparently, he has left the country and his location has not been identified."

"Mr. Steiner. Can you tell us the name of this person?"

"We won't release the name of the suspect until we find the person. It is difficult to track people outside of the United States. However, we are working closely with authorities in other countries to locate him."

Miles nods her head, and asks, "Tell us about the document found in Dr. Killian's room. How does it implicate Mr. Thomas Kolb and the Vatican?"

"The Manifesto was slid under the door of the room," Detective Steiner responds. "Perhaps, by the murderer, but we still do not know for sure. The deliverer of the document was careful not to leave any fingerprints or other evidence."

"What was in the document?" She asks.

"It was interesting. The Manifesto commented on a political agenda and the heresy of research that questions the word of God. It also named Dr. Leonard Kolb as the Messiah, and indicated that the Pope was involved. The links cannot be overlooked."

"Do you believe Mr. Kolb was involved in the murder?"

"I cannot comment on that," Steiner says.

The shot cuts to a video clip of the front of Mr. Kolb's high-rise headquarters in downtown Dallas. There is a background narrative by Miles. "Mr. Kolb and his companies have supported several non-profit political action committees, termed superpacs, including the Freedom Group. This group supports political candidates whose agenda is to reduce the size and control of the government. They have clear goals as described in their Freedom Manifesto. They want their corporations to be free to do what is best for them to generate profits, regardless of its consequences to the people or the environment. They have supported many anti-government movements, including gun lobbyists, anti-climate change theories, the Right-to-Life movement, anti-pollution control, repeal of healthcare laws, anti-gay marriage, voter registration, and a reduction in regulations in general. They also support eliminating social programs like Social Security and Medicare, environmental protection laws, and open immigration, while giving more tax breaks and cash incentives to corporations in the name of more jobs." The shot cuts back to the interview with Steiner.

Miles, a tenacious reporter, continues to probe him for answers, "Mr. Steiner, do you believe the murderer is involved in any of these organizations?"

The camera pans to a close-up of Steiner. "We have interviewed the leaders and members of the organizations. They have discussed several people who have yet to be interviewed. We are working on every angle, but have no information yet."

The camera pulls back to view both of them in front of the Science Museum. The wind blows her blond hair, and she brushes it back. "How was the Vatican implicated in this Manifesto?" She asks.

"Among many other claims, the killer's Manifesto specifically references the need to stop anti-religious research and return to the traditional teachings of the church. The words of the Pope were mentioned several times in the document. We have contacted the Vatican, and they declined to be interviewed. We do not believe they had any role in the murder other than to be mentioned in the Manifesto."

She raises the microphone closer to him. "Mr. Steiner, tell us about the *Prophecy Scroll* and the research related to it. Why would this incite such angst?"

"You probably know more about it than I do, Cindy. All I know is that it was written two thousand years ago, and is the last of the *Dead Sea Scrolls* to be discovered. The manuscript predicts apocalyptic changes to our current world. It appears to be the research on the last scroll that triggered the controversy and, perhaps, the murder."

The camera turns back to the reporter with a growing crowd from the museum gathered around, listening to the interview. The camera changes its angle and the crowd comes into view. "What do you mean by the controversy caused by the research?" Miles persists.

"The researchers in Italy are trying to answer one of the greatest puzzles of all time. What force makes life different than death? They are the first to measure the energy associated with the human spirit and are using the religious manuscripts to validate it. This research, the Manifesto claims, is wrong and is bringing on seven plagues through the wrath of God. Perhaps, there's also a political agenda at work using religion as the pretense. We just don't know."

"What do you mean political agenda?" She wrinkles her forehead.

As the crowd watches his every move, he becomes more self-conscious and stands more erect. "It's interesting. The Manifesto's political agenda was nearly identical to that of Mr. Kolb's political action group."

"You mean the language in the killer's Manifesto comes directly from Kolb's Freedom Group?"

"Yes." He says definitively, knowing it will raise ire among some viewers, but it may break open the case and reveal evidence to help solve the case.

"This implicates someone in Kolb's Freedom group. Is that correct?"

"I'm sorry, Cindy. I cannot comment on that. Thank you." He looks away, indicating the interview is over.

"Thank you for your time today, Detective Steiner. We wish you luck in the investigation."

"You're welcome, Cindy."

"Next, we cut to an interview with Mr. Jonathon Black, spokesman for the Kolb Foundation's Freedom Group. Our correspondent, Robert Jonas, is in Dallas, Texas for the interview. Hello, Robert."

"Hello, Cindy," Jonas turns towards the camera and narrates, "We are standing in front of the luxurious Kolb Industry Headquarters in downtown Dallas where Mr. Black, Executive Director of the Kolb's super Pac, the Freedom Group, has agreed to be interviewed about their recently released Freedom Manifesto. The Manifesto includes the group's latest plans to strengthen the culture of prosperity with a specific political agenda. With the sweep of the elections, and majority control of Congress, this agenda will most likely become law."

The camera turns towards Mr. Black, a handsome, well-groomed middle-aged man. Jonas states in the microphone, "We have the pleasure of speaking with Mr. Black today."

Black is dressed in a single-breasted suit created by Alexander Amosu, the luxury designer for the rich and famous. With this first question, Jonas is looking for blood. He brings the microphone close to him, "Mr. Black, thank you for your willingness to be interviewed today. You look nice. Mr. Kolb was cited as the Messiah in a killer's Manifesto. This document is similar to that of your Freedom Manifesto. Is the killer part of the Freedom Group?"

Mr. Black's discomfort at the pointed question is obvious. His voice cracks as he responds, "Mr. Jonas, we have no knowledge of the killer, and Mr. Kolb does not consider himself a Messiah of any sort. Many people find our Freedom Manifesto inspiring. It lays the groundwork for returning the United States to economic prosperity. There are many people who respond to this message and appreciate his leadership. However, he is not the Messiah and has never claimed to be. Obviously, the killer who wrote the Manifesto is disturbed and needs to be apprehended. There are a lot of people out there ready to prey on innocent people with money. They simply need to find their own path to God's blessing."

"Tell me about that," probes Jonas.

"Mr. Kolb was in a terrible plane crash and was the only person to survive. He was badly injured and recovering when a routine physical exam led to the discovery that he had early stage cancer. The cancer was cured with surgery, and subsequently, he felt he needed to reconsider his life. He asked God why he was saved and Mr. Kolb was inspired. He has been busy ever since, making money, supporting the cause of freedom, and doing all of the good work that God intended for him. The Freedom Manifesto is about that."

"What's in the Freedom Manifesto," Jonas asks. "Perhaps, that would reveal something that could help the investigation."

"The Freedom Manifesto for America's Prosperity was produced by a group of American leaders who are tired of being whipping boys for all of the country's ills. They do not want the government taking over every part of our lives, emptying the taxpayer's pockets, and not having the conviction to balance its books like every taxpayer must. The government bureaucrats spend our tax dollars on ineffective programs that not only make more people dependent on government dole-outs, but also take away an individual's opportunity to control his or her own destiny. This has to stop. This country was built on freedom. We have a choice to sink or swim. Let's keep it that way."

"What are the Manifesto's major points?" Jonas asks.

Mr. Black smiles to himself. He is happy to discuss the country's new agenda over a major national news channel. "We have seven legislative initiatives that will literally revolutionize economic freedom in the world. Now that we have control in the legislature, our leaders are writing new laws right now based on these concepts. The Responsible Science Act eliminates funding of research that is inconsistent with our moral teachings and our economic profitability. The Bright Minds Act ensures the brightest future for our students by shifting public funding of education to the private sector. The Health and Retirement Freedom Act transfers health care and retirement programs from the government to the private sector. The Economic Prosperity Act protects small and large businesses from high tax rates, stringent regulations, and red tape. The Unlimited Natural Resources Act protects the fragile corporate climate and expands the use of our unlimited natural resources. The Terrorist Abolition Act protects our way of life by tightening immigration, reversing anti-discrimination laws that protect terrorists, and makes the conceal and carry guns and stand your ground laws national. Finally, the Freedom from War Act shifts most government spending from expensive social programs to expanding the world's most powerful military. We need to protect our way of life and ensure our mastery of the world's economy."

"Thank you for sharing this with us. I have one final question. Why are there so many people protesting against your efforts?"

"Freedom of speech is one of the beautiful laws of our country. People can say what they want. We fought hard to lift restrictions on corporate funding of political campaigns so that our companies, with their unlimited wealth, can change the political landscape of America. We worked hard to ensure that our election process in every state has the highest integrity by requiring government IDs to vote. Both of these laws have helped elect leaders who will support freedom and economic prosperity. The protestors are most likely unemployed. I would protest, too, if I didn't have a job or a future. But if they're working hard in their job, they won't have time to complain and protest."

"Thank you for your comments, Mr. Black. This is Robert Jonas, reporting from Dallas."

Cindy Miles, now sitting in her studio behind the anchor desk, comes back in view. "We now go to Harvard University in Boston with Dr. Julia Stone. Dr. Stone was at the conference when Dr. Killian was murdered and her research has dovetailed with that of Dr. Killian's. She has visited Italy to review the research that Dr. Killian was supporting. "Dr. Stone, thank you for speaking with us today."

Dr. Stone sits behind her desk in her office at Harvard for the tele-interview. "You're welcome, Cindy."

"What happened at the meeting while Dr. Killian was speaking?" Miles asks.

"Well, he was giving a brilliant lecture on the scientific basis for a new revolutionary approach to understanding health and illness based on measuring the electromagnetic energy fields that surround the body. He was half way through the lecture when he fell over. The toxicology report says he had ingested a slow acting poison at breakfast, evidently placed in his coffee by the murderer."

"Why would he be murdered?" Cindy asks.

"I don't know. Apparently, Dr. Killian's research is threatening to some people's religious and political beliefs."

"Was Dr. Killian a naysayer, predicting the coming Armageddon?"

"No, he was only telling people what the *Prophecy Scroll* says. He was presenting the facts of the research, the emerging Plagues, and how to prevent them through the secrets to the seven Blessings of life. You need to make your own conclusions. Perhaps, this is what was threatening. I don't know."

The shot breaks back to Cindy Miles sitting at her desk.

"Now, here is a story that is steeped in intrigue and controversy. Research on the essence of life. Secrets from the last *Dead Sea Scroll.* An apocalyptic prediction of seven Plagues. Seven Blessings from an ancient manuscript to save the world versus seven principals from Mr. Kolb's Freedom Manifesto to save our economic freedom. Which will lead us down a path of salvation or to our destruction? You decide. This is Cindy Miles of National News."

Chapter 23. The Rules of the Blessings

Among the participants during the morning session, one person is particularly concerned about his mission to save the world. After sitting quietly among the participants, the Messenger stands up and slowly walks out of the Great Hall alone. The opening sessions confirmed what he suspected. This heretical research opposes the Manifesto and will only bring death and destruction to our world. It must be stopped. But he knows that he needs to be patient in finding the best opportunity to do so.

Oblivious to this impending threat, Ryan steps out of the Great Hall with Cicci close by his side. He carefully looks around to see if Vanessa is there. To his relief, she must be back in her office. He takes a deep breath and walks with Cicci over to the path along the river. Cicci is dominating the conversation while Ryan thinks about meeting Julia, Vanessa, and now Cicci. He realizes his potential for a romantic life has already become more confusing than he wants it to be. However, as things go, none of the relationships will likely be sustainable for so many reasons. Furthermore, he is not here for romance but rather to learn about the knowledge that this surprising project will reveal.

As Ryan returns from his walk with Cicci and enters the Great Room, he is relieved to find Vanessa still not there.

Cicci follows Ryan to their circle of chairs and stays glued to him throughout the session. She continues to ramble on while he smiles politely at her.

Ryan ignores Cicci and listens to Linda as the next session begins.

"Welcome back," Linda says. She looks around to see that everybody is back. Cicci and Ryan are sitting together. Bob and Beatrice right next to them. The circle continues with Eliza, Mona, Jack, Wayne, and Trent.

"Are you ready to tackle the *Rules of the Blessings?* The Rules provide a practical framework to understand and enhance your energy. Once you learn them, they can become an integral part of your daily life. When this happens, it's addicting. Any questions before we get started?"

The group is silent waiting for the discussion to begin.

"The seven *Rules of the Blessings* present the basic principles on how life energy flows in each Realm. The first two rules are the *Rule of Doing* and the *Rule of the Keys.* These tell you how to boost your energy and how the energy flows between Realms. Everyone, please take out the copy of the *Rules* manuscript from your materials. Read along if you like."

The group pulls out sheets of paper and sorts through them to find the two Rules documents.

Linda explains, "The *Rule of Doing* states what we know intuitively." She reads, "For those who know the *Rule of Doing* can learn actions that bring strength of light into a Realm and shun actions that weaken the light in a Realm. For when light is brought into each Realm the angels will come and the demons will be banished."

She looks up at the group. "As Dr. Venetre said earlier, if you take the action suggested in each Realm, you will promote your energy there."

Eliza asks in her quiet voice, "So, this energy is available to anyone who does these things? It's as simple as that?"

"*Si, molto facile.* It's easy," Linda responds. "Your potential to achieve high energy in each Realm is not dependent on circumstances outside of your control such as your family, genetics, personality, social status, income level, job status or any other seemingly permanent situation. Anybody and everybody can achieve high energy by simply doing the actions in the *Seven Realms of Life* and following the *Rules of the Blessing.* In fact, the more you promote your own energy in each level, the more the world will pull itself together, banish the Beast and its demons, convert zombies, and achieve the *Seven Blessings* in your life. For example, as noted in the *Seven Realms of Life,* the action to enhance energy in the Body Realm involves exercise. Our research has found this and there's much research that suggests that exercise will improve health and prevent many chronic conditions. You simply need to do it regularly."

"That's a no brainer. If I exercise, I'll get healthier," Bob replies with sarcasm. "All the doctors tell me that. Unfortunately, I've been eating like a pig most of my life. It's hard to change. What else can I do?"

"You just need to do it, Bob," Beatrice rolls her eyes.

"Understanding the *Rule of the Keys* will help," Linda adds.

"What's that?" Bob responds quickly.

"This rule is complimentary to the *Rule of Doing* because it suggests that the key to boosting energy in one Realm can be done not only through the primary Realm, but also through an adjacent neighboring Realm that is in directly connected to the primary Realm. Let me read it."

She looks down at the copy of the manuscript and reads, "For those who know the *Rule of Keys* will know how to bring strength into a Realm by bringing light in from its neighboring key Realms."

She explains, "This Rule suggests that the energy in all Realms is connected to other Realms and that energy can move from one Realm to another. Each Realm has two key Realms that will directly enhance the energy in the neighboring primary Realm. Here's a word of caution. The neighboring Realm can also deplete the adjacent Realm. Energy flows back and forth between Realms. Our research agrees with this. We found that taking actions in the key Realms will directly enhance the energy in the primary Realm."

"I'm confused," Mona says. "To enhance my energy in the Body Realm, I need to focus on actions in all three Realms?"

"*Esattamente,*" Linda affirms Mona's understanding. "The key to achieving the *Blessing of Health* is not only through the Body Realm, but also the closely connected Way of Life and Nature Realms. This *Prophecy* symbol illustrates the *Rule of Keys.*"

She shows a slide of the seven-sided heptagon.

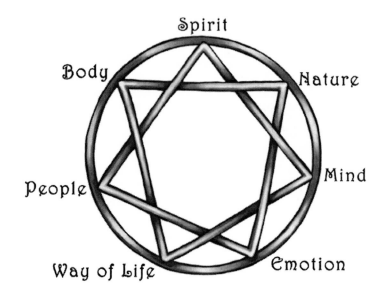

She explains, "You can see from this symbol that each Realm connects with two other Realms. These are the Key Realms for the primary Realm. The energy from these connected Realms can directly strengthen the primary Realm. The *Blessing of Health* requires maintaining high energy in the Body Realm, but also the Way of Life and Nature Realms. Promoting energy in the Way of Life Realm is done through a modest healthy diet, sleeping well, and staying active. The scientific evidence for actions in the Way of Life Realm have clearly documented that these actions, like exercise, also improves health. For the Nature Realm, it suggests that you need to be organized and orderly, clean and careful with the natural environment. Again, the scientific evidence shows that keeping yourself and the environment clean will enhance health. According to the U.S. Centers for Disease Control and Prevention, environmental changes such as clean water and improved sanitation—and not necessarily advances in medical technology and health care—have accounted for at least twenty five of the more than thirty years added to the human lifespan during the twentieth century."

"So, if I boost my energy in the Way of Life Realm, it will also improve my health?" Eliza asks. "So, I need to focus on all three Realms. I can do that. According to the symbol, I could also achieve the *Blessing of Prosperity* by working on the Mind, Body, and Way of Life Realms."

"*Si. Capisci.* You understand," Linda nods in encouragement." There are three Realms for each Blessing. One is primary and two are secondary."

Trent, who has been quiet most of the day, finally decides to speak up. "What about those things that drain energy? What are they?"

"Good question, Trent," She detects an attitude, perhaps related to his life problems. "In contrast to boosters, these actions are called depleters. Please learn what or who they are in your life." Linda says emphatically. "There are many energy depleters. In the Way of Life Realm, a poor diet of refined sugar, high calories, processed foods, and fat are all depleters. Research has shown that this type of diet contributes to heart disease, obesity, diabetes, cancer, osteoporosis, and many other conditions. You are what you eat. In addition, studies have found that poor air quality is a depleter leading to asthma and lung disease. In addition, toxic chemicals, some viruses, and radiation in the natural environment is a depleter leading to cancer."

"What about people?" Trent continues. "Are they depleters?"

"Yes, zombies, with their low energy, are depleters," she smiles. "They suck the energy right out of you. And you know who they are because of their many vices. They can be angry, mean, and abusive, or stupid and selfish. They can be lazy, unclean, and disorganized, or deceitful and dishonest. These concepts bring up the *Rule of Being*."

"Is it like 'be here now' or some other philosophical mumbo jumbo?" Trent asks cynically in a failed attempt at humor. Nobody laughs.

"Trent, it's more of a tool than a philosophy," Linda responds. "It's something you observe. When you have high and low energy in a Realm, it's reflected in the characteristics of a person called vices and virtues. It's like having a people barometer. It provides you a way to see what's inside a person. Let me read this rule."

She looks down at her copy of the manuscript. "For those who know the *Rule of Being* will see virtues in those with angels from the strength of light in a Realm and vices in those with demons from weakness of light in the Realms."

"Talk about these demons," Wayne asks. "They cause vices, ya say? My mamma and brother says I 'ave lots of those. Does that mean I have demons crawlin' around inside me? That's pretty creepy."

"The Prophecy talks about demons that live in people when their energy is low," Linda replies. "Like the Beast, demons are symbols to help explain why people act badly. Have you heard the expression—he's got demons?"

"Too many times!" Wayne exclaims. "Are they for real? Do they actually get inside of us?"

"If I look carefully, I can see some faint red beady eyes inside you," Linda says with a quizzical look and raised eyebrows, playing into Wayne's naiveté and sense of humor.

"My brother said he could see the demons of addiction in me and my drug friends," Wayne says. "That's when I said no to drugs and to those friends."

"Good idea. When a person has low energy in a Realm, there is a tendency for them to compensate for this through these negative characteristics called vices. These vices reflect your demons. You can see them in people every day. People who are dishonest, demanding, lazy, disrespectful, sad, disorganized, dirty, intolerant, careless, and uncaring. These demons have beady red eyes that are crouched over inside, irritating you. When I see a crabby person, I can almost see the demon inside them. Obviously, I stay away."

"And what do angels do?" Wayne asks.

"Angels reflect positive energy in people and show up as virtues such as being honest, sincere, respectful, happy, helpful, clean, organized, tolerant, careful, caring, and many more. These as caused by angels with white wings, bright eyes, and a radiant glow that supports you in achieving the *Seven Blessings* in your life."

Ryan watches each member of the group. Most members of the group are surprisingly active in the discussion. What an odd collection of people from small town café owners, a pretty Italian divorcée, and a former prostitute to an obese single Londoner, a veteran with PTSD, an abuse victim, and former drug user. It will be a challenge to save this group from their vices. This continues to be a fascinating day.

Linda continues, "Using this information you can tell if a person has high or low energy in each Realm. Everybody has some vices that annoy people and announce their demons. Likewise, everyone has virtues that people appreciate and announce their angels."

"Ah-ha. So I have a big fat demon of gluttony inside me," Bob responds as the group laughs. "Can anyone see it?" Nobody in the group indicates they can.

"Some people, visionaries, clairvoyants, say they can see demons that inhabit people," Linda replies. "They say they see angels and energies too. Maybe, they are for real. I don't know. We are venturing into unknown territory here. We didn't know for sure that our spiritual energy existed either until we started measuring it. Maybe, we will be able to measure the presence of angels and demons in the future. I don't know. Meanwhile, I would use the vice and virtues of a person as your measure of low and high energy in people."

"How do you suggest we get rid of these demons?" Bob asks.

"Demons can spread inside you and deplete energy from other Realms. They can also spread to other people by annoying others and creating conflicts."

"How do we deal with people who are mean and abusive?" Eliza asks. "I couldn't just ignore them."

"Doing that would just lower your own energy," she replies. "There are lots of things to do, but whatever you do, don't blame them. They don't choose to have demons and be zombies. They have low energy from difficult life situations, lifestyle choices, or negative relationships. How you gain and lose energy to the challenges in your daily lives is a complex process, and we are only beginning to understand it. This brings up the *Rule of Challenges*."

"Dealing with these challenging people?" Eliza asks.

"*Si*. This Rule helps you understand how to respond to your daily problems, and, of course, negative or annoying people," Linda continues. "It determines whether you deplete your energy or maintain it when confronted with a challenge. Listen."

She finds the paragraph in the manuscript and reads, "For those who know the Rule of Challenges will understand that when challenged by problems or others who take away the light from your Realms, you will have no strength when you respond by taking light from your Realms, you will have more strength to respond when you bring more light into your Realms, and you will have the most strength to respond when you bring light into the Realms of all people who gather with you."

Ryan scans the faces in his group, and most look quite puzzled. Linda recognizes the need to explain further. "This fourth Rule is one of the most difficult to understand and follow. Let me explain."

"Yea, like what to do with my drug buddies!" Wayne says. "Should I stay away from them or try to help them? I doubt that's even possibility. Or, should I let my brother just keep them away."

"It's difficult to decide how to deal with these negative people in your life," Linda explains. "First, this Rule warns you not to lose your own energy to these zombies by getting angry, revengeful, or over critical of them. It's better to avoid them. But if you can't avoid them, ignore them and make sure you maintain your own high energy through your daily booster actions. Third, the Rule says that if they are willing, help them understand how to gain more energy and rid themselves of their demons. Care about them. Let your positive energy spread to them. Teach them what to do. It may not be easy, but it is what a Prophecy warrior will do."

"Some people have such low energy," Mona complains, "My boss and my soon to be ex-boyfriend to name a few. They're mean and verbally abusive. It's terrible. I feel so bad around them."

"Let me explain it in another way." She wants to ensure they understand. "The *Rule of Challenges* states that there are three levels of change that you can make to respond to people like that. We call them first order, second order, and third order changes. If you respond with a *first order change*, you take energy from other Realms to deal with it. But this depletes your own energy. For example, after a fight with your soon to be ex, most people respond to by shifting energy from the adjacent Realms such as the Emotional Realm by developing anger, the Spiritual Realm by developing hate, the Way of Life Realm by eating and sleeping poorly or becoming disorganized in the Nature Realm. It's a chain reaction that can deplete all Realms and make you miserable."

"That's exactly what happens to me," Eliza complains. "I feel so weak when I'm around negative people. I internalize conflicts, and don't deal with it. It pulls me down for a whole week. I feel depleted. I can't sleep. I eat junk food. I stop taking care of myself. How do I change this pattern? It makes me so angry at myself, but I can't control it."

"That's true of many people. A better way to respond to the challenge is through a second or third order change."

"What's that?" Eliza looks puzzled. "It sounds like physics."

"It's easy. When someone sucks your energy, say from your People Realm, instead of pulling energy from one of your other Realms, you simply focus on a *second order change* by doing booster actions in either your challenged Realm or an adjacent Key Realm. For example, you could do something creative for the Emotional Realm, help others in the People Realm, meditation or prayer in the Spiritual Realm, or exercise in the Body Realm. Even if you do not deal directly with the person in resolving the conflict for whatever reason, these actions will help you recover the depleted energy in your Realms and help you better deal with the conflict."

"The conflict I have right now is with my boss at work," Mona complains. "It involves not only me, but other employees also. It's a no-win situation for all of us. I could end up being fired."

"There is also a *third order change* that you could try. You will have the most strength if you respond by bringing energy into the Realm of all of the people involved. In the case of a conflict with a friend, this would involve doing something to help the friend or exercise together. Be direct on ways to resolve the conflict. Help them boost their own energy. And do it with kindness and understanding. You've heard the old adage; 'You can help yourself by helping others.' Think of what they need, and help them achieve it. Be creative to boost all of your energies. Or simply show that you care about the person by sending a nice card. In this way, your action boosts your happiness and that of your friend or group also. This also leads us to the *Rule of Balance.*

"This is pretty interesting stuff," Mona comments. "I've had so many people in my life drag me down. Now, I know what to do. It makes sense."

Linda smiles. "I agree. The Rules are insightful. Most people don't apply them regularly. However, once you do, it just clicks. These daily challenges happen to everybody. Just a couple of years ago, I was involved in a bad relationship. I was sad, depressed and had little energy. My boyfriend's energy levels in many Realms were even lower. He had lots of demons. He was insecure, angry, controlling, and drank too much. He sucked the energy right out of me. He would threaten me when he was drunk and had really low energy. I could never meet his needs. I was too weak. It was bad." She shakes her head.

The group is surprised that even Linda had problems like theirs and is willing to share it with them. She tells them that it still can drain her energy just thinking about it. Talking about it helps boost it back up.

"I was lost until I met someone who went through this program. I became a warrior. I came here for just a week, but it woke me up to the reality of my situation and how the *Rules of the Blessings* work. It was a remarkable transformation. I boosted my energy in each Realm, and felt better, clearer, and happier. Did I blame him? Well, I wanted to, and I hated him for being such a jerk. But now, I see that he alternated between high and low energy in the Emotional Realm. As they call it in psychiatry, he was manic with dramatic mood swings. One minute, he was the life of the party, then the next, he would become extremely angry. His angels and demons were fighting. I realized that he was pulling energy from the people around him to feed his weak Emotional Realm. He was so out of balance. Balance requires working on all Realms and not just a few."

"It seems like there's a Rule in there somewhere," Wayne laughs.

"Foresight becomes you quite nicely, Wayne." Linda says with encouragement. "It's called the *Rule of Balance.* It's simple. Let me read it." She opens her notebook and reads the passage, "For those who know the

Rule of Balance will know that to have equal strength in all Realms will bring more fullness and goodness to life."

The group nods in agreement. "That makes a lot of sense," Eliza says.

"In other words, make sure that there is sufficient energy in all of the Realms, or you will fall into the same trap as my boyfriend," Linda continues. "Despite having a dominant Realm, it is important to strengthen every Realm to achieve a balance. It's like a wheel with seven spokes. When all spokes are equal, the wheel will roll smooth. But when one spoke is too long or too short, it wobbles. Wobbling for a short time is tolerable, but if you wobble for long periods, you will lose your balance and your wheel will fall off. Thus, above all, don't wobble. When balance is achieved, you have more resilience and adaptability to bring energy from one Realm to the next if one is challenged."

"I love the word wobbling. Can you give us an example? I have a feeling I do it all the time." Mona asks with a worried look on her face. "Is that the same as hobbling or waffling?"

"Clever question, but not the same, Mona," Linda replies. "If you are challenged by a conflict with a friend or family member and significant negative energy is pulled from the People Realm to deal with it, you will usually pull energy from another Realm such as the Emotional and Mind Realms, allowing you to think through the challenge and remain calm. However, if you are wobbling on unbalanced Realms, then you'll have a tendency to hobble along with weak Realms. You may become dishonest with yourself and others and unhappy. You're more prone to becoming angry and say stupid things when energy is pulled to deal with the conflict. That's when you waffle. Waffling is simply being indecisive. You can't figure out what to do so you become wishy-washy and avoid making a decision, avoid doing something about it, and avoid commitment. And, then, there is wallowing. When wobbling causes conflict and things go to hell, you may find yourself wallowing in your own misery and become self-pitying and self-indulgent which lowers your energy even more. It's a downward spiral. I'm sure you have all experienced wobbling, hobbling, waffling, and wallowing even if you don't know it. But, if you can, try to avoid it. It's not a pretty site." She laughs.

Ryan laughs to himself at the simplicity of the concepts. He has noticed himself doing every one of those things at some point in time. And Linda made it fun and easy to remember. He writes it down so he can bring it to his patients. Wobbling, hobbling, waffling, and wallowing. Onomatopoeia! What clever poetry. The words sound like their meaning.

"Tell me how to apply this Rule," Bob asks.

"First, it's important to realize when you're wobbling with uneven Realms or have a tendency to hobble along in life or even waffle with indecision. Once you recognize your own weak Realms, you can work on actions that will boost them, such as helping others in the People Realm, learning and being honest in the Mind Realm, or meditation and prayer in the Spiritual Realm."

"It's easy to lose balance," Bob replies. "Then, I hobbled and waffled along every day. When our café was busy, I could only focus on work. I neglected exercise, eating, and sleeping, and to most people's surprise, even having fun. It was busy, intense and demanding. I was miserable and wallowed in my own self-pity every day. I'm glad I'm out of it, but many people are stuck wobbling and hobbling. What happens if you're stuck?"

"That happens a lot with work," Linda responds. "With all the e-mail, social media, computer work, time pressures, and demanding and insensitive people around us, it's easy to wobble and lose balance. Then, as you say, you hobble and waffle. Your energy and health can be affected directly. Your muscles may ache, your immune system weakens, you get sick, you become irritable, and may complain to those close to you, or worse, you may deny the problems and stuff it inside. You may fall prone to wallowing by feeling sorry for yourself and indulge in eating, drugs, alcohol, and other vices, which lowers your energy more. It's a vicious cycle. The question you need to ask yourself is this—would you be more effective and efficient at work if you took care of your energy levels each day and maintained balance? Personally, I've learned to maintain my energy levels first, and then, focus on work. When I do this, I'm more creative, effective, efficient and cheerful at work. People respond to me better. I do a better job. Of course, I do work here. Not a bad place to work. All work environments should be so supportive. Si?"

"I'm looking for work. Any warrior positions open?" Wayne replies followed by laughter from the group. "Or, maybe, we should forget about work and focus on booster actions all day?"

"You know the answers," Linda laughs. "No and no! We don't have any positions available. And you can get too much of a good thing. This leads us to another Rule. The *Rule of Moderation*."

The group finds the Rule in the documents they each received. They follow along as Linda reads, "For those who know the *Rule of Moderation* will take care to not bring too much strength into one Realm for this can weaken other Realms."

The group nod in agreement as they already know the importance of this.

"Like too little energy in a Realm, too much energy may not be good either. When a person spends too much time strengthening one Realm, you will neglect other Realms. For example, when someone eats too much food, even if it's the best quality natural food you can find, you can get sick. If you exercise too much, you may injure muscles or joints leading to problems. It's all about moderation to maintain energy. When you push too much energy into a Realm, you will lose balance, and you know what? Si! You get wobbly and hobbly again—you run off the road."

"Each of these rules make sense, but how do you apply them to groups?" Jack asks, agonizing over his experience with war. "Dr. Venetre indicated that our energy levels effect others. Tell us about the Rule that involves communities and nations. Can it help achieve peace between nations? Good luck on that."

"Jack, your timing is perfect," Linda replies. "You bring up the next rule, the *Rule of Gatherings*. I personally believe that this is the most important Rule because it tells us that our energy levels will influence the energy of others and our communities. We have an impact."

The group turns to the document as she reads, "For those who know the Rule of Gatherings will understand the light of one person will spread to strengthen or weaken the light of those people around him. For when a third of the people bring positive light together in a gathering, their light will show brightest in changing the gathering for the better.

"Whether you want to or not, your energy spreads to others around you," Linda explains. "Your energy is contagious. And the collective energy of a group is greater than the sum of each individual's energy. This is important to know! Our energy not only spreads but also is synergistic. People feed on each other's energy. We have observed this in our research. When at least a third of the people in a group have high energy, it generates greater energy for every person in the group. However, be warned. The converse is also true and can be dangerous. When a third or more of the people in a group have low energy, it can deplete or drain the energy of the whole group more quickly. The low energy of a few will pull down the rest of us. Then, we have a group or even a nation of zombies. There are so many examples throughout history of whole nations who became zombies. It's terrible situation when that happens." She says shaking her head in her most somber tone.

"Can you give us an example of how this Rule works?" Jack asks. "If we can use it to prevent war, it could be revolutionary."

"*Si*. You can have an impact on any size group," Linda explains. "Whether it be small groups such as a couple, family, or work place or larger groups such as neighborhoods, towns, nations, and, even the world, our positive energy will spread in a chain reaction. For example, in small groups, the collective energy of the group will explain why families have harmony or some companies are productive. The converse is true too. This collective effect is the reason why divorces occur or companies fail. On a larger scale, the collective energy of the population explains why revolts occur in a country, why fads can sweep a nation with a crazy idea, and why social media is so important."

"But there must be a critical mass of people in a group or a country to make a change, is that right?" Jack ponders.

"Exactly! This states that if more than a third of people in a group have low energy in a Realm, a plague will occur in that Realm, whether it is widespread hate, illness, drought, or war, it will become a reality. This has serious implications. Likewise, when you have at least a third of the people in a group with high energy, it will enhance the entire group and the Blessings will come true, almost magically. Thus, if you are bringing together a group, it is important to choose the individuals and leaders in the group wisely. If you are part of a community or nation, everybody benefits when a minority of the population and the leaders of the group have strong energy. Every individual person has either a positive or negative impact, whether you like it or not."

"I like this Rule," Wayne says with a laugh. "I can just sit back and soak up everybody's glowing energy."

"Don't laugh!" Linda counters. "It's true that you will receive great energy from a high energy group. But your energy will influence the whole group also, whether you say anything or not. If you bring negative energy, it will bring others down. You are still the key to influence the group. You can't leave it to others."

"I like that idea," Beatrice comments. "Even if I don't say anything, I'm still having an impact on a group just by showing up with positive energy. People will pick up my energy and vice versa."

"It's true," Linda says. "And we've confirmed this in our research. It's the energy of your presence that talks. This is why mass demonstrations, if they are peaceful, have a powerful effect. If they are not peaceful, the opposite is true."

"It makes me want to shy away from groups if you're a zombie," Eliza says with a sigh. "You don't want to spoil it for others."

"I wouldn't see it that way," Linda replies "We all live as a part of groups—friends, families, work colleagues, and communities. These groups receive your positive energy and can give you positive energy back. Thus, you need to surround yourself with people who have high energy. You will know these people based on your sixth sense and by seeing their virtues. Hang out with people with lots of positive virtues since they will give you and your group energy even if you have yet to achieve high energy."

Trent, who has not said much, speaks up, "I assume you also need to avoid people with low energy and many vices, right?"

"Si, they're energy thieves," Linda says with seriousness. "We will talk about energy thieves later. And be quite wary of low energy groups. Many companies or organizations are low energy simply by the way they treat their employees. They will bring you down."

She pauses and looks at the time. "Let's take a fifteen minute break. Then, I will introduce you to Deanna D'Amico, our facilitator. She will teach you about the *Blessing of Health*. You may be surprised at how elegant and simple it is, yet powerful in enhancing your health."

Chapter 24. The
Blessing of Health

Ryan excuses himself from the confines of Cicci's attention, explaining that he needs to send some emails. In truth, he simply would rather just spend some time alone to consider the knowledge that Linda reviewed. He returns to his room to jot down some notes. He does not want to miss anything. The Rules are so simple but have such deep truth. And they all can be applied to his patient care. He lies down on his bed and checks his emails. He gets a few from his friends, saying they miss him on the fishing trip. His mother sends a message telling about her day's activities. Nothing from Julia yet. He's sure she is swamped with work. He responds to his mother's email and leaves to return to the Great Hall with a few minutes to spare.

As Ryan walks into the large stone room, Cicci sneaks up behind him realizing that she needs to step up her advances towards him. He's obviously a slow learner in new relationships with women. She places her puckered lips close to his neck and blows her sweet breath towards his ear. "Did you enjoy that session?" Cicci whispers in a low voice. "*Molto interesante. Si?*"

Ryan, startled, turns around to see Cicci's smiling face almost nose to nose with him. He steps back with a look of bewilderment. "What the… Oh, *si*, Cicci. It was good," Ryan replies with irritation, "I guess it makes you re-evaluate not only what's important in life but what you do every day."

"I've been here before, and each time, I feel my energy growing," she says. "Can you feel my energy?"

Ryan wants to be polite, but rolls his eyes at the loaded question. "I'm not sure I can feel other people's energy yet. Maybe I'm a slow learner, or I don't have those butterfly genes."

"Well, I think you have a very nice energy about you," she says seductively.

"You can see it?" He asks.

She bats her big eyes and smiles. "I can feel it deep inside me. Right here," she holds her hand to the middle of her ample breasts.

"Are you sure that's my energy?" He tries not to be too sarcastic, but cannot avoid it. "Maybe you have indigestion."

"I know it is, because every time I get close to you, I get this tingly feeling and my heart beats faster."

Ryan is feeling awkward about the direction this conversation is heading. He remembers an older female patient, Dorothy. The lady had persistent romantic fantasies about him and scheduled an appointment with him nearly every week. She told him how much she loved him and would wear special undergarments to show him. Finally, he had to have a talk with her to help her get over her fantasies and look for real love in her life. He knows how important it is to be kind and respectful to people who are emotionally vulnerable. But he is not sure he can put Cicci into the emotionally vulnerable category. She seems to take care of herself quite well.

"I wouldn't read too much into those feelings quite yet," he says in an attempt to buffer her advances. "And we still have a lot more to learn."

Luckily, Linda walks back into the Great Room accompanied by a stout middle-aged woman with face that exudes maturity, understanding, and sincerity. She has long brown, wavy hair and is dressed casually with black tights and a loosely fitted white cotton pullover shirt with a colorful pattern of flowers across it.

Ryan takes a chair, and Cicci follows him like she's his best friend.

"It's my pleasure to introduce Deanna D'Amico," Linda says. "She is one of our skilled trainers, and will help you understand the *Blessing of Health*. You will like her and find this Blessing remarkable."

Deana has a broad smile and a slight furrow in her brow that shows she has both a playful and serious side to her. She has a big heart, and transfers her abundance of positive energy to anyone and everyone around her. Yet, she works hard at maintaining a strong balance in all Realms.

She is particularly gifted in helping people understand how to boost and maintain high energy.

She takes over from Linda to guide the group. "*Grazie*, Linda. *Tu sei molto simpatico!*" she says with a smile in Italian, and continues in English with an accent that gradually disappears, "It ees a pleasure to be 'ere with you today. Eet ees also my responsibility to do anything and everything to help you boost your energy."

She looks around the group and makes direct eye contact with each of them. She raises her hands above her as if she will hug everyone. "*Per favore.* Letta me 'elp you, Si? It ees my pleasure to do so. And maybe you learn a little *Italiano*, too. *Domande?* Questions?"

She pauses for a minute for any questions. "*Molto bene!* You must know each other by now. So, I ask you to introduce the person sitting next to you and tell me a little of their background. This will help me know you better and boost your People energy."

They shift a little in their chairs, not sure what to say about each other. Then, beginning with Ryan, they go around their little circle and tell what they remember about the person's background. Ryan introduces a glowing Cicci as the fur shop owner in the next town of Faenza who grew up here and is now looking for the secret to happiness and love. She then introduces Bob as the previous owner of a café who is here with his wife. This is their first visit to Italy and he is on his way to a full recovery to robust health. They each take their turn until Beatrice, Trent, Jack, Wayne, Mona, and Eliza are introduced.

"Bravo! It is a pleasure to know each of you," Deanna replies. "As you now know, life energy is available to each of you by following the actions in the seven Realms. And you cannot buy the seven Blessings. Spiritual energy is not for sale. It is only available to those who practice them regularly. Don't forget, you are never stuck where you are. Your success is based on what you do to boost, not deplete, your energy. It's not about who you know or how much money you have. It's all about your energy, *Si? Pronto?* Ready to get started?"

The participants smile and nod in agreement. They have heard this before and will likely hear it again. Repetition is the key.

"Okay. Let's review the first Blessing manuscript that has been assembled and translated, the *Blessing of Health*." Deanna takes out the manuscript from her folder, and asks the others to do the same, "This Blessing is pretty easy to understand since it follows the same concepts from the Realms and Rules manuscripts."

The group shuffles through their documents to find the two-page manuscript. She reads the first part.

"And Behold, the *Blessing of Health*. For those who want health and to be well is through strength of light in the Realm of the Body. To strengthen this Realm is to be active, to walk, to run, to stretch, to use the body well."

Deanna looks up at the group. "These statements are pretty straightforward and consistent with the actions in the Realms document. To be healthy, you need to focus first on your body. This means you need to stay active every day. Being lazy will not promote health or energy. And it is not only important to focus on being active, but also on exercising and stretching to maintain good range of motion. And don't overdo it. Remember the Rule of Moderation. Let me read more about the other Realms that are important in health."

She continues to reads, "And the keys to bring more light into this Realm is through the Way of Life and the Nature Realms. For those who are modest in eating and drinking, to have pure food and water that rises directly from the natural springs and soils of the earth, to breath clean air, to work steady, have good sleep, are organized and clean, to take care of and waste not the abundance that you have, for the spirit flows freely from these Realms into the body and strengthens you in health and wellness."

"So! Exercise is not enough," Bob laughs out loud. "I also gotta eat and drink well, sleep better, stop smoking, stay clean, get organized, and go skinny dipping in the Roman spa. I don't know what else. Couldn't I just take a pill?"

The small group laughs with Bob. Deanna shakes her head in doubt, "Oh, you want the easy pill, Si? Many people want the quick fix. We all wish for that. Unfortunately, there are no quick fixes in health. Remember, the *Rule of Keys*. There are always at least three Realms to boost in order to achieve each Blessing. You can do this. It's not *scienza missilistica* you know, rocket science. And, what is skinny dipping?"

Bob sighs, and then says, "I guarantee that there is nobody in our group who wants to see me *tutto nudo* in the spa."

"Did Linda teach you some *Italiano*, Bob?" Deanna smiles, "I'm impressed. But, *per favore*, keep your clothes on. Our energy is at risk." Deanna laughs along with the rest of the group. "Next, remember the *Rule of Being* with its angels and demons? It applies to the *Blessing of Health*."

The group looks back down at their manuscript as she reads, "For strength of the spirit in this Realm will bring you angels that are evident as virtues to others as you show strength of the flesh, be regular and routine in health, be steady and resolute, and show courage and boldness."

Ryan thinks about how well she would work in his clinic. She exudes a patience, clarity, and understanding that everybody can respond to.

She continues, "With high energy, you will not only be healthy, but you will show many virtues. Strength, steadiness, resolve, and courage are all for the taking naturally. And the vices and plagues are not pretty. Listen."

"She looks down and reads, "Beware, for weakness of the spirit in this Realm will bring demons to live here and show as vices to others with weakness and fat of the flesh, be unsteady and cowardly with no control, and have sickness that comes easily."

She looks around the group for understanding. "If more and more people deplete their energy in this Realm, we will see the Plagues from the Body Realm." She reads on, "And lasting weakness of the spirit in this Realm among the people will bring plagues of afflictions, pain, and sickness of the flesh."

"That pretty much explains my situation," Bob says flippantly. "I owned a café. I ate constantly. I slept poorly. I thought walking around the cafe was enough exercise. I guess not. I need to change this while I'm here."

"Bob, you are like millions of others in the same situation," Linda explains. "I know these may seem hard for some of you but it's a lot easier if you do it as part of your daily life. It becomes routine just like your bad habits, only they are good habits. And you will feel much better, like eating a good Italian meal when you're hungry."

"I'm sold, but how do I do this?" Mona says with a deep breath. "I need to exercise more, eat fruits and vegetables, eat less fat, sugar, and caffeine, work hard and steady, and sleep well. It sounds like me mum is yelling at me. Mona, eat your vegetables! But I've tried this for years. Is there any hope for me?"

"It's just like everything else in life. If you work at it, you can do anything," Deanna says with assurance. "But if you don't work at it, then no. We want to help. We can't do these for you, but we will do them with you and help you integrate them into your daily lifestyles when you return home. When you do them here, you'll see how they immediately boost your energy and make you feel better. Most people find that quite motivating."

"That may work here, but will it work when I go home?" Mona says anticipating the common relapse.

"We cannot control what you do when you return home. We will work with you individually to overcome your challenges and barriers. I bet you'll be surprised at the results by the end of the week. You will start feeling good, really good, in just one week. Feeling good is a motivator. And the bonus is that it doesn't rely on any drugs, mood enhancers, energy pills, or alcohol."

"Well, Miss, You know I'm on vacation right now," Bob says as he looks at Beatrice. "Can I actually do these exercises?"

She directs her comments to the whole group, "People lose energy when they sit on their butts, watching television, playing video games, and eating junk food. You're not doing any of that here. We will help you, exercise, eat well, sleep well, and be active each day. They activities we have you do have much science behind them and your doctor would recommend. They will naturally boost your energy. *Hai capito?* Do you understand?"

"Enough chatting, then," Bob says with the impatience learned from years of running his cafe. "When do we begin?"

Deanna smiles at his eagerness and energy to move on.

"Any other questions? *Bene. Adesso.* Here's how it works. We teach you a variety of booster actions that will give you energy in each Realm and how to avoid the depleters that will reduce your energy. You choose what activities that you feel will work the best to improve your energy. We then measure the changes with the SERF technology that we will distribute tomorrow. It's simple. We want to see how these actions in the seven Realms change your energy levels. The list is included in your materials."

The group pulls out their list and reviews it. She pauses to ensure everyone is on the same page. *"Per favore.* I'll lay it out as easy as possible. In the Body Realm, we have four types of exercise that you should do for different reasons. They include stretching, posture, strengthening, and conditioning. There are many forms of individual or group activities that can replace the exercise. They include biking, running, walking, yoga, and swimming. We suggest that you develop your own routine and practice it at least thirty minutes per day."

The group nods in understanding. They have all heard these recommendations before but most have fallen into lifestyles in which they do not get them done.

"Then, in the Way of Life Realm, we found the energy is boosted through eating natural foods and drinks that are close to harvest, and filled with energy. Thus, while you are here, we would like you to eat a modest diet of natural foods including fresh fruits, vegetables, beans, whole-wheat, and nuts with limited meat, sugar, fat, and chemical additives. The natural drinks include simply water, fresh juice, milk, or natural teas. Even one meal of healthy food can make you feel better if you do not eat too much. Despite our love for cappuccino and pasta in Italy, we found that when we detoxify ourselves from chemicals including caffeine, refined sugar, fatty foods, soft drinks, energy drinks, and flavor enhancers, your *Way of Life* energy will go up. We also found staying busy all day will allow you to sleep well at night and both will boost your energy."

"The food part is a bit more difficult," Mona says. "That's my downfall. But I'll try."

"You need to start with the right attitude or it's all over before you even begin," Deanna replies. "For some, these changes can be a challenge. But remember, simply doing them will make you feel better. It's naturally self-reinforcing. We are also particularly proud of our dining facilities here to help you. We have a four-star restaurant, as well a fresh food deli, to serve you only the most natural local cuisine. We also have cooking classes to take these menus home with you. Any questions?"

Ryan looks around the room to see the reaction. These are many of the changes he would like to see his patients make. But, most people can't follow through. There are so many distractions. And being in Italy is a huge distraction. But, perhaps immersing themselves in a healthy environment, like the Terme Spa, is the way to go. As he said before, this will be an interesting week.

"Then, in the Nature Realm, we have found that when you spend time outside in nature taking in the fresh air, the sun, and recreational activity, your energy goes up. In Brisighella, you can enjoy the natural therapeutic benefits of the hot sulphur springs here. When you take a bath in the mineral hot springs, you absorb minerals and water, take in negative ions from the air, and get rid of toxic waste and metabolic by-products. The osmotic qualities, the mineral concentration, the steam, and the Ph level of the springs here are near ideal for health. You may also want to go on hikes in the country, bike riding in the hills, or work in the orchards, vegetable, and flower gardens. We have many other outdoor activities including bird watching, golf, and horse-back riding."

"I enjoy getting out in nature," Ryan says encouraging the group. "This morning I biked around countryside. The wine country is beautiful. I recommend it."

The comment reminds Wayne to ask about the wine, "That's right! With all these natural grapes around here, is wine off limits too?"

"Good question, Wayne." Deanna replies. "A limited amount of wine or beer is actually quite healthy for you. It not only enhances your Way of life Realm but also the People and Emotional Realms."

"And, you have ample amounts available?" Wayne continues.

"Of course, we do," She replies. "The wine here is great. But, remember the word 'modest' when eating and drinking. Too much of anything will deplete your energy."

"Other questions?" She looks around the room. "Okay. The energy in the Nature Realm is also enhanced if you keep yourself and the environment clean and organized. Just getting organized will make you feel better. Organize your days. Set your life priorities. Resolve nagging problems. They all work. You get the message."

"What about the other four Realms, the Mind, People, Emotional, and Spiritual Realms?" Jack asks. "Should we do those actions too this week?"

"Yes, they are not primary or secondary Realm for this Blessing but still can boosts your energy," Deanna replies. "I know that Dr. Venetre reviewed these before but let me briefly summarize again. They are each important and can easily fit into your daily life. For example, in the Mind Realm, we have many classes and training sessions for you to learn something new every day. In the People Realm, we want you to feel the 'helpers high' every day. You can volunteer in our day care center, the local food shelf, the senior center, the homeless shelter, or simply help others at the Terme. The key is to be sincerely helpful and appreciated by others. You will feel the energy immediately."

"Can we help in teams?" Cicci looks at Ryan and smiles.

"Si. That will boost both of your energies," Deanna replies. "Then, to boost your energy in the Emotional Realm, there are endless opportunities to be creative here at the Terme. You can play or listen to music, sing in our choir, play games, creative cooking, create pottery or artwork, write a journal or even a personal letter… This is Italy. We love creativity here."

"What about the Spiritual Realm?" Cicci asks as she looks at Ryan. "That boosts our love energy, doesn't it?"

"Si, the Spiritual Realm is the most important Realm because it is closely connected to all Realms including the Blessing of Health," Deanna explains. "And, yes, Cicci, it does enhance the capacity to love yourself and others."

Ryan feels embarrassed as he notices that others are beginning to wonder if a little romance has developed between the two. He tries to ignore Cicci's attention.

Deanna continues, "In this Realm, we recommend meditation and prayer every day. There are many different practices we can teach you including contemplative prayer, mindfulness meditation, relaxation techniques, tai chi, self-hypnosis, and others. Do whatever fits into your beliefs and preferences. Meditation and prayer will also boost all other Realms."

"I'm not the religious type," Eliza asks. "Is that a problem?"

"Most religions promote meditation and prayer, but doing them does not require a religion. Prayer is the process of asking for help or guidance while meditation is calming yourself and seeing your life more clearly to gain insight into your issues. We have a prayer and meditation room and personalized training in developing skills in this area."

Ryan notices that that most of the group is already overwhelmed and exhausted. This is a lot of material to cover in a small period.

"We know this may seem daunting to some of you at first," She says sincerely. "But, let us help you. I'm also personally available to each and every one of you to help. After you review your first few energy measurements, you'll have many questions. Just remember, by following your seven Realms you'll feel your energy soar even after a few days. I can guarantee it. Let's take a break."

Chapter 25. Energy Thieves

At the break, Ryan finds Cicci flirting with Jack, another unsuspecting target of her female attention. Ryan immediately escapes outside to get some fresh air and warm sun. He checks to see if Vanessa is around and is disappointed to see no sign of her. As he walks across the campus, he thinks about the sessions so far. They have been relevant, thought provoking, and a bit overwhelming. And it's still only the first day.

It's late afternoon and the sun has crested above the distant hills and tall pines creating a magical glow in the sky. He sits down at a bench along the river, and soaks up the sun. He looks out over the river to see the old town in the distance and the three towers above it.

He is surprised to see Brian Johnson, the on-again, off-again participant with a cynical attitude, walking towards the center of town. Ryan thought that he had left the Terme and gone touring. Evidently, he is sticking around, but not participating in the groups. How strange. What is he up to?

Ryan watches him for a few minutes as he walks along the street, and then ducks into an old building on the outside of town. Johnson comes out with a long thin package, and then walks around the corner out of sight. He wonders what's in the package—a gun, perhaps—but then quickly dismisses the thought and walks back to the Great Room to find his group. He will need to talk to Vanessa about this as soon as he has a chance.

He finds his group assembling around their circle of chairs. He notices that Cicci is now talking to both Jack and Wayne. It is good to see her mix it up a little to see which man becomes the catch of the day.

Deanna reconvenes the group, "Now, let's talk about that most difficult topic, challenging people with low energy. The zombies of the world! How do we deal with these energy thieves?"

Deanna loves this session on challenging relationships and considers it her most important lesson. "We all have these people in our lives and they can suck our energy dry." Deanna explains. "Do not let them! Remember the *Rule of Challenges*. Most zombies do not recognize that they are energy thieves. And when they do, they often don't have the motivation, the time, or perhaps even the insight to change. Or they feel trapped because they've not developed their own personal sources of energy. This is particularly true if the person is too busy or in a position of power."

Jack, feeling confident after his conversation with Cicci, speaks up, "What do you do if they're part of your family or worse, they're your boss?"

"It is often more convenient for zombies to steal energy than to boost their own," Deanna responds. "However, taking energy from others is not the best practice. It not only makes them unpopular, but people avoid them like a plague. Then, they frequently lose their source of energy, unless they're the boss."

"Exactly!" yells Mona. "My boss is a zombie!"

"Some zombies seek positions of power so they can steal energy from those who are subordinate to them," Deanna explains. "When this happens, they can become excessively pushy, micromanage everyone, and be authoritarian. Or worse yet, they can be manipulative, dishonest, or even abusive just to keep their source of energy. This can happen in business, politics, religion, and of course, in families too. It is particularly difficult if you are close to a zombie, or married to one."

"I saw this in the military all the time," Jack agrees. "It seems that every leader needs to take a course in understanding how our energy works. There are few who seem to know what they're doing."

"This is what the *Rule of Gathering* is all about," Deanna continues. "As discussed earlier, this Rule facilitates the enhancement of collective energy. If disagreements occur, they are easily worked out through discussion, compromise, and mutually agreed upon win-win decisions. I love to see this when it happens."

"Politicians, in particular, need a good dose of energy boosters," Jack comments.

"So true," Deanna replies quickly. "But their virtues and vices tell who they truly are. If they have strong energy in each Realm, they can win over any constituency and bring the polarizing effect of different political parties to productive results. However, the reverse is also true. A leader whose energy is low requires a dishonest, deceiving, and negative strategy to win. They choose to focus on single polarizing issues, and as they say in America, lots of mud-slinging."

"What happens when a person with low energy votes for a leader who's an energy thief?" Jack asks.

"As you'd expect, people with low energy often vote for someone like themselves. When you have a leader with low energy, they use poor judgment based on ignorance and low insight. They often insist on an ideological position without regard to what is good for the people and their energy. The community begins to decline into disagreements, conflict, and gridlock. They avoid compromise. This reinforces the most important principle. Maintain your own high energy and you will spread this to others. You will then make good choices regardless of your political orientation."

"I just need to stay away from zombies," Eliza states.

"*Si*, it is best to stay away from those who steal your energy," Deanna replies. "But you may work with them or they may be a friend or even your family. Sometimes, you're married to them."

"What a hassle that is! I know," Mona comments. "I dated many. And my best friend is married to a zombie. The guy's a jerk. She's miserable and tired all the time."

"You can try to help them by giving them some of your own energy. However, this is not the best practice because a co-dependency can develop. This occurs when one person is routinely dependent on another for their energy. You must be careful if you're around these people for extended periods of time because they can steal your energy to a point that you may also become a zombie."

"What if you're married to a zombie?" Beatrice asks, looking at Bob.

Bob shuffles in his chair and glares back at her. "I'm not talking about you, Bob," Beatrice counters.

"If you're married to a zombie, most people simply try to avoid them. However, this can lead to possessiveness, jealousy, and efforts to keep the person close so that they can use their energy whenever they need it. Others lower their own energy to the level of their zombie spouse and they both have miserable lives. Others sit in the relationship for long periods of conflict and do nothing but try to adapt. Ultimately, their own energy levels will be depleted and they develop an illness like cancer or become depressed. Not good."

"Well, what should we do with zombies when they are intimately involved in our lives?" Mona asks, "Sometimes, you can't just leave them?"

"The best solution is to help the person learn about the *Seven Realms of Life* and the *Rules of the Blessings*," Deanna explains. "First, they need to recognize which of their Realms are weak. Review the concept of vices with them but let them figure out if any vices apply. Most people do not recognize their own vices or may deny them. They get defensive. It's not good to point out their obvious vices and flaws because it only lowers their energy further. Help them understand the concepts in the *Prophecy*, the actions in the *Seven Realms* and the *Rules of the Blessings*. Give them information and explain it so they can learn about it themselves. Encourage them to participate with you in boosting their energy. This will gradually help them change from a zombie to a warrior. It's such a relief when that happens. Almost euphoric!"

"Zombies seem to gravitate towards me, particularly men," Eliza continues. "I don't know how to keep them away. What can I do?"

"Some people are more sensitive to gaining and losing energy than others," Deanna explains. "As I noted, you may become their source of energy. If you are sensitive, you have to be very careful when you're around a zombie. Best to recognize them and stay away."

"But what can we do with zombies who don't want to change?" Eliza continues.

"These people can and will change once they understand that they can be as happy and content as others. Zombiehood is not a permanent condition. They simply need to focus on becoming more virtuous with a lifestyle that regularly brings in energy into their weak Realms without having to steal it from others. Eventually, they will get it and begin to change."

"When somebody screws me or gets angry with me, it's hard not to feel anger back," Jack says with frustration. "Sometimes, I just want to clock 'em. How can I avoid losing my energy in the process?"

"It's natural to feel anger when someone steals your emotional energy. However, you need to recognize that anger is a quick loss of energy. If it happens, and you know it will, you simply need to quickly boost it back up. The best thing to enhance the Emotional Realm is to do something creative, something that will make you happy. The anger will pass and your energy will come back."

"What happens when everybody starts following the *Rules of the Blessings?*" Trent asks as he sits slouched in his chair.

Trent has been quiet during the entire discussion. He has a history of depression and Deanna wonders if this has been too much for him. Is he taking any of it in?

"Good question. I was wondering when you would speak up," Deanna says. "I know you can add much to our discussion."

Trent sits upright and ponders her comment, "It makes me think about my problems back home. I've known so many people who were zombies."

Deanna tries to engage Trent more, "Don't worry. If you just take care of your own energy, it will influence those around you and vice versa. As more people do this, the common currency will shift away from monetary gain and material possessions into focusing on life's energy, our spirit, and maintaining high energy in each Realm. Everyone wants to feel good and have a good life. It is a basic drive for all people. And a growing number of people in the world are waking up to the realization that money has no intrinsic energy by itself and does not guarantee a life of happiness, health, and peace."

"But it can help," Eliza says. "I didn't like being homeless and selling myself on the street. Poverty is terrible. I would love to be wealthy."

"So would I," Jack agrees. "Money can bring us a comfortable life."

"Working is important and the money does allow us a more comfortable lifestyle that brings energy into Way of Life Realm," Deanna explains. "However, what you do at work, and how you do it, may either boost your energy or deplete it. People can make money on all kinds of things that deplete energy. Like swindling, selling drugs, prostitution, and insider trading. Money by itself is energy neutral. It is not an end in itself, but rather a means to an end. Money can be used to do things that boost or deplete energy. It is still your choice."

"I'm not sure I agree with you, Deanna," Cicci says. "I like people with money. Their life is so much simpler."

"Our society is still evolving," Deanna explains. "Money is still the primary driver of people's actions in the world because it brings prosperity to your life. But if the economy continues to grow and more people become middle class allowing our basic needs for food, housing, mobility, and safety to be met, then, enhancing our energy will become the more important focus in our lives. People will want to live a long happy and healthy life with positive relationships, beauty, and inner peace. The pursuit of money can actually hamper this goal and complicate your life. When a person achieves a high energy in each Realm, it feels so good. And when it is maintained over the long term, it becomes the core of each person's being. We will not only want to continue to maintain energy, but we will spread it to others around us. It will be the thing to do. Look around you. It's happening right now with the wellness movement."

"So, we can just give our money away?" Jack laughs cynically.

"Now, don't get me wrong," Deanna replies. "I'm not saying to throw away your money. I'm saying keep it in its proper place. An adequate income is important for many Realms and allows us to buy good food, have daily freedoms, and material comforts. However, people who spend all their time making money to the neglect of other Realms will feel ultimately feel out of balance, wobbly, and unfulfilled. They may fall into the power trap. Their happiness becomes based on external power and control and not inner satisfaction and happiness. Having material wealth can then become a burden that may deplete their energy."

Deanna is happy to see a lot of discussion. Although an overwhelming amount of information was covered today, the more people know about the knowledge in the *Prophecy*, the more they want to know and the faster they learn. "I greatly appreciate that you are all active learners. You ask a lot of good questions. Before we end for the day, are there any final questions?"

"Deanna, I don't mean to be disrespectful," Jack says scratching his head. "But these ideas focus on the individual and small groups. Maybe, I'm just dumb but I still don't know how they can lead to world peace."

"We must always start with the individual," Deanna says. "You can only change the world one person at a time. If enough people embrace the Blessings and maintain high energy in each Realm, the world will change."

"But this is not happening," Jack looks directly at her. "The world is filling with more and more zombies. The Plagues are getting worse. Dr. Nobili reviewed this. Twenty percent of people are depressed. Over twenty percent of all women have been raped or abused. Hate and guns are everywhere. Over thirty percent of people are obese. Global warming, severe weather patterns, and massive droughts are predicted. Over twenty percent of countries are at war. All of these threaten the lives of millions of people throughout the world."

"This scares me," Eliza says with a weak voice. "I feel my energy draining out just thinking about it."

"We're not saying these things to scare you," Deanna responds. "We're just being honest about the reality. We need to wake up. It's a good motivator to change things. We need more warriors like you."

"But most people are not doing these things?" Eliza pleads. "Aren't we losing ground?"

"Some people are doing some of these things some of the time. But, on the whole, the data points to a collective loss of energy in most Realms. Perhaps, you are right, the zombies are coming."

"The *Prophecy* is a good reality check on simple personal goals," Ryan finally speaks up and adds to the conversation. "From what I learned today, it is not too difficult to maintain high energy and achieve the blessings of a good life."

"But the people of the world are not doing this," Mona complains with a sense of futility. "If they are so simple, why are predictions in the *Prophecy* coming true? Why are so many people fat, depressed, angry, and hateful? We have such a modern technologically enlightened society with so much knowledge, affluence, conveniences, and prosperity. We should be able to solve these problems. Why is this happening now?"

"I don't know exactly why," Deanna shrugs her shoulders. "Maybe, people don't have the time or motivation to do them. Maybe, they're lazy and complacent, and just don't care. People can get stuck in low energy. But it is clear. We are headed in the wrong direction."

"I'll tell you why," Bob says emphatically with the instructive tone of an aging man who has been kicked around the block a few times. "Life is too complex, too busy, too commercial, and too materialistic. People have lost their core values and a sense of themselves. Our daily activities are no longer focused on enjoying a good life, but rather on making money to buy all the materialistic possessions that everybody wants and needs to keep the economy going. We get divorced and lose our friends, our marriages, and our children. We drink too much. We have trouble sleeping. We are sold on eating processed, poor quality fast food with more and more fat and sugar, geared for our taste buds and not our health. That's why I'm here. To learn how to change."

"I agree with you, Bob, but it is more than that," Ryan shakes his head. "There also seems to be a deep-seated unrest due to the inequality between the haves and the have-nots. The richest one percent has the wealth and live in luxury, and the bottom ninety nine percent are losing ground fast. I've seen both sides in my clinic. Many people, the elderly, the middle class families, the young are losing ground and becoming disillusioned."

"This is predicted by the *Prophecy*," Deanna says. "When large numbers of people deplete their energy, the *Rule of Gatherings* applies in a negative direction. Not only are we going downhill, but we also heading there faster and faster as everybody's energy runs down. It is sad and scary. But I'm an optimist. There is an easy way out. Become a warrior and let the energy spread. Each one of us, one person at a time, can change the world. We have the knowledge and the responsibility to do so. And I'm hoping that's why you're here."

"All of this seems too overwhelming," Bob says with a big sigh. "How can I possibly learn all of this in just one week? And then change the world? Ha! I'm retired. I need a month or a year to even begin."

"How about a lifetime?" Deanna responds with assurance. "The Terme is just the beginning of a good life for those who want it. Let me tell you an old anecdote about three travelers who came to see the beauty of Rome."

The group quiets down. They all like to hear stories about Rome.

Deanna continues, "The travelers went to see the Pope who asked of the first visitor, 'How long are you going to be here?' The man said three months. The Pope said, 'Then you will be able to see much of Rome.' The second traveler said that he could only stay for six weeks. The Pope said, 'Then you will be able to see much more of Rome. The third traveler said with disappointment, 'I will only be in Rome for two weeks,' to which the Pope said, 'You are so fortunate, because you will be able to see everything there is to see!' The three travelers were puzzled at the Pope's comments. They didn't understand the mechanism of the mind. If you have a life of a thousand years, you would miss many things, because you would go on postponing things to the next day because you have so much time. But if your life is short, only seventy or eighty years, you cannot afford to postpone. You need to live life now. I'm confident that in one week, you will learn all that you need to learn and will be able to apply it to the rest of your life."

She stands up and stretches. "You've had a busy day. Now, go! Take the rest of the day off. Think about the concepts we talked about today. Begin to do those things that boost your energy in whatever Realm you please. If you need advice, come to see me. I would love to help. Don't forget about the reception tonight at 8pm. I want to see each of you there. Come ready to celebrate your initiation as warriors of the *Prophecy*. And thank you for being here."

Chapter 26. The Reception

Ryan has a couple hours to kill before the reception tonight, and his thoughts center around what Brian Johnson was up to earlier. Without Cicci at his side, he is free to wander alone to town and check out the building that Brian went into. He walks across the Lamone River and turns left at the main street looking out for Brian or other participants. He walks down the road to find the old stone row house that Brian entered.

He looks up at the nameplate. It's a hunting and fishing shop. He peers in the store window and sees several deer heads, boar heads, guns, fishing poles, tackle, and baits hanging from the walls. What would he be carrying out of this shop that is long and thin? A rifle? A fishing rod? Maybe Johnson decided the Terme was not his cup of tea and wanted to take in some fishing. Or maybe, he is planning an attack on Drs. Nobili and Venetre. He dismisses the thought as ridiculous.

He walks up and around the piazza, and stops in a clothing store to purchase a new Italian shirt to go with his sport coat. He stops by the Hotel La Meridiana and asks if Brian Johnson is staying there. He is not. End of investigation. But he is still concerned about the possibility that Johnson is planning something sinister. He heads back to his room and prepares for the reception. He must stay alert and find out more.

The welcome reception in the Great Hall of the Mind is a Monday night tradition to welcome new arrivals and enhance the energy in most Realms.

There is theatre and music to enhance the Emotional Realm. Socializing to get to know each other in the People Realm. Dancing to music in the Body and Emotional Realms. Good food and wine in the Way of Life Realm. Invitations went out to participants, staff and locals who volunteer in the day care, senior center, food shelves, vineyards, and orchards. It's a real bash on the two Monday nights a month when new guests arrive.

Ryan dresses up in his recently purchased light blue dress shirt and sport coat with the collar turned up in the back, black dress pants and comfortable Rockport shoes. He hustles over to the reception, excited to see Vanessa again. He arrives on time, about 8:00 pm. As he walks into the room, he realizes that most participants have already arrived and are getting their wine and appetizers. Like most Americans, by the time evening rolls along, they are starved. They want something, anything, in their tummies. However, no Italians were there. They typically arrive fashionably late.

A six-piece dance band from Faenza is playing in the back of the hall below the second floor old wooden beams as people arrive. The music is upbeat, energetic, and lovely. The hall is all decked out with an Italian cinema theme with photos from major movies from Fellini's La Dolci Vita to Benigni's Life is Beautiful. Ryan recognizes photos from Cinema Paradiso, Il Postino, and The Fall of the Roman Empire with Sophia Loren. A couple dozen round tables are on one side of the room with a dance floor and a stage above it. The tables are decked out with white tablecloths, white cotton napkins, and centerpieces of beautiful local flower arrangements. There are no name placards on the tables so Ryan immediately finds a seat at one of the tables closest to the food and wine. There is an open bar, with local beers and wines. Ryan's stomach grumbles as the aroma from the Italian food at the buffet table arrives his way. Ryan goes to the wine table and asks for a glass of Sangiovese di Romagna, the local red wine that he had last night. He also eyes the Malvasia dei colli di Parma, a dry white wine that is a blend of Malvasia and Moscato, and several other red and white varieties. He must try the Malvasia next.

He sits down to savor the scene and wait for Vanessa to arrive. He gulps his wine and notices that the flavor of the wine seems somewhat enhanced. It's just his imagination. What could have changed him in one day? He laughs at how suggestible he is.

He then sees both Vanessa and Cicci walk into the room at the same time into the Great Hall. Both women, dressed elegantly, see Ryan sitting in the distance. Recognizing the dilemma, Ryan decides to simply sit, drink his wine, and watch the scenario unfold.

Cicci is dressed as if she's on a model runway in a Moschino bright yellow low cut wrap around evening dress with broad loose ruffles and a waist wrap that accentuates her figure to the maximum. Her hair is flowing about her shoulders, highlighting her bright red lips, black eyeliner and mascara. She wears a symbolic red cross around her neck to represent her piety, but it has a large gold cross, embedded with red stones on a delicate black chain to reflect her eccentricity. She covers all the bases to ensure she gets the attention she wants from the men attending.

Vanessa, on the other hand, is dressed elegantly, but professionally, in a beige flowing Dolci Cabana evening dress that is accented with a long string of pearls and Prada heals. She wears minimal makeup, sheer lip gloss, and a tiny accent of mascara.

Cicci hustles over to say hello to Ryan while Vanessa mingles among the staff and participants. He was expecting Cicci to shift her attention to Jack, Wayne, or even Trent after their meeting this afternoon, but that is not the case.

Vanessa, on the other hand, refuses to compete for Ryan's attention despite her desire to have it. She thought about him and their dinner together last night for a long time before she fell asleep. They were nice thoughts. But she tells herself defiantly that he needs to make it apparent if he is interested in anything beyond a professional relationship with her. It is not her style to chase after any man, especially an American, who may follow the stereotype of having no clue about romance and little understanding a woman's needs, especially Italian women.

On the other hand, Cicci knows what she wants and aggressively pursues her target to solidly hook him in tonight. She considers an American doctor exactly who she wants to be with tonight, and hopefully, forever. And she knows how to please men, particularly American men. She considers them among the easiest to manipulate with her beauty, charm, and sensuality. Plus, she knows they will become her precious *burattini* puppets until they wake up. By then, she's got them snared in her web.

Cicci approaches Ryan with a smile and a compliment, "*Buona Sera!* Ryan, you look so handsome tonight."

Ryan stares at her sensual dress and voluptuous figure. "Buona Sera, Cicci. You look very nice tonight, also." He can't keep his eyes off of her round breasts flowing out from her dress.

She looks directly back at him and says, "*Mi stai spogliando con le tua mente?*"

"Excuse me. What did you say?" He asks, confused at the Italian.

"I said, are you undressing me in your mind?" She smiles.

"No, no," he says, embarrassed at the accusation. "I was just startled at how beautiful you are. Have you been to these parties before?"

"Si. To the credit of Dr. Nobili and Venetre, they know how to facilitate positive energy and help participants get to know each other. We didn't have time for vino today, but now is a good time. Can we share a glass together?"

"Oh, si. Let me bring you some. *Roso o Bianco?*"

"You're Italian is coming along, Dr. Laughlin. *Roso per favore.*"

He walks over to the wine table and retrieves a glass of red wine for Cicci.

"*Grazie.* Tell me about you and your clinic. What type of doctor are you?"

"I'm an internist with a general practice. All kinds of patients. Young and old. Sick and healthy. Some easy to work with while others who are so complex it's difficult to understand all of the problems they have. How about you? What are you involved with?"

"*Grazie* for asking," she takes the opportunity to reel him in. "I'm so sad. Now, that I'm single again, I feel lonely all the time." She goes on to repeat the story of her past husbands and their infidelities, which he already heard earlier today. Although she paints the picture of herself as a saint, in reality, neither she nor her husbands were saints.

Ryan resists the urge to get snagged into this charming woman's web, and maintains a gentleman's attitude. He respects the need for people to tell their story simply to better understand it. He has learned to be a good listener. Cicci has interesting stories and he is happy to simply let her do the talking.

They notice the food is about to be served and Cicci is happy to be finally at his side for a meal. Food is one of the secrets to a man's heart. Although he is an intent listener, she is not sure if she has hooked him yet. She must be patient. "Ryan, *sei affamato?* Are you hungry?"

"Famished," says Ryan. He raises his eyes and nods affirmatively. "I'm interested to see what's on the menu tonight. My energy needs a boost with some Italian cuisine."

"*Bene. Andiamo,*" she takes Ryan's arm. He looks around uncomfortably. He knows he has to stop this one sided relationship pretty quickly if he is to spend any time with Vanessa. They stroll over to the buffet table and gaze at the feast of Italian cuisine. Cicci tells him about the local antipasti including *pecorino cheese, salami rustico, prosciutto, formaggio, mortadella, olivos,* and other local finger foods. She explains the main entrée tonight consists of *fusilli pasta con sugo del rosa y carne* and *tortoloni,* a larger version of *tortellini* with a ricotta spinach and herb filling. They are also serving it with *raguí del pomodore* with a sprinkle of *Parmigiano.* She tells him not to forget about the *insalata con pomodore, olivos verde* and *nero, onion de dolci* to boost his energy.

She talks about the delectable Italian treats as the walk through the line. He takes one of just about everything and they walk over to the table together. Ryan listens and eats, as Cicci continues to talk. He becomes increasingly restless, not wanting to lose the opportunity to spend time with Vanessa this evening. A waiter comes around and asks if they would like some Limoncello or sweet Moscato wine to finish their meals. Ryan orders the Limoncello, but also wants to try the Moscato. Fortunately, Cicci orders the Moscato and loves the opportunity to share it with him.

Ryan sees Vanessa in the distance, staring at him. He smiles at her and, then, frowns, hoping she realizes that he is in a challenging situation with Cicci's unrelenting attention. Ryan needs to take the initiative if he is to talk to anybody but Cicci. After dinner, he politely excuses himself and tells Cicci that he needs to talk to others in his group. The look from Cicci could break a dozen mirrors.

"Oh, Ryan," she says displaying an exaggerated, pouting frown. "I'm so lonely here. I know nobody. Will you come back?"

"Cicci. There are many nice people here," he says. "You will enjoy meeting them and I'm sure that they would love to meet you too. Thank you for the conversation. I enjoyed it."

With that, he stands up and walks away—to her continued dismay. The music plays in the background. There is a buzz of conversation among the hundred or so attendees, but nobody is dancing. As usual in gatherings, there are a lot of shy people attending the reception. The staff recognizes this and always comes up with something to counter it.

Suddenly, the Terme staff, in a well choreographed move, steps on stage and asks the band to play the Blues Brothers' song, *Everybody Needs Someone to Love.* The staff is dressed in black hats, white shirts, loose black ties, and jackets. They dance to the song with a wild gymnastic routine. They are ridiculously bad, falling over each other, but have fun doing it and make people laugh. The crowd loosens up, and then, to their delight the band moves right into the contagious dance song, *Celebration* by Kool & the Gang.

As the song moves past the first stanza, a few people in the audience cannot resist the beat, and start dancing like there was no tomorrow. The energy spreads to nearly everyone. The *Rule of Gatherings* in action.

Ryan cannot resist the musical energy and walks over to the busy Dr. Venetre, apologetically interrupts her conversation, and asks her to dance. She looks at him with those warm eyes and a sweet accepting smile and excuses herself from the people with whom she is talking. At first, she is serious and somber, trying to resist any jealous feelings. But, then, she is simply relieved to be by his side and begins to loosen up. She smiles as they dance together with well-synchronized beat and grace. It's apparent that she was waiting all night to dance with him.

After a few songs, Ryan gets his own private wish. The band plays a popular Italian song that caters to slow dancing. *Con te partirò*, Time to Say Goodbye, always brings tears to his eyes. He holds Vanessa close and whispers in her ear, "This is the best part of my evening. Thank you." Then, Ryan looks out beyond her and is startled to see who is here.

"Do you see who I see?" He asks.

Brian Johnson is standing by the wine table watching the celebration. He appears to be enjoying himself as he watches the Italian women display their fashion and figures on the dance floor. He looks more relaxed than he appeared earlier. Perhaps they misjudged him and the jet lag simply made him irritable.

However, Vanessa immediately becomes stiff and alarmed. She sees Dr. Nobili on the other side of the room, and alerts him. She stops dancing, takes Ryan's arm, and leads him to the opposite side of the dance floor. "Ryan," she whispers, her mouth to his ear, "You need to go over there and make some conversation with Johnson. See what he's up to. Tell him that we noticed his absence at the sessions this morning. Ask him if he's feeling any better?"

"What if I find he's a maniacal killer," he says with a smile. "Should I take him out with my James Bond routine or simply have him arrested?"

"Ryan! This is not funny," she says. "We may be in grave danger, and you're making jokes."

"Vanessa, if he was a killer, would he be here dressed in an elegant sport coat watching the Italian women? He's here to party. Right now, he looks more like a religious misfit than a nutcase."

"Nonetheless, do this for me. *Per favore.*"

Ryan finally agrees and walks to the wine table, gets another glass, and wanders over to where Johnson is standing. He passes Bob and Beatrice

Baker and says good evening. Then, he stands next to Johnson watching the dancing and sipping his wine. He turns to him and says, "Hello. I'm Ryan Laughlin. We met on the plane coming over. What do you think of the Terme so far?"

"Yes, I remember our conversation. The staff and participants are very nice. They're helpful," he says. "And the participants all have such interesting backgrounds. I guess a project like this pulls in all types."

"We missed you today at the group sessions," Ryan says in a friendly tone. "I hope you're feeling well. Your questions earlier today raised some eyebrows."

Johnson looks at Ryan directly and says, "Well, I realized that the research was not what I expected it to be after flying all this way to be here."

"What do you mean?" Ryan asks.

"Well, I don't mean any disrespect, but I was just hoping the use of the *Dead Sea Scrolls* was more religion than science. In our religious circles, we don't believe you can, or should, use religious documents in research. We are also not enamored by the idea of testing the validity of sacred documents. However, there is much to see and do in Italy."

"What sightseeing will you be doing?" Ryan asks.

"Florence, Venice, and Pisa are a quick train ride from Brisighella," he replies. "Seeing the Vatican in Rome has always been a dream of mine. I don't know. I have a week. I'll see where I end up. What about you?"

"I'm a physician with more of an interest in the science than religion," Ryan probes a little, hoping to trigger comments about Johnson's possible intentions. "I see potential in this research to help my patients improve and maintain their health. I believe religion and science can exist together. Science can help us understand what we know about the world and religion helps us have faith in what we don't know. I see it as one continuum."

"From what I've seen so far, the research part of this project is dangerous," Johnson says with disdain. "Com'on. It uses sacred documents to get media attention, and I suppose, more funding. It's a circus act. Trying to measure the soul is a waste of our federal dollars."

"I suppose you don't agree with research on stem cells, global warming, and human evolution, either," Ryan tries to provoke him further. "Should we just stay in the dark ages and let fear of the unknown drive us? We each have our opinions."

"Yes, we do," Johnson replies, recognizing his need to calm himself. "But this project is not about research. My visit has confirmed what our group feared about this project."

"What's that?" Ryan asks.

"The Terme project is worshiping the anti-Christ, plain and simple. There are dire consequences to our world if it continues. And those who are believers, and follow the righteous path, will be saved. And the rest will be left behind. My advice is to avoid this research. It could be the beginning of the end for all of us."

Ryan's alarms go off, but he remains more cool than emotional. "As with all research, the funding will eventually end. Papers will be written. People are slow to adopt the results. If I were you, I would back off comments like that. Did you know there was a murder in St. Paul related to this research? You don't want to be implicated in that mess."

Johnson becomes quiet and looks away. He says politely, "That's my point. It can be dangerous. But your suggestion is accepted. Excuse me. I just saw my date over there and must go to greet her. "

"It was nice to see you here. Enjoy your travels," Ryan says.

"Same to you, and stay safe," he says with emphatically.

Johnson crosses the dance floor, and introduces himself to one of the local women whom he met in town and they begin to dance. Ryan thinks about his conversation with Johnson. Perhaps, Vanessa was correct. His strong religious beliefs aside, he is unusual at best. His energy was low. He needs be considered a suspect until proven wrong. The authorities should be alerted. He walks over to Vanessa and whispers to her as is she talking to some participants.

"*Scusami*, Vanessa. *Un momento.*"

She excuses herself and says, "Ryan. *Che cosa?* What did you find?"

"I don't want to alarm you, but this Johnson is a religious extremist. He was way too negative about your research. We need to keep an eye on him, but I doubt that he is a murderer. He does not look the killer type. Look at him. He's dancing with an Italian lady. I don't think killers do that. They just kill. . . but I could be wrong. Nonetheless, we need to be cautious."

As they talk, they look over to find Johnson, but he is gone. Vanessa calls the local *polizia* immediately, and alerts them that a person at the Terme may be a possible suspect in the murder in St. Paul. The polizia take the information over the phone and say they will need to assign an investigator on Tuesday.

Despite the worry, she does her best to enjoy the rest of the evening with Ryan, dancing, eating, drinking, and more importantly, learning more about each other. Right now, she wants him close, and he enjoys it. They have a few more glasses of wine and talk about each participant they see.

Ryan notices that Cicci is spending the rest of the evening with Jack. He's handsome, courageous, single, and needs compassion, if not passion. He is a war hero. Good choice! He's been through a lot and has a maturity about him that matches Cicci's diverse relationships. Who knows what could happen? With a murderer on the loose, he is glad she's found some companionship.

As the reception winds down, Ryan and Vanessa says their good byes and walk from the Great Hall to the bridge over the River Lamone. They stop to watch the moonlight shimmer across the water and light up the distant vineyards and orchards. It is a romantic evening, and their energies are high.

"Vanessa, I enjoyed the evening immensely," Ryan says sincerely, hoping she forgot about Cicci's smothering of him earlier. "Thank you for spending extra time with me. I feel kind of selfish for dominating your time when there are so many others who wanted to be with you tonight."

The wine has loosened her inhibitions and she says what's on her mind, "Ryan, I was looking forward to your companionship tonight. It just took a while with that piranha hanging on you." Then, she looks at him and holds his arm. "A companion who I enjoy immensely. Perhaps, it is I who is selfish. With a murderer on the loose, I need someone who can watch my back this week. I should thank you for at least this small sense of security."

"The research you are doing here is so innovative yet practical. There is such a need," Ryan looks her in the eyes. "Publishing your results could revolutionize strategies for not only understanding our health and wellness, but also understanding the very nature of life itself. You must be congratulated."

"You are so kind and flattering," Vanessa holds him tighter. "Are you trying to work your magic on me. Do you want me to fall madly in love you? It will be no easy task, you know. As I said, I don't really trust men." She smiles and turns away.

Ryan laughs and ignores the comment. He knows that she has an attraction towards him that is equal to the attraction he has for her. Right now, in his eyes, she is a radiant Sophia Loren in some romantic Italian cinema. He wishes he had the charm of Marcello Mastroianni right now. He smiles back and says, "As I asked last night, is there any wiggle room?"

She looks at him with her big brown eyes. She wants to provide some encouragement, "Ryan, you can have all the wiggle room you want. I enjoy being with you. I feel safe and secure with you. You're a good person and I appreciate you being here. Thank you."

Ryan smiles and lets her talk. "To go back to your comment about publishing," she says. "Yes, we are publishing the results as broadly as possible. Dr. Killian, before his passing, was one our biggest supporters and a major source of inspiration and encouragement. His loss is devastating to us. But we must persevere. There is too much at stake." She bows her head to hide the tears that well up in her eyes. "He was a true visionary and was so sweet to us."

Ryan, without hesitating, puts his arms around her and holds her closely.

She looks up at him and says, "I spent many hours with him discussing and editing our grant before we submitted it. He was the one who encouraged us to use the teachings in the *Prophecy Scroll* as a basis for the human studies in our research. He also believed this would stir controversy, but would bring needed attention to our research. He was so brave. He was the visionary, not us. He loved helping people, particularly researchers. It's sad he's gone. I still cannot believe it. He would tell us over and over again that the *Prophecy Scroll* is one of the most important ancient documents ever to be discovered. He would say our research and our warriors will set the world on a path of recovery." She looks at Ryan and says with a hint of angst in her voice, "You are a lot like him, Ryan. Idealistic fools."

Ryan is taken back by her comment, knowing that he is as practical as they come. "What do you mean by that?"

She realizes that with the wine and the fatigue from the first day, she just let the cat out of the bag. She decides to throw caution to the wind, "You're always thinking about everybody else, but I fear that you're not looking out for yourself," she says. "You are sweet, kind, and generous. People take advantage of you. It's a cruel world and you need more of an edge. You need to be more suspicious and say no sometimes."

"What do you mean? I say no all the time," Ryan says defensively.

"I don't know you that well," she tries to explain herself despite the wine. "I see your personality. You may say no to yourself, but you want to please people. You want to help them so much that sometimes you put yourself at risk. This is an admirable quality that would make our world a better place. If everybody did this, the Blessings would rise, the Beast would be destroyed, and the Plagues would be gone."

"That's the whole point of your research, right?"

"Yes. It is," she says with a sigh. "But I just worry about the people I care about. I don't want them to be at risk and end up hurt or worse, dead."

She looks away at the moon for a few moments. Then she turns back towards him, takes his arm and pulls him away from the bridge. "Sorry, I'm not making any sense. My insecurities are showing. I need to go to bed."

Ryan realizes that she is rambling some, but likes the direction of the conversation. It is such a new relationship that any confirmation of feelings towards him is revealing. Yet, he recognizes the need to just let it go for now.

"Yes, let's get to bed," he says. "I assume there is much to do tomorrow. We both need a good night's sleep."

They slowly walk back to her apartment, talking about their lives, their loves, their tragedies, and their hopes and dreams. When they arrive at the apartment, he looks into her eyes and desperately wants to kiss her.

But instead he looks away like a schoolboy saying goodbye to a female teacher he has a crush on. He gives her a big hug with a kiss on each cheek. He says good night and walks away. He is content to have spent another enchanting evening with her. He also knows that any relationship that is important is worth being patient for.

Chapter 27. The Lessons

Ryan wakes up to sunny skies, both outside and inside. He slept well and is in a great mood with a wonderful energy about him. This is the beginning of his second full day at the Terme. Although it is 12:30 midnight, his time in Minneapolis, he has adjusted nicely to his new time zone. Promoting energy in each Realm also seems to work for jet lag. He thinks about his first day at the Terme and the two evenings with Vanessa. The content in the *Prophecy* was so simple but comprehensive and inspiring, but it was the time with Vanessa that made his thoughts linger. How strong are his feelings for her or is it this new knowledge that has made him feel this good? He admits that both are more intriguing than he had expected.

He is excited to see what's in store for today. He looks at the schedule and then at his watch. The first gathering is at 8:30 am. All of the participants in Ryan's group need to meet in the Room of Wisdom to take baseline measurements. He steps out onto the balcony and watches the morning mist still hanging over the Lamone River. He looks behind him and sees the sun creeping above the distant hills. He gets dressed in comfortable grey sweat pants with a white t-shirt, white socks, and his running shoes. He will do his biking this afternoon. Per instructions, he also defers his traditional breakfast and coffee routine, and instead drinks a full glass of spring water.

He leaves his room and walks slowly across the Terme's grassy promenade and follows the other participants to find the Room of Wisdom adjacent to the Great Hall. He walks into the room and smiles to acknowledge the members of his group who are there. Like the other buildings on the Terme campus, this room also has large beams on the high ceilings, dark wood trim around the windows, and paintings of the countryside, food, and people of Italy. The large windows overlook the adjacent orchards, vineyards, and hills in the distance. This is clearly not a research room.

As he enters the room, he is not surprised to see Cicci eagerly awaiting his arrival. "Buon Giorno, Ryan. *Come stai?*" She says with a polite smile.

"*Buon giorno*, Cicci. I hope you enjoyed the reception last night," he says, wondering what happened last night between her and Jack.

The answer is clear when Cicci immediately sits right next to Ryan. The others in the room also greet Ryan with a series of good mornings. Jack walks into the room and stares at them with what may be a touch of jealousy. He sits on the other side of Cicci, who is delighted at the extra attention. Everyone is excited to get started in measurement of the energy in each Realm.

In addition to Ryan, Jack, and Cicci, the other participants in their group—Wayne, Mona, Bob and Beatrice, Eliza, and Trent—are all here sitting close within the larger group. He does not see Brian Johnson among the participants.

Drs. Nobili and Venetre are there with Deanna to explain the study and how the technology of measuring the energy works.

"*Boun giorno* to each of you," Dr. Nobili says. "I hope your first day at the Terme has been enlightening. I know you're most likely hungry since we asked you not to eat or drink this morning before taking the baseline measurements. I also know that you most likely have many thoughts and questions from the first day. We can answer them during your individual meetings later. Right now, we want to take your baseline recordings within the SERF measurement rooms and calibrate your wrist recorders to collect your daily energy readings in each Realm."

Deanna passes out a wrist magnetometer and a cell phone device to each of the participants while Dr. Nobili tells the group how they work.

Dr. Nobili shows them the small cell phone-like device on which they'll need to write a brief description of their activities. He walks them through how the app works, "We want you to categorize the activity and indicate whether you believe it has enhanced or depleted your energy. This should be done at breakfast, lunch, dinner, and before bed. It does not need to be detailed but the category is important and your opinions are important."

Ryan is impressed with the sophistication of the technology used in the project. After further discussion, each participant, one by one, is accompanied into the laboratory adjacent to the Room of Wisdom. It is lead lined to protect the equipment from adjacent sources of magnetic fields. The laboratory assistant, Roberto, arrives at Ryan's name on the list. He is a dark, muscular Italian man wearing a tight tan t-shirt and jeans. He walks into the room and says, "Dr. Laughlin. Are you ready to get your baseline measurements?"

Ryan waves his hand and they walk together into the lab. The lab is a twelve-by-eight foot room off the Room of Wisdom with a glass window on one wall and a large tube in the middle of the room. From the end of the tube extends a bed that rolls into it like an MR scanner. A red laser beam is coming out from the tube giving it an eerie science fiction look. Ryan can see another staff member with a white coat through a window into the observation room. He is sitting at the console of stacked equipment with flashing lights and wires monitoring the readings.

Roberto asks Ryan to get onto the bed, lie down, and be still in the reclined position. He checks to make sure that Ryan has no metal on his clothes and asks him to breathe slowly. He slides the bed, with Ryan on it, into the scanner. Roberto leaves the room while Ryan stays still. In a few seconds, the equipment starts to send laser beam like lights within the tube in all directions. The scanner moves up and down along his body, buzzing softly. This takes about three minutes.

After the baseline scanning measurements, Roberto explains how to work the wrist magnetometer. "Please wear this watch at all times while you are in the study. It records your energy levels in all seven Realms. In addition, it measures the slope of energy flow—in other words, whether the energy is increasing or decreasing with your activities.

"Can I see the measurements?" Ryan asks. "How's my energy level now? Am I still alive?"

Roberto, who's heard every wisecrack and stupid question, responds with a straight face, "I'm sorry, Doctor, but your energy levels are so low that we will have to isolate you to prevent you from becoming an energy bloodsucker to those around you."

Ryan smiles and responds, "Well, could you at least send in someone with high energy to balance my deficiencies. It sounds like it's urgent. How about Dr. Venetre?"

"Si! *Ho capito*. I understand," he winks. "*No problema*. I will call her immediately for an emergency energy infusion."

The thought of an energy infusion from Vanessa made him smile, but the smile was quickly was replaced with a feeling of foolishness in making it obvious that he has romantic fantasies towards Vanessa. Roberto has seen many participants with an infatuation for Dr. Venetre and Ryan's comment will spread like wildfire through the rest of the Terme, and ultimately to Dr. Venetre's attention. Discretion is not the better part of valor here.

When those in Ryan's group have been measured, Vanessa comes back into the room to address his group. She smiles at Ryan, but gets down to business. "Thank you for allowing us to get baseline energy measurements for each of you. Before you leave this session, please schedule a time this morning to sit down with me and review your baseline results and develop your own personalized plan for boosting your energy. In this way, you will get the most out of your efforts. Deanna will begin the training for both the Body and Spiritual Realms next."

Deanna walks to the front of the room and takes over from Vanessa. "Thank you, Dr. Venetre," Deanna turns to the participants. "For the rest of the morning, we will focus on the booster actions for these two Realms. The actions are simple to do, but difficult to maintain in your daily routines. However, if they are followed regularly, they help you maintain high energy every day and then focus on other Realms. Are there any questions?"

"How structured are we in our schedule?" asks Mona. "Do you want us to do certain things every day?"

"Each of you has different energy strengths and needs," Deanna responds. "We've reviewed the general concepts and Rules about boosting energy in each Realm. It's not so hard. Remember, children have some of the highest energy levels and naturally do things that boost their own energy every day. As adults, we lose some of this capacity because we pick up so many bad attitudes, habits, and relationships that depletes our energy daily. It helps to find the child in each of you."

Deanna spends the next thirty minutes reviewing and demonstrating each type of exercise to boost energy in the Body Realm, and indirectly in all Realms. She discusses how different types of exercise will reduce different health problems including pain, stress, anxiety, depression, high blood pressure, and obesity. The group does them with her. Most keep up but Bob, Beatrice, and Mona are struggling.

At the end of the introductory session, she says, "I can see that you are all at different levels of skill. So, please sign up with a personal trainer to review what exercise routine is best for your individual needs. We personalized your program depending upon your level of fitness, experience, and existing health issues. No two people are alike. A trainer will review your strong and weak Realms and teach you how to integrate booster actions into your daily routine. In the next session, Linda will review the Spiritual Realm. Before, we move on, are there any questions about the exercise program?"

"Deanna, how can I fit these into my daily routine," Mona asks, frustrated. "Some days, I barely have enough time to eat!"

"Time management is an important issue that cannot be minimized." Deanna explains, "With the endless bombardment of intrusions into our minds, lifestyles, relationships, and emotions, many people are swept into a bad routine. But as I mentioned, each person is unique, and thus, needs to develop his or her own individual solutions. For example, try setting aside at least a half hour to perform your own personal routine in the morning. Call it something such as the good life routine. Include an action from each Realm in your routine each day. Seven actions for seven Realms. Once you get into the routine, you will gain insight into how best to fit it in. Even after a week, you will become pretty addicted to feeling good after your routine. I can almost guarantee it."

Chapter 28. The Deep Calm

Linda takes over for Deanna in the Room of Wisdom off the Great Hall. "Thank you for taking your measurements and learning about your energy in the Body Realm. Make sure you schedule with Dr. Venetre to go over the readings. Roberto can do that for you." She points to Roberto, the dark, sultry lab assistant who took their readings earlier. He smiles to the group.

"*Adesso!*" She continues. "Let's move on to the Spiritual Realm. I'm delighted to train you in boosting your energy in this Realm. I believe it's the most important of all the Realms, so we focus a little more attention on it."

"Why is that?" Bob asks.

Beatrice frowns at him and says to him quietly, "Because it's religious dummy! You go to church. You should know."

Linda ignores the slight and continues. "Let me explain. The use of meditation is one of the most effective ways to boost your energy in all Realms, especially the Spiritual. However, prayer can also be helpful. We call it meditation, but there are many other names for it including calming, meditative prayer, mindfulness, stress reduction, relaxation, and tai chi. What you call it is your decision as long as it includes several things. You need to relax your body, calm your mind, discard negative emotions, and most importantly, develop a deep awareness of yourself and your energy in the moment. Avoid any judgment and do not strive for anything. Just be still, inside and out."

Most participants are looking confused since this idea of doing nothing is the opposite of what our production-oriented society encourages. Furthermore, few of them, other than Jack and Ryan, have had any serious health routines, and none of them have practiced meditation before.

"What does that do?" Wayne blurts out, asking the obvious question that most participants are thinking. "It seems like a big waste of time to just sit there and do nothing."

They always know where Wayne sits on any issue. Linda explains, "There have been many studies that support the use of these calming practices to improve your health and well being. Regular practice can boost brain function, mental acuity, the immune system, and heart and artery health and decreases the need for medication for many conditions. It is as close to a panacea as you can get."

"So, you're saying that by zoning out for a few minutes every day, it will cure whatever ails me?" Bob asks skeptically. "I thought that's what sleep was for."

"Sleep is important, but that boosts your energy in the Way of Life Realm. We want you to also enhance your Spiritual Realm. You will find that with regular practice, you will be better able to tap into your own deep inner resources for learning, growing, and gaining insight into your past and future. It can also enrich your everyday experiences by learning to be fully present in the moment."

There are lots of puzzled looks around the room. Linda continues, "It will also enhance the *Blessing of Love.* Both love for yourself and the capacity to love others."

"Now, you're talking my language," Wayne replies with a laugh. "How does it work?"

Cicci looks at Ryan and gives him a wink, "Did you hear that, Dr. Ryan. Love is around the corner."

Ryan pretends not to hear the comment as he keeps a straight face and focuses directly on what Linda is saying.

"It's quite powerful for other Realms too. It does so many things for you that it is hard to imagine," she says enthusiastically.

"Name a few, *per favore,*" Wayne asks politely.

"You are learning some Italian!" she replies. "I'm impressed. Meditation can bring greater clarity and understanding to everything you do so you can function more effectively and know how to see beyond your own self-imposed limitations. It allows you to respond creatively to issues, rather than reacting mindlessly to them with negative emotions. It helps you understand your senses to their fullest, and to detect warning signs for problems in any Realm. It can heighten and expand the experiences of pleasure and vitality and help overcome addictions or self-destructive behavior patterns. And, of course, as I mentioned, it enhances love."

"But I have a hard time concentrating," Wayne complains. "I'm just restless all the time. I can't sit still. I just want to go out and whoop it up. How the heck am I going to sit quiet and do meditations?"

"Wayne, I'm sure you're like a lot of young guys," she says. "You have lots of physical, hormonal, and social energy, but not much spiritual and way of life energy. These Realms become weak by eating lots of sugar and junk food, drinking too much caffeine, taking drugs and alcohol. Many guys think that this will make them happy, but usually you simply get a hangover and feel worse, particularly if you acted stupid while intoxicated."

"I'm guilty as charged," Wayne replies. "But everybody does it. That's our entertainment. I just grab what's there is to eat. Usually it's junk food, sugar, fat, and caffeine. Okay, so how do I do this?"

"*Adesso.* Let me show you," Linda begins. "This is a simple meditation technique that can be practiced easily every day whenever you have a few minutes or when you feel your energy is low. It's easy to learn. Right now, there's nothing for you to do but listen. Listening to me means that you trust me to guide you through this technique and protect you on the way. But if you have questions or concerns, please ask me now before we begin."

"Let's go for it," Wayne speaks up. The rest of the group nods in agreement.

"At the Terme, everything we ask you to do is based on your own free will. Thus, during the next few minutes, you can do whatever is necessary to feel more comfortable and relaxed. My role is to simply talk to you about becoming relaxed and bringing in more energy to every Realm. Again, there is nothing for you to do but listen."

She pauses and looks at the group, ascertaining their level of acceptance. "One of the best ways to achieve a deep calm is to allow yourself the pleasure of being physically relaxed. Adjust yourself to the most comfortable position whether it be sitting or lying down."

Linda adjusts herself and the rest of the group follows her lead. They shift around in their chairs, slump down, let their breath out, and try to relax.

"Are you there?" She asks. "Feel free to adjust yourself as many times as you need to as I talk to you. Now, as you continue to become more physically relaxed, take a slow deep breath. That's right, a very slow very deep <u>breath.</u> Breathe in and then out. Now, notice the air flowing in through your nose or mouth as you inhale. Then, let it all out as you exhale completely. That's right. Try it again. In and out. Excellent. Remember, right now there is nothing to do, no one to please, and no one to satisfy. Just be here now. Wonderful. Now continue to take four more very deep and very slow breaths. And with each slow deep breath, just notice how you feel. That's right, nice and slow. Notice how it enters through the nose or mouth, and how far the glowing energy of the breath travels in your body. Perhaps it fills your chest. Perhaps it travels down to the belly. Maybe, it goes all the way to your toes. The only thing that matters right now is your comfort and relaxation. And all you need to do is notice how you feel when you breathe in and breathe out. Breathe in all the way down to the top of your lungs, and then let all the breath out down to your belly. Excellent. Now, sit quietly, and notice how you are feeling for a minute as you continue to breathe slowly and deeply."

The room is already so quiet you could hear a pin drop. Wayne has his eyes open and is looking around trying to follow her suggestions. It's difficult for him.

"Now, with each breath, notice if anything is happening. Perhaps, you're just beginning to let go, perhaps you notice that the noises around you become more distant and become part of your experience of relaxation. Perhaps, you realize this is one of the few times you can just sit there, do nothing, please no one, and just relax. Perhaps, it's the first time you had an opportunity to relax today. Perhaps, it is the first time you relaxed all week or even all month. The only thing that matters right now is your comfort and relaxation as you continue to breathe, slowly and deeply."

Linda pauses to look to see who is relaxing and who is struggling. The whole group has caught on quite well. Even, Wayne, who was restless a moment ago, is settling down with his eyes closed.

Now, she builds on the initial relaxation. "As you continue to breathe slowly and deeply, I want you to keep your eyes closed and imagine, in your mind, a golden staircase of five steps. You can see one step, several steps, or all five steps. Now, picture standing at the top of it, looking down. Imagine it any way you would like. Whatever you see is fine. It's your staircase."

She pauses to let the imagery become clear for everyone. "Now, I would like you to take a step on that staircase. When you do, see yourself stepping on the staircase, feel yourself stepping on that staircase. Go ahead. That's right. Take the step in your mind. Very good. Now, step down that staircase. See yourself, feel yourself go down that staircase. And with each step down the staircase, just notice what you feel. Perhaps, you feel even more relaxed, even more comfortable than before. Perhaps, your energy makes you feel light as a feather, so light that perhaps even the slightest movement is effortless." She looks around to find they are all quite still, sitting calmly and relaxed, with their eyes closed breathing deeply. "And now, two steps down that staircase. Deeper down the staircase. Deeper feelings of relaxation and comfort. Perhaps, you feel a tingling in your hands or a coolness of your forehead. The feelings and sensations allow you to become even more relaxed, as well as more sensitive to the subtle energies of life. Perhaps, you are beginning to enjoy this experience for the first time. Feeling so relaxed, comfortable, light, with energy coming into you. Perhaps you feel the warmth of the energy flowing through your body, moving from your chest to the arms, from your head to your toes. Maybe it feels like warmth or perhaps it feels like coolness. It does not matter. You are simply relaxing here with no one to please, no one to satisfy and no one to do anything for. Just relaxing and enjoying the experience."

Bob is beginning to snore. The rest are in a deep state of relaxation.

She continues in a low calm voice, "Three. Three steps down the staircase. Take another step further down the staircase, closer to the bottom of the staircase, closer to restoring warm healing and healthy energy to every part of your being. Perhaps, you begin to see things you have not seen before, images of the past, or images of the future. Maybe you have feelings of happiness and pleasure. Maybe you have feelings of confidence as you continue down the staircase. I want you to enjoy each moment of this experience."

Jack is moving about, trying to get comfortable. His muscles and joints have been so tight since the injury and surgeries. But the relaxation is coming. He can feel it.

"Four, four steps down the staircase. Continuing to feel calm and relaxed as you go further down the staircase, deeper and deeper down the staircase, with nothing to bother, nothing to disturb. Perhaps, you are feeling more calm and energized than you have been for days. Maybe, you haven't felt this relaxed for weeks or even months. Just notice the positive warm energy coming in so easily. Notice the glow of angels with warm healing energy moving throughout you, tickling different part of you. It brings out the strength of your body, the clarity of your mind, and uplifts your emotions. The glowing energy pulses and tingles. It builds up, and then, comes down. It flows from your heart to your hands and feet and then up to your head. You have awakened your ability to be aware of the subtle energies within you. Your fingers may tingle. Your forehead may be cool. Your arms may be heavy or feel light. The only thing that matters right now is your relaxation, comfort, and letting the energy naturally enhance you."

Linda is enjoying the feelings as much as the participants. She feels the same boost of energy that they feel. "And now, the final step. You're at the bottom of the staircase. Completely relaxed, comfortable, and feeling calm with a loving energy pulsating through you. And while you're at the bottom of the staircase, I would like to talk to you about your past, present, and future. Just as the visions of your past and present are clear to you, your visions of the future are the same as you continue to relax and feel the energy flowing through you. You can see yourself in the future and the path to get there becomes clear. Your past, present, and future all become part your present reality."

The group is quiet and still. They are all in a state of deep physical calm with their minds filled with visions of the past and future.

"As you enjoy this experience, I wonder if you will be surprised to notice how easy it is to bring in more energy. When you need more energy, you simply take four very slow, very deep breaths, and just notice the energy coming in with each breath. You may be delighted to notice just how comfortable you can be when the energy fills you with warmth. Surprise. Delight. Comfort. I'm not sure exactly what you'll feel, but just let yourself experience it. Maybe, the energy will come in quickly or flow in slowly or maybe just appear. The only thing that matters is that the energy will flow in each and every time you practice your breathing, your relaxation, and your deep calm. And all you need to do is take slow deep breaths, and with each breath let the positive energy come in. The angels will come in and the demons will leave. Angels come in and demons go out."

Ryan's mind has been released. He is in an altered state of consciousness. He sees a vision of himself in a strange place. It's a scary place. An ancient town with a labyrinth of narrow winding cobble stone streets. There is a crowd of angry people with masks and costumed characters, like a carnival, moving down the street towards them. They are yelling insults and chasing after him. They have clubs and sticks. He doesn't know where he is, but he is afraid. He's alone. He's trying to get away from the crowd as they chase after him. He sees a familiar woman down the street in the distance who is yelling at Ryan. He cannot be sure who it is, just a familiarity.

"Come this way," she yells, alarmed. "Hurry or the crowd will get you."

Ryan is running, trying hard to follow her. Then, she turns the street corner, and he sees only a fleeting glimpse of the woman. He continues to run after her as the crowd is getting closer and closer, and more noisy and unruly. He sees her again in the distance. Come this way she waves. He can't keep up. The streets are a maze. He cannot find his way. The crowd is loud and threatening behind him. He must get out of here. Fear grips his heart. His heart is racing and a panic overwhelms him as the crowd catches up to him.

Suddenly, he hears a voice close by, and he comes back to the room he's sitting in. The vision is gone, but the memory lingers. He cannot fathom how this vision could come through so much positive experience of calm and relaxation. Who was the woman? Was it Vanessa trying to save him? Was it Julia? His mother?

"Now, I'd like you to come back up the stairs to be awake, alert, and refreshed," Linda says slowly and calmly. "As you go back up the staircase, notice the return of your normal feelings and sensations. Take a step up the staircase. One step up the staircase, going up at your own speed. No need to hurry. Two steps up the staircase. Coming back to all normal feelings and sensations, but still keeping all of the healing energy that you brought into your Realms. Three steps up the staircase. Continue to be relaxed, but aware of the people around you, the room you are in. Four steps up the staircase and feeling normal, but still relaxed and energized. And finally, five steps to the top of the staircase and back to normal feelings and sensations, being ready to tell us what your thoughts and feelings are."

She pauses to let the silence of the experience resonate with each person. "How did it feel to you?" Linda waits a few seconds for people to come around and wake up. "Would anybody like to share their experience?"

"It seemed like it lasted an hour, but my watch says fifteen minutes," Eliza says with astonishment. "It was so uplifting and energetic. I quickly became calm and peaceful, and then quite suddenly, I felt emotional like something was released. I was in the clouds high above the earth. I felt loved, protected, and safe. My stress level feels about zero. I expect my energy to have skyrocketed. I feel good."

Jack adds his perspective, "I cannot remember the last time I laid so still for even fifteen minutes without falling asleep. I was worried that I wasn't relaxed enough. Then, it didn't seem to matter so I just let it go. The only noises were the hum of the building and a few whispered conversations. I saw a golden light moving up through my body bathing in the glow of healing energy. It was all very restful, like spring sunshine seeping through the blinds. I woke up and have no pain in my legs and body. I feel great. That was amazing."

"When I got to the top of the staircase," Mona says, "I could see right into heaven. My whole life seemed to flash before me like having my life on a video. I could fast-forward or rewind. I could see a vision of me as a child, and then, I could go forward and see my future working at a job that I'm only training in right now. My mind opened up and I could even feel my energy moving up and pulsing like a light flowing through my system."

Linda looks around the room and notices that Wayne is having a hard time returning to an awakened state. Many people who are restless and have difficulty relaxing can have a difficult time returning once they achieve it. It's not that they can't return. Their state of being is so comfortable that they often do not want to return. She leans towards him with a smile. "Wayne. Earth to Wayne. Are you still with us?"

Wayne opens his eyes and smiles, "Wow, was that a trip. I have never felt so relaxed in my life. What did you put in this drink?" There is mild laughter throughout the room. "My mind stopped racing. My body felt like I was floating. It was better than any drug I've had. And I loved your soothing voice. Can I get a tape to listen to daily? I like how I feel right now."

"Yes, we did record it," Linda says. "Playing the recording often helps when you return to this calm state."

As they sit in a circle, the group continues to discuss this morning's session and how to apply it to their daily lives. The challenge is to find an hour a day to do their routine. Here, at the Terme, it will be easy. When they return home, it may be more difficult.

Ryan, on the other hand, remains silent. He is alarmed by the vision and is not sure why he had it. Is it an ominous sign that something is wrong at the Terme or is his past misery rearing it's ugly head again? He will need to discuss it with Vanessa.

Chapter 29. The Lunch

L inda wraps up the morning session by reminding them to meet with Drs. Venetre or Nobili and have their energy measurements reviewed. They have the rest of the day to focus on practicing what they learned and developing their routines to boost their energy.

Linda reminds them, "*Per favore*, don't forget to wear your SERF recorders. Members of the staff are available all afternoon to help you find your optimal routines. Any more questions before we break for lunch?"

"Speaking of lunch, how does food impact our energy?" Mona asks forgetting that she went the whole morning without a snack.

"As you know, what we eat is critically important for both our Way of Life and Body Realms," Linda explains. "It can either raise or lower your energy depending on what you eat and how you eat it. We have conducted several small pilot studies on the impact that eating has on the energy level. We found that the energy of each person is influenced by different foods."

"So, I can eat and gain energy at the same time?" Mona asks in hopes of hearing an affirmative response.

"It's personal and individual. However, there were certain trends. For example, vegetables and fruits clearly generate more energy than meats. Eating a larger meal, particularly to the point of feeling too full may reduce energy compared to small meals. Drinking alcohol in limited amounts seems to bring in more energy in the Way of Life Realm and not unexpectedly in the Social Realm. However, larger amounts of alcohol lowered energy in the Way of Life Realm and in the Mind Realm, again not surprisingly. Thus, the menus at the Terme are focused on natural foods, and we offer small quantities on small plates. But the taste is out of this world. Are you hungry? Let's go have lunch. *Boun apetito.*"

With that, the group breaks up and Cicci tags along with Ryan and carries on her one-sided conversation with him. "Wasn't that a great experience? I love coming to the meditation session. I feel so relaxed and energized afterwards. I can even feel my love growing. I enjoyed spending time with you last night at the reception. Sorry you had to leave so soon. I did get to know some other participants. Jack's a nice guy. He's been through a lot, but has a big heart. Are you having lunch right now? I would love to share lunch with you. Will you, *per favore?*"

Ryan would rather not be alone after the alarming vision in the meditation session. His attitude on this trip is to go with the flow. "Ah, *si*," he says with quiet reservation. "That would be pleasant."

"Delightful. I'll tell you more about our Italian food."

They walk over to the dining building together and talk about the meditation session this morning. He follows Cicci through the buffet line. She does everything possible to show that he and Cicci have a special relationship. She bats her eyes, bends down to show her ample cleavage, and walks as close as possible to snuggle up to Ryan. She explains each of the local foods. To her, Italian food may be the secret to Ryan's heart.

Ryan, of course, wants to sample all the delicious offerings.

"Look at this!" She points to the tray of meats. "They even have *Mortadella di Bologna*. It's pork that is first cured in salt and spices, and then, cooked in a dry air stove to mellow its taste and create the pink color. It's very low in fat to keep the waistline tiny. I like it, but I'm still a salad girl. I use *aceto balsamico* from the province of Modena with extra virgin olive oil on my salads. The flavor is so rich, sweet, and intense. . . like me."

They both laugh, and she studies Ryan to ensure he is enjoying her attention. She can be funny and charming. He smiles back.

"It also goes well with *Parmigiano* cheese and the local *panne* bread," Cicci loves to talk about the Italian food. "Do you mind if we have some wine for lunch? The wines here are different from the rest of the country. They're more sparkling and frothy."

Ryan succumbs to the peer pressure of having only a light lunch and takes some *Mortadella* sausage on a salad of carrots, tomatoes, and sweet onions. He sits down and Cicci follows.

Vanessa comes in the dining room and sees them together. She walks directly over to their table. With a somber tone, she asks Ryan to step out a second.

He excuses himself from the table and asks her, "What's wrong? Did something happen? It's Johnson, right? I knew it was him. Did you bring in the police?"

"No. Nothing happened," she says flatly. "I stopped by to tell you that I'm available immediately after lunch if you want to go over your baseline readings."

He takes a deep breath in relief, and then responds with a smile, "You came over here to tell me that? Thank you. That works for me. I need to find out where I'm hot and where I'm not," he says in an awkward attempt at humor.

She ignores the comment and, then, stares directly into Ryan's eyes. "Remember what I said about Cicci. She has gone through three husbands already, and has become rich doing it. She is targeting a sweet American physician right now. Please be careful that you do not become number four."

"Don't remind me. It's difficult to keep her away. To her credit, she knows a lot about the food here."

"That's her little trap. She gets men by recognizing their biggest areas of low energy. Their stomach and their *pistolone*. She's trying to make a nice *pistolone* dinner for herself."

"What's a *pistolone*?" He asks, puzzled.

She laughs and then looks at Cicci from a distance, "Figure it out. She looks pretty innocent, but she's quite skilled at managing a man's *pistolone*."

"Cicci is just friendly," Ryan counters with some defensiveness. "She means well. Do I detect a hint of jealousy?"

"*Gelosa*, no. I just don't want you to get hurt by our little black widow from Faenza. I can't keep her away from here, but I can warn people who I care about."

As he is about to respond, he realizes that she just said that she cares about him. "Thanks for the warning," he responds with sincerity. "I'll finish having lunch and be right over to your office, say, in thirty minutes?"

"Ugghhh!" Vanessa quickly turns and says to herself. "Men, you can never trust them."

Ryan finishes lunch with Cicci. He finds that she is charming, smart, and funny. He enjoys her company and is not sure why she's called the black widow. And what is a *pistolone?* He dare not ask Cicci. When he's done, he thanks Cicci for the entertaining and informative lunch, and then stops at his room before going straight to Vanessa's office.

The sun is shining, and there's a warm breeze blowing across the Terme campus. The hilltops in the distance are bright and rich with color in the afternoon sun. He thinks about Vanessa's comments about caring for him as he walks over to see her. But Vanessa's jealousy seemed out of place. They had special evenings the last two nights and he was hoping to spend more time with her. But they just met. They barely know each other. The Festival is Thursday night and spending it with her would be a great way to finish the week before he heads home next Tuesday.

He arrives at her office and finds the door open. He peaks his head in and says, "*Boun giorno*, Vanessa. I'm here."

She does not look up from her desk. So, he knocks on side of the door to get her attention.

Then, she looks up at him with a cold, apathetic glare. "Oh. You. Yes. I told you I would be going over your baseline measurement. Here, sit down. I don't have much time before the afternoon session."

She brings up his recordings on her computer, but refuses to smile and avoids eye contact with Ryan. She prints out the report and hands it to him without looking up. "Here are your results. Tell me if you have any questions."

Then, she looks back down at her work. Ryan is startled by this cool reception and tries to figure it out. Is he actually getting the proverbial cold shoulder? He can't believe it. He didn't even know if people do that these days. He's heard about Italian women's positive and negative *passione*, but this is ridiculous. They just met two days ago. He admits that he is attracted to her, but this is too much. What ever happened to being simply civilized?

He is lacking in knowledge and experience when it comes understanding Italian women in the affairs of love. He doesn't realize that they often use the proverbial *big club* to hit a guy over the head to maintain their attention. Neither does he know that women here have all learned that you can never fully trust men to keep their heart in their shirt and their *pistolone* in their pants. They must hold those who are precious to them as close as possible. Ryan is simply trying to figure this out on the fly, and is not being particularly successful.

He reads the report, and then, looks up to say, "Excuse me, Vanessa. Sorry to bother you, but I thought you had time to go over my readings. It says that I'm high in my Mind and People Realm, but lower in my Spiritual and Way of Life Realms."

Vanessa responds without looking up, "That means you eat too much and have no clue about love."

Ryan raises his eyebrows and looks at the results again. She continues to do her work. This raises Ryan's ire. He responds with his typical impatience, characteristic of low energy in the Way of Life Realm.

"Vanessa. Is that it? Is that all this research is about? Well, then, perhaps I wasted my time coming here. I was hoping to find a little more truth and understanding, but instead, I find the cold shoulder. Does this have anything to do with me having lunch with Cicci?" He stares down at her with a menacing look.

She looks up with a thin smile on her face, and says calmly, "Ryan, you need to learn about Italian women. I enjoyed the last two nights, and you never know where a relationship will go. I have no expectations. However, I'm not going to let some octopussy screw up any potential relationship here. I'm simply protecting my territory. *Capisci?*"

"Vanessa, I have no interest in Cicci. She is a friendly participant here who asked to have lunch with me. I have absolutely zero interest in her." He shows a zero with his fingers, and says emphatically, "Zippo, *niente, nada, aucun* interest in her. I'm not some Italian guy who falls in love with every beautiful girl who comes by."

"So, you admit she's beautiful?" Vanessa asks sternly. "Does that mean you're attracted to her? Did you like her big and very real boobs shaking in your nose? Or, did you like her tight buttocks from the years of holding a coin between her butt cheeks?"

Ryan looks at her, flabbergasted, and says, "She does what?" He slumps his shoulders and looks at the ceiling. He is learning that Italian women are relentless.

Vanessa continues for a few minutes with her *brutta faccia*, and then, she smiles in a more conciliatory fashion. "Let me tell you a story about *mia mamma*, and maybe you won't want to get to know me better anyways. My older sister brought home the man she hoped to marry to introduce him to *la famiglia. Mia mamma*, who only goes by her first name, Guiliana, said to him after the initial welcome, 'It's so nice to meet you. You seem to be such a nice man. I'm sure you'll be very kind to my daughter.' The man nods his head in understanding."

Vanessa pauses, looks up and says, "*Mia mamma* says to him with a straight face, 'The last guy whom she brought home cheated on her and my daughter was very sad. Can you see that thing floating in the jar on the kitchen shelf between the olive oil and dried garlic?' The man squinted to see what looked like a thick brown sausage sitting in the jar. Then, she said, 'That's his *pistolone* in there. That's what we do to men who cheat on my daughters.' My sister was not amused, but the man got the point. They are still married today, and I must say, he has never cheated on her."

Ryan looks as if he has seen a ghost. He gains his composure and says, "Well, in any case, I'm not attracted to Cicci. In fact, I have a difficult time opening up to any woman. You know my circumstances. I also enjoyed our evenings together and would like to get to know you more. And your mother doesn't scare me a bit. If I had a daughter, I might say, well, not the same thing, but I'd be protective. You get my point."

She smiles and realizes that she has made her point. "Okay. I accept your apology. And, by the way, the Brisighella Medieval Festival is here Thursday to Saturday. I accept your invitation to have dinner together on Thursday, and then, I will show you how the medieval people of Italy party."

Ryan does not remember when in the conversation he had invited her. He thinks a beautiful Italian woman, who is way out of his league, may have just had her way with him. But in some morbid way, he enjoyed every bit of it. To get any attention from Vanessa is uplifting, even if it borders on manipulation. He particularly liked the jealousy part of it. It's a sign of a strong woman who knows what she wants. "Great. It's a date. Now, could you spend a little more time explaining my baseline readings? What do I need to focus on here?"

"Well, let's see," She smiles agreeably. "The readings can be quite revealing, and even unsettling to the unprepared. Almost as good as Taro cards, tea leaves, and palm reading with a little science thrown in."

He laughs at her uncharacteristic sarcasm.

She studies the readings on the form carefully. "As I mentioned, you do have high levels in the People and Body Realms while it is nice to see that your Nature and Mind Realms are also high. However, the Way of Life, Emotional, and Spiritual Realms are quite low. This means that you most likely have demons in these low energy Realms. Your vices demonstrate this. In the Way of Life Realm, your vices include being excessive and impatient with a tendency towards gluttony. In the Emotional Realm, you may become depressed or anger easily, and may create conflict between people due to your cynical nature. You also have vices in the Spiritual Realm, such as having doubt in your life with little faith and hope, ultimately leading to a path of disdain, or even hate for yourself or others. This does not sound too promising for your relationships. You better get your act together."

Ryan ponders this revealing and surprisingly accurate information. He knows that he can be excessive, impatient, greedy, and depressed—with anger, doubt, disdain, and hate thrown in for good measure. His energy reading made him sound like he's totally screwed up. Her directness lowered his energy even more. He has always thought of himself as a good person who gives to others, but this new version of him is disturbing. He is sounding more like a zombie, walking around dead, than a caring physician who is compassionate and understanding.

"The booster activities that would enhance your *Way of Life* energy include eating a modest, and more natural, plant based diet, and working on sleep quality. In the Emotional Realm, you need to participate in more creative activities such as music, art, or writing daily. To promote your Spiritual Realm, you need to practice meditation regularly. Did you have a good experience with Linda's session today?"

"It didn't go too well," he said nervously. "I had a weird vision. An angry carnival crowd chased me through a town maze of old stone streets. A familiar woman was guiding me. Not sure who it was. I have no clue to the meaning of any of it."

"It means that you're afraid of going too deep into your soul. And it is possible that you may see a woman as someone who can bail you out. What do you do regularly to boost your energy?"

"Well, I do yoga. I bike regularly, and I read a lot."

"That's a start, but understanding your mind is not the same as understanding your soul. It's common for those who have pursued advanced education to neglect their Emotional and Spiritual Realms. People learn intellectual discipline with an emotional distance, but this doesn't do much for these two Realms. Don't feel alarmed. Almost everyone has areas they need to work on. You're not a zombie, but you do have some work to do. And I'm happy to work with you to improve those areas. *Capice?*"

Ryan fakes a smile, as if he was a kid whose father just yelled him for breaking the living room picture window with a baseball. "Yes, I'll take this information as my assignment for the week," he says. "And it would be nice to work with you on it. I need to go. Our next group meeting is in a few minutes. I'll see you later."

He smiles at her with a mixed bag of fear, awe, and appreciation. He leaves feeling worse for wear than when he arrived. Still, he needs to just go with the flow. This is good for him.

Chapter 30. The Boost

Ryan heads to his room to reflect on the implications of his readings. He lies on his bed looking out the window at the sky beyond. He thinks about the first two days. It feels like a week has passed. He realizes that the Terme Project will bring him down a few notches from his almighty doctor horse to reality.

So be it. He needs to change something. The energy readings even the playing field for everybody. Rich or poor. Young or old. Doctor or receptionist. They all can maintain high energy with the right routine or fall into the pits with low energy. Then, his thoughts move to Vanessa. She is one intimidating lady. He does not quite know how to react to her. Her spunkiness and demand for high ethical standards and moral positions are admirable, but he's not sure he agrees with her methods. Apparently, she has been burned by Italian guys one too many times and has learned to protect herself. Maybe it's more than that. Perhaps, her virtues of honesty and directness are a result of maintaining energy in each Realm. It's all fascinating.

He carefully plans the rest of the day to boost his energy in each Realm. He starts with his favorites, exercise and learning the materials. Then, he will practice his meditation in the Terme spa and walk into town to find a volunteer opportunity. This will be followed by a modest healthy dinner, alone this evening, and then, hopefully, a restful night's sleep. He gets dressed in his bike pants and shirt to prepare for his early afternoon bike ride. His goal is to bike to the town of Modigliana to see the sights in the valley on the other side of the hill. He packs a light jacket, water bottle and snack, and then, heads out.

As he rides up the winding hill, the sun is a golden glowing sphere high in the sky. As he pushes to the top of the hill, he thinks about how the energy works. As he exercises, he is gaining spiritual energy even though he is burning caloric energy. It's opposite to his training as a physician. It is an interesting, and perhaps, revolutionary concept in thinking about health and well-being.

The morning breeze cools his face as he continues to climb past the herd of sheep, the old stone farmhouse, and the stone church at the top of the hill. When he hits the crest of the hill, he stops on the narrow stretch of road to take in the view of both the south and north sides of the hill.

Then, he walks across the road to look north over the steep green hill. He can see the stunning aquamarine aquifer tucked away between the mountains in the distance. He stops and stares into the distance, as he thinks about his time here and his situation in Minnesota. Despite the up and down experience this week, a series of over-riding questions repeat over and over again in his mind.

What happens when he returns to life in Minnesota? Will he forget these lessons in the busy routine of his life? Will the habits of drinking too much, avoiding commitments, waffling on decisions, and working too much change? Will the nightmares and anxiety come back? Does he really want his mother to be the main woman in his life? How can he apply this knowledge to the lives of his patients? These are questions that he needs to forget right now. He wants to simply enjoy the present. After all, this is his vacation, and so far, he has enjoyed nearly every moment of it. He is content with that.

He rides by the entrance to one of the many old family farms that sell fruit, wine, cheeses and other locally produced foods. The sign says— *Benvenuti a Fattoria Leccio*. He decides to pick up some fresh cheese and fruit to share with the others. He considers the messages in the *Prophecy*. Take in natural foods that rise directly from the springs and soils of the earth. Sounds like this place fits the bill.

The Terme staff said the farm sells a tasty peach juice and two special brands of cheese, caprino and pecorino cheese, made from goats and sheep grazing on the hillside. They told him that the cheese has anti-inflammatory and cancer-fighting properties and reduces the risk of arteriosclerosis, diabetes, and tumor growth.

He walks his bike up the long dirt entrance road that rises above the paved road and looks around to see if anyone is there. The door to the little shop in the old stone house is open. He walks in and smiles to the young Italian girl who waits on him behind the counter. She is about thirteen years old with deep brown eyes, fine olive skin, and dark hair. She is wearing jeans, a soft pink sweater, and open sandals. She looks down shyly, but then, lifts her head and smiles at him.

She recognizes that he is American. "'ello. May I 'elp you?" She says with slow, but proper English.

Ryan does not want to sound too much like an American tourist, so he responds with a smile and the broken Italian that he learned via the tapes on his flight over to Italy. "*Grazie. Si. Tu hai un formaggio per favore? Pecorino e caprino. Anche suco de pesca?* Peach juice? *Si?*"

"*Si, si, aqui.*" She relaxes a bit knowing that he knows at least a little Italian.

She shows him where the cheeses are, and he picks out a medium package of both goat and sheep cheese. He also sees peach juice and a local wine called *Inspirata*. He looks at her. She nods her head and smiles to confirm that it's very good.

He pays the girl for the items, and puts them in his backpack. He opens the peach juice immediately. It has a tart, but sweet taste and satisfies his thirst more then he could ever have imagined. The girl tries to make conversation with Ryan to practice her English. "You go to *le Feste domani* in Brisighella?"

"*Si, e tu?*" He responds.

"*Si,* each year it ees event *especiale* for town. We dress up."

"What mask will you where?" he asks.

She looks at him puzzled, not sure what *mask* means. Then, he moves his hands to the sides of his face to illustrate a mask. She smiles and proceeds to describe the mask with many hand gestures and the excitement that comes from knowing she has something more unique than her friends.

"*Lo ho un maschera di veneziana*—a mask of Venice. It ees *bianco*. White with a gold crown, pink swirls on white cheeks, and red blush with large red lips. We have black cape and hat with red and white... How do you say? *Di ucelli.*" She points outside and flutters her hands.

Ryan smiles before replying, "Oh, feathers from a bird, you mean?"

"*Si,* feathers."

"I look forward to seeing you there tomorrow. *Grazie, signorina.*"

He says goodbye to the girl recognizing the high energy that comes naturally in children who are loved. He places the cheese, juice, and wine in his backpack and walks to a clearing by the side of the road. He stops to admire the view of the eastern Tuscan hills, rolling off into the distant horizon, silhouetted as multiple layers of green shadows.

He continues on his journey to Modigliani. The road crest becomes a downhill, winding road with mirrors at each side of the curves to see who is coming. The slope is steep, and he picks up speed, banking around the curves. The flight down the hill is fast, exhilarating, and dangerous.

It takes only few minutes to get down the hill. He slows down to pass the café outside of Modigliani. He can see the town in the distance nestled in the middle of the Tramazzo Valley, where three rivers join to form the River Marzeno. He bikes over river on the Bridge of San Donato and stops to read the tourist description. It says that this is one of the few elegant hump-back shaped bridges built in the eighteenth century in the province of Forlì-Cesena. The water is flowing fast, but is not high at this time of the season.

He bikes into the Piazza Pretoria, and looks in awe at the Fortress of the Counts Guidi, called the Roccaccia, that rises above the town. It's an imposing ancient stone castle structure that housed the royalty of the region for centuries, and has been rebuilt recently to maintain its history.

Ryan looks at his watch and realizes that time has passed quickly, and he still has a full agenda for the afternoon. He puts on his helmet and takes a drink of water. He hops on his bike, and takes off out of town and back up the steep hill. As dangerous as the hill was going down, it is equally physically challenging going up. He has as strong a quadriceps as any competitive biker, but he finds it's still a grueling test of his strength and conditioning.

He slows down to shift into a higher gear, and picks up an even pace as he pumps harder to move faster up the hill. He arrives at the crest of the mountain almost as quickly as he came down. When he reaches it, a blast of fresh wind, scented by the pine trees on the distant lush hills, hits his face. He squirts water into his mouth from his container. He notices how beautiful a day it is with the warmth from the sun, the cool mild breeze, and the aroma of countryside. It's glorious.

His fatigue is gone. His energy levels are high. He feels better today than he has all year, and it's only Tuesday. But he still needs to avoid zombiehood, and work on his weak Spiritual, Emotional, and Way of Life Realms. He is excited about documenting his actions and events this afternoon to see how they influence his energy levels.

He crests the hill, and the winding road becomes straight and flattens out. He can see the horizon in all directions. The hills are sprinkled with red poppies, rows of lavender with metallic silver foliage and purple flowers, and yellow wild daisies.

He begins the descent to Brisighella. He is vigilant in watching for ongoing traffic. He can see the Terme in the distance along the River Lamone. He finishes the last kilometer of the ride, and arrives at his apartment feeling more refreshed and energized than when he started.

After returning, he is excited to take his first dip in the Terme spa. He puts on his bathing suit, robe and sandals and quickly hops across the Terme green to the weathered old stone and wood beam building. He walks in, picks up a towel at the reception desk, and slowly makes his way down the mosaic ceramic tiled steps into the large cavern-like room. The room is mostly comprised of a steamy dark blue pool that is decorated with matching colorful blue and green ceramic tiles on the ceiling and recessed sconces that cast an eerie shadow on the wall.

When he arrives at the base of the spa stairs, he notices several other bathers are quietly talking on the distant side of the pool. He steps into the steaming pool and the warm sulfur water tingles as the heat moves up his legs into his body.

He immediately feels relaxed, breathing the healthy negative ions from the humid air, and sits down at the other end of the pool. He spends the next twenty minutes meditating to Linda's slow melodic voice in her meditation soliloquy. He achieves a deeper calm with each breath. In contrast to his last time in meditation, his visions now bring him to see his past as if it was yesterday and his future as it will be tomorrow.

He sees Sophia and his father before they passed away. He feels the joy when he was with them and the strength that they gave him. He feels the emptiness when they were gone. The visions quickly moved on into his present life. He sees his clinic and his patients. They're so much a part of him and his life. He feels their pain and their grief when they describe their problems and their joy and relief as their health and pain improved.

The vision moves into a picture of his future. He sees a family to love and share his life with. He sees two children, a boy and girl, running up to him and hugging him tightly when he comes home from work. He sees having meals together, doing homework, watching movies, telling stories, playing games, biking together, and laughing. He sees the life that he has always wanted, but that he thinks may have passed him by. He comes out of the session feeling optimistic and hopeful about making this future a reality, however distant it appears right now.

He realizes that he needs to prepare for the evening, and gets out of the spa and into the shower room to wash off before he leaves. Once dried, he puts on his robe and slowly saunters up the stairs and back across the green to his room.

As he prepares for the rest of the day, he thinks about both women he has met recently, Julia and Vanessa. In either case, a long-term relationship just does not seem likely. But then he wonders if the hurdles he sees are real or is he simply avoiding a deeper relationship, and the complexity that comes with either of these intense professional women. He concludes that he simply needs to be positive and go with the flow. If something develops, so be it.

He reads the *Seven Realms of Life* and *Rules of the Blessings* documents again. He thinks how novel and practical they are. He recognizes these are universal truths that all of us need to learn sometime in our lives. Unfortunately, our relationships, habits, fears, and environment can deplete our energy and send us off in directions that create problems. Life becomes more complex as we age, and we lose sight of these principals and how they can help us enjoy a good life. We simply need to re-learn these habits, incorporate them into the routines of our daily lives, and be reminded of them repeatedly. They are easy to do here at the Terme, with all the support one receives. But the challenge is overcoming the inertia of avoiding them when he returns to his real life.

But he is here now and he will make the most of it to boost his energy. He has had a light healthy lunch with Cicci, met with Vanessa to understand his weak and strong Realms, has exercised with his bike trip in the fresh air and sun, completed his meditation in the natural spa, and learned more about the manuscripts. He addressed the Way of Life, Body, Spiritual, People, and Mind Realms.

Now, he needs to work on promoting his energy in the remaining Realms so he will do something creative in the Emotional Realm. He heads over to the Brisighella activity center, and decides to have fun wallowing in the mud of the pottery wheel. On his way back, he plans to stop at the senior center to find what opportunity he might have to help them out. Finally, he will have a pleasant dinner by himself focusing on a small portion of his favorite pasta and a simple salad from the deli. All in all, he plans a splendid afternoon and a quiet evening leading to a long, deep sleep. Things are looking up right now for Dr. Ryan Laughlin. He is feeling optimistic and the fear and despair have passed. It's a good feeling to savor.

Chapter 31. The Visit

As Ryan wakes up in the morning, he is happy to recall that his previous day was exactly what he had in mind for his vacation—a productive afternoon, a quiet evening, and a superlative sleep. He steps out onto the balcony and stretches his arms, legs, and back in satisfaction as he gazes out at the sun rising in the eastern slopes of the hills overlooking Brisighella. Another glorious day has arrived in the Lamone Valley and he is fortunate to be part of it. He showers and dresses in a white shirt and jeans, and then carefully prepares a small fruit plate and whole-wheat muffin for breakfast, supplemented by the peach juice he bought yesterday. No caffeine today, he thought to himself. He will need to get his energy from his booster actions.

Ryan decides to visit Vanessa in her office on his way to the readings. He does his homework by jotting down a few notes about his activities yesterday afternoon. He checks his watch and realizes that he does not have much time. To his pleasure, her door is wide open, and she happens to be working on the computer. He watches her from a distance and is again taken aback by her beauty. She is dressed in jeans, a white blouse with the two top buttons open, minimal make-up, and gold hoop earrings. She looks up, sees him, and gives him the sweetest smile he has ever seen. He is surprised that it brings him such a rush of positive energy and emotions of joy.

"Good morning, Ryan. What a pleasure to see you. What brings you over to my part of the Terme this morning?"

Ryan smiles back as he stands behind her desk. "*Boun giorno.* I thought I'd stop by for a moment to share some of my experiences with you. I'll also have you know that I practiced the actions in my weak Realms that you so aptly pointed out yesterday."

Vanessa waves her hand to welcome him in. "Si, si. *Viene qui.* I'm interested in what you think. Tell me."

"It's been very interesting," Ryan says with the brightness of a child's face. "It's a great vacation so far. Just what the doctor ordered. I meditated in the spa, and had the most pleasant vision of my life, both past and future. I biked to Modigliani then ate modestly last night, despite my addiction to Italian food. I ate small portions of pasta instead of stuffing myself. I detoxed from caffeine, and slept like a rock last night. I re-read the *Prophecy Scroll* and started some creative writing. Then, I helped out at the senior center. They are great folks. Are most of the people in Brisighella over seventy? And where are all the women? Is there a women's center?"

Vanessa laughs. "We do have a geriatric crowd in Brisighella, and all over Italy. The birthrate here is low. The women stay at home. Right now, they're most likely cooking, baking, and cleaning up after the men and their pets. The old men have time to hang out at the senior center and café on the piazza. It's their form of fun. They love to see the Terme participants, particularly, the young women. I'm sure you were warmly welcomed."

"True. I felt as if I was a buddy of theirs for years. They said they needed my virgin tongue to taste their different wines. They love to sing, and to my surprise, even roped me into a few rounds of *O Sole Mio.* It's easier to sing after tasting a few glasses of their best wine. I feel my energy levels are rising. My sixth sense is coming around. I feel uplifted and lighter. And it's only my third day here. I'll admit there is a little bit of happiness shining through. It's a nice feeling. Thank you."

Vanessa looks at him fondly. "It can happen quickly. In a couple of days, with the right practice. Promoting energy in a Realm is simple if you give up the fear of change and set up your routine to do actions every day. As you found, even one day of practice will lead you to feel better. The problem is that most people don't do them. There are always lots of excuses. Too stressed, too busy, too little time, too lazy, don't know what to do or don't agree. I'm sure you heard them all in your clinic. People get out of balance and become unhealthy in many ways. Now, the knowledge in the *Prophecy Scroll* is not a cure all, but the actions can make anyone happier and healthier."

"I was surprised at my ability to become deeply relaxed during the meditation," Ryan says. "I tapped into parts of my brain that I never accessed before. I felt like an enhanced Ryan with surprising clarity about my past, my present, and what I envision to be the future. It was exhilarating. My mind was organized and clear. I felt like I could save the world if I needed to. Or, at least save myself from the doldrums."

Vanessa smiles. "*Maravillosa*, Ryan. I'm hoping the others in your group get the same reaction. You're remarkable in your ability to adapt and change. Most people have more difficulty. We throw a lot of things at people during the first two days and many get confused. Some people do well and some people do not. We don't fully understand what factors lead to success versus failure. Perhaps, you can help us there."

"I expect there are some patterns that lead to failure," he replies.

"There are," she says. "For example, some people feel good quickly. They think they just drank from the fountain of youth. They have new insight, confidence, and conviction. Unfortunately, they may not remember the *Rules of Moderation* and *Balance*. They push too much energy into a Realm and find themselves out of balance and wobbling. One or more Realms become depleted and they develop problems. They don't understand it. They feel it's not working. Fear of failure takes over and they lose their focus and confidence and go back to square one. Your friend, Cicci, has done that several times. People need to understand and follow the Rules. It sounds like my mamma speaking, but it's true."

"How do you know when an action is too much?" He asks.

"It's not difficult," she explains. "You learn to recognize when you're losing energy because you don't feel as good. You become irritable, don't sleep well, worry too much, get a headache, or simply feel down. You'll know when enough is enough. Most people around you will know because you stink." She holds her nose, and they both laugh.

He feels better than the last time in her office. He never knows whom he'll meet when he sees her. Up and down. He hates to admit it, but he has a desire to please her.

Vanessa continues, "When a person achieves high energy in each Realm, it feels so good that it's addicting. It changes a person in fundamental ways. They begin to feel alive, focused, energized, and more confident. They live in the extended moment. Daily hassles become easy to forget. Each day feels longer and becomes more eventful. Time does not fly by because you feel it so well. The activities that you choose each day can promote energy in each Realm. There is no such thing as a wasted day."

"I love the concepts," Ryan says with enthusiasm. "There is no such thing as a wasted day. And you can boost our energy any day if you need it."

"Then, the best part is that your positive energy will spread to the others around you also," she says. "Don't you just love the concept behind the *Rule of Gatherings*? You can feel the shift in energy when you're in a group with positive energy. Of course, the opposite is true too. A few negative members can drag the whole group down. What did you see happen yesterday?"

"My group started with pretty low energy," Ryan replies. "Their stories were a remarkable collection of sadness, abuse, bad decisions, and bad luck. Except for a couple of them, they were a mess. Yet, by just sharing their experience among others who sincerely listened, they felt better with more energy. We'll see what happens today. By the way, I did not see Brian Johnson anywhere. Perhaps, he realized this is not his cup of tea and left."

He looks at his watch. He would like to spend more time talking, but is excited about what he may learn today. "I need to get over to my group," he says. "Let's have dinner again tonight. Are you busy? "

For a moment, a dread flashes across Vanessa's mind but she quickly dismisses it and smiles. She likes how she feels with him and will not let fear diminish her energy. Their energies seem so synergistic and the attraction is clear. "I have plans, but I can change them. Does 7:00 pm work?"

"Great." He looks at her like a kid who's found a new friend in the neighborhood to play ball with. "I'll pick you up at your apartment." He says goodbye and smiles to himself. Maybe there is something there. He's willing to be patient to find out. Just go with the flow.

Chapter 32. The Conflict

This is the third session for Ryan's group. They are gathering to discuss the progress they've made this week and download their readings. They all look up to Ryan as he walks into the room. As a physician, they hope that he may have answers for them. Most people do not realize that physicians have many of the same problems that their patients have, but rarely acknowledge it. They are also trained to focus mainly on the body, and often miss or avoid the other Realms, particularly in their own lives. And they believe they are there to help others, not themselves. It may be both a blessing and a curse.

And Ryan is no exception to these realizations. Though he has struggled in the past two years, the experience at the Terme has renewed his energy in moving his life forward. Yet, Ryan realizes that their problems dwarf his own. In many cases, the traumas of participants such as those suffered by Trent, Eliza, and Jack were due to circumstances beyond their control. Now, here they are, ready to turn around these major problems, and hopefully, achieve a better life.

They sit down with Linda's stealth guidance and discuss their progress and hopeful redemption at the hands of the *Prophecy Scrollis* wisdom. Ryan recognizes that some could slip down the path to more tragedy. He thinks about his own situation. He is lucky to have grown up in a life focused on education, generosity, kindness, and abundance. His father, an engineer, did not express himself much, but he was always there to provide a loving and supportive family environment. He grew up feeling safe and protected and ready to learn as much as he could, to explore the world, and make a difference in helping people. Most members of his group are working hard to achieve a good life, that in many ways, Ryan has already achieved. But he still feels there is a long path ahead to the life he's always dreamed of.

After the discussion, Ryan downloads his readings and finds out that he, in fact, has boosted his energy considerably in all Realms. He is not surprised since he in on vacation and working hard at the booster actions in each Realm. He feels good too. Maintaining these levels when he returns to Minnesota may be another story but will be a priority. He must consider how realistic his daily routine will be when he returns and if it can become routine in his future lifestyle.

After the morning sessions, he walks down to the piazza of Brisighella to say hello to his new geriatric drinking buddies. He has one glass of wine, but no more. He wants to stay energized for his dinner with Vanessa tonight. He spends part of the afternoon helping some seniors clean their rooms and get organized. He then walks back to his room to read and write more. He hopes to get in another sulfur spa and a bike ride before meeting Vanessa. He bikes up the hill from the Terme to the small old stone church at the crest of the hill that he visited his first day here. He stops briefly standing on his bike as the sun is setting in the distance. Ryan imagines that all of his fears and faults will sink behind the hills with it.

He heads back to the Terme to get ready for dinner with Vanessa. The dusk is beautiful as he rides down the now familiar hill to the Terme. An uncharacteristic peach scent is in the air from the adjacent orchards. This is a divine place.

He walks over to Vanessa's apartment and knocks on the door. She opens the door, greets him with a smile, and they kiss each other on both cheeks. She is dressed in a Max Mara camel silk open sweater with sheer matching low cut blouse that shows just enough of her bosom to gain attention. She wears a matching leopard skirt, a darker matching brown coat draped over her shoulder, delicate gold laced earrings, and matching animal print purse. The dress is unique in that he cannot decide if she is dressed more for elegance or for fun. Either way, he simply enjoys being with her.

"Vanessa, you look elegant as usual. Are you trying to raise my energy levels or whatever? You know it can lead to that blessed curse of love."

"Ryan, *grazie* for the compliment. I'm sure that regardless of how I look, that curse will pass me by. However, I do like to dress up for fun. Don't read too much into it. Everybody expresses the *Blessing of Beauty* in his or her own way. I don't do it to influence anybody one way or another. And you look your dapper self, as usual. I consider it a real treat to have dinner with you three nights this week. Some people would actually accuse us of dating."

"Heaven forbid," he says sarcastically. "If they knew us though, they would know that it's strictly business. No hanky-panky."

"Well, where are we going tonight?"

"I made reservations at La Grotta," He replies. "You must have been there. Tell me about the restaurant."

"Good choice. I love the place. I know the owner. We go way back. It is built into the side of the hill where an old cave existed right under the Donkey Way. It was originally used to store food and wine. As the town evolved, it became a wine shop and now a restaurant. The food is unique. The atmosphere is romantic, with dim lights lining the walls of the cave. Stalactites and stalagmites line up like guards protecting the diners. They have a special wine made from grapes grown near the old church above the Terme."

As they walk to the restaurant, she holds his arm above the elbow tightly and pulls him toward her, to his enjoyment. Ryan uncharacteristically dominates their conversation as he describes the effects of his activities on the energy readings and the discussion with his other participants in his group.

Suddenly, Vanessa stops in her tracks and throws up her arms. "Enough is enough! I prefer not to talk about work all night." She smiles as she looks at him with sincerity, "Let's simply enjoy the evening together."

"Grand idea," Ryan tries to think of another topic and his mind goes blank. Then he says with a grin on his face, "Did you see how the Minnesota Twins are doing this year?"

She asks with a puzzled look, "Who are the Twins? Is that a football team? Is that all you can think of?"

They both laugh together as they cross the Lamone River Bridge and walk towards the Piazza. They pass by the older gentlemen who are still sitting at the small tables of the corner bar. As they walk by, the men look up to see the two of them together again with Vanessa holding Ryan's arm. All five gentlemen in their best shirts, jackets, ties, and hats turn their heads to watch her as they do for every attractive woman that walks by. Then, the face of one of the gentlemen brightens when he recognizes Ryan from the

Senior Center. He shouts out. *"Buona sera, Dottore Reeian. Come state? Vedo che le piace la Dottoressa Venetre. Si?"*

Ryan is embarrassed, not knowing what the man just said, but assumes it had something to do with Vanessa. He replies in his broken Italian and American accent. *"Si, la Dottoressa Venetre e bella e intelligente. Io sono molto fortunato."*

The men laugh at Ryan's comment and are delighted that he is learning some Italian words. They sense that Ryan is a good man. The men discuss the couple among themselves, and conclude that they all hope Ryan gets lucky tonight. They know Vanessa is a good woman and a good match for Ryan.

Vanessa watches the interaction between Ryan and the older gentlemen. She knows that she just received their understated approval to pursue this good man, and agrees that this is a good idea. She hopes that others do not ruin it.

They arrive at La Grotta directly below the arches of the Donkey Trail. They enter the restaurant and Ryan is surprised that it is literally a large cavern built into the side of the selenite cliffs that the town is built on. Friz, the Maître' di and owner, knows Vanessa and the two greet each other with big hugs and kisses on the cheek. He jokes with Vanessa in Italian about their youthful adventures together.

He takes them to a quiet table in the back and brings them menus. The waiter, who is dressed in a casual Armani black shirt with white stripes and a broad collar complimenting his comfortable jeans, comes over and greets them.

"Boun Giorno. *Mi chiamo, Lorenzo."* He recognizes Ryan is American and shifts to English. "Let me review a few of the menu options for you." He goes through the menu, highlighting the house specialties. "And finally, there's *passatelli* with bread, eggs and *Parmigiano* cheese cooked in a clear capon broth and *pasta la carbonara* made of eggs, bacon, pasta, and olive oil."

"Sounds like my energy is going to take a hit tonight," Ryan replies. "I would like to try them all."

"They do have a lot of salads and vegetable options also," Vanessa tries to help him out.

"Si, we have selected locally grown vegetables and salads served with various sauces including a local citrus dressing, oil, lemon and capers, and of course, our well known balsamic vinegar."

"You've got my mouth watering," Ryan responds. "What about dolci? I'm sure you have sweets that will blow the top off of any diet."

"Of course, we have," he says, "You must see our after dinner buffet of desserts. We have exotic fruit skewers, strawberries with warm chocolate sauce and whipped cream, our traditional watermelon, pineapple, and melon, as well as an array of tasty pastries. Can I get you some wine or a cocktail while you decide?

"We'd like the Albana di Romagna," Vanessa replies.

"Yes. Let's have a bottle," Ryan replies proudly remembering the faux pas of ordering only a glass at L'Infinito.

The waiter has an irritated look implying there is no need to tell him to bring a bottle. He always does.

Ryan looks at Vanessa and says, "Thanks for coming with me tonight. This whole trip has been remarkable so far. I feel at home here. My energy feels good. Is it the research, the vacation, or you? You tell me."

"There are many reasons that make you feel good here, the least of which is me. But thanks for including me in your options. You're our special guest and it makes me happy to see you enjoy it. We try to make it special for everyone."

The waiter brings the bottle of wine and pours two glasses.

Vanessa raises her glass and says, "*Salute.* This toast is to you, and maybe, us. I like you too, Ryan. You're a good man. I enjoy being with you. I hope we can spend more time together before you leave."

Vanessa looks at Ryan. She liked him from first moment she saw him. Despite her attraction to him, there are a lot of walls to climb and barriers to overcome. The distance between their homes, the dedication to their careers, and their mutual cautiousness about relationships should be enough to kill any romance. So, she must be patient and let it happen if it's going to happen. He is a good person and will not hurt her intentionally. And, of course, he invited her to dinner again so she knows that there is a mutual attraction. She feels good about lowering her walls for him.

"Thank you, Vanessa. It's mutual," Ryan replies. "I enjoy getting to know you better."

The waiter comes and asks if they have made a selection. Ryan motions to Vanessa to go ahead.

"I'll have the squid and shrimp salad with cherry tomatoes and arugula. Also, please bring some *panigacci* and *formaggio.*"

Ryan orders the homemade pasta with eggplant, zucchini and fresh tomatoes sounds delicious. He continues, "Add the *passetelli* soup and a small salad as an *antipasto, per favore.*"

As they drink their wine, they realize that even though they wanted to avoid discussing work, the participants in Ryan's group were simply too compelling to avoid talking about. Ryan starts them down that path, "Most of the people in my group have major trauma histories and suffer from post-traumatic syndrome. These people are suffering, and a week at the Terme will not solve their problems."

"Yes, that's why we are careful to tell participants that this is not a clinic," Vanessa replies. "We are not treating their problems, but rather measuring their energy levels in response to their daily activities. We don't want all supermen here, but rather, we welcome people with low energy so we can see change. We work with them to strengthen their energy and believe that when they achieve higher energy, it will take them past their traumas and help them achieve the life they want. But that is not our primary goal. We hope each of them has had care for their problems, but if it is only focused on one Realm, it limits their potential for success. Working on all Realms can be powerful and transformational."

"It will be interesting to see how I can apply this to my patients in Minnesota. They are not too dissimilar to the participants here. There's much suffering going on there also."

The comment triggers an anxiety that is just under the surface. "Ryan, I'm still alarmed about the possibility that the killer is among us. What if it's Brian Johnson? Your conversation with him was strange. The police have yet to find him."

Her comment reminds Ryan of the purchase that he saw Johnson making at the hunt and fish shop yesterday. "He is strange," Ryan agrees. "He shows up one day and then disappears. He was creepy. I did see him yesterday when he went into the hunting shop down the street and came out with a wrapped package. I thought if might be a gun."

"A gun!" She yells. "Why didn't you say this earlier?" Her anxiety just stepped up a notch higher.

"As I thought about it, I decided to check out the shop. It was more of fishing shop than a gun shop so I concluded he bought a fishing pole."

"There is no fishing around here, Ryan!" she states loudly. Others in the restaurant look towards their table.

"I didn't know that. Anyway, he is not the killer. He does not match the profile. Do you know if they have any leads on the case in the U.S? Do they know who killed Dr. Killian?"

"Ryan, we cannot rule him out. To me, he looks the part. Who knows! His position was similar to the killer's Manifesto. At least, you should have told me and he should be checked out. And I have not heard a word from the *polizia* here."

"Sorry. I forgot. Who is on the case in the U.S.?" Ryan asks.

"A guy named Steiner from St. Paul was assigned to the case. And the National Institute has assigned a new program officer for our research. I worry about his safety too."

"We should contact them then," Ryan states emphatically.

"Si, and we need to alert them about Brian Johnson," she says. "I will call the *polizia* again."

"I'll also give Julia Stone a call, and see if I can find out more from her. I know she has been interviewed about the murder."

"We need to be proactive if there is even the slightest chance that the madman is in Italy," Vanessa says persistently.

To avoid souring the mood any further tonight, Ryan needs to change the subject. "Agreed. But let's talk about more pleasant things. Tell me about the festival tomorrow night. Can I go with you and Paolo?"

"Of course," she answers pensively and takes deep breath. She needs to calm herself. "The annual festival, called le *Feste Medioevali*, is held during summer weekends in June and July. It's just a big party in the name of historical reconstruction. Those who attend feel as if they're living centuries ago. Everybody dresses up in costumes and mask. You'll meet knights, monks, merchants, bandits, musicians, and entertainers, all of whom act as if they lived in the village 700 years ago. They become a bunch of drunken hooligans, but it is fun."

She takes another deep breath and tips her glass of wine a few times. She also doesn't want to spoil the mood. She continues, "*Le Feste* is somewhere between reality and illusion. The local merchants are there on every street to show off their art, crafts, and antiques. The ancient music of the times is played loud, raucous, and festive. They have theatre and shows. It's very authentic. Sometimes, too much so."

"If there are going to be hundreds of people crowding the streets, maybe it would be just as fun to park ourselves at a restaurant and simply watch the events unfold?"

"This is a seven-hundred-year-old tradition, Ryan," She says passionately. "It's something you immerse yourself in."

Ryan laughs. "Vanessa, I'm not sure it's my cup of tea. I passed my adolescence over ten years ago. But I suppose it could be fun and boost my Emotional Realm."

She is feeling better as Ryan successfully distracted her from the possible threat from Brian Johnson.

"Ryan, don't be such *vecchio ramoscello nel fango!* How do you say in America—a stick in the mud. *Le Feste* averts evil spirits and helps purify the city, thus, releasing health and fertility among its people."

"Now, that makes it sound a lot better to me," Ryan says with a smirk. "We have plenty of evil spirits around, and I would like to try enhancing fertility some."

Vanessa blushes. "Are you flirting with me? We better slow down."

She gives a playful glare, and blushes more.

The meal comes and they eat with great attentiveness to the exquisite salads, breads, cheeses, and pasta. They talk about the rest of the week and what their plans are for Thursday during the day. The conversation has shifted to the jovial and sweet. To those in the dining room, the love is apparent between these two. They cannot get enough of each other. Everything brings laughter and their body language shows a true physical attraction to each other.

As they enjoy their dining experience at La Grotta, Ryan's cell phone rings. He does not know who it is so he excuses himself and answers. That was a big mistake. It is Cicci Beretta on the phone.

"Hello Ryan. This is Cicci Beretta. How are you tonight?"

A wave of panic goes through him, and his heart starts pounding. Why is she calling at this time?

Vanessa notices Ryan's discomfort immediately after he answers the call. She wonders what is wrong.

"Ah, well, hello. Oh, I'm fine."

Cicci replies on the other end, "Good. I was just thinking about you and thought we should get together again. I called to see if you are interested in getting some vino later tonight."

"Ah, well," Ryan stammers. "Thank you for invitation, but I'm pretty busy tonight. Perhaps, another time."

"Oh dat's too bad. Are you with someone?"

"Yes, I'm having dinner with Dr. Venetre. It's about the Terme and the results of the research."

"Oh, maybe I can join you?"

"Well, no, not tonight," he pauses. "Thanks for calling. Ciao."

Vanessa, by now, knows who called. She sits quietly fuming. "Who was that, Ryan?"

Ryan contemplates the best way to handle this. There are lots of land mines in his response. He remembers the *Rules*, and cannot figure out which one applies. He concludes it is best to be honest and direct. This is what any woman expects, as hard as it is to say. Explaining a call from Cicci is a no win situation that will blow up in every possible angle. He might as well take the knife in the chest and reply in the only ethical way out.

"That was Cicci. She wanted to know if I was busy tonight. I told her that I was having dinner with you."

"You know, Ryan. I warned you about her motives. She can be sweet and charming, and very adept at getting the attention and love she needs. She uses her many talents to snare unsuspecting men into bed, and then into their hearts and wallets, with great sophistication."

"I know you warned me. She's not a bad person. She needs to talk to someone. My personality is such that I don't turn away people in need. Even you acknowledged that she needs help. As I said before, I have no interest in her romantically."

"Don't give me that bullshit, Ryan. You gave her your cell number. You would not have done that if you had no interest. *Hai capito?*"

"Not true," Ryan wallows in his guilty-looking innocence. "I gave it to her because she knew about the restaurants in the area, and I told her that I was going to dinner. She is not trying to manipulate me into bed. I resent that you would even suggest it. I can control my desires nicely."

"Come on, Ryan. You can do better than that. Well, I'm done. I'm going home," she screams. The rest of the patrons at the restaurant look at them and confirm that, yes, they are in love.

Then the silent treatment comes, that impenetrable wall of silence that comes with the territory of angry women. They finish their entrees without a word. Vanessa does not look up. The waiter comes and asks if they would like dessert. The waiter picks up the tower of tension looming over their table. He rolls his eyes. He understands that Ryan blew it, and he seems to have no clue about Italian women. He should have simply lied. Ryan looks up at the waiter with an exasperated look, and says with a low, somber voice, "I guess not. *Il conto, per favore.*"

They both slowly get up from the table, avoiding eye contact. He walks her back to the Terme, and the silence gets even denser. The black cloud hangs over Ryan as he wracks his brain trying to think of what to say. Many thoughts race through Ryan's mind. Damn it. He could kill himself for giving Cicci his cell phone. Why on earth did he do that? How would he know that she would call in the middle of dinner with Vanessa?

Perhaps that was her intention. Maybe, she is manipulative. It was such as romantic night, until she called. Damn it. Damn it. Damn it. He is doomed when it comes to women. Vanessa is right. His Spiritual Realm is in the pits, lower than the bottom. Love will pass him by. He simply cannot do it right. He is such a wimp. And she is such a damn challenge! Maybe he should assume the relationship is over and not going to happen. Should he just forget about her?

As they arrive at her apartment, she turns to him and says, "Ryan, if you want to pursue Cicci, go ahead. I don't blame you. She is beautiful, sexy, and knows how to handle men. She has been a victim so long that she knows how to protect herself. I simply do not know how to do that. I'm vulnerable that way. I cannot and will not play games. It's too hard."

As she says this, she desperately tries to hold back her tears. She is surprised and angered by the emotions that Ryan provokes in her. "I'm . . ." She hesitates. "I'm sorry, Ryan. I like you, but I can't put myself at risk. I just can't be hurt again. I don't know what I'll do if that happens. Good bye." She makes it sound final.

As she says this, she avoids eye contact, turns, and marches inside of her apartment. Ryan is trying to say something, anything, but nothing comes out of his mouth. His brain is frozen. As the door is closing, he finally says with the pathetic voice of a mouse, not even loud enough to be heard, "Vanessa, wait. Please wait. I have no interest in Cicci. Zero. Zippo. Niente. Vanessa," his voice trails off slowly as the door shuts close. "I'd never hurt you. I love you."

He stops in his tracks and thinks about what he just said. He has not said those three words since the death of Sophia. Did he really mean it, or did he just want her affirmation and approval. Obviously, it was a desperate plea. But he said it like a wimp. There was no conviction. Why is it so hard to say it if it's in his heart? Is it the truth? How can he love someone whom he's just met? Be real. Or, does he really love her but is afraid of the commitment and the risk. Maybe, it is him who is afraid of getting hurt or afraid of hurting others. Of course, she did not hear him. Did he not want her to hear it? And if she heard it, would she come back to the door? What's wrong with him? Now, he clearly recognizes what wobbling and waffling are. He's living it and it's pathetic. He is the epitome of them. He is sabotaging a potential love, perhaps to avoid commitment, or out of fear that he will get hurt again. He is so confused.

He walks back to his room wallowing in his misery and self-pity. And he even recognizes it. He is so discouraged. He stops on the bridge over the River Lamone and looks up in the lighted sky of a million stars. He expects there's a thousand hearts that feel like his right now. And he hates it. How could he have such high energy today, and then sink so low so quickly? And he doesn't even fucking care. He wants to feel miserable right now. He deserves to be punished for his stupidity.

He now knows how it feels when the energy drains out, the demons take over, and he's back to square one. He could do a booster action of exercise, meditation, or prayer for God's sake, but forget it. He has a lot to learn about life, his energy, failure, and redemption. But now, he only thinks about Vanessa and how he blew it. He doubts that this love will take him anywhere.

As Ryan heads back to his room, the Messenger is watching him carefully from his balcony. Dr. Laughlin can be quite a nuisance. He will not leave Dr. Venetre alone and this makes his task that much more difficult. He needs to be sent a message that if he keeps it up, he will be in danger also.

Chapter 33. The Suspect

Harvard University
Boston, Massachusetts
Tuesday Morning

Dr. Julia Stone has a busy morning planned. It's 8:30 am, and she is scheduled to give the first lecture of the summer course entitled, *Ancient Manuscripts and Their Implications for Health*. She is dressed casually, atypical for Harvard faculty. But she rationalizes that it is, after all, summer. She wears a loose fitting colorful flowered silk blouse, a red sheer scarf around her neck, tight tan dress slacks, and comfortable open platform sandals. As she hustles across Divinity Avenue into the Peabody Museum Hall, she finds students lining up to see her after all of the publicity surrounding the murder of Dr. Killian. There are at least fifty students registered for the class, but today she already has nearly one hundred twenty who have shown up, and there is still fifteen minutes before the lecture.

"Shit," she says to herself. "Just what I needed today. A swarm of paparrazi students trying to snap a shot of my butt for their Facebook pages."

As she prepares the final slides for her lecture, her cell phone rings. She notices that the number is blocked. She hesitates to answer because she's not finished with her slides, but curiosity gets the best of her, and she answers it. "Hello. This is Dr. Stone."

"Dr. Stone, this is John Steiner again. We talked the week of the murder. I apologize for calling you, but we have an urgent matter, and I need some more information."

"Yes, Mr. Steiner," She replies slowly and quietly. "How can I forget? What information?"

"We need to know if you recognize a man who was at the lecture that you attended with Dr. Killian. We have reason to believe that a man by this description boarded a plane to Amsterdam this past Sunday. We want to do what we can to ensure there are no more incidents."

Julia's heart pumps hard, and her energy drops. Dreadful images of the conference go through her mind. Is the killer on the loose in Italy? Who will he kill? Are Vanessa, Paolo, and Ryan safe? She must call Ryan right away, but she has to get through this lecture first. Or, should she cancel the lecture? She regains her composure, realizes that she must go on. "Mr. Steiner, I'd be happy to talk to you, but unfortunately, I have a hundred students waiting in their seats for a lecture from me right now. Can I call you back as soon as I'm done?"

"Certainly, of course. I'm sorry to interrupt you."

"No problem. In fact, we need to do everything we can to get this madman off the streets before he kills again."

"I look forward to your call."

She turns to the slides already on the screen. She is visibly upset, but has to go on. She turns to the students and looks up at them staring down on her, like demons putting her on trial. "Good morning. Thank you for attending *Ancient Manuscripts and Their Implications for Health*. Registration information only notes that fifty people are registered for this course, but I see over a hundred students here. If you are not registered for the course, and are just a curious bystander in the murder mystery of Dr. Jack Killian, I ask you to leave right now. However, if you have a genuine interest in the course, you can stay, but you will need to be registered by the next class session."

About twenty people leave now. The students shuffle out with comments mainly about her appearance. "Yeah, she's a looker with brains." "She's so uptight. I'm getting out of here." "She is nice on the eyes, and the class seems interesting. I may actually register."

The remaining students hear the same introductory lecture that she gave last year. She reviews the goals, rationale, and content of each of the twelve lectures focusing on the wide range of health related ancient manuscripts from the *Bare-Foot Doctors Manual* in China, the *Mayan Madrid Codex* from

Guatemala to the *Bible* and the *Dead Sea Scrolls*. The *Prophecy Scroll* is lecture number eight. She spent the rest of the hour discussing the parallels between ancient and contemporary knowledge and how insightful some texts were despite not having the benefits of scientific methods of discovery. The students seem attentive and interested. She feels an urgency to get back to Mr. Steiner, but at the end of the lecture, she has to answer some questions about the schedule and examinations from a couple of students.

Finally, one of the students asks, "We have heard a lot about the murder of Dr. Jack Killian on the news, and you were the one who was interviewed. Do you know who murdered him?"

At this question, she packs up her bags and says succinctly, "I cannot comment on that at this time. You may want to check with the police. This ends the questions for today. I'll see you next week. Remember, the assignment is chapter one and two of the text."

As the students filter out of the classroom in the front, she leaves out the back exit, and heads to her office. She wants some privacy when she calls Steiner back. There are too many nosy students, and she dislikes being the target of publicity. She also thinks about Drs. Nobili and Venetre, and how distressed they will feel when they find out the killer is in Italy. And then, there's poor Ryan. He's on vacation. The last thing he needs is to be the target of a killer. She should never have told him about the Terme. Once she arrives at her office, she calls Steiner immediately.

"Thanks for getting back to me. How did your lecture go?" Steiner asks, trying to make conversation.

"It was fine until they began asking questions that would have been better answered by you. I gave them all your cell phone number," she says smiling to herself. "I hope you don't mind."

There is a few seconds of silence on the other end of the phone, and then she hears an abrupt, "You didn't."

"No. I'm kidding," she says with a quick laugh. "But the publicity about this case is getting out of hand. I'm tired of it."

"Not funny, Dr. Stone. This is no kidding matter," he says seriously. He sits in his office in the police station with papers cluttered across his desk. "We all get tired of publicity, but we need to manage it. That's part of the job. The reason I called again was that we have reason to believe that the person who murdered Dr. Killian was actually at the lecture that you attended in St. Paul. Have you had any contact with anyone or could recall anyone who acted particularly strange."

"There were a lot of weird people in the room," she says as she braces the phone on her shoulder and organizes the stack of scientific papers that were slightly askew on her desk. She has a penchant for organization and cleanliness stemming from her high energy in the Nature Realm. "I do remember one fellow sitting near the front of the room, not far from me. He asked a number of accusatory questions that Dr. Killian handled quite well. He had a strong jaw, short-cropped blond hair, and an intensity about him that made me a bit uncomfortable. He was reclining back in his chair. No computer. No note taking. No brief case. He was just taking it in. However, there are a lot of eccentric scientists in this field who look dubious and ask pointed questions. It's part of the Socratic method of teaching. This man did ask several questions about the relationship between the manuscripts and the research."

Steiner becomes more interested. "I'm going to text you several pictures of possible suspects. One of the men is a member of the Kolb Foundation's Freedom Group and was registered at the same conference in St. Paul. We identified him by matching names across registrations. But he was also at a dinner honoring Mr. Kolb in New York on that same Sunday evening. How he could be in St. Paul earlier the same day is surprising, and makes him an unlikely candidate, but we need to check him out. The strange thing is that the Manifesto found in Killian's room overlaps with that of the Freedom Group's. I need to know if his face is familiar to you, and if you saw him at the lecture."

"Yes, please send it to me."

Within a few seconds, she switched to her cell phone messaging, and was staring at photographs of three men. She was astonished to see that one of them looked like the blonde gentleman who had attended the conference. The more she studied it, the more she believed it was him. After viewing the photos, she got back on the phone with Steiner. "The second picture is the same gentleman who was asking the questions about the manuscript. Is he a suspect?"

"We do not know quite yet, Dr. Stone, but we're trying to locate him. If you or your colleagues have any contact with him, we appreciate if you would contact me immediately. We did the usual background check and nothing came back. He has no psychiatric history, but those who worked with him said he had some anger management issues. He does have a military background and was a weapons expert. He had lived with his mother in St. Cloud until recently. I called her and she said he was working around the country. She reported that he did attend church regularly. We talked to the clergy there, and they said that Trevick had some kind of religious revelation."

"Do you know where he works now?" She asks.

"He apparently works for the Freedom Group," Steiner replies. "But we can't trace any check deposits. He simply cashes them. The employees who work there vouch for him as a hard worker with strong convictions. We scanned this photograph into our system and matched it with people in the last week that went through security at the major airports. It came up with one match on a plane heading to Amsterdam from Chicago. However, there was no one by his name on the passenger log. "

"Do you suspect that he traveled to Italy? Do you think he might murder the other investigators?" Julia asks. A feeling of dread overcomes her.

"Dr. Stone, we do not like to accuse someone without cause. He is one our suspects, but until we find him, we cannot rule anything out. If you find out anything about him from the people in Brisighella, please give me a call. You have my number."

"Yes, I will. Thanks for calling me," Julia's alarms go off. She needs to call Ryan immediately. She checks her computer to see if Ryan is on Skype. He is not. She notes that it's about 5:30 pm in Brisighella, and he would most likely be out. She calls the Terme and there is no answer. She leaves a message. "This is Julia Stone from Harvard. Please have Dr. Laughlin call me right away. It's urgent."

Chapter 34. The Omen

When he arrives at his room after the disastrous dinner with Vanessa, he sees a message on the floor that was slid under his door. It's from Julia Stone. She said that it was urgent, and to call her right back. A feeling of relief passes over him. It's nice to hear from a woman who is not angry with him. Despite the brief foray at his house and the communication in between, he is fond of, if not quite attracted to Julia. He would love to talk to her. He notices that it is 11:00 pm here in Italy, which means that it is 4:00 pm in Boston. She should be up and about. He dials her cell number. It rings several times before she answers.

"Hello," she says hesitantly since it was a number she was not familiar with.

"Julia. It's Ryan."

"Ryan, what relief! It's been a nightmare of harassment from the media since the murder."

"Sorry, I was out for dinner with Vanessa. I didn't get your message until now. It's good to hear your voice. What's up?"

"Ryan. They have a possible suspect," she says with dread in her voice and a pensive look on her face. She stands next to her desk in her third floor office of Sever Hall, looking out the window at the students walking along the Harvard grounds. "His name is Anton Trevick. He is about thirty years old, tall, muscular, blond hair, and a strong jaw. He has a strange history and recent religious fanaticism. He was at the conference in St. Paul when Dr.

Killian was murdered, and then, on the same night, he was in New York at a Gala where he met his employer, Leonard Kolb. Apparently, he works for Kolb's Freedom Group as a door-to-door political salesman. Someone of his description flew to Amsterdam about the same time that you did. Another thing. The Manifesto document left in Dr. Killian's room and the published goals of the Freedom Group are similar. Steiner fears that the Terme is his next destination."

Ryan is silent. A million thoughts run through his mind, but the only person that sticks in his head is Vanessa. "I'll alert Paolo and Vanessa," he says. "If you can send me a picture of him, I can pass it around. Thanks for calling, Julia. By the way, this is an amazing place and a remarkable project. I've learned much. I feel good here."

"I know how you feel. It was a wonderful experience for me also. A game changer."

"It's late here," Ryan replies. "So I'll call you again after I find out more. It is so good to hear your voice."

They hang up and Ryan sits on the upholstered chair in his room. He is not surprised at this development. He thinks about Brian Johnson. Although the descriptions are different, there are enough similarities to consider him. He needs to talk to Vanessa immediately. He rings her apartment. No answer. He tries again. No answer. Obviously, she is either asleep or she wants to be alone. He decides to go over to her office first thing in the morning.

After a failed attempt at a good night's sleep, Ryan suddenly wakes up with his stomach in knots. His throat is dry and his heart is pounding. Sweat is running down his face. He had been dreaming. Another nightmare. This time, he was being chased through the Festival. There were odd people with grotesque masks yelling at him and a masked man with a sharp knife chasing him. He looks at the clock. It's 5:00 am. His nightmares are returning.

But that should not be happening. Except for last night, he feels good and his energy recordings in most Realms are getting stronger. He feels happier and more at peace. He's been biking, eating well, enjoying himself, helping others, exercising, meditating, and organizing his life. Is he regressing or was it the conflict with Vanessa, the threats from Johnson, or the killer on his way here causing the ill visions? Who was the masked man with a knife, and what does it mean? Was the dream a premonition? Questions run through his head as he drifts in and out of the morning sleep.

After an hour of restlessness, he decides to get out of bed to try to forget about the quandary. He decides to go biking again today. He knows that he'll feel better with the fresh air, the exercise, the beauty of the countryside, and the boost in his energy. He gets dressed, eats a good breakfast, equips himself and takes off on his rented bike.

He climbs the hill above the Terme quickly, trying to shake off the fatigue from his poor night's sleep. He pumps harder and faster as he goes up the hill. When he arrives at the top, he already feels stronger, with more energy. He has no specific destination planned, but the ride is invigorating. His anxiety is dissipating, yet, every few minutes, he looks behind him to see if the man who chased him in the dream is there. He quickly dismisses the action as folly.

He decides to get off the bike and relax at the old stone church at the top of the hill. He walks to the big yard in the back of the church for the best view of the many dark layers of misty Tuscan hills off in the distance. He feels the heat from the morning sun warming his back while the light is brightening the rolling hills in the foreground. He closes his eyes and lies on his back in the grass. He opens them to view the cumulus clouds moving slowly across the blue sky.

He breathes slowly and deeply, and can hear Linda's soothing voice as he steps down the golden stairs to sink deeper into a meditative state. Scenes of the women in his life run by his mind like a movie screen. There's his mother and Sophia talking to him. Then, there is Julia and Cicci. Finally, there is a smiling Vanessa. His mind drifts to the disastrous ending last night. Although her response to Cicci's call was out of line, it was still her natural reaction, perhaps amplified by the wine. He has to rectify it today by apologizing to her as soon as he gets back. He will simply say he's sorry, if that's what she needs or, he will even grovel, if it comes to that. Most importantly, he needs to tell her about Julia's call.

He gets back on his bike and heads down the hill. On his way back, he sees a car coming towards him. Ryan slows down to avoid colliding with it while rounding the corner. He is surprised that the car is moving too fast to make the curves going up the hill. At this time of the morning, it is unusual to see any car, let alone one that is in a hurry.

As the car passes, he looks at the driver. He has a menacing look on his face, but Ryan cannot identify who it is. He looks back to see that the car has stopped. At first, he dismisses it, but then the car turns around and is coming back for some reason. What's he doing? The car speeds up and is driving too fast to stay in control, down the steep decline directly behind Ryan.

Ryan speeds up as he heads down the hill to avoid being overtaken by the speeding car. He recognizes the danger of banking around the sharp turns at too high a speed. If another car comes up around the curve, it would kill him. He slows down to move off the side of the road and let the car pass but the car slows down also and comes within a few feet of him traveling down the narrow winding road.

He cannot make out whom it is. The car appears to be following him and then swerves toward Ryan as it tries to pass. Then the car backs off. Ryan is startled. What the fuck is the driver doing? Did he actually try to hit him? Ryan speeds up and the car picks up speed also. The car is close on his tail again. Ryan pumps at his top speed and cannot stay ahead. The car speeds up and is nearly touching his back tire as they approach the next sharp curve.

Ryan begins to panic as he rides even faster. He knows that he is moving too fast to make the next curve. He quickly thinks through his options and decides he needs to get off the road. To prevent a disastrous crash, he sees a field of grass ahead right at the curve. In a split second, he decides to drive his bike straight off the road and hopefully save himself by tumbling in the soft grass.

The bike goes off the road and he jumps from it, curling up in a ball. His bike careens further down into the gully. He does several rolls on his shoulder and back without hitting a rock. He ends up in the grass and lucky to be alive.

The driver, who Ryan still cannot see clearly, stops on the side of the road, and yells out the window in English, "Serves you right. Stay out of the way. This is your only warning!"

Ryan gets up off the ground, brushes himself off, and checks for injuries. He has a few scratches and bruises, but is more startled than anything. Thank God for helmets. He cannot believe what just happened. The guy appeared to try to kill him. What the hell did he do that for? He gets back on the bike and rides slowly and cautiously to his apartment.

When he arrives, he checks his watch. It's about 8:00 am. He is still quite upset over the incident. He runs up the stairs into the apartment. Before heading to his session this morning, he wants to stop by Vanessa's office and apologize about the call from Cicci and tell her about the call from Julia and the possible threat to his life. He showers, patches his cuts and scrapes, and gets dressed as quickly as possible. He heads over to Vanessa's office before the group session to see if she is there.

He thinks about the incident on his way over, now that he has cooled down. He still is perplexed about why the driver ran him off the road. Maybe, he was trying to scare him, but for what reason? If he was the murderer, why didn't he finish him off? And wouldn't he still be after him? Or maybe, the driver was an angry zombie with low energy trying to taunt bikers to be more careful on the road. Nothing makes sense.

Vanessa's door is open and she's working on her computer. She is concentrating intensely, but looks up as she hears someone approaching. Ryan comes into the office. She stands up to greet him with a sad look on her face. She has dark red eyes, as if she's been crying all night.

He stops across from her desk and says, "Did you hear what I said to you after you closed the door last night?"

"No, Ryan, I didn't," she says with an apologetic voice, looking sincerely into his eyes. "I was too upset to listen, and I'm so sorry. It was uncalled for. I lost my emotional energy so quickly with that phone call. You're right. I know Cicci needs help, and you're so kind to help her. Many people would take advantage of her, but you have such a caring soul and a big heart. The energy in your People and Mind Realms are always high. I know that you're not here for romance. I should have known this, but my energy dropped so fast that I didn't recognize it. What did you ask me?"

"I said that I'll never intentionally hurt you," he said. "Never. And, then, I said something that startled me. I said I love you." He looks at Vanessa, tears welling up in his eyes. He can't help it. The tears have been so long in coming–since he loved Sophia so deeply and then lost her. He cannot hold the emotions in any longer. He cannot deny his need for love. Vanessa is a wonderful soul, and he wants to spend more time with her. He knows that it is premature to say those words, and maybe it will scare her away. But he said it anyways.

She looks at him with a startled expression. They only met on Sunday, and they hardly know each other. They have never even kissed. How could he say this now, this morning? Surprisingly, she feels good to hear it. He is like a long lost soul. Their energies are synchronized. She knew this from the beginning. Could it be love at first sight? Of course not. Is he for real? He cannot be. Furthermore, she has told herself over and over that she will not hurry into any relationship. Let it unfold naturally. So what should she say? It is only 8:30 in the morning. She needs to say something, and not just stare at him like an *idiota con la bocca aperta*, an idiot with an open mouth.

"Ryan, those words are hard for me to hear. I have protected myself so well for the past few years. Then, you come here to the Terme and knock me out of my shell. I don't know what to feel. I'm vulnerable right now. I'm up and down. I'm fearful. I'm not sure what to say. You're a good man. I know you will not intentionally hurt me. But I'm not ready. Let's start again, and I will try to trust you more if you are willing."

He looks directly into her sad eyes with a business-like seriousness. He is not thinking about her feelings right now, but rather considering how to protect her from serious harm. Vanessa immediately detects his emotional change, and her doubt is replaced with anxiety. She forgets her English, "*Tutti bene? Problema, Si? Per que?*" She looks at him with the vulnerability of a little girl.

"Vanessa," he says in a quiet voice with no emotion. Since I left you last night, it's been a steady stream of bad news." He steps around her desk to be closer to her. He tells her calmly, "I talked to Julia Stone last night after I dropped you off. She called urgently, and said they have a suspect. His name in Anton Trevick, and he's got a military background and, supposedly, he's a religious fanatic. It is possible that he is headed here to Italy. The detective on the case, Steiner, doesn't know for sure, but regardless, we need to be cautious and vigilant. He will send a photo of him and we can see if it matches any participant here."

"Oh, *Mio Dio*," she says, alarmed. "We must do something. I need to talk to Paolo."

"On top of that," he explains, "I had a bad dream last night. I was at the festival in the piazza and there was an amazing array of performers making people laugh. An unknown man with a grotesque mask was following me. I ran up to La Rocca to escape. The faster I ran, the closer he got, until I reached the top. Then, he took out a knife and thrust it into my stomach. I lay in shock, bleeding on the floor. I woke up in a panic."

"Ryan, you're not making sense," she says with a shaky voice. "Was this true? Not for real, si?"

"It was a dream, but it was unsettling. Then, listen to this. I went on a long bike ride up into the hills to forget about the dream early this morning. I stopped at the old church on top of the hill to meditate. My mind could only focus on visions of you. On my way back, I passed a car, but could not make out who was driving. I said to myself how strange it was to see a car so early."

"Was this part of your dream?"

"No, this was for real, just a half hour ago. The car turned around and came back towards me driving as fast as he could. I started biking faster and faster. Dangerously fast. Then, as he got close to me, he drove me right off the road. I don't know what the hell he was doing, but Vanessa, he threatened and maybe tried to kill me."

Vanessa falls back into her chair. Ryan sits down on the desk.

"Was it Dr. Killian's murderer?" She asks.

"I don't know. Maybe, I'm just getting paranoid. Why would a killer travel all the way to Italy to murder a physician he doesn't even know. It doesn't make sense."

Vanessa's voice is shaking, "Ryan, are you sure? Maybe, he was just looking at the scenery and didn't see you. Did he say anything?"

"Yes, he did. He stopped on the road and yelled to stay out of the way. I don't know if he recognized who I was. I had my helmet on. It was so strange. He sounded volatile with very low energy."

Vanessa's face goes white. Her heart beats fast and her mind goes blank. All she can feel is a shaking anxiety. He pulls her up with her arms and holds her tight.

"Oh, *Mio Dio*, Ryan. What should we do? I'm afraid. I'm worried about those who are here. Remember the mass murderer in Norway? He could kill us all." She grabs the cross around her neck and says a little prayer. "*Mio Dio. Per favore*, save us from this monster."

Ryan holds her tightly as he thinks through the situation and what should to be done. "Don't overreact," Ryan says trying to be calm. "We don't know for sure whether Anton Trevick is here or not. They don't even know if Trevick is the killer. And we don't know if Brian Johnson is involved in any way. I know Johnson's past comments and the package he carried out of the shop do incriminate him, but we just don't know. We don't want to be misled or be unprepared. We need to call Steiner and ask him to find out who Brian Johnson is. If he doesn't exist, we're in trouble. There are most likely a thousand Brian Johnson's near New York or Chicago. It will be hard to track him down. We also need to call the police again and find out if they know anything."

"I'll talk to Paolo and the police," Vanessa replies. "If he tried to kill you, I assume there is sufficient grounds to bring him in if we can find him."

"Should we still go to the Festival tonight?" Ryan asks.

"I don't know. It's important to show up. It's the big opening night for the participants. Let's play it by ear. I'll talk to Paolo."

"Be alert, Vanessa. Don't do anything alone. Stay with the staff and the participants. Okay?"

"Thanks, Ryan. I do feel better with you here. You're like an angel sent from heaven to help us."

Chapter 35. The Doubt

BRISIGHELLA, ITALY
THURSDAY AFTERNOON

Ryan spends the morning with his group, documenting his energy readings and log, and cautiously goes about town helping his senior friends and finishing his writing and ceramic projects. By afternoon, he's calmed down. When he gets back to his apartment at about 5:00 pm, he calls Vanessa. "Hi. I'm just checking in about the Festival tonight. Are we still going?"

"I talked to Paolo and he indicated that we should not change our plans until some firm evidence arises. It will be busy with lots of people around. Company breeds safety. So, we should all go, but we still need to be cautious."

"Okay. I'm just checking. What time should I come over?"

"I'll be ready in forty-five minutes. It'll be fun." Ryan says with some doubt in his voice.

"It sounds like you don't want to go," Vanessa probes, "Don't go if it's not for you."

"No, no. It's not that. I want to go, especially with you and Paolo. It's just that I talked to Julia Stone in Boston again this afternoon. She was in touch with Steiner again. I'll tell you more when I get there."

'Do we have a killer on the loose in Italy or not?" She asks.

"It's not good news," He says quietly. "I'll be over at seven. We can talk."

Ryan showers and gets dressed. He thinks about the dream he had last night, the bike accident, Trevick and Johnson, and about Julia and Vanessa. What is he doing here? For safety sake, he should stay home tonight, or better yet, leave the Terme early. But how could he leave Vanessa, Paolo, and the Terme when they need him most. The Festival sounds fun despite his dream. He shakes his head. He does not have to control everything, particularly since he has little control right now anyway. Go with the flow.

Ryan decides to wear his jeans and an untucked white short sleeve dress shirt that has embroidery along the front buttons. He walks across the Terme courtyard to Vanessa's apartment. The sun has set and dusk is bringing a mask of darkness over the distant hills. The streets of Brisighella are coming alive with the noise from *le Feste*. The sun setting on the old stone buildings gives an eerie look to the town.

He can hear the revelers whooping it up in the village, singing and shouting. He does not like crowds, particularly if they have been drinking too much. Still, he is curious about *le Feste* and the raucous and lively atmosphere that it generates. He has been to medieval festivals several times, and enjoyed the re-creation of fun and games of that historical time period. He also admits that he ate and drank too much while he was there. He needs to avoid that tonight to maintain his energy, but he plans on stopping short of being a complete teetotaler.

He walks over to her apartment. She lives in one of the old historic buildings, just above the Donkey Way. She can see the clock tower off her kitchen and the bedroom upstairs.

When he knocks on her door, Vanessa opens it with a big smile. She's dressed casually with blue embroidered jeans, leather flat shoes, and a white silk blouse with colorful embroidery across the front, ruffled sleeves, and a broad collar. She skips the formality of kissing both cheeks, and gives him a long hug–longer than expected, to Ryan's pleasure.

He walks into the apartment and is impressed by how beautifully restored the two-century old building is. There is an old fresco painted at the top of the curved walls that extends onto the arched ceilings. She has decorated it with modern colorful furniture to suit her taste.

"Well, my Dr. Laughlin. Are you ready for a fun evening?" She laughs as she closes the door behind him. He notices that her usual composure and caution is gone. "So, Dr. Ryan, what's your big news from the States? Did they catch the killer?"

"No, but they identified the main suspect while he was going through the airport. Julia sent me a picture. Here, look at this!" He shows Vanessa the picture on his phone.

"His name is Anton Trevick," he continues. "And he may be in Italy right now. There appears to be a little resemblance to Brian Johnson. Don't you agree?"

"Brian Johnson? Nope. That's not him. We know Brian won't be a problem." She giggles, "He's just a surly teddy bear."

"What do you mean a teddy bear?" He says defensively. "Get serious. He could be a cold-blooded killer. We don't know for sure."

"Oh, then, we can just blow 'em away," she laughs uncontrollably. "That'll get rid of him." She continues to laugh.

"Vanessa. Did you have some wine before I got there?"

"Oh, just one of those half bottles. I had to get in the mood for *le Feste*. We all do that. Can I offer you some?"

"I suppose. But just a little. Someone has to be alert."

She pours him a big glass of red wine. He sits formally, like a teenager, on the contemporary, dark red Morano sofa. She comes over, hands him the wine, and snuggles up close to him.

"Have you changed your mind about going to *le Feste*?" He asks. "Do you still want to go with a mad man on the loose?"

"Well, Dr. Laughlin. You'll save me, won't you?" She laughs as she puts her arms around his neck and looks him in the eyes.

Although he has known her so briefly, he has yet to see this new side of her. How much wine did she have? He responds, "Ah. Yes, of course. You know that I have a second job as a trained bodyguard," he smiles. "And I'll save you, if you save me here at the Terme."

"Of course, I'll save you right back, my darling doctor. As long as you don't wander too far away," she says laughing. "Or get caught in a web by Cicci, the gun!"

"Well, then. We're all set. We will watch each other's backs." He drinks a large gulp of his wine. He realizes that he needs to loosen more to match Vanessa's energy.

"It's glorious," she says. "The age of chivalry is not dead. My knight in shining armor is here." She raises her glass and says, "*Salute*. Cheers to Ryan, my handsome, sweet, and, sometimes too serious doctor. Here's so we won't all get killed." She laughs and finishes her glass.

Ryan does the same. He's beginning to feel a little less worried about the evening. Go with the flow, Ryan. Then, he says with a more cavalier attitude, "I don't expect Brian and Anton, or whatever his name is, to do anything at a busy festival. And if he does, we'll just have to kick his butt. And we'll have fun doing it."

"I called Paolo earlier, and he is going," she says. "He doesn't fear any of them. He also needs to have some fun and be there for the participants."

They leave the apartment with Vanessa holding Ryan's arm. They walk the few blocks to the piazza and are both laughing at nothing. Their mood is one of nervous giddiness from the tension and wine. When they approach the top of the stairs that descend from the Donkey Way towards the piazza, she stops them. They stand in the archway overlooking the town and can see the festivities going on.

She doesn't say a word as she watches them for a few seconds. Then, in a serious tone, she says, "Actually, Ryan, I'm kind of worried. Maybe, I'm getting paranoid, but now that I'm out here, I keep thinking about creepy guys who might be watching me." Then, she says with more alarm in her voice. "I know he's after me. Why wouldn't he be? I'm one of the main investigators of the study. He killed our Program Officer. It just hit me, Ryan. I'm so totally screwed." Tears well up in her eyes and she holds his arm tight. She looks at him, waiting for him to come up with some explanation for why they should continue to *le Feste*. She does not get it from him.

Ryan states, "Frankly, I'm not sure we should go. First, I get that ominous call from Julia. Then, I have this bizarre nightmare being stabbed at the festival. A maniac who runs me off the road and now, we even have a picture of the murder suspect. This day does not have good energy any way you look at it. We may want to just go up to L'infinito, have some wine, pasta, and salad, and let the night be a quiet one. What do you think?"

"But I can hear the excitement at *le Feste*," Vanessa says. "It's pulling me there. I want you to see it, but my common sense is pushing me away from it. Do you think he's around?"

"Brian's around. And if he is Anton, he is here for a reason. The *polizia* have to find him. Are they looking for him? How do you feel about being bait?"

"Bait? What do you mean? I don't want to be bait. That makes up my mind. There is no way I want to be bait. I don't want to go."

"I agree. It's too dangerous. What about Paolo?"

"I'll call him. He'll understand."

"Let's at least walk by the festivities so I can get a glimpse of the excitement. That will be enough for me."

"Let's hope that it will not be the end of us." She says pessimistically.

Chapter 36. Le Feste

Ryan and Vanessa walk arm in arm to the piazza. The streets are filled with vendors, in a packed open market, organizing their tables to sell their wares. There are antiques, toys, and trinkets; ancient, used, and new books and magazines; beautiful artwork, ceramics from the local artisans; practical household products; fine wines and spirits; and enticing Italian foods including olive oils, *prosciuttos*, *formaggios*, *panes*, *bicottis*, and nearly anything that would sell, on display to peruse. There are games, palm reading, tarot cards, and crystal ball gazing to lure tourists in and predict their future. The performers, jugglers, orators, and singers with colorful makeup and clothes from the era, are preparing for their shows tonight. Exotic dancers with revealing costumes and alluring masks are setting up their stages.

There is a growing crowd of revelers and drunken villagers walking up and down the streets, laughing and yelling, excited to see what adventures are in store for them. The loud and raucous music almost hurts the ears, with a mixed bag of musical sounds from accordions, recorders, horns and trumpets.

The scene, as intriguing as it is to Ryan, is too reminiscent of his nightmare. He is glad they've decided to settle into a more tranquil evening. They walk up the Donkey Way and cautiously tread down the dark winding path to L'infinito. The view from the hill overlooking the town is eerie. The sky is darkening and the clouds are moving fast across the sky. The full moon is slipping in and out of the dark clouds to faintly light their walk. The distant festival noises, the bright moon, the cool evening, the ominous three towers, and a mad man on the loose all tighten their stomachs and sends shivers up their spines.

They arrive at the restaurant safely. Maria Theresa greets them on this wild Thursday night. She stares at Vanessa with forlorn look on her face, wondering why she is here at her *restorante* during *le Festeis* opening night. When she sees Ryan, she understands. She gives them both a kiss on each cheek and then gives Vanessa a hug.

"My somber-looking friends, you're worried. You should be at *le Feste*. It's opening night, and so much fun. It will liven you up."

"Maria. Si. Si. I know," Vanessa says with quiet concern in her voice, and not wanting to get into it with her. "Ryan and I decided to get a quiet dinner together before we consider heading down there."

"Of course, I can set up the most romantic table outside."

"Can we sit inside tonight? I'm a bit chilled."

"Vanessa, *che cosa?*" Maria detects her low energy. "What's wrong? You're so upset."

Vanessa could not hold back. She starts to sob uncontrollably, and hugs Maria even harder.

Maria looks at Ryan with suspicious eyes. "*Che cosa hai fatto?*" Maria states sternly.

Ryan looks back with a 'Who me?' expression.

"Maria, no, no, no. *Mia vita*! My life is in danger. Ryan is simply helping me. *Un uomo pazzo*. A crazy man is here in Brisighella, and he wants to kill us."

Maria says with a flip of her hand in the air. "There are many crazy men here. I could not even name all of them. I'll start with the A's. There's Adriano, Alesandro, Aldo, Alfonso. Then the B's. Bernardo, Bruno, Benno. I could go on. All of them, *pazzesco*, crazy."

Vanessa interrupts, "No, seriously, Maria. It's not them. I know they are jerks. There is a guy from the States who murdered an officer of the National Institute of Health because of the research we are doing here. And now, we find out that he may be here in Italy. We are convinced that he is out to murder us."

"*Impossibile, mi amore. Chi è questi uomo?* Who is responsible for this?"

"We don't know. We are hiding out here for the evening. We're afraid."

"No problema. I will send my friends, Mario and Giuseppe, to check this guy out. What does he look like?'

"You are so kind, Maria, but this is in the hands of the *polizia* now."

"Polizia do nothing! They are just *bambini* fulfilling their government obligations. Vanessa, we need to take this into our own hands. Do you have a photo?"

Ryan opens his cell phone and shows the picture of Trevick to Maria.

"Please text this to my phone," Maria states emphatically. "Don't you worry, we will find this bastard. This guy is dead meat."

Ryan is taking this all in. He sends her the picture, and then smiles to himself. He knows this is not funny, but it seems like he's in the middle of an Italian mafia movie right now. Does this truly happen in modern Italy? Can she help them? They need to try anything, and Maria must have experience in this kind of thing. He looks at Vanessa to see if she is serious.

"Let's feed you," Maria puts her arm around Vanessa and sits them down at a nice table in a quiet corner inside. An open wine bottle was prepared for them. "You just sit. I make you feel better." She smiles at Ryan. Then, she sits down with the two, pours three glasses of wine, and explains how food can get rid of whatever ails you. "You're both physicians so you must know about the four humours of the body. These are the principles followed by most of the physicians, healers, and intellectuals of the middle ages to treat illness. Much of the knowledge has been lost by our modern medicine but the chefs here still pass it down through the generations."

Vanessa nods in agreement. Ryan looks puzzled and asks, "I'm not familiar with that system of health. The four humours?"

"Ryan, you need to know this. *Sei un medico, si?*" She asks.

Ryan nods affirmatively and listens intently.

She continues, "All things, man, animals, the four seasons, planets, everything exists under the effects of the four humours. These are like the spirits that inhabit the body. They are melancholy, choler, phlegm, and blood. We are all influenced by the bodily presence of these humours. An excess of any one of them can affect your personality, your feelings, and your behaviors. Right now, you and Vanessa are under the influence of melancholy and choler."

Ryan is bewildered by this conversation, but he says, "Okay, tell me more."

"Melancholy has the properties of cold and dry, and is linked to the God Saturn," she explains. "If you have melancholy, you'll be prone to delusions, depression, and heightened sensitivity. Then, you need *loveth and desyre* to cure it."

"I can see that," Ryan smiles to himself and nods seriously. He is now much more intrigued by the conversation. "Continue, *per favore. Molto interesante.*"

"*Parle Italiano?*" She asks.

Ryan quickly replies, "Oh, no, no. Just practicing. Please continue."

"Choler is a hot and dry condition, and is ruled by Mars, the God of War. It makes you unkindly, wrathful, and unstable. Phlegm is a cold and moist condition, and part of the Moon Goddess. It induces laziness and slothfulness. These people are often affected by obesity and choked in extremities. Blood is a hot and moist condition that is ruled by Venus. It is characterized by heat, quick tempers, and passion."

"How do you treat these conditions?" He asks curiously, raising his eyebrows. "Is it all cured through *loveth and desyre?*"

"No, no, *stupido!*" She laughs. "Are you sick in the head?"

The waitress brings them their food. They did not even order yet, but Maria knew exactly what they needed.

"These four humours are influenced by food, of course," she continues. "In the medieval days, cooks were advised by physicians to prepare foods that were properly balanced with these four humours for each patient. It's similar to balancing the nutrition from our four food groups. For example, fish, which are cold and moist, need to be served with spices or sauces that are hot and dry to prevent excess phlegm humour. Eating foods that are properly balanced makes you feel better. It can be a cure-all for whatever ails you. You heard the expression, 'you are what you eat.' The four humours explain this. All of our menus are arranged with the light foods first, heavier foods later. They all need to be spiced and prepared to treat whatever excess of humour is present. Now, both of you are melancholy, so you need to stay away from leeks, onions, and garlic."

"What about the *loveth and desyre* part?" Ryan asks trying to shift the mood away from the impending threat. "Should we follow that?"

Vanessa looks up and, then, stares at Ryan with the evil eye.

"Si! You need a lot of that," she says with a smile, and quickly adds, "But leave that for after dinner. This food will make you better now."

Maria pours their wine, and they spend the rest of the evening drinking the wine, eating specially prepared pasta, roasted vegetables, and salad to heal their souls. They are not surprised to find they are both more relaxed, and actually back to laughing and smiling, despite the circumstances.

"Maria, you're a culinary genius," Vanessa says. "I do feel much better now. *Grazie.*"

"And better yet, you two romantics, this is *complimentaria*. You heal your way, and I heal mine. They both work. You take care. And don't worry about the *uomo pazzo*. Mario and Giuseppe will try to find this guy. Nobody threatens my friends." She pauses for a few seconds and then says, "Oh, and don't forget your second course of healing. *Loveth and desyre* is dessert and will top off the night. That's my prescription for both of you."

They smile as she leaves to take care of her other guests. "I like her philosophy, Vanessa," Ryan nods with a smile. "She is quite a talented and insightful lady. But I wouldn't want to be on her bad side."

They sit alone for a few minutes listening to *le Feste* going on and wondering what is happening amidst the crowd. They are glad they are here and not there.

Le Feste is the wild event of the season and lasts for several nights. The first night brings out the crazies. Most people are dressed in costumes and running run through the crowd.

Paolo and his wife, Roberta, are walking down towards the streets of Brisighella dressed in jeans and colorful matching shirts, but wearing no masks. They choose to be observers tonight rather than participants. They understand the potential danger with a killer loose, but they are walking together with several Terme staff for safety. As they do every year, they love the festival atmosphere. Yet tonight, they are cautious enough to study each person carefully, being particularly suspicious of anyone with a mask. But the crowd is increasing in size and rowdiness and there is lots of pushing and shoving from drunken revelers.

As their group enjoys more of the free flowing wine, they gradually lose their caution. They are increasingly swept up in the excitement and activities of *Le Feste*. They examine the wares for sale, watch the performers with their magical talents, and listen to the ancient music. It is as classic and authentic a medieval festival as they have in all of Europe.

An exotic dancer, dressed in long flowing brightly colored silk scarf loosely covering a bikini top and blossoming pants, comes up to Paolo. She weaves a dance around him while looking up at him with the mask of a colorful peacock. She then disappears in the crowd. They watch a ropewalker practicing his juggling and flame swallower startling the audience. Women are running and screaming in the delight of being caught by young, masked men. Accordions, bells, and drums are playing in the background.

The streets are so crowded with villagers and tourists drinking and laughing that the crowds move as one up and down the streets. There is a lot of pushing and shoving. One masked reveler runs into Paolo, and shoves him. He feels a sharp pain in his arm where he was pushed. He doesn't think anything about it, and continues to walk through the crowd, enjoying the entertainment, food, and wine.

Within the hour, Paolo notices that his arm is sore and swollen. His mouth is dry and he's become more fatigued. He complains to Roberta, "Carissimola, I don't feel well. I must have eaten something bad tonight. The crowd, noise, wine, I don't know. It all seems to have gotten to me. We should think about leaving soon."

As they slowly make their way through the crowd, he tells her that his mouth is dry and he needs some water. His chest tightens, and he is having difficulty breathing. He stops in the street for a moment to catch his breath. He feels nauseous and holds his stomach. His head begins to spin and feels dizzy. He staggers forward and, then, falls to the ground moaning. He begins to lose consciousness.

Roberta screams in a panic, "*Per favore! Aiutami! Aiutami! Per favore!*"

A crowd gathers around, and a doctor steps out of the crowd and says, "*Io sono medico.* Please give us room." He checks Paolo's pulse and breathing.

His breathing is shallow and pulse is rapid. The doctor is surprised and says, "*Non lo so cosa sta accadendo!* I do not know what is happening!"

They call the paramedics who arrive quickly. Paolo, lying on the ground, twitches and jerks uncontrollably. Roberta tells the doctor that he does not have a history of a seizure disorder. The doctor opens his airway and starts CPR and continues until the paramedics arrive.

The paramedics get a stretcher, and quickly transport him into the ambulance with Roberta. The lights and siren sound as they take him to the nearest hospital, in Faenza. The crowd is stunned, but eventually disperses.

Ryan and Vanessa are leaving L'infinito and hear the disturbance at the edge of town. They walk over to where the crowd is leaving. They ask one of the people what happened.

"Dr Paolo was ill. He went into a seizure. He did not look good. They took him to the hospital."

Vanessa and Ryan stare at each other, and cannot speak. A moment later, Vanessa calls Roberta on her cell phone.

"Roberta, *Cos'è successo?* What happened?"

Ryan watches Vanessa. Tears come to her eyes. Then, as she listens to Roberta, she begins to cry uncontrollably.

She turns to Ryan and says in an uncontrolled sob, "Paolo's dead. He died on the way to the hospital. They think he was poisoned." She hangs up and can't stop crying. Ryan holds her securely in his arms. It has been a bad day. They hurry back to the Terme, paranoid that they are next. If he was killed, Vanessa has no doubt that her life here at the Terme is in serious danger. If this is the case, the question is not if, but when, will the killer strike again.

Chapter 37. The Departure

Vanessa and Ryan hurry back to her apartment. Paolo is dead. The killer is here in Brisighella. Vanessa knows that she is next. She needs protection. When they arrive, she insists that Ryan come in. Vanessa heads to the kitchen and pours herself a glass of wine. The kitchen is small, but has a brick fireplace on one side and pans hanging down from the long aged wood mantle. There is a solid antique wooden table in the middle with four chairs. The large window in the back door of the kitchen shows a small *terrazza* and a stunning view of the three towers. She offers a drink to Ryan, who turns it down. He expects he will need all of his wits and calm.

She sits down at the table and drinks her wine. Ryan pulls out a chair and sits down. He places his warm hand on hers. She looks at him with a drawn face and creases in the middle of her forehead. She is overwhelmed with fear for her own life and riddled with guilt about Paolo's death. "Ryan, I should have been there. I could have saved his life. I can manage a seizure. How could this happen? Who would do this?"

"Don't make assumptions. We don't know how he died. They'll do an autopsy. Call Roberta again to find out what happened. Just in case, we need to think about our own safety."

She dials Roberta again on her cell phone and Roberta answers, knowing it is Vanessa calling. "Roberta. I'm so sorry! Do they know what happened yet?"

Roberta is crying, but tries hard to regain her composure. "Vanessa, *Ascolta*! Listen to me! They did some blood tests and evaluated his status."

Roberta hears Vanessa crying. "*Ascolta*! Listen! Vanessa!" She yells at her on the phone, "The seizures weren't natural. They believe a needle stick of a fast-acting nerve agent, Sarin, or some derivative of it poisoned him. It was in his blood. He told me that he felt a sharp pain in his arm when someone in the crowd pushed against him. The arm got sore over the next hour."

Roberta has known Vanessa and her family for most of their adult life. They are close family friends. Their parents knew each other. Both Paolo and Roberta consider her to be like a daughter. They have always been protective of her and have helped direct her education and training as a physician. She says to Vanessa in a serious demanding tone, "Vanessa! *Ascolta*! You must get out of town. You're vulnerable here. It's possible that the killer is after you too. It was fortunate that you did not come to *Le Feste*. You may be dead too."

Ryan watches Vanessa. A look of horror comes over her face. She is in a panic, breathing with short quick breaths. "Okay, Okay, Roberta. *Si! Si! Andiamo adesso. Si. Grazie. Grazie.* I'm so sorry about Paolo. I wish I could hug you right now."

Roberta responds seriously, "Vanessa. *Vai! Vai!* Go! Is there someone who could go with you? Someone who could help protect you? Who could watch your back?"

She looks at Ryan and her face goes pale. She wipes the tears from her eyes, and says to Roberta, "Si. Ryan Laughlin. He will come with me. We'll go to Rome and stay with Gabriela. We'll call the *polizia*—again."

"*Bene!*" Roberta says. "You simply cannot be alone at this point. You need protection. Vanessa, please take care of yourself. I love you, and I could not bear to lose anyone else dear to me. *Ciao, ciccia bella.*"

Vanessa shifts from frantic to serious. She looks Ryan directly in his eyes with a face of resolve. "They suspect that Paolo was poisoned and died from the seizures. We need to call the *polizia*. Also, I'm sorry, but I need someone to come to Rome with me. I cannot be alone right now. There are many protests going on there now, but the big city will make us hard to find. This maniac is not only crazy, but also smart. He knows chemical compounds, and is under cover. We still do not know who he is. I may be next. I need to disappear. Are you in or out? Do I need to find someone else? I cannot be alone."

Ryan thinks a moment, "Yes, of course, I will come. As I said before, I'm here to help you. We need to think this through. We do not want to put you at risk. Who else can help? What about Maria's friends?"

She puts her hands to her mouth pensively praying. "No, no, you can't come. I will get one of my friends. Yes, Maria. This maniac may kill anybody who supports the research, including those who are helping with the manuscripts. You may be at risk too. You should not come. Maria can get her friends."

Ryan says defiantly, "No, I'm coming. I'm here. I will stick with you all of the way. Your work is important. It must go on. I have no fear," he says to assure her, despite the conflicting thoughts running through his mind. This vacation is turning into a nightmare.

She flashes him a taut smile, knowing that she would prefer having Ryan with her than anyone else right now. She shifts her thoughts. "I need to warn Gabriela, and the scholars, before the killer finds them," she says. "You call the *polizia* and I'll call Gabriela. Since you're an American, maybe they will pay more attention to you."

Vanessa stands up from the table and looks out onto the *terrazza* while she dials Gabriela Gaetti's number in Rome. She answers, "Gabriela. This is Vanessa. I'm so sorry to call you so late. A terrible tragedy has occurred tonight. Dr. Nobili is dead. He had a seizure last night at *le Feste di Brisighella*, and the lab report found that he died from poisoning. We can't believe it."

"Where are you? What happened? How could this have occurred? Who did this?"

"It may be the same killer who murdered Dr. Killian, our program officer. He may be here in Brisighella. We do not know if he is a someone attending the Terme or not."

"Vanessa, are you safe? You must get away from there. Come and stay with me. We can discuss what to do next. I need to alert the Pope and his inner circle to make them aware of this threat to us all."

Vanessa turns away from the window in the door and paces across the kitchen. "What about the protests in Rome. Is it safe there? Its sounds like its crazy scene on the streets."

"Don't worry about that. You know Italians. They love to protest and make noise. Then they make love."

"I don't know what to think or do right now. I'm in danger here. I need to go somewhere. I can't imagine continuing on without Dr. Nobili. How can I? He is the brains, the heart, and the soul of this research."

"Vanessa, listen carefully!" Gabriela says clearly. "I know you and the research. As much as I love Paolo, you're as much the heart and soul of this project as him. You do most of the teaching. Right now, the world needs this research and its knowledge. You need to continue no matter what. Be strong, and most importantly, be safe. We cannot afford to lose you. Is there anyone there who can help you?"

She looks at Ryan sitting at the wooden table talking on the phone to the *polizia*. "I have a very kind doctor visiting here from United States who insists on coming along. His name is Ryan Laughlin. He's here for the research and a vacation. Ha! What a vacation! He's not a typical American. He is willing to come with me. And he's sweet."

"Good. You simply cannot be alone at this point," Gabriela says emphatically.

Vanessa pauses to think about Gabriela's last comment. She cannot be alone. Thank God for Ryan.

"I understand," Vanessa says. "*Che macello! Che macello!* What a mess! What should we do about our current research participants? How can we ensure that our staff, our participants, and the scholars are safe? I'm worried about your safety also, Gabriela."

"Vanessa, don't worry about me. We are not the target of the killer right now. You are. You need to get out of there. Now!" She yells. "Pack your things and come here first. We'll figure things out. Your staff are excellent, and they can push on until they find the killer."

"Okay. Thank you, Gabriela. You're a dear friend. I will talk to you later. I will be on the first train out tomorrow. It goes through Florence."

She hangs up and turns to Ryan. "What did the *polizia* say?"

"I talked to the chief detective there, a Francois Legrand. The *polizia* are all over the Terme. Listen to this!" He pauses to be sure she hears. "Linda found a document in the Great Hall and gave it to the *polizia*. They did not release the content, but is titled the Manifesto. It confirms that Paolo was murdered, and the killer may be anywhere. It may be Brian Johnson, or somebody else. LeGrand wants to talk to us as soon as possible, tonight or the first thing in the morning."

"Come with me. We need to make plans," She stands up and walks into the *soggiorno*, the traditional sitting room of her apartment. She sits down on the bright red sofa and Ryan follows. Both are anxious and exhausted but can not handle a detective from the *polizia* grilling them right now. And, despite their desire to sleep, they are too wired to do so. Vanessa turns to Ryan and takes his hand. She says, "Ryan, you're very kind to help me now.

Thank you. I don't want to be alone. Will you please stay with me tonight? I have an extra room you can stay in. It's clean and comfortable. I have some pajamas you could wear. Are you okay with that?"

"No problem," he says with an odd déjà vu. He remembers the night Julia slept with him after a similar threat. There must be some type of synchronicity in the energy that can explain this, but he has no clue right now. "We can swing by and get my things from my room tomorrow on the way out of town."

Vanessa stands up and walks up the old wooden stairs to show Ryan the guest room. He follows curiously. She walks into a small room on the second story with a view of the clock tower.

"You have a nice place here, Vanessa. How long have you lived here?'

"I moved in three years ago, after I went through the divorce. I did some remodeling and upgrades to restore the original rooms and frescos. The *terrazza* is my favorite place. Look!" she points to the tall window. "The sun comes through right there and keeps me warm all winter long."

He looks out the window into the *terrazza* below and the clock tower above. There is a large wall of stunning white selenite stone face that rises five meters above the old clay tiles of the *terrazza*. The accent lighting on the wall displays the richness of the selenite rock. She has potted flowering plants and several weather tarnished Italian statues dispersed about the space. He is impressed with the natural beauty of it all.

"The sheets are clean and the bathroom is off the room to the right. I will be downstairs if you need me."

Ryan stays in the room and prepares for bed. Just like he did with Julia, he needs to go with the flow. Keep her calm and stay on track. Say good night and go to bed. If she needs him, she'll come and get him.

After getting dressed in the faded blue cotton pajamas pants, apparently made for the shorter Italian men, and his white t-shirt, he walks back downstairs and over to Vanessa's bedroom. He knocks on the door and she answers, wearing a long flowing white nightgown under a robe that is untied and left slightly open. Her hair flows over the robe and frames her olive skinned face. Ryan is struck with her beauty and sensuality. She notices his gaze and fastens the robe to cover her body. Her eyes are swollen, teary, and red. He sees a vulnerability and gentleness about her that was difficult to see previously through her academic shell.

"*Escusame*," Ryan says. "I just wanted to say good night. If you hear anything during the night, call for me and I will come down. We need a good night's sleep. *Buona notte*."

She does a quick scan of him wearing the short pajama pants that belonged to Vanessa's ex. She smiles and says, "They don't fit, do they?"

"They're fine," he quickly replies. "How are you feeling?"

"I'm a little better now. I'm just happy to have you here. Thank you, Ryan, for being here." She turns to go to bed, and then turns back to say, "I really don't like how you look in those pants. Reminds me of my ex. He was too short."

They go to their respective rooms, close their doors, and go to bed. Ryan turns his light on and looks up at the ceiling. He is exhausted, but can't sleep. After a few minutes, he turns the light off. He is restless and only doses on and off. In the middle of the night, he hears footsteps coming up the stairs. The solid wood floor squeaks as she walks closer to his room and opens the door. He pretends that he is asleep. She lifts up his covers and quietly slips into bed with him.

Ryan says nothing and stays still with his eyes closed. He smiles to himself that this is the second time in a month that a beautiful woman has crawled into bed with him. Perhaps, his life may be turning around. That is, of course, if he does not get killed in the process. She gets close to him, and he pretends to wake up. He puts his arm around her and pulls her close.

"I'm sorry. I can't sleep. I'm worried. I need company," she says quietly.

"No problem. Just relax. You're safe here."

He holds her tight and kisses her head, recognizing the subtle Fendi fragrance of Vanessa's perfume. He is surprised that it's one of the same fragrances that Sophia enjoyed. Vanessa's soft skin and the warmth of her embrace help him relax. She quickly falls asleep in his arms, exhausted from the day. He stays awake for a while as he feels the arousal from holding her so close. He dreams about making love to her, but doesn't act on it. Is this the best or the worst fortune? He can't decide.

After a restless sleep, Ryan wakes with Vanessa snuggled close to him. A cell phone is ringing. He lets it continue until it stops. Then, a few seconds later, it rings again. Vanessa is still sleeping soundly.

Ryan slowly sneaks out of bed and answers it quietly, "Hello. This is Dr. Laughlin."

"*Ciao!* This is Francois Legrand, the detective on the Nobili case. I talked to you last night. Would you and Dr. Venetre have some time this morning?"

"Ah, si. We are headed to Rome on the morning train. When can you come?"

"I'm headed over there right now," LeGrand answers, "Are you both up? I'll be there in ten minutes."

Ryan urges Vanessa to get out of bed and get dressed. They are both fatigued and irritable but scramble to get ready to meet LeGrand. They need to hurry to catch the train to Florence on the way to Rome.

In ten minutes, there's a knock on the door. Vanessa answers. LeGrand is a handsome man of medium height with a strong jaw and short sporty haircut. He's wearing a tight red Ralph Lauren polo shirt, stretched over his bulging arm muscles, black dress pants, and Prada Gucci shoes.

He speaks English with a French accent, *"Buon giorno.* Dr. Venetre? I'm Detective LeGrand from the Faenza *polizia."*

"Si, per favore. Entra," Vanessa welcomes him in. "Sit down. Can I get you anything? I was beginning to think the *polizia* didn't exist. I'm pleased that you are taking this more seriously, now that a death has resulted," she says sarcastically. "What have you found?"

They all sit down in the armchair and red sofa in the *soggiorno.*

"Well, we do the best we can, Dr. Venetre," he starts, defensively. "We take all deaths seriously, particularly when there is foul play involved. At first, we were not sure about Dr. Nobili's death. It seemed to be a seizure disorder, but without any history, it would be unusual. Then, we received the report from the hospital's toxicology department. The labs came back with sarin in his blood. It's a common seizure-producing compound. You would not find that in food. It was injected.

"We also received some help from your staff, Dr. Venetre. A document was found in a meeting hall last night. One of our officers picked it up. It was a Manifesto ranting about religious ideology and a political agenda. They are examining it now for fingerprints and DNA."

To Ryan and Vanessa, the Manifesto further reinforces that it was, in fact, a murder. LeGrand takes out his notebook and scribbles some notes. "I'm sorry to take your time, but I'm hoping either of you could fill in some background to help us investigate Dr. Nobili's death. We need to narrow down the suspects. Were there any participants at the Terme who we should follow-up on?"

"We went over this with someone at your office yesterday," Vanessa sighs. "I'm relieved to have someone listen and write it down this time. Brian Johnson, a new participant, has acted strange all week. He came on Monday and questioned the research. He considered it anti-Christ, just like the Manifesto. He came to the reception Monday night, and Dr. Laughlin had a strange conversation with him. Then, Ryan saw him carry a long thin package out of the hunting and fishing shop."

Ryan pours some coffee, and offers some to LeGrand. He waves it off.

"You're a Frenchman, right?" Ryan asks. "How is it that you're working in Faenza?"

"Oh, it's a long story. I wouldn't want to bore you," LeGrand says, taking a deep breath.

"Now, you've intrigued me," Ryan replies. "Summarize. We'd like to hear."

He rolls his eyes impatiently. "I was playing for the French rugby team here in Italy a few years back and fell in love with this woman from Faenza. We corresponded, and then, I moved down here to be with her," he says shaking his head. "She dumped me a year later for some other guy. I had this detective job, and so decided to stay until I get on my feet planted elsewhere."

"What's her name?" Vanessa asks curiously.

"Cicci Beretta. Like the gun," he sighs and lowers his head. "Do you know her?"

Vanessa laughs. She walks over to pack her bags. "We all know Cicci Beretta. She comes to the Terme to find unsuspecting husbands. Dr. Laughlin understands what you've been through. He was recently under her spell, but I hope that he was able to break free. Most men can't."

LeGrand frowns and looks at Ryan with empathy. "I couldn't resist. And she cleaned out my bank account. I try to forget. Dr. Laughlin, tell me about your conversation with Mr. Johnson."

"Yes, let's leave Miss Beretta out of this," Ryan says quietly to him. "It's a sore point." Ryan continues, more loudly. "Yes, I met him on the plane coming here from Amsterdam. He made some awkward comments about the research. Then, I talked to him at the reception. He said the research was a sham, was sacreligious, and should not be continued. He was adamant. He said he would not stick around, and instead, would do some touring of Italy, perhaps go to Rome."

LeGrand jots down the information.

"Then, something odd happened yesterday," Ryan hesitates. "I was riding a bike in the countryside outside of the Terme. Someone passed me. I couldn't see whom, but maybe it was Johnson. He saw me, turned around, and then to my surprise, he tried to run me off the road. He stopped and yelled at me. I don't know if he recognized who I was with my helmet on, but of course, I was angry. What did I do to bring that on?" Ryan pauses a moment, takes out his cell phone, and shows it to LeGrand. "My friend Julia Stone texted me a picture of the suspect in St. Paul. His name was Trevick. Anton Trevick. Although the hair and beard are different, I suppose you can imagine some resemblance to Johnson. Julia Stone and the detective from Minnesota, someone named Steiner, know more about this. Have you been in touch with them?"

LeGrand takes his phone, and looks over the picture. "This is the first I heard that they have a suspect. Steiner, you say? Can you send me the picture and the cell numbers for Steiner and Stone? Here's my number."

He hands him a paper. Ryan types in the number and forwards the photo and numbers to him.

"Yes, but right now, I would find Johnson for questioning," Ryan answers. "He's the most likely suspect here, and we've lost track of him."

"Do you know where I could find him?" LeGrand asks.

Vanessa replies, trying to be helpful, "We have his home address at the Terme. He said he was from New York. I'll call them from the train to tell them you're coming. He told Ryan that he left town to see more of Italy. It may be difficult."

"*Grazie* for this information," LeGrand replies. "Sorry to take up your time. What about your safety? Do you feel you need protection?"

"Yes, we need protection!" Vanessa says, "But I'm not going to sit around waiting to be killed. We need to stay one step ahead of the murderer."

"Well, Dr. Venetre. It's difficult to protect you if you are traveling about. You're a much easier target then."

Vanessa shoots him a dirty look. "I'm not sure I agree with you there. I doubt that it is wise to sit in my apartment, or anywhere, for that matter."

He scowls, "At least tell me your itinerary. We can stay in touch, and if something comes up, we will be there immediately."

"Fair enough," Vanessa replies encouraged that someone in the *polizia* is attentive to their circumstances.

"Here is my card," LeGrand says. "If you see Johnson, or anything else related to the case, don't hesitate to call me. And if you see Cicci, don't say hello from me."

Vanessa smiles and looks at Ryan, "Understood."

LeGrand begins to leave, and then turns to Ryan to ask, "Can I have a word with you?"

Both Vanessa and Ryan look puzzled by the request. Ryan says, "Sure."

"Come with me."

Ryan walks with LeGrand to his Renault R5 Turbo. LeGrand opens the car door and retrieves a leather case. Ryan's eyes light up in astonishment as he opens the case and takes out a handgun.

"Don't worry. I don't plan on using it. I want you to use it, if needed," he says. "I was in the French military as an undercover agent during my athlete years. I used this compact Beretta 92 for most of the operations. Here take it."

Ryan puts the Beretta in his hand and admires the feel of the handle. He looks up at LeGrand.

LeGrand smiles at him. "It's a compact weapon with a light-weight aluminum frame. It doesn't hit as hard as Cicci, but it's sufficient to stop a killer if you need it." He laughs.

"I can't carry a weapon in Italy. Can I?" Ryan asks. "Wouldn't I be arrested?"

"You know," LeGrand says. "I have sympathy for those who support the Stand your Ground Movement in America. I love Dirty Harry's line. "Go ahead, make my day." It's a strong statement. When you're threatened, you need to protect yourself. Even in Italy, we're beginning to be more assertive. Here take it. See what it feels like. I'll let you borrow it. You need protection."

He hands Ryan the gun. "Use it, if necessary," he says. "But don't show it to anyone unless you need to. Even Dr. Venetre will most likely not approve." LeGrand shows him how to load, aim, and shoot the gun.

Ryan thanks him for loaning him the gun, and they say goodbye. He walks in and puts the leather case in his luggage.

Vanessa, obviously curious about their conversation, asks, "What was that all about?"

"He wanted to show me some strategies to protect us in case the killer confronts us," he replies. "It may be quite helpful."

"Thank goodness that someone is looking out for us," she goes back to packing.

They have to hurry to finish in order to catch the afternoon train. They throw their luggage in the Vanessa's Fiat 500, and drive first to the main Terme office to meet with the staff about what to do now after Dr. Nobili's death.

Vanessa explains to the staff that Dr. Nobili had poison in his blood from a needle stick and foul play is suspected. An investigation is under way with Francois LeGrand from Faenza. She encourages them not to let fear control their lives here at the Terme. It only feeds the killer's motives.

In fact, they will expand the research to include each Blessings document when they have been translated. She reminds them of Dr. Nobili's most important mission, to train *Prophecy* warriors and spread the knowledge around the world. And they are the key to continue this mission.

Linda brings up the manuscript she found. "Last night, as I was setting up the meeting room, I found a manuscript laying there on the front desk. I didn't think much about it at first. I thought someone had left their Terme notebook. Then, I picked it up and started reading. The document was very strange."

"What was in it?" Vanessa asks as the rest of the staff are glued to her every word.

Linda goes on, "It was filled with confusing language about freedom, politics, strangling government, anti-Christ research, conquering the Beast, and much more. It stated that people will be hurt. It sounded like a fanatic wrote it. With Dr. Nobili's death, I decided to call the police. They came out and picked it up right away since it may be evidence. As you know, a similar manifesto was found after Dr. Killian's death. I hope it was the right thing to do."

As much as Vanessa wants to read the document, she assured Linda that calling the *polizia* was the only alternative. A worried look came over both Ryan and Vanessa's faces. She recovers quickly and explains that she is leaving town for a week to retrieve the Blessing manuscripts, and will be off the radar. She does not tell them where she is going, but formally thanks Dr. Laughlin for accompanying her on the trip. She hugs each staff member before they leave. She does not speak of her concerns for her own life, knowing this would lower their energy considerably. But they all know. She is the next target.

Chapter 38. Rome

BRISIGHELLA, ITALY
FRIDAY MORNING

It is a cloudy morning in Brisighella, in more ways than the weather. They leave a somber staff at the Terme, and are late in leaving. They need to quickly drive the few blocks to Ryan's room to pick up his things before they can get to the station and catch the train to Florence. They hurry through these tasks and arrive with ten minutes to spare.

The train originated in Ravenna on the east coast, then came through Faenza, and now, is headed to Florence, where they will need to transfer to a train to Rome. This steam engine is from a historic line, dating back a century, when railways were the major form of transportation around Italy. As Ryan approaches to get on the ancient train, he is surprised at its shoddy condition. He has only seen steam engines in the movies, and this one has seen better days.

As they board the train, they scan the crowd, watching everyone carefully. They see no one who resembles Johnson or Trevick. They find seats next to some Italian teenagers and their parents traveling to Florence for the weekend. The teens are excited and chatty. Ryan and Vanessa are tired and quiet. They do not talk about last night, but rather, stare out the window at the panoramic view of the countryside, occasionally watching the other passengers for anything worrisome.

They see nobody suspicious. Ryan tries to relax by starting idle conversation with Vanessa. "This train must have a long history of service," he says diplomatically. "Do you know much about it?"

"These old steam engine trains are almost like toy trains. They're not fast, nor comfortable, but they bring back many memories of a time lost. A lot of people ride them for the nostalgia that comes with experiencing the relics of old Italy. It's one of very few left."

"Despite its run down condition, it does bring some memories," Ryan replies. "Have you ridden this train often?"

"Si. Many times. As a teenager, we went to see the cultural riches of Tuscany and Venice. Unlike the teens of America, none of us had a car to take us places. So, we took the train everywhere. This train started in the early 1800s, when the Grand-Duke Leopold of Tuscany wanted to link the east and west coasts of Italy. It was a symbol of Italian unity, and now a symbol of old Italy."

After a half hour, the train slows down and comes to a stop in a small town in the mountains.

"Where are we now?" Ryan asks.

"This is the last station before reaching the heart of the mountains through the Marradi Pass. You would like it here. Marradi is known for its ancient chestnut trees and its myriad of exquisite dessert recipes based on the chestnut. The recipes are jealously guarded secrets in memory of the past generation who developed them. They are all made with the marrone chestnuts.

"Sounds delicious. Can we stop?"

"We have no time for dessert right now. You will have to satisfy your sweet tooth in Florence."

Ryan rolls his eyes and frowns like a kid pouting over being deprived. He returns to gazing out the window. The train starts to roll again. As it leaves the forest, the train passes through vast fields of wheat, soybeans and sunflowers.

"Look at the beautiful villages with their old row house, walls, and churches," Ryan comments. "They look like the pictures of old Italy."

Vanessa points out the window. "That's Ronta. It's the first town in the Mugello Valley. The next one will be Borgo San Lorenzo. It has the ancient Abbey of St. Lawrence and the Parish of St. Cresci in Valcava. You can see the parish on a hilltop in the distance."

The scenes of ancient, walled towns, surrounded by rich fields of flowering sunflowers, mountains in the distance, age-old vineyards and olive groves is stunning. The beauty of the Tuscan hills and towns, at least temporarily, replaces their troubles.

They arrive at the station in Florence and feel less worried knowing they are away from the killer in Brisighella. They run to find the train departing for Rome. The scene is chaotic generating more anxiety. People are racing to get on the trains before they depart. Italians do not believe in orderly lines. Most seats are secured on a first come, first serve basis, so there is always a push to get on the train and find a seat.

Ryan stops to look at the menus above the bakeries and cafés next to the train tracks. For a few moments, his hunger displaces his fear and caution.

"Ryan, we have no time for that right now," Vanessa says. "Remember, maintain your energy. We need to make haste, or we will miss the next train. Pigging out does not qualify as an activity that maintains your energy."

Ryan had imagined this trip to Italy would at least bring him some sight-seeing and food-tasting while in Florence. He was wrong, and his stomach grumbles. They are vigilant as they find their seats, carefully checking each passenger to see if anyone resembles Johnson. Their anxiety returns as they worry whether the killer may be following them despite their precautions. They let nobody know where they are going.

After they settle into their seats, their fatigue overwhelms them both, and they sleep for two hours in route to Rome. Their dozing is restless. They are easily startled by even the slightest noise. As they arrive in Rome, they wake up and watch the hustle and bustle of the large city out of the train window.

Vanessa alerts Ryan that they will need to be prepared to get off the train quickly. A few minutes pass as the train slows. Then, without a word, Vanessa gets up, grabs her bag, and walks briskly to the exit while Ryan hustles to keep up. She wants to be first in line to get off the train, and expects him to be right behind. She looks both ways for Johnson or other suspicious characters and sees none. They find a taxi outside the station. She calls Gabriela as the taxi leaves the station with them safely inside.

The taxi weaves its way through the streets of Rome to Gabriela's apartment near the Piazza di Spagna by the Villa Borghese. Villa Borghese is the largest public park in Rome and has a lake, temples, fountains, statues and several museums. It has become a haven for the weekend athlete and the tourist alike. They can also see the church of Trinita dei Monti, with its twin towers that dominate the skyline above the steps. They find her apartment entrance and push the button to alert her to their arrival. They look around, and see no one following them.

Gabriela responds via the intercom. "Ciao, Vanessa, I'll be right down." Gabriela arrives at the door, and gives Vanessa a big hug and kiss on each cheek. "Oh, Vanessa, Vanessa. *Che piacere vederti! Stai bene?* Are you okay?"

They go through the introductions with Ryan and she takes them up to her apartment at the top of a building. The apartment is a two story flat with a cast iron spiral staircase that winds up to a guest loft. The main floor has a canopy ceiling with old frescos of angels with trumpets sounding. A kitchen is off to the side with a large old, wooden dining table with wooden chairs.

"Gabriela, you've done more to your place since my last time here. Look at your *terrazzo*. It's beautiful," Vanessa recalls.

"*Viene qui*," she says. "It's a room with a view!"

The loft opens to a large roof-top terrace. Gabriela has planted large pots of palm trees, umbrella trees, snake plants, and there are several arrowhead vines falling over a tall pedestal. Blooming flowers are scattered around the trees. The rooftop has a broad view of Rome, high above the Spanish steps.

"It's like a jungle out here," Ryan says, "And what a beautiful view."

"I like it here," she laughs. "I have a jungle, but no pesky monkeys, unless you include the tourists."

"What is the fountain at the base of the steps?" Ryan asks, pointing.

"That's *La Fontana della Barcaccia*, also called the Fountain of the Boat. The flooding of Tevere in 1598 inspired it. It's been in many movies," She points to the top of the steps. "And up there. That's the French church, the Trinità dei Monti. See the rooftop garden over there. Eugene Unico lives right over there. He is one of the Vatican scholars working on the *Prophecy Scroll*. You must meet him. Delightful person. You must be tired."

She walks off the terrace and says, "Please bring your things and let's get you settled. You're safe here. I'll open a nice bottle of spumante to help you relax. You've been through quite an ordeal. What would prefer? Red or white?"

She directs Vanessa to the spare bedroom downstairs and Ryan to the loft. They unpack, change into more casual clothes, and gather at the table. Gabriela opens the delicate sparkling wine called *Rose Spumante Veneto* from Lamberti. She knows it's a favorite of Vanessa's, with a fine mousse flavor and aromas of both flowers and banana. "Vanessa, tell me everything that led up to Paolo's death. Are you sure someone killed him?"

"It's too much of a coincidence. He was strong as an ox. Never had a history of a seizure disorder. He's a physician, and knows his own body. His wife, Roberta, told me to get out of town because they suspected foul play in his death. We have a theory that the main suspect is a guy who showed up on the first day at the Terme. His name is Brian Johnson from New York," Vanessa reports.

"Dr. Julia Stone, from Boston, texted me a picture of Anton Trevick, one of the chief suspects in the States," Ryan adds. "There are some vague similarities to Johnson." He tells her about the conversations on the plane and at the reception, the suspicious package, the bike incident, and the Manifesto left at the Terme. "Now, he's disappeared. It's all strange."

"Okay. Let's say he's the killer," Gabriela says with a concerned look on her face. "What do you think he is going to do next?"

"If his goal is to stop the research, he'll be looking for me," Vanessa says.

"Do you know if he's following you?" asks Gabriela.

"I don't know," Vanessa says. "We did our best to get out of town quickly and quietly. If he is following me, I want to keep one step ahead of him. Who else knows where each of the manuscripts is located?"

"Primarily my colleagues, Gene Unico and James Monsein." Gabriela says. "I suppose some of our Academy staff and the Pope's inner circle."

"Have you warned them?" Vanessa asks. "And do the *polizia* here know about the threats?"

"Yes, Dr. Unico and Monsein know about Dr. Killian and Dr. Nobili. I also alerted the Vatican Swiss Guard, and they will fill in the *polizia*. We are covered here. Now, about the other *Prophecy Scroll* manuscripts. Only a couple are completed and they're in Sardinia and Pisa. The scholars would enjoy meeting with you and reviewing them. But we still need approval from the Pope to do that. Unfortunately, that may be hard to get. If he does support us, you will need to visit a couple of beautiful Italian towns and meet some interesting people to get copies. Are you up for that?"

"Ryan, you may get your tour of Italy after all," Vanessa smiles.

Gabriela continues, "The *Blessing of Prosperity* and the *Blessing of Love* have been completed. You will like the scholars who are translating them. They are authorities in their respective fields, and understand the ancient Hebrew from which the *Prophecy Scroll* was written. Dr. Ambra Antonioni is an organic farmer in Sardinia who happens to have a PhD in Economics. She is translating the *Blessing of Prosperity*. Then, there's the handsome movie star priest, Fabrizio Brizi, in Pisa. He is a young, highly educated priest who changed careers. He went from a handsome movie star to becoming a priest. He's an expert in ancient manuscripts. He's translating the *Blessing of Love*."

"Can't wait to meet them. They sound intriguing," Vanessa says. "What about the other manuscripts?"

"Sorry, but they're not all ready yet," Gabriela apologizes. "They'll be done sometime in the next couple of months. Father Cyprian Bandini works in the Gran Sasso Laboratories in the mountains east of Rome. He has a PhD in nuclear physics and is translating the *Blessing of Wisdom*. Brother Thomas D'Angelo runs a parish in Asissi with Sister Marie Clare. They're a humorous pair of entomologists and ecologists with a talent in butterflies. They're translating the *Blessing of Beauty*. Then, there's the charming Vincenzo Bernacchi of Spoleto. He's the lead tenor in the *Phantom of the Opera* performance, and an expert in translating old manuscripts. He is translating the *Blessing of Happiness*. I also know Lella Gelossi from San Marino quite well. She is the Dean of the Vatican Diplomatic Corps here, and is translating the *Blessing of Peace*. She is San Marino's ambassador to the Pope, and helped get the manuscripts to the Vatican. She is organizing a conference on world peace next month with leaders from the major religions. A great lady."

Gabriela looks at the both of them and says, "You look like you could eat something. It's 7 pm. Although I know it's early, we better leave for dinner now to avoid the tourist crowds and the protestors."

"We'll go to Settimio all'Arancio. It's a quiet place known mostly by the locals. It's near the river near Ponte Cavour, the Piazza San Piedro and the Vatican. I called a taxi, and hopefully, he can avoid the unruly crowds. Not sure that's possible though."

The taxi arrives and they take off through the main streets of Rome, trying unsuccessfully to avoid the mass of people gathering for the evening protest. Yesterday, thousands of protestors took to the streets as the unions launched a two-day general strike against the government's austerity measures.

Vanessa watches the crowd as the taxi moves through the streets, and says with sorrow in her voice, "I fear that these protests are just the beginning of a deteriorating world. More evidence of the truth behind the *Prophecy Scroll*."

"It's hard to be an optimist these days," Gabriela sighs. "But I'm quite hopeful that the majority of the people will embrace the principles in the

Prophecy Scroll when they see the universal wisdom in them. Your work is so important. You'll see."

"My hope has been dampened considerably by the death of Paolo," Vanessa replies. "I may not even see the future. My concern is to survive right now."

"Well, that makes two of us," Gabriela agrees. "Point well taken."

The taxi passes by the Ponte San Angelo walking bridge across from the Castelo San Angelo in an attempt to avoid the protestors. Unfortunately, the timing and path of the Taxi's route could not have been worse. The protestors are marching from the Vatican, down Via Della Conciliazione, across the Ponte San Angelo and down to the River Tiber. They walk down the street shouting "*Occupare! Occupare! Occupare!*" They smash shop windows, torch cars, and hurl bottles. As the driver turns to avoid the procession, the Italian police fire tear gas and water cannons at the crowd to disseminate them.

They pass Ponte San Angelo safely, and Gabriela tries to distract Ryan and Vanessa from the conflict. "Amidst all of these protests and the hate, there is still some room for love. Do you see all of the lover's padlocks on the bridge handrails? It's a tradition that stems from Federico Moccia's sentimental love story of Roman teenagers. Lovers tie a padlock to the handrail of the bridge and throw the key in the Tiber River to symbolize their everlasting love. As usual, the government has banned the practice to protect the bridge."

Vanessa holds Ryan's arm and looks up at him. "Well, I would throw caution to the wind, ignore the law, and clip a padlock on for you. You are so kind to be here with me. I understand the risk that you're taking."

"Yes. It is precious of you to be here now," Gabriela agrees. "Vanessa really needs you."

"Well, I appreciate the thought, but let's skip the padlocks for now," he says. "We're in enough hot water. We don't need to get arrested too."

Ryan knows that he could get himself killed by helping Vanessa, but what can he do. She's vulnerable right now. She is a remarkable person who needs someone to be here with her. He should have thought about the safety issues before he came to Italy. He remembers the research that demonstrated feelings of love suppresses activity in the area of the brain that controls critical thought. Definitely. He can see it. His critical thought is not working too well right now. He must be in love. He recalls Shakespeare, 'love is blind and lovers cannot see.' Maybe, love is stupid also. There's only one thing to do in matters of the heart. He must help her any way possible.

They arrive at the restaurant and decide to eat inside to avoid being seen at the tables on the walk. Their paranoia is running high. Vanessa and Gabriela each order a pizza margherita with tomatoes, mozzarella di bufala, and basil. Ryan orders the pizza quattro stagione with potatoes, asparagus, zucchini and olives on the pizza. They pick a nice white wine that compliments both. They're famished, and the pizzas and wine go down quickly. The wine relaxes them enough to talk about their lives, the research, and the manuscripts.

Gabriela looks at Ryan. "Why did you come to the Terme? You knew about the murder in St. Paul. Did you not think that this might happen here?"

He looks at Vanessa's painful expression knowing that she is worried about his response. "I asked myself the same question, many times. I had my own issues. My wife passed away two years ago, and my job and my patients, at times, were overwhelming. My personal life was going nowhere. I had trouble sleeping. I was even a little depressed. I don't know. Then, I had this dinner with Julia Stone, who has been here. It just clicked. It was powerful. Maybe, I was just feeling the power of the *Prophecy Scroll*. When you hear about it, you must admit that it's hard not to want to learn more. If you are searching for more meaning and happiness in life, you take a few risks."

"It does possess you," Gabriela admits. "I also want to know more about the results. The research is very compelling."

"I'm as motivated as Vanessa is in completing the research and seeing those additional manuscripts. So far, I have not been disappointed in coming to the Terme. And as a bonus, I met this lovely lady. I think she's pretty special, si?"

Vanessa smiles at him as she feels herself falling for this man's charm.

Ryan can see the signs of the affection she has for him and his male ego rises. "As far as danger, I can handle myself," he says confidently, though his bravado doesn't convince him anymore than it does the others. "And it's harder to get to two people than to one."

They finish their meals and walk to the corner of the street. The protests have passed, and the streets are quite. They flag a taxi and head back to Gabriela's apartment. When they arrive, they turn on the television news to see the extent of the protests.

The shot shows heavy smoke billowing into the air from downtown Rome. People are scrambling to escape the tear gas and *polizia*. The protests left dozens injured as tens of thousands, who nicknamed themselves 'the indignant,' marched in Rome. The reporter proceeds to say that most major cities across Europe have protests against the government financial policies that favor the wealthy. The camera then pans to several scenes including a parked car on fire during a demonstration, protestors clad in black with their faces covered carrying clubs and hammers, protestors throwing rocks and flaming bottles at the banks, and the Rome *polizia* in full riot gear.

The newscaster tells of the crisis, "They destroyed bank ATMs, set trash bins on fire and assaulted at least two news crews from Sky Italia. In the city's Basilica of St. John Lateran Square, police vans came under attack, with protesters hurling rocks and smashing the vehicles."

The shot shifts to Jesse LaGrecio, a leader of Occupy Wall Street. He speaks of the spread of the protests around the world, "We are seeing our future stolen away from us while the wealthy elite become richer and richer. People are finally participating in our democracy."

As they watch the news, they find themselves exhausted from the day and the turmoil in the world. Ryan climbs to the loft and falls asleep within minutes. Gabriela and Vanessa talk about Ryan for a few minutes.

"You know that Ryan's a special person, si?" Gabriela asks Vanessa quietly. "He's not full of himself like some men."

"Well, I'm not thinking about him right now. I just want to survive this ordeal. He's kind enough to help me. Last night, I crawled into bed with him because I was afraid. I was surprised, and maybe a little disappointed, but he kept his hands off of me. I guess my mother's sausage in the jar story threw up a few red flags."

"Vanessa, you didn't tell him that story, did you?" She laughs, and then, tries to stifle the laugh to avoid waking Ryan. "That can kill any relationship. You should know better."

"I don't care," Vanessa says. "He'll see through a story if he wants to. Remember, the greater the barrier, the greater the passion."

But only if the motivation is there," Gabriela quickly replies. "Don't kill the motivation."

"I think it's there. A challenge is good for relationships. If you're easy, the love dies easily. In the end, if the relationship works, it works, if it doesn't, *ei la vita!* That's life."

"You must know what you're doing," Gabriela says. "As a nun, I have taken an oath to avoid the whole question. Now, the big question is whether you really want to pursue the two manuscripts that are available. If so, first, you will need approval from the Pope, and then you'll need to travel to Sardinia and Pisa to get them? If you are followed, it will be a harrowing journey. Are you afraid?"

"Yes, I'll be afraid until they find the killer. But I don't want to sit somewhere like a *facile bersaglio*, you know, a sitting duck. We need those manuscripts."

"I assumed as much. So, I went beyond my comfort zone to schedule it," Gabriela says with her face shining brightly.

"Schedule what?" Vaness replies.

"I have arranged for you to meet with the Pope tomorrow afternoon about the research."

Vanessa is shocked. "You arranged what? The Papal? *Vero? Si? è incredibile che!*"

"He wants to hear personally about the research since the Vatican has been implicated in the murder in the U.S. He knows people's lives are at stake, regardless of whether the research continues or not. I believe he understands the power of the knowledge in the *Prophecy Scroll* for the world. He wants to meet you."

Vanessa sits back, trying to fathom this request. "I'll be so honored to talk to him," she says. "But I'll be so nervous I won't know what to say."

"You'll do fine," Gabriela continues. "Just be yourself. You're remarkable. You'll know what to say. There's a lot of pressure on the Pope to do something about the violence, political unrest, and unfairness of the world. He feels a strong responsibility to help improve things. His decision will be controversial either way, both inside and outside the Holy See. But the Vatican has also been besieged by a continuous stream of leaks of confidential documents, political infighting, and a reputation as a secrecy-obsessed tax haven. The unrest at the Vatican reflects the growing problems in the world. The sensation generated when the murder broke in the news makes it a delicate time for him. Now, with a murder here in Italy, it's urgent. We do not know what he will say, but we must remain hopeful."

Vanessa's anxiety, already high with a killer on the loose, has just doubled in anticipation of meeting the Pope. "With all of the worries he has in the world, I have little hope that he will support science over religious doctrine. With Paolo's death, it is the end of this research. He will not support it." She shakes her head in doubt.

"Vanessa, *tu se stanca.* You are very fatigued," Gabriela says. "You have a big day tomorrow. Get some good sleep. You'll need it. And you know what else you may need?"

"*Che cosa è quello?* What?" Vanessa gives her a dirty look. "I thought you've sworn off thinking about men."

"Si, but you have not!" Gabriela laughs at Vanessa.

"What are you thinking?" Vanessa laughs. "*Tu se una mente sporca è erotica!*"

"That's not what I was suggesting, Vanessa," She exclaims. "You must have sex on your mind! My only thought was that perhaps it would help if Ryan takes you shopping along the most famous fashion street in the world, Via Condotti. With all this stress, I believe you'd feel a lot better to get something special to wear for the Pope."

They both laugh at the truth of both ideas. Vanessa says good night and thanks Gabriela. She crawls into bed and, as she thinks about Ryan for a few minutes, she falls deeply asleep. Fatigue trumps all.

Chapter 39. The Shopping Trip

ROME, ITALY
SATURDAY MORNING

The next morning, Vanessa and Ryan awaken slowly and get dressed for the day. Gabriela rose early and prepared an exquisite breakfast of *panini* and *brioche* pastries, fresh from the oven, with an array of cheeses and fresh grapes, peaches, and melon. She sets out the marmalade and Nutella for the pastries, and has a steaming café latte for each of them waiting as they slowly roll out of bed. The tasty breakfast sets an uplifting mood for the day. They will need it.

"Buon giorno, you two sleepy-eyed travelers," Gabriela says melodically, as she opens the morning conversation. "Come, sit down. I prepared some breakfast for you." They drag themselves into the kitchen and sit down at the wooden table to sip their first morning café latte. Gabriela sits across the breakfast table from them and tries to stifle the scheming smile on her face. "Ryan, you're such a sweetheart to take Vanessa for a brisk walk down the shopping mecca of Via Condotti this morning. You will need this boost of energy before we meet with the Pope."

Ryan opens his eyes in astonishment. "I agreed to do what? The Pope? Shopping?" He is not quite sure what he actually agreed to do last night. But with all the wine, protests, and intense conversation, he could have said just about anything. But he knows that he never heard a word about meeting with the Pope. "I'm not sure what you mean?" He says as he pushes back from the long wooden table to get a second café latte. His energy already feels weak, so what the hell, he will have a second.

"I arranged a meeting with the Pope about the research for this afternoon, so you and Vanessa need to go shopping down Via Condotti. You want to dress appropriately, right?"

"Sure," he says staring at a smiling Vanessa. "Where is Via Condotti?"

They both laugh at his lack of awareness of the street's international reputation as the fashion center of the Italy.

"It may be risky for the checkbook," Vanessa replies. "Via Condotti is at the base of the Spanish Steps, and is lined with shops carrying the latest offerings from the Italian fashion industry."

Ryan knows that his fashion sense is practically non-existent, and that no matter what he puts on his lanky six foot three inch frame, it hangs there as if he just got out of bed. "I'm not exactly a fashion plate, but I would enjoy shopping with you. Maybe, I can learn something."

"Great. You'll like it," Vanessa says. "All the top names have shops here. Giorgio Armani, Gianni Versace, Fendi, Gucci, Max Mara, Kenzo, Jimmy Choo, Louis Vuitton, you name it. They're all here. Even the least materialistic and fashion conscious person can enjoy via Condotti. Are you up for it?"

"I guess," He says trying to hide is reluctance. "Do they have men's clothing also?"

They laugh. "Yes, of course," Vanessa replies. "The stores are not just for ladies. Some men care about how they dress too. Maybe, we can find something that fits you."

Ryan looks down at himself with his jeans and beige pull over cotton sweater with rolled up sleeves. He is dressed as an American in every way. Despite their indirect slight about the clothes he wears, he believes his attire is what he intends it to be, rugged, packable, and adaptable enough to be suitable for a tourist's wardrobe. Nevertheless, he is open to any suggested upgrades from this self-proclaimed fashion queen, particularly, if he is to meet with the Pope. Wonders never cease if you go with the flow.

They step out onto the terrace to check with weather. It's a cool summer morning in Rome so Vanessa puts on a sweater. She looks up and down at Ryan in his boring outfit. She shakes her head," You certainly could use some help in the fashion realm. I'm open to giving you some suggestions, if you're interested."

"Well, I guess. If it's needed," he looks down at himself.

They take off down the Spanish Steps to begin their shopping adventure. As they stroll down Via Condotti, Vanessa wanders in and out of each boutique, pointing out why they are famous. "Ryan, here's Giorgio Armani. Look at these dresses. They're so understated, so elegant. I would feel quite at ease in one of these evening designs. What you do think?"

She holds one up in front of her. Ryan knows his role this morning. "You would look stunning in that dress. Why don't you try one on?" He looks at the price tag, and takes a step back. "I must be in the wrong business."

She eyes him with the forlorn look of a shopper who has run out of money. "Fashion is part of the charm of Italy. In Rome, they say 'If you can afford it, flaunt it.' Unfortunately, on a researcher's salary, these are all off limits for me. Maybe, someday, this research will bring me fame and fortune. But I won't hold my breath though. I just need to be creative in less pricey ways."

They continue to walk down Via Condotti, forgetting about the eminent danger for a few moments. Vanessa is excited to show him the fashion, and Ryan is happy to be playing along while he watches their backs. Vanessa picks out a nice dark brown jacket for him, and he tries it on. With her encouragement, he purchases it reluctantly, shocked at the price tag. Meanwhile, he tells her how good she looks in several dresses she tries on. They act as if they have been a couple for years.

"Ryan, you'll like Gucci. It can be described in two words—unbelievably sexy. They lead the world in luxury avant-garde designs. They even pay attention to the evolution of your lifestyle with the transformation from youthful pretty to grown-up sexy."

"I may be in the over-the-hill and do-not-care phase of fashion," He quips.

She laughs at the truth of it. She takes a Gucci design off the hanger and walks to the mirror to look at it in front of her. A minute later, she's in the dressing room and returns with it on. "Look at the detail on this dress. This is so me. Do you like it?"

Ryan recognizes the loaded question, and tactfully avoids lighting any verbal fuses, "I like the unbelievable sexy part. You look great in it."

Vanessa smiles as she watches herself twirl around in the mirror and then looks over her shoulder at it, "It's so simple, with a touch of unique elegance. Perfect for a romantic dinner and dance with you sometime. I enjoyed dancing with you at the reception. Did you?"

"*Si.* Very much," He assures her. "I discovered that dancing boosts your physical, emotional, and social energy simultaneously. How can you beat that? Sophia and I used to go out to live music downtown regularly. Lots of fun, but I haven't done much dancing in the last few years—other than the reception. And I especially enjoyed the dancing with you part."

Vanessa lights up, "You're sweet. Then, we must do it again." She returns to the dressing room and changes back into her casual jeans and sweater. She exits the dressing room without the dress. There is a touch of disappointment on her face.

Ryan is surprised and inquires, "You're not going to get it? I think you look fabulous in it. The Pope will like it."

"Ryan, this is for partying, not the Pope. And I have no Christmas bunny to bring me clothes or money," she replies with a forlorn look. "I'll have to wait another day for that one."

Ryan is puzzled by the comment. They spent all of this time and she's not even going to buy anything? He doesn't get the shopping part of buying. He prefers simply to buy something when you need it. Regardless, he's goes along with her, learning what Italian women love to do. They spend the rest of the time window shopping and simply being together to see where this love will take both of them.

They head back to Gabriela's apartment. As the walk back, they both recognize how much they enjoy each other's company. Once they're back at the apartment, Gabriela reminds them that the appointment with the Pope is at one in the afternoon.

"Do I have some time to go for a run through the park?" Ryan asks. "I'm in desperate need for an energy boost. I can't miss my daily routine."

"You have an hour before we need to leave," Gabriela replies. "Go ahead. Vanessa and I have to catch up on *la storias di la familgia*. You know, our family gossip."

Ryan gets his athletic gear on and heads down the steps. Gabriela tells him how to get to Villa Borghese for the best run.

They watch him from the open terrace as he takes off. "That's surprising," Gabriela comments. "He said he was going to the Villa, but he went the opposite direction. I hope he doesn't get lost and make us late. You know men and directions. They don't always go together too well." They laugh and move into a more lively conversation about *la familgia and amici*.

Finally, they shift their conversation to the more overriding topic of the day—the upcoming visit with the Pope. They know that it is a day of reckoning regarding the future of the Terme project. If he supports it, she and Ryan will travel to Sardinia and Pisa to retrieve the two completed manuscripts. If he does not, the project will be nearly dead before it really had a chance to flourish. The killer's goal will have been accomplished. Either way, Vanessa is not sure she wants to continue the research without Dr. Nobili, and without her, it will die. Gabriela insists that he will support it. He must.

Ryan completes his run and sneaks back into the apartment with a bag in his hand. He says hello to the ladies, as he quickly passes them on his way up to his room. He showers and dresses in the most formal outfit that he brought—his dress pants, a formal button down white shirt, a striped blue and brown tie, and his newly purchased jacket. He looks in the mirror. It's still too casual to wear to a meeting with the Pope, but who would have thought this would ever happen now, or ever. He is not there to impress anyone—He will have little to say and they may not even notice he is there. This meeting is about Vanessa, Gabriela, and the research, but he is delighted to come along for the ride to observe. He needs to make sure that he does not open his mouth and blow it for Vanessa.

Vanessa dresses conservatively with the non-descript brown pants and jacket outfit that she brought along. She is perfectly content that she did not spend a lavish amount on a new outfit for an hour meeting with the Pope. It's just not worth it. Although Gabriela usually wears casual clothes to work, today she wears her traditional brown robe with a long shoulder wide scapular over it that hangs to the ground in the front and back like an apron. Ryan feels better about his attire after seeing how boring they are dressed. They quickly head to the base of the Spanish steps and flag down a taxi to drive them over to the Vatican.

As they approach the Vatican, they see St. Peter's Basilica situated on the eastern section of the Vatican Hill with its historical building and lush gardens. A road leading around St. Peter's Basilica approaches the Vatican Palace, the personal residence of the Pope. The covered way leads from the Cortile di Belvedere to the Cortile della Sentinella. After the taxi drops them off, they walk across St. Peters square and around the stoic Bernini colonnade to the entrance at the side of the palace. The Swiss Guard at the gate greets them. Gabriela tells them that she has arranged clearance for her two guests. After checking their passports, the guard gives them security badges, and waves them through. They continue to walk towards Clementine Hall, the Papal's reception room

"If we have time, we need to take Ryan up to the cupola of St. Peter's," Vanessa suggests to Gabriela and then turns to Ryan. "You can see all of the Vatican Palace, its gardens and buildings, and even much of Rome from there."

"Well, right now, we have to make the appointment on time," Gabriela replies with haste. "It's a rare event to meet with the Pope."

"So true! How do I look?" Vanessa asks, catching a glance of herself through the reflection in a window.

"You look perfect…very boring, Vanessa," Gabriela laughs. "It is best to be subdued when addressing his Excellency. It's all about first impressions. He is a very modest man."

Chapter 40. The Pope

THE VATICAN
ROME, ITALY
SATURDAY MORNING

Gabriela and her two visitors walk through the long stretch of edifices connecting the many courts of the Vatican, ending in a row of smaller connected buildings, before which stands a great loggia, known as the Nicchione. To the right and left of the loggia, and at right angles to it, are two narrow buildings, which are connected by the Braccio Nuovo. These four buildings are enclosed around the Fontana della Pigna, a gigantic pine-cone bronze statue, preserved from the old St. Peter's chapel. The former Roman fountain decorates a vast niche in the wall of the Vatican facing the Cortile della Pigna.

There is a covered way that leads from the Cortile di Belvedere to the Cortile della Sentinella and then on to a exit door, situated at the back of the palace, that is used only for official purposes such as the meeting today. The Cortile di Belvedere is decorated with a fountain with a woman holding a vase above her head and water flowing out of the basin below.

The view from the windows and galleries of *Li*Appartamento Borgia and the Stanze di Raffaello shows half of the Roman skyline. They walk over to the eastern wing of the palace. "We're going to the second floor," Gabriela says quietly. "This is where he works and receives visitors. He lives up on the third floor. I've never been there."

They take the stairs to the second floor reception rooms, through the broad wooden arches, wall frescoes, and paintings leading to the Clementine

Hall, called Sala Clementina. This room is used by the Pope as a reception room and in some cases, a site for various ceremonies and rituals. The Swiss Guard keeps watch at the entrance to the papal apartments. Gabriela talks in a hushed tone, "His Excellency is in mass and has only a half hour to spend with us. We must be efficient."

"I'm surprised he would make any time for us on a Saturday morning," Ryan comments in his usual tone.

"Please keep you voice down here," Gabriela says apologetically. "Sorry, we treat this area like a library."

Ryan looks embarrassed. She answers, "He takes the time today because this is an important issue for him. He wants the Vatican to stay abreast of the most current and controversial areas that affect the church. This, of course, includes an array of issues from evolution, new life forms, birth control, homosexuality, abortion, use of stem cells, the use of sacred documents, and of course, measurement of the human spirit. They do not want to be accused of ignoring science and embracing ignorance. For example, a few years ago, the Vatican hosted a conference on Charles Darwin to debunk the idea that it only embraces creationism or intelligent design. They don't want the Church to stand in the way of scientific realities. They believe there is a wide spectrum of room for belief in both the scientific basis for evolution and faith in God the creator. This applies to other areas of science also."

"I'm actually quite surprised at that," Ryan comments. "I've always held the impression, albeit perhaps incorrect, that the church is narrow-minded and mired in deeply entrenched traditions and rituals."

"In fact, the opposite is true," Gabriela responds with a smile. "In the past few years, the Vatican has acknowledged that it will not stand in the way of scientific realities. Even the Pope has emphasized that there is no inherent incompatibility between faith and science. That's why I'm hopeful that his position on the research will be positive. But there are some traditionalists in the Pope's inner circle that vehemently oppose any change in Church doctrine. The discussion will be interesting to say the least."

As they wait, Gabriela tells them more about the palace. "The Vatican Palace was not originally intended as a residence. Only a comparatively small portion of the palace is residential. The remainder serves the art, science, and administrative aspects of the official business of the Church and for the management of the palace. My office is in the building next door. The Vatican is more of a huge museum and a center of scientific investigation than a church. The residential portion of the palace is the Cortile di San Damaso and includes the quarters of the Swiss Guard—

the gendarmes charged with civilian police duties at the Vatican. There are a thousand rooms in the whole palace and only two hundred serve as residential apartments for the Pope and those officials in close attendance to Him."

The Swiss Guard comes out from behind the closed door, and announces that the Pope is ready for their meeting. Gabriela briefs them on proper etiquette to address His Excellency. As she describes this, Vanessa and Ryan can feel their hearts racing with anticipation. They hope they do not become fools at the hands of the more traditional members of the inner circle.

Just two weeks ago, Ryan was complaining that his life was going nowhere. Now, he's about to be received by the Pope. Life is unpredictable, and maybe, it can only be understood in a broader spiritual plane. Is it better to just go with the flow of energy and let destiny unfold. Or, in contrast, should he work hard to define his own destiny? Right now, he has no clue.

The Swiss Guard leads the group through the court and into the work room of the Pope. Three huge Gobelin tapestries, presented to the Vatican by Louis XV, adorn the walls. Between this and the Sala del Trono is a smaller room, which serves to accommodate the Noble Guard, and leads to the Pope's private chapel. The floor of the throne room is covered with a specially manufactured Spanish carpet presented to Pope Leo XIII in the late 1800s. The room is simple while giving both an impressive look and a comfortable restful effect.

Without much pomp and circumstance, the Pope enters the room with the Camerlengo, Archbishop Santos Castellengo. They sit down around the large wooden table in this throne chair. Cardinal Martinelli and the Pope's two secretaries, Monsignors Grandscheid and Guissani are also in attendance. The Pope smiles as he sits down. He is dressed in his traditional uniform—a zucchetto skullcap, the white zuchettos, a short white mozetta cape, a gold pectoral cross, and his red papal shoes. Gabriela takes the lead and crosses the room to greet him. She kneels down and bends her head to kiss his hand. Vanessa and Ryan follow suit. They note the gold Fisherman's Ring that he wears in honor of St. Peter.

Ryan whispers to Vanessa, "This is the most powerful religious figure in the world. Yet, look at him. He looks so modest and subdued. There are no feelings of condescendence, control or dominance. I can feel his energy—calming and reassuring. It's uplifting."

Vanessa ignores Ryan and gives all of her attention to the Pope. The Pope sits down in his throne at the end of the table. "Please sit," he says in excellent English. "Welcome to Rome and the Vatican. I'm sorry that today I'm too busy. I wish I had more time to spend with you. However, I understand there is some urgency to this request."

He looks sincerely at Vanessa, and says, "Gabriela has told me of your plight. I'm very sorry to hear about the death of Dr. Nobili. He was a great man who understated his many accomplishments. His loss is a tragedy for all of us. I've said a blessing for him this morning at our service."

Vanessa looks worried. "Thank you, Your Excellency, for your condolences. I'm very saddened by his passing. He was like a father to me. I'm also sorry that our research has brought a storm of controversy to you and the Vatican. It was unintended. I'm sorry for this."

The Pope replies calmly, "This is not your fault, my dear. This may be true of people who are weak in spirit. But we know that science and religion are sisters to each other. Religion seeks the truth through spiritual insight and revelation. We rely on faith, ritual, and sacredness of the presumed truth. Science also seeks the truth, but through the scientific method to test theories on how the world works. In science, we rely on reason and empiricism to validate that which we observe in the world. The problem arises when scientific and religious concepts clash. When science proves something in religion that historically we needed faith to know exists, it's unsettling to some."

Ryan and Vanessa are startled at the clarity and intelligence by which the Holy One speaks. They are listening intently as the Pope continues. "People fear that science may prove that some of the basic tenets that underlie their faith are different than reality. Look through history and you will find science has challenged and changed many religious views that were sacred to our church. Take, for example, Galileo and his belief that the world revolves around the sun. He was not very popular with our church and was tried by the Inquisition. He was forced to recant, and spent the rest of his life under house arrest. Many are threatened by the role of science because they rely on faith for strength. Fear is a common method of control and influence by those with weakness of the spirit. We believe that enlightenment is achieved by promoting our spirit. Tell me more about the *Prophecy Scroll* and what your research has told us about this divine knowledge."

Vanessa bows her head and nervously tells him about the research. Gabriela listens to her careful descriptions, but understands her role as a scholar and not a change agent. She was originally doubtful that any woman can thrive in the Vatican, but she is surprised how well she has been received. However, she does not want to speak up in fear of reprisals from the large number of conservative Cardinals within the inner circle. Vanessa must speak for herself and her research.

There are a few questions about the research results but the conversation did not venture yet into controversy. Vanessa does her best to respond to questions and comments.

One of the most outspoken critics of the research is Monsignor Grandscheid. He has yet to express his opinions and is looking for his opportunity to thrust a knife in the back of this research, and twist it.

The Pope looks at Grandscheid, and responds, "There are those even in our inner circle that believe that we must be cautious in interpreting changes that impact our religious faith."

Grandscheid acknowledges His Excellency's request for him to speak with a nod. He looks directly at Vanessa with a sneer on his face and states emphatically, "My dears, we have a heavy responsibility as leaders of the Church. We need to provide direction and support for the followers of God. We have had heated discussions about this research. I believe that we should not have released the *Prophecy Scroll* because it questions the Word of God. What happens if the research does not agree or even tears down God's message? As I said before, and I contend now, this is coming back to haunt us. People are dying over what we have done. It must be stopped now."

Vanessa, hearing the scathing criticism of the research, finds her eyes filling with tears. She tries to remain calm. But the nervous anticipation, poor sleep, and pent-up emotion cannot be contained, "We are doing nothing wrong here. Yet, I fear for my life. I don't want to die. This is not what I expected from a life of science. I can't take it. I'm not that strong." She bows her head and covers her face with her hands. She can't stop her silent sobbing.

Those in the meeting are surprised at her lack of stoicism and control. They have little understanding of what she has been through. Monsignor Grandscheid shakes his head, confirming his opinion of her and the research.

Ryan bends down with his lips close to her ear and whispers to her quietly, so that only she can hear, "Vanessa. You're crying in front of the Pope. This is not the time for that. Can't you control your emotions?"

She looks back at him and silently shakes her bowed head. It's been too much for her.

Ryan decides that he must speak up, "Monsignor, in my humble position here as a physician, and as a new visitor to your beautiful country and the glorious Vatican, I have seen first hand the power of the *Prophecy Scroll*.

This research has shown that science and religion are, as you say, sisters. They can and should work together to elevate our understanding of the world. This research supports many of the wonderful practices espoused by the Church. It supports the efficacy of prayer, almsgiving, singing, eating healthy, developing values, and protecting nature, all actions that will enhance a person's spirit. It promotes the advancement of virtues and elimination of vices to banish sins and plagues. This is a powerful message that the Church must embrace. It's not heretical, but rather, it's spiritual and consistent with God's message to mankind. The research brings these messages to so many more people."

"I know it is difficult," the Pope says to Ryan. He then directs his attention to Vanessa. "You must be strong, dear. Those in religion need to pay close attention to our scientific discoveries and ensure that what we teach in religion is also consistent with our scientific and natural understanding of reality. Of course, science is evolving and sometimes the scientific principles of reductionism, where science only sees part of the picture, can be a problem. Religion fills in the whole picture. We all know that faith is one of the most important principles of life. With faith, we can explore the world, send people to the moon, conquer fears, and see how the tiniest particles of the universe act."

He pauses to let his words settle into the minds of those present. Everyone is waiting for his next words. "We are climbing the scientific walls of time, and our understanding of the principals in the Universe are evolving. We can take the case of Noah as an example. Through a vision, God told Noah about the upcoming flood and its terrible consequences for the world. Noah was inspired to help save all species on earth. This knowledge of what will happen is called faith. He had faith that what he was doing was the right thing. Everyday, our actions are based on the belief that we are correct in our understanding of the way the world works. We have faith that we are doing the right thing. Now, when science gives us more information to base our reality on, it's a good thing. If we can measure the elusive spirit, it can confirm our faith and helps us interpret the *Prophecy Scroll* as words from God."

He pauses a few seconds before he says the next words. "But my dear, like Noah, it is not without risk." He says with a sorrowful look on his face. "When the early Europeans traveled across the seas to the new world, it was not without risk. When Galileo demonstrated the earth revolved around the sun, it was not without risk. When, the astronauts traveled to set foot on the moon, it is not without risk. The research you are doing has risk."

Cardinal Martinelli speaks up, "I studied the papers that you have published, and found the results of the research at Brisighella to be remarkable. The research demonstrates the power of this ancient wisdom from God and continues to support our Church's view of authentic spirituality. I believe we need to make this knowledge available to all. I see no conflict here. Even though we intuitively know that prayer is associated with heightened spiritual energy, it has never been confirmed until now, with your brilliant research. This is a breakthrough and shows that science supports that which we know through spirituality. It's not surprising that the insights they had two thousands years ago still apply to our era. I fully support this research."

Vanessa tries to hold back her emotions as she says, "Then, why are people so opposed to our research?"

Monsignor Grandscheid quickly answers with disdain, "Science has brought us stem cells from killing unborn children, the atomic bomb from understanding the secrets of the atom, enhanced disease by manipulating genes, chemical weapons, and dangerous new microbial life forms. Not all science is good for the world, and consistent with the ways of the Lord. Take for example, new age philosophy. We have distanced ourselves from this philosophy because as we understand, it blurs the distinction between good and evil and creates the mindset that we cannot condemn anyone no matter what they do. They believe that nobody, regardless of what they do, should feel guilt or need forgiveness."

Grandsheid looks at each member of the circle to let the next concept sink in. "This is wrong. We are constantly battling evil on earth and this philosophy doesn't seem to recognize this dichotomy. New age philosophy states that any believer can connect with divine spirit of the cosmos and allows people to ascend to a higher sphere by following enlightened masters. It appears that your research is similar. Your research suggests that anyone can have a powerful spirit, without believing in God. We believe that spiritual life is based on our relationship with God through prayer. We need to listen to the words that God brings us. This and only this will enhance our spirit and guide us through life, not simple actions and new age philosophies."

Ryan, frustrated at his uninformed opinion, speaks up to defend Vanessa and the research, "Monsignor, with due respect, you are simply wrong. New age strategies are not science. It cannot be compared to the research in Brisighella. There is not a shred of scientific evidence that links crystals, psychic healing, iridology, and other new age strategies to improving health other than placebo. Yet, the research done on the actions suggested by the *Prophecy Scroll*, and implemented at the Terme, is not only of the highest quality, supported by the National Institutes of Health, it is consistent with decades of clinical trials on how meditation, prayer, exercise, healthy diets, creativity, and clean environments improve health and well-being. This is real science, not some mumbo jumbo trick to control you through so-called masters of the universe. Furthermore, as a practicing physician, I see first hand how strategies in the *Prophecy Scroll* can improve health. If you can not see this, then you're ignorant of science."

The Pope raises his eyebrows at Ryan's strong language. Grandsheid stews at this accusation and impudent show of disrespect. Then, Camerlengo Castellengo, a close colleague of Grandsheid's, speaks up, "Now, Dr. Laughlin, I can speak for Monsignor Grandsheid's extensive knowledge of both science and religion. Science can be wrong sometimes, and it will bring a firestorm of dissent against you when it is discovered. You are simply seeing the tip of the iceberg with the conflict regarding your research. I fear for Dr. Venetre's life, and yours, as well. You have your careers ahead of you, and it would be wise to move into a new line of research that does not push the boundaries between religion and science. The world is not ready for this. We must rely on religion to understand the divine spirit, and not science. I'm sorry, but it is you that is ignorant if you do not recognize the broad realm of religion."

Grandsheid appreciates the direct way that the Camerlengo handled Ryan, and he calms down.

Ryan is quietly thinking how arrogant and self-righteous the uniformed can be.

The Pope, frustrated at the discourse, replies, "Enough! We all know these are risky times and many people don't know where to turn. They often grasp for the newest or most convenient philosophies, without regard to science or divine knowledge. The words of the *Prophecy Scroll* present insight that has been passed to us from those who lived at the time of Christ. Our knowledge of the divine spirit is as old as mankind, and the *Prophecy Scroll* has been given to us to help us live a life of goodness. The application of science to measure it is novel, but cannot, and should not, be denied. The human spirit can be seen as a common language for which the people of all worlds can come together. Some people call English the world's common language, but it is not."

He pauses to let the next statements hit hard. "The human spirit is truly the common language, and the scroll presents a way to understand this.

When people are unified in a common language and understanding, we can finish resolve the confusion and conflict. We can accomplish this dream for all of mankind. It is here for us to embrace or discard as leaders and as individuals. Thus, I believe the Church must act to expand our knowledge of the *Prophecy Scroll* despite the conflict associated with it. It's a path we must embrace. For these reasons, we need to continue this mission. Gabriela, please contact each of the scholars around Italy and tell them to share their manuscripts with our colleagues here. Dr. Venetre and Dr. Laughlin, it is a pleasure to have you here today. My best wishes to both of you and the research you are doing. I know that it is not without risk, but I am confident that the Lord will show you the right path and protect you."

With that, the Pope slowly rises and walks back into his chambers. The group sits, stunned at this unusual departure from his conservative consensus-built opinions. The Camerlengo and secretaries follow him. Grandsheid sits, shocked, not knowing what to say. Vanessa smiles through her tears. They each think about the implications of this decision. They will now confront the evil head on. It will not be easy.

As they walk out of the meeting accompanied by the Swiss Guard, Vanessa turns to Ryan, with affection in her eyes. "Thank you, Ryan. I'm not sure what happened to me in there, but I couldn't maintain my composure. It's been too much to cope with, and I just lost it. I couldn't stop crying. It's not like me. I blew it. And you saved the day. I couldn't believe that you told the Monsignor Grandsheid that he was ignorant."

Gabriela defends Ryan's comments, "Well, he was ignorant of science. The church cannot, and should not, be ignorant. They, above all others, must be willing to see the big picture for both religion and science. I'm glad it worked out. I appreciate you speaking up, Ryan. There are not many people who could have done what you just did. I know the Pope was conflicted about this research, and you changed his mind. That takes courage."

Ryan, his emotions still stirred, replies to Gabriela, "I responded with my heart. He was simply wrong. They need to support this research. It's a no brainer. I was not worried about the Pope's decision, but I am worried about this maniac trying to kill us to stop this research. We must be careful—and vigilant. I fear we have not seen the last of him."

Chapter 41. The Threat

Ryan, Vanessa, and Gabriela walk out of the Vatican's second floor reception room, and again, through the broad wooden arch of the hallways leading from the Clementine Hall, then down to the guarded entrance to the Pope's quarters. Gabriela wants to show them the famous Vatican Apostolic Library of the Holy See, which contains one of the most significant collections of historical texts including the *Prophecy Scroll*.

They walk through the covered walkways to the library, and enter with their security clearances checked carefully. She walks into a vault with a glass covered display box that contains the final completed *Prophecy Scroll* manuscripts that have been assembled from Scroll fragments. She points out that they are held in a closely controlled and monitored environment that stabilizes the humidity and light, and keeps the artifacts from further deterioration. She walks over to the offices of Drs. Unico and Monsein from Notre Dame University and introduces them. They review the pains-taking process of assembling the fragments like a giant ancient puzzle.

Ryan and Vanessa are impressed with their detailed work and the quality of the final manuscripts that have been sent to the scholars around Italy. The tour and their meeting with the Pope have buoyed Vanessa's energy and her anxiety is slowly passing. She is excited to proceed to the next phase of their journey.

"What do we have to do next to retrieve the two manuscripts, the *Blessing of Prosperity and the Blessing of Love?*" Vanessa asks Gabriela.

"I will call the scholars and tell them to expect you in the next few days," Gabriela replies. "You need to go to Sardinia first, to meet with Sister Ambra, and then to Pisa to meet with Father Fabrizio—Fabio for short."

"Tell us about them," Ryan asks.

"Sister Ambra is a rare breed among clergy. She calls herself an organic foods farmer. But she's much more than that. She has a PhD in economics from the University of Vienna, and has led international efforts on the sustainability of our agricultural system to feed the world. Father Fabio needs no introduction. He's the heartthrob of an entire female generation. He's an Italian movie star turned priest. Unusual man."

"Can't wait to meet them both," Vanessa responds.

"And remember Aldo? He will pick you up at the ferry station."

"Not Aldo Pessari!" Vanessa exclaims.

"Yes, the one and only."

"Are you serious?"

"Si, he's a professor now, at the Universita Degli Studi Di Sassari. He's doing research on the lifestyles of the local people. You know about the Blue Zones? There is a high percent of people who live to be over a hundred years there. He's researching the diet, lifestyles, and genetic variations that contribute to this."

Vanessa laughs at the thought of meeting up with Aldo again.

Gabriela smiles at her. "Don't laugh. He will be very helpful. He'll drive you around, show you the sites, and introduce you to Sister Ambra."

"I'm sure Aldo would like to do more than just be helpful," Vanessa says quietly to Gabriela. "He's your basic unapologetic Italian male chauvinist. He tried to seduce me many times in med school, on the ruse that he wanted to get to know me better."

Gabriela whispers back, "Maybe he's matured and tamed his *pistolino* by now. He has a fiancé. Give him the benefit of the doubt."

"Well, I'll believe it when I see it."

"Anyway, you won't be alone. Ryan will be with you."

"Did you already call him?"

"Si. He's excited to see you. In fact, he said he couldn't wait."

"I'm sure of that," Vanessa rolls her eyes.

Gabriela speaks louder to catch Ryan's ear, "Aldo is an international triathlete who competes across the world. His research is outstanding too."

Vanessa turns to Ryan to add her two cents about Aldo, "I must apologize to you already for Aldo's behavior. I knew him in med school. He's charming, and can sweep you right off your feet, and for women, right into bed. I wasn't interested then, and I'm not now."

"Maybe, that's why he's so fond of you," Gabriela quickly responds, "You have been a formidable challenge to his male ego, and for some men, that's tough to take."

Ryan takes this conversation in stride, realizing that Aldo discovered the same attraction for Vanessa that he has. He has heard about Italian men, but has not seen them in action. This will be an interesting trip to Sardinia.

Gabriela indicates the need to stay at the Vatican to continue her work, but says she will call both scholars and facilitate the meetings. "Ryan, you'll get that brief tour of Italy you wanted. You will like both Sister Ambra and Father Fabio. And Aldo too! Each is charming in their own right. Call me if things change, or if any trouble occurs here, especially with Aldo. I know how to keep him in line."

Vanessa convinces Ryan to spend the remainder of the day renting Vespa Italian scooters to see the spots of Rome. He shakes his head, thinking it is exactly the wrong thing to do if they want to stay safe. He does not quite understand her thinking but goes along to avoid an argument. Gabriela directs them to the Vespa rental place a few blocks away. They kiss each other's cheeks to say goodbye. Gabriela also gives Vanessa a long hug and tells her to be careful and attentive.

She pulls Vanessa close to her and says, "Ryan's a good man. He'll protect you, but you must also protect him. Let's pray that the trip will be non-eventful. Take care. I love you. And call me when you get to Sardinia."

Ryan and Vanessa walk over to the Vespa rental shop just down from the Vatican, along the Via della Coneliazione.

After querying about the availability of two Vespas, the man at the desk recognizes that Ryan is American, and sees an opportunity to sell him on them. "Nothing exudes the European retro style more than a Vespa. And it's more than a personal declaration of style, its practical too. You average thirty kilometers to the liter. That's about seventy miles per gallon in the U.S. It's easy to park and perfect for urban transportation. Is this your first foray into the two-wheeled world?"

"I bike a lot, but there are not many scooters in the States," Ryan says reluctantly. "Some consider them dangerous because American drivers don't see them on the road."

"I've rented them many times here," Vanessa says. "It is the best form of transportation in Rome. Quite safe. Drivers and pedestrians look out for them."

Without saying word, Ryan's expression makes it clear that he doubts this contention.

The Vespa man continues his sales approach, "We have several models to choose from. We even have pink one for the beautiful lady." He walks them out back where the scooters are stored. He finds two matching Vespas that should suit them, pink for Vanessa and bright orange for Ryan, to announce to other drivers his inexperience as a Vespa driver.

Ryan rolls his eyes, and realizes that this is fast becoming a true Italian vacation. He hopes he survives it to appreciate the fond recollections of it. "Sounds fun," Ryan smiles. "…if I don't kill myself. Okay, show me how these babies work. Any rules which I shouldn't break? Is it like a bike?

Vanessa smiles, "Ryan, it's just like a motorcycle."

"Si, like a mountain bike with a motor," the man says. "Teenagers use them all the time."

For some reason, that statement doesn't help Ryan feel any safer. The man reviews the controls with him. Ryan sits down, and manipulates the controls.

"Your arms should be stretched without having to lean forward. Your brake levers are on each side of the handle bars, just like your bike. Your right hand controls the throttle. You simply twist it, like this, and off you go."

Ryan twists it as instructed and he pops a wheelie and takes off down the parking lot, barely under control. He is surprised with its acceleration.

"*Aspetta*! Wait! You need this. It's the law." The Vespa man picks up a fashionable helmet and runs across the parking lot to give it to Ryan. "Please wear a helmet."

"It's easy, but where's the exercise in this," Ryan says with a smile.

"There is none," Vanessa laughs. "It's an Italian thing. Don't be a maniac on it. You're safe if you're careful and attentive to the cars and people around you."

"*Andiamo*. Let's go." Ryan twists the throttle again while holding the break.

The man shakes his head as he watches them head out. He makes a Sign of the Cross before and after a brief prayer, hoping to save the American's life on a Vespa.

They drive a few blocks to the Vespa museum, look through it for a few minutes, and then take off to see Rome, the Vespa way. They hit the popular tourist spots including the Coliseum, the Roman Forum, and the Arch of Constantine. He enjoys not only the Vespas, but also the time spent with a relaxed Vanessa. In retrospect, it is precisely what they both needed to do.

Vanessa points out the historical relevance of the Arches. "This is one of three surviving triumphal arches in Rome, situated between the Coliseum and the Palatine Hill. The first one was the Arch of Titus that was built in the first century to celebrate the conquering of Jerusalem. That invasion was the reason the *Prophecy Scroll* was written and the religious leaders sealed it away with the other *Dead Sea Scrolls*."

They grab some *paninis* and water at a local café, and find a sunny spot for a picnic in Palatine Hill Park overlooking the Coliseum. The view of Rome from the park is spectacular, unlike any view of Rome he has ever seen. As he stares at the Forum and Coliseum buildings, he can imagine the crowds of ancient Romans gathering to see the gladiators' event of the day.

As they lay on the blanket, Vanessa and Ryan talk about all of the positive activities of the day, each of which has boosted their energy. They are in a good place now, far from any threat to their lives.

Ryan lies back on the blanket and stares up at the white clouds as they idly move across the blue skies of Rome. Saying that Rome is a romantic city is like saying the Mona Lisa is a beautiful piece of art. Words cannot describe it. He realizes how special it has been to be with Vanessa today.

He has been successful in distracting her from the real threat to the research and to her life. In the process, he is doing things that, just a few weeks ago, would have been beyond his most vivid imagination. Despite the conflict and emotional turmoil of the murders, he has found an inner peace that reflects his own high energy in many Realms. He thinks about Julia and how lucky he was to meet her, and how fortunate it was that she encouraged him to go on this trip. Is this all part of going with the flow or is it the synchronicity of his energy with that of the world? He has no clue, but does not care.

Linda and Deanna at the Terme were correct. The feelings of high energy are intoxicating. Once you feel so good, you don't want to let it go. And it becomes easier and easier to return to this uplifting state of being. This is the way life should be. Or, maybe he is just fooling himself. Does he feel good because he is simply on vacation, or worse yet, because he's falling in love?

Who knows? It's a good feeling any way you look at it. But he does acknowledge some credit to the ideas of the *Prophecy Scroll*. They are magical and can seemingly transform a person's life. Despite this, right now, he still must not forget the looming threat. He must continue to be vigilant and protective. He recognizes that they are not safe until the murderer has been apprehended and put away.

They finish lunch and continue on through Rome. They park their Vespas to see one of the most famous fountains in the word.

"The Trevi Fountain was built in the 18th century at the request of the Pope," Vanessa explains. "It was the site of the Roman Empire's Aqua Virgo aqueduct. They say it has magical qualities. If you want a wish to come true, you simply toss a coin into the fountain." She turns her back to the fountain, closes her eyes, thinks of a wish, takes a coin in her right hand and tosses it in over her left shoulder.

"So what did you wish?" Ryan's curiosity is peeked.

"I can't tell you, or it won't come true," she says definitively.

"I see. I'll give it a try," Ryan insists. "I need a wish or two to come true."

Standing in front of the fountain, Ryan turns around and spontaneously tosses in a coin. Then, he asks, "Do I need to do something special after I toss it in, or can I just think about the wish?"

"No, no, no! You blew it! Do you always act first and think later?" She laughs. "All men do that, don't they? *Ascolta!* First, you must turn your back to the fountain, and then, close your eyes and toss the coin—using your right hand over your left shoulder. If you don't do it right, your wish won't come true."

"Okay! Okay! Do I detect a hint of superstition in you?" Ryan says with a smile.

"Most Italians are believers. We recognize that what happens to you in life is not only by chance. There are subtle powers, energy perhaps, at work that exists beyond chance. It's like the concept of synchronicity. It can go with you or against you. I simply like to hedge my bets in whatever little ways I can—to make it go my way."

Ryan then turns around and throws a second coin into the fountain using the correct technique.

"*Oh, Mio Dio!*" Vanessa exclaims. "That's embarrassing. I completely forgot about the other tradition. If you toss two coins into the fountain, it will bring you marriage." She laughs out loud.

"Did you do that on purpose? Is there anything else I should know about this fountain?"

"Well, yes. You should also know that if you toss in three coins, you'll get a divorce."

"Well then, that settles it. I'll stick to two coins. It's hard enough just to find romance, much less marriage." He grins suspiciously, and studies her to see what she is up to.

"Ryan, don't give me that look," Vanessa says. "I did not do that on purpose."

"It's a curious idea, and one that I'm sure didn't pop into your mind just by chance. It must be synchronicity!" He laughs as he walks back to his Vespa. She returns the smile. There is much that she likes about this man.

"Where should we go next?" Vanessa asks. "Rome is big and we've only hit a few of the tourist sites. We can push on, or simply go to a café, sip wine, and enjoy some conversation. Your choice!"

She studies him with sincere eyes. "Ryan. I want to thank you again for being here with me. I feel so much safer and it's much more fun."

"It's my pleasure," Ryan says. "I'm also enjoying this unexpected tour of Rome. What time do we have to get to the ferry terminal? Are we not going to Sardinia tonight?"

"You're right. As much as I would like to sip some wine at a local cafe, we need to keep moving. We should get our things and catch a taxi to the train that will take us to the coastal ferry in Civitavecchia."

On the way to return the Vespas, a Fiat 600 smart car comes up behind and follows them a bit too closely for Vanessa's comfort. They cannot make out the driver, but think that, perhaps, they may be going to the same place. However, the reckless bumper to butt driving raises an alert in both of their minds. They look at each other as they decide to drive faster to move out ahead of the Fiat. As they do this, the Fiat also moves faster, staying close on their tail. Ryan motions to Vanessa to pull over and let the impatient driver pass. As the car passes, they get a glimpse of the intense driver.

Ryan yells, "Did you get a look at that guy? Didn't he look like Johnson?"

She nods affirmatively, and yells, "Follow me!" She takes them along Largo Pietro Di Brazzà, and then onto Via Stamperia. They cross over Via del Tritone and look behind them.

The Fiat pulls out from a corner spot and comes up behind them again. The driver gets close enough to nearly bump them. What is the driver doing? Vanessa stops to see who it is, but the Fiat takes off as fast as possible down a back street, almost hitting two pedestrians. They give the driver the fist in the air, and yell, "*Vaffanculo!*"

Vanessa tries to lose the car by quickly taking off down a narrow side street. Ryan has a hard time keeping up. Vanessa heads down Via Del Nazarone and then takes a right on Via Bufalo. The Fiat is still following them, so they turn left onto Via dei Due Macelli, and drive the wrong way onto Via di Propaganda, on their way to the Spanish steps. They seem to have lost the car as they arrive at Gabriela's apartment. They park the Vespas and use the keypad to quickly get into the apartment.

They call the police, but they're of no help. They tell Vanessa that there are crazy drivers all over Rome. They leave a note asking Gabriela to return the Vespas. As they leave the apartment with their luggage, they see the Fiat parked in the distance. The driver sits in the car, watching them. Ryan heads over to give the driver a few words, but the car quickly departs, as Ryan gets close. They flag down a taxi, throw in their luggage, and head to the central train station.

They arrive in time to board the train to Civitavecchia with only minutes to spare. As the train leaves the station, they find a couple of seats in the corner, as far away from people as possible. They throw their luggage in the rack above them, and flop down in the seats. They are out of breath. They watch the aisle and out the window for Johnson, the driver of the Fiat, or anyone who looks suspicious. Tonight, going somewhere, anywhere but Rome, is paramount.

Chapter 42. Sardinia

Ryan and Vanessa are relieved as the train arrives in time to catch the late afternoon Ferry from Civitavecchia to Sardinia. The Sardinia Regina caters to tourists and includes bars, a la carte restaurants, a swimming pool, a solarium and several shops. It travels fast and smooth across the warm Mediterranean Sea, and arrives in Sardinia relatively quickly. Tonight, with the calm, warm evening, the ferry should arrive in Cagliari in time for Aldo to greet them and, perhaps, go out to dinner.

They walk across the boarding deck onto the large boat. They find some quiet seats on the top front deck, away from the crowded inner deck. They settle into two choice seats with a nice view of the sea for the three-hour trip.

The boat quickly leaves the dock and picks up speed as it departs the harbor. They both stand to watch over the front railing. The wind blows through their hair as they stare at the diminishing shoreline of cranes, docks, buildings, and adjacent hills as the ferry heads out into the open sea.

Vanessa turns to Ryan and says, "I need to call Aldo to see if he will actually pick us up at the station. It's too windy here."

She steps away from the deck to get shelter from the breeze in the top foyer. He watches her closely, but expects nobody to have followed them to the ferry. She dials Aldo's number and he answers, "Aldo, this is Vanessa Venetre. Remember me? How are you?"

"Vanessa, how could I forget? It is so good to hear your voice. Gabriela said that you were coming to visit about the *Prophecy Scroll*. I've been following your research. It's remarkable. I was hoping we could connect to discuss it. I'm also so sorry to hear about the death of Dr. Nobili. He was a great man. It's so tragic. He will be missed. I still can't believe it. Are you okay?"

"Thank you for your concern, and your help. It's been a rough week so far, but our meeting with the Pope was encouraging. He's expressed continued support for our research in using the manuscripts."

"That's surprising," his astonishment can't be hidden. "It's tough to get support from that old paisano. When are you arriving?"

"We caught the last ferry out of Civitavecchia and should be there by 7:00 pm. Aldo, we toured Rome on Vespas, and were almost run over by a stranger in a smart car! We'd feel a lot safer if you can pick us up at the ferry station and take us to the hotel."

"Of course. Who else is with you?" He asks. "You have an escort?"

"He's not an escort. He's a physician from the States who was attending the Terme. He has been so kind and generous to help me, despite the risk he's taking. I just couldn't be alone."

"O, *hai uomo Americana*, eh?" He says with a seductive voice. "I'm sure he is quite helpful. Is there romantic inclinations that I detect."

"No, Aldo. He's not like you. He's simply a colleague who was visiting the Terme. He's a nice guy who doesn't always have sex on his mind. His name is Ryan Laughlin. You'll like him."

"What do you mean by that? I'm not like that anymore. Anyways, I look forward to meeting him. After I pick you up from the ferry, can I talk you into coming out to dinner with me."

"Not if we're alone," she states emphatically.

"No, no, I want you to meet my fiancé, Francesca. *Sicuramente*! Bring the doctor along. It will be fun."

"Okay, then. We're famished. We'll arrive about 7 pm. Thank you for helping."

"I'm happy to redeem myself after my bad behavior in med school," Aldo replies apologetically. "I had a few too many drinks on that night."

She laughs at his last comment. "I'm surprised you remember. But, to be accurate, it was several times. It's hard for me not to forget. I'll see you at the docks. Bye."

Vanessa hangs up and walks back to join Ryan standing on the front railing as the ferry continues to speed along. She turns to Ryan and says, "Aldo was nice over the phone. Perhaps, he's changed."

"What was your relationship with him?" Ryan asks as neutral as possible.

"He wanted to date me, or more likely, just have sex with me. He was attractive, smart, athletic, and full of himself. I wasn't interested. He's not my type. But he was very persistent and crossed the border from 'boys being boys' to sexual harassment a few too many times. After I said no about ten times, he eventually got the message. I'm more direct with men now. Maybe too direct. I hope you do not think I'm. . . How do you say? Anti-men?"

"I don't see that at all," Ryan says trying to be honest with her.

"After my husband cheated on me, I'm just a bit *particulare*, you know, particular. If there's one word which you need to know about Italian women—*gelosa*! It means we get jealous. We're not polyamorous. We are not good at sharing partners with other women. But I'm patient and I will find the man of my life sometime. I have a lot to offer. Let's sit down and relax."

As they sit down out of the wind, they watch the waves of the sea flowing by and the playful sea gulls flying overhead.

Ryan thinks about his wife, Sophia, and how lucky he was to have this type of relationship with her. "Vanessa, I understand. You don't need to explain. Most of us have had bad experiences in relationships, particularly, in college. I've been no angel with some women. I know I've hurt people because I was not clear about my intentions. I regret some of my behaviors, but I've learned to control my desires. I expect Aldo feels some guilt about his unwanted pursuits. Nobody wants to hurt others."

"Maybe he does regret his past behavior, but I doubt it," Vanessa replies. She stops and stares at Ryan with those big brown eyes. "You're not like him, Ryan. You're respectful and considerate of the person you're with. As I said before, I'm lucky to have you here with me. Thank you, again." As she says this, tears well up in her eyes. Surprised, Ryan wonders if it was something he said. She wipes the tears and takes Ryan's hand in hers. She holds it tight. "What are we going to do, Dr. Laughlin? I've brought you into a serious situation. I'm so ashamed for doing that, but I cannot be without you right now. I feel so guilty."

Ryan tightens his grip on her hand. "It's okay. If I didn't feel strongly about you and the research, I wouldn't be here. We're in this together. I'm learning more than I expected. We're on a mission, and we'll see this through. We'll get the manuscripts, apprehend the murderer, and bring sanity back to our lives. You will be back to tranquil Brisighella on Tuesday, all safe and sound."

She squeezes his hand for a brief moment and leans her head against his shoulder while the sea moves rapidly by. He always seems to know what to say. It will be hard to leave this man when he goes back to America.

"Would you like something to drink?" He asks.

"You're sweet," she smiles. "A little vino would do wonders for me right now. I'll come with you."

They head over to the bar, and wait behind an overweight American couple. The couple is occupying all of the attention of the bar staff, complaining about the lack of the junk food they want. The man rips into the bar attendant, "What kind of a ship is this? You have no nachos? Every ship in the Caribbean has nachos. I thought Italians were such food connoisseurs. Well, do you at least have some Cheetohs?"

The attendant, who is patiently trying to meet his demands, calmly says, "No sir. Again, I'm sorry, but we have no Cheetohs, either. We do, however, have some excellent potato chips and pretzels. Will that do?"

The fat man storms off, with his hefty wife following him, shaking their heads in disgust. "Let's get out of here. This cruise line is so inept!"

Vanessa turns to Ryan and says, "Did you feel it?"

"Feel what?" He asks.

"Did you feel that depressing feeling when your energy is drained by the sinkhole of low energy that surrounds that guy? He has all the trappings of a zombie. He's overweight, with little self-control. He eats a bad diet, is inflexible, angry, ignorant, and most likely suffers from many chronic conditions. He tries to compensate for his low energy by shifting energy from other Realms or stealing it from others. In the process, he becomes irritating and difficult to be around."

"We see these types at my clinic all of the time," Ryan replies. "What a little exercise, change in diet, creative outlets, and meditation could do for him. Unfortunately, I'm sure these activities are as foreign to him as he is to the Italians!"

They each get a glass of merlot and go back to the top deck to sit quietly for a few minutes, drinking their wine slowly. They continue to watch the entertaining sea gulls coast along in the air as the ferry flies over the sea—getting closer to Cagliari.

Vanessa asks, "Have you been to Sardinia?"

"No, but I know it's a blue zone. People live a long life on this island."

"My family used to vacation here. The natural beauty and history is an attraction to many tourists. It's a mountainous island that is shaped like a kidney bean and is about the size of Sicily," Vanessa explains in her academic tone. "It's the second-largest island in the Mediterranean Sea and sits on the west coast of Italy."

"I suppose it has a rich history with Rome so close by."

"Like all of Italy. The prehistoric Nuragic tribes lived here for thousands of years, well into Roman times. They lived behind a well-hidden natural cavern in what is now called the Lost Valley of Lanaittu. The whole cavern collapsed creating a huge crater with tall stone walls. Dinosaurs no longer live there," she laughs. "But there are two old stone villages with many artifacts that are still intact."

"Did the Romans invade here, too?"

"Surprisingly, the Romans did not get here until the third century because the Carthaginians dominated the island. After the mercenaries on the island revolted, the Romans were able to defeat the Carthaginians.

"Let's pray for no revolts while we're here," He makes a futile attempt at humor. "Where does the ferry land?"

"We'll be arriving in Cagliari. It's the major city of the island. It was built on seven hills, with the oldest part of the city, Castello, cresting the highest hill. We should climb it. There's a stunning view of the Gulf of Angels from the peak. The ancient Romanesque Cathedral of Cagliari is also there. It's a beautiful island and will take your breath away."

Time flies as they talk about the people, sites, and landscape of Sardinia. To their surprise, they arrive at the harbor a few minutes early. The sun is just setting over the mountainous horizon. They stand and watch the boat's arrival. They can see the city of Cagliari getting larger as they get closer. With its church steeples and mix of historic and modern buildings, it's a beautiful city to introduce arriving tourists to the island.

The minute that the ferry ramp is laid down, they walk briskly down it to disembark from the ferry. They see Aldo and a young lady coming to greet them. He is a tall affable man, with short light brown hair, and a dark tanned face. His muscular frame, from years of bench-pressing weights, stretches the sleeves of his short-sleeved shirt. The top three buttons are left unfastened, to bare his broad, hairless chest. His smile is fixed. He kisses Vanessa on both cheeks, shakes Ryan's hand, and then, introduces his fiancé.

Francesca, ten years younger, is an athletic beauty, with a comparably tanned face and long flowing blond hair. She, too, has a gym-built body, and is dressed casually, with loose flowing island pants and a cotton pull over shirt with colorful embroideries. They both are impressive human specimens, with muscles sculpted to near perfection.

Aldo opens his arms towards Vanessa and Ryan. "Welcome to our island! You have come at the right time. The *La Cavalcata Sarda* festival is this week. Thousands of people are coming from all over Italy to see our Sassari parade. The locals dress in costumes, and ride hundreds of our best Sardinian horses—and the occasional donkey."

Vanessa, thinking she needs to avoid another festival like the plague, is relieved to have an excuse to head out of town immediately after retrieving the manuscript. "I'm sorry. We have to meet as soon as possible with Sister Ambra Antonioni about the *Blessing of Prosperity*. We wish we could stay longer, but can only stay one night before we head to Pisa to get the next manuscript."

"That's unfortunate. I wanted to spend more time with you. Perhaps, you can plan better next time. While you're here, you are our guest, and we are happy to help you do whatever you need to complete your mission. The Pope has also authorized me to meet every whim and wish you desire." He laughs.

Vanessa rolls her eyes and realizes that some people never change.

Aldo and his wife escort them to their car, and drive to the Hotel del Villa Cagliari, in the old town. It's a three-story carved stone hotel built in the nineteenth century for the aristocracy from Europe to visit the Island. The hotel is perfectly restored, with large tapestries on the wall, ornate gold trim, and bright red runners down the hall.

"You are staying at the best hotel in Sardinia, as our guests. Don't worry. We've already made reservations for you." Aldo nods at Vanessa as she and Ryan exit the car, get their luggage, and head into the hotel. They agree to meet in the lobby for dinner in a half hour.

At the front desk, the clerk greets Ryan. "Welcome to Hotel del Villa Cagliari. What name is your reservation under?"

Before Ryan can say anything, Vanessa steps in and says, "Aldo Pessari made the reservation for two rooms."

The clerk replies, "I see, but we have only one room reserved."

"But we need two rooms," Vanessa says. "Do you have two?"

The clerk responds, "Oh, no problem. I understand." He looks busy as he pushes papers. When Ryan is not looking, he tips his head up and winks at Vanessa to indicate that he understands the relationship is not one of husband and wife. After locating two rooms together, he hands Vanessa the two keys.

They need to make haste in getting dressed for the evening dinner. Ryan goes to his room and Vanessa to hers. He retrieves the bag he brought back from his run in Rome and knocks on Vanessa's door.

She opens it. "Ryan, I'm nowhere near ready," she frets. "I have nothing to wear that is decent. I'll be so embarrassed."

Ryan smiles and says, "Maybe I can help."

"What can you do?" She looks disdainfully at her wardrobe selection in the luggage. "Despite all the things that happened this week, at least, I wanted to look good, especially to Aldo. But that's not to be. Excuse me, Ryan. I need to get ready." She begins to close the door, and Ryan puts his foot in the opening to stop it from closing.

"What? Do you need something? I don't have any clothes for you. Or, for me either—for that matter."

"But I do," Ryan hands the bag through the crack in the door.

Vanessa opens the door and grabs the brown, nondescript bag. She looks at it, shocked. "You didn't! Did you buy that outfit I tried on? No, it couldn't be. Ryan, you shouldn't have. When did you have time?"

"I'm a fast runner. I hit the Villa Borghese, and Via Condotti, this morning. Do you like it?"

"It's gorgeous. Thank you so much. I can't believe you did this! You are such a sweetheart. *Tu se mi amore!*" She gives him a big long hug while Ryan soaks in the positive energy.

Ryan heads back to his room to finish dressing. A few minutes later, he picks up Vanessa, in her stunning new outfit, and heads down to the lobby. Ryan, wearing his casual jacket, and Vanessa, in her new Gucci design, arrive to the smiles of Aldo and Francesca.

"Vanessa, you look stunning tonight. Is that an Armani design?" Aldo attempts to impress her.

Ryan smirks, and tries to outdo his competition for Vanessa's attention. He says, "No. This is Gucci. I bought it earlier today for her."

"Oh, my mistake. I've never been able to tell the difference," Aldo admits. Francesca rolls her eyes at his ignorance.

"Well, I may not know fashion, but I do know restaurants," Aldo tries to save face. "We will be taking you to Su Combidu Carasau, in the old town. They serve native cuisine and wine grown and prepared from the farms here in Sardinia. Their most popular meal is the *porcheddu*. It's a young pig that is slowly roasted over local timber and frequently basted with drippings to make it very tender. Also, you must have the *culurgiones*. It's *fantastico*! It's ravioli pasta filled with *pecorino* cheese, mint, and other ingredients that have been kept secret by the family for generations. There's nothing like it in the world. Trust me."

"Thank you, Aldo. Sounds wonderful," Ryan says, hoping to maintain the group's energy.

They arrive at an old two story stone building with a lovely vine-entangled edifice to the restaurant. The concierge, dressed in formal evening attire with a bow tie, greets them. They are immediately seated. Like magic, a bottle of the local Cannonau wine appears at the table.

"The wine here is rich and healthy," Aldo explains, "The grapes grown in the countryside produce a delicious red wine that's both dry and sweet at the same time."

"How do they do that?" Ryan asks.

"It's the special grapes and the ideal climate for them, here on Sardinia," Aldo replies.

"I'm excited to try it. And thanks for picking us up and hosting us while we're here," Ryan tries to build some rapport with Aldo. "It's my first time to Sardinia."

"*No problema*," Aldo says. "Vanessa is our special guest, and you're here with her."

Ryan ignores the slight. "I heard you're quite an athlete, and doing some remarkable health services research?"

"*Si!*" He smiles, seeing an opportunity to impress Vanessa. "I'm an international tri-athlete. But I must maintain the highest level of health to compete at that level. So after medical school, I took a faculty position here at the Universita Degli Studi Di Sassari. Sardinia is one of the Blue Zones where many people live to be over one hundred years old. Their longevity and lifestyles are truly amazing and worthy of study."

"I'm familiar with the Blue Zone book. It's by a Minnesota author, Dan Buettner. What have you found in your studies?"

"Along with genetics, it is clear that exercise, diet, and social support contribute to their longevity. Everybody walks, talks, and eats well here. It's a way of life. The typical Sardinian diet contains beans, nuts, whole-grain breads, fruits, garden vegetables, and mastic oil. All quite natural and eaten soon after harvest."

"What's mastic oil?" Ryan asks.

"It's oil from the evergreen shrub that produces pistachios. You know, the nut. A diet of mastic oil has been shown to absorb cholesterol, lower high blood pressure, and decrease the risk of heart attacks. It also seems to have anti-bacterial and anti-fungal properties based on some of my research."

"Do you follow the same diet?" Ryan asks as he follows his pattern of deflecting any questions about himself.

"I do my best, but like most men, I have difficulty sticking to any diet. Especially, when it comes to good wines. But the Canoneau wine here is quite healthy. It makes it even harder to control consuming much of it."

Aldo seems like a sensible guy. Perhaps, he's changed over the years, and has settled down in his relationship with Francesca. The waiter comes and takes their order. Ryan admits that he is a pasta addict, but decides to add a natural green salad to his order of *Culurgiones* ravioli. He also has a special request, in acknowledgement of Aldo's research. "Also, could you give me generous portions of mastic oil."

Aldo moves his attention to Vanessa. He tries to be sincere and empathetic. "Vanessa, please tell me how you are feeling. Are you okay?"

"Not good," Vanessa sadly states. "The loss of Paolo has been difficult. You know it was a murder and I may be next. Ryan has been helpful. This trip will allow us to stay ahead of any pursuer but also acquire more of the remaining *Prophecy* manuscripts for our research. But our future is threatened and seems so empty without Paolo."

Aldo misses this opportunity to enhance Vanessa's energy as he inappropriately ogles her shapely body while she is opening her heart. To top it off, he leans over and says quietly in her ear, so as not to let Francesca and Ryan hear, "You know, Vanessa. I was so infatuated with you in med school. I'm still disappointed we didn't get together. Is it not too late?" He gives her the soft 'I want you' eyes.

Vanessa returns it with her big 'quit it' eyes. Vanessa recognizes the need to nip this in the bud. She says quietly but firmly, "Aldo, you're a good person, but I was never attracted to you. You were not even on my list. So, drop it, will you."

Aldo mimics a poor little boy's pouty face, and then puts his hand on hers without regard to Francesca and Ryan's reactions. He leans close to her ear and whispers, "That's sad. We could have made the best couple together. It's your eyes, your figure, your intellect, and your passion. It's a powerful combination. I really adore. . ."

Vanessa turns and interrupts him abruptly and loudly, "Aldo, zip it. If you know what is best for you!"

The arrival of the dinner gives her a break from Aldo's unwanted attention. Both Francesca and Ryan have been watching closely.

Ryan ignores the flirting, but Francesca thinks differently. "Aldo, if you want to continue to fawn over Vanessa, I might as well go home. You decide."

Aldo holds up his hands, shrugs his shoulders, and says, "What are you talking about? I'm just paying the respect that a woman like her deserves."

Francesca says angrily, "If you don't pay your respects somewhere else, you'll find this meat on your head where it belongs, you *bruta* meathead."

Ryan and Vanessa laugh out loud at her comments. She'll be good for him. Some men just don't change much unless pushed by their lover.

Vanessa looks at Ryan, discreetly. He is a different sort of man. Kind and gentle. Respectful and unselfish. He's not so egocentric like many men. But there is a sadness about him. It must have been difficult to see his Sophia die.

Aldo improves his behavior as the conversation shifts to comparing his research with those results of the Terme Project. Both found that the same healthy lifestyles could enhance a person's well being. In the Terme Project, it enhanced a person's energy while Aldo's research it enhanced their longevity. The dinner conversation moves to one heated question—if you enhance your own energy, will it contribute to a longer life? Aldo indicates that the meeting with Sister Ambra may shed the best light on this.

As they wrap up dinner, Aldo is careful with his words and suggests that they collaborate more. Vanessa appreciates his efforts to minimize his flirting, but it does not matter. The bridge is burning and he has to do more than talk to put out the flames. She will see what happens tomorrow.

Chapter 43. The Dilemma II

They arrive back at the Hotel del Villa Cagliari, and say goodbye to Aldo and Francesca. Vanessa tries to avoid the cheek kissing and hugging that Aldo wants to lavish on her. They walk up to their rooms and discuss the evening.

"I just don't like being around him," Vanessa complains. "He drains my energy."

"I can see why," Ryan empathizes. "He couldn't keep his hands off you. I understand his infatuation with you, but it was inappropriate, especially in front of Fancesca. She did straighten him out some. That will be good for him, but I doubt that he will learn much."

"Aldo is a classic example of wobbling in the *Rule of Balance*," Vanessa's tries to be positive. "Could you detect his strong and weak Realms?"

"He seemed to have high energy in the Body, Mind, and Way of Life Realms," Ryan surmises.

"Si! And low energy in the Spiritual and People Realms," she concludes. "He pulls energy from his strong Realms to boost his weak Realms and his attempts at love and affection become distorted."

"He falls off balance and wobbles," Ryan agrees. "How would you apply the *Rule of Challenges* with him?"

"Aldo is intelligent and perceptive," Vanessa says. "I would skip the first and second order changes, and focus on helping him learn to boost his weak energy. He's not hopeless."

"You're such an idealist," Ryan laughs. "Do you actually think you can change Aldo? He's a macho guy. An international athlete. He's entrenched in his ego. But I give you credit for considering it."

"He simply has to work on meditation and prayer in the Spiritual Realm, and genuinely think about how to help others more than himself in the People Realm," she smiles. "That would work. He could become a warrior instead of wallowing in life as a borderline zombie."

They both laugh. As they approach the doors to their two rooms, neither of them wants to initiate the next step in their relationship and invite the other into their room, particularly after the discussion about Aldo. Although they skirt the issue, they know that the past week's events have sealed their fate together like *pasta* and *ragù*.

They stand outside of their room doors. Neither of them takes the initiative to invite the other into their room. But neither wants to leave the other alone either. Small talk prevails and Ryan asks, "What's our schedule tomorrow?"

"At about noon, we'll meet with Sister Ambra Antonioni at the Cathedral of Santa Maria Assunta in Oristano, and review the *Blessing of Prosperity*. Hopefully, she'll be ready to give us a copy to add to the teachings. Then, we need to quickly catch the ferry back to Civitavecchia, and the train to Pisa to meet with Father Fabio about the *Blessing of Love*."

"Can't wait to hear about that," Ryan smiles. "Maybe, we can learn something. Where are we meeting?"

"Fabrizio Brizi works in the Cathedral of the Duomo in Pisa," she laughs. "The Vatican has him there for a reason. As Gabriela said, Fabio is *molto famoso*, and is every woman's dream. Maybe, someone will fall in love." She laughs again.

"Why are you laughing?" Ryan asks. "Because he's a priest? That's his choice."

"No," she says smiling. "He's gay."

Ryan's eyes light up as he laughs, "You're kidding. He actually knows that he's gay and admits it? Isn't that a faux pas for a priest?"

"I don't know the details. But it'll be interesting to meet with him. Have you been to Pisa before?"

"Yes, once before, with Sophia. She loved the Piazza of Miracles and the Leaning Tower. I'm still amazed that it's not fallen over."

"The history, legends, and even the views from the top are remarkable," She replies. "Did you go up?"

"Sophia did. I didn't. I know this sounds juvenile, but I have a fear of heights. I don't know why. Maybe, something happened as a kid. It's one of those fears that have no basis in reality. I've never fallen off a cliff or out the window, but I get dizzy when I'm up high looking down. I don't even like looking out of a tall building despite being protected by glass. I get vertigo and almost fall over. I even had a hard time going up into St. Peter's Cathedral in Rome."

After ten minutes of talking in the hallway, an older woman in the adjacent room opens the door a crack and stares at them with a stern look on her face. "*Silencio!* Shhhh! *Sto cercando di dormire.*"

Ryan stifles his smile and tries to appease the lady. "Sorry. *No problema.* We go." The complaint breaks the stalemate, and Ryan invites Vanessa into his room. "Come in. We don't want to disturb the lady any more."

She is surprised that it took Ryan so long to invite her in. She walks in and plops down on the antique armchair. "We all have our fears. I hate snakes and spiders," she laughs. "They simply creep me out. If I see a big one, I literally freeze and scream at the top of my lungs. It's a woman thing. It's hard to explain. But right now, my biggest fear is the killer that's on the loose. Aren't you afraid of him?"

"As I said before, we're in this together. And if a spider comes along, you'll need me." He pauses to look out the window, and then, shifts his stare into her brown eyes. "And if the Prophecy Killer shows up, I'm not afraid of him either. I might even get to use this thing."

He flashes the leather case with the small Beretta that he pulls out of his luggage and says, "It's a guy thing."

"What do you mean—it's a guy thing? That's illegal here," she says shocked. "Where did you get that thing?"

"LeGrand. He wanted us protected."

"Giving you a gun is not protecting us!" She exclaims. "Do you even know how to use it?"

"I'm a Minnesota hunter and from America. We all grow up with guns. I've been through a hunter safety course."

"So you're one of those gun-loving macho American men? Ryan, this is not hunting! I doubt you could use it if you had to. I'm disappointed. I didn't think you were that type of guy. And don't be showing that off or you'll get arrested."

LeGrand was right. He shouldn't have shown her the gun. It raises her anxiety and she thinks he's a nut case. But they both know they are safer with a gun.

She calms down some. "If you kill the spiders, I won't ask you to climb the Leaning Tower to save me from the evil villain."

"Agreed. And I won't use the gun on the spiders unless forced to," he laughs and then changes the subject. "I remember Pisa as being quite beautiful. Tell me more about it."

"Si. The Campo Santo, the Duomo Cathedral, and the Leaning Tower are among the most famous group of buildings in the world."

"We should explore them while we're there. Remember, I'm still on a relaxing vacation seeing the sights of Italy. I'm just a simple tourist."

"With a gun! I don't think simple is the right word," she replies.

"Did you know that the Leaning Tower of Pisa is not the only leaning building?" Ryan says as he tries to change the subject by reading from the tourist book. "The Baptistery, next to the Duomo Cathedral, is also leaning. All of the bell towers in the area are leaning."

"Si. This area of Italy is not good for tourists who have a fear of heights," She laughs. "I'm sorry. I shouldn't be laughing. There are plenty of spiders here also."

"I'll simply stay away from bell towers," he replies. "Before I left Minnesota, I was hoping to see more of Italy. I'm delighted to be getting my wish, even if it is a bit tense at times."

"It's not much of a tour," Vanessa says sarcastically, "Dear Sir, I invite you to risk your life to protect a near stranger from a crazy man on a murderous rampage, and then, if you survive, you will embrace your fears at the top of an unstable leaning bell tower."

He laughs. "Well, you're not a total stranger, and I have enjoyed seeing Rome and will enjoy seeing Sardinia and Pisa. Hopefully, we've lost the killer. How will he know to track us here?" He assures her, "We'll be fine."

Vanessa stands up and says she needs to go to bed. They say good night and she goes back to her own room.

Ryan stays up and reads the four manuscripts again in anticipation of seeing the others this week. He is still impressed with those who wrote these. They had a deep insight into the modern human condition with all of our problems and hopeful solutions. It is simple, divine and universal knowledge.

As he sits reading on his bed, Ryan hears Vanessa's cell phone ring next door. He walks over to the door and listens. "What? Tell me. What? Oh, mio Dio, mio Dio." Then she listens quietly to the caller.

Ryan tries to decipher what she is saying. He knows something terrible has happened. Then, he hears a knock at the door. He answers it.

Vanessa's face is as white as a sheet. She's breathing quickly and is emotionally taut. "I can't believe it. That was Gabriela on the phone. One of Gabriela's scholars in residence, Eugene Unico, was found in his apartment. He was dead. An overdose. Someone may have followed him home. Nobody saw him enter or leave his apartment. They do not know if it was a murder or not. There was no manifesto or other evidence left. What should we do?"

"My God. This is a nightmare," Ryan says horrified. "If he did kill Dr. Unico, he may know we're here, and most likely, will try to find us," Ryan says. "We must leave tomorrow afternoon, immediately after our meeting with Sister Ambra, and try to stay one step ahead. I don't like being a target. Right now we need our rest. Tomorrow will be another challenging day."

"How can I sleep, especially alone?" She asks. "Do you mind?"

"*No problema*," he says with a straight face and no hesitation. "We're definitely safer together."

Vanessa gets her things and moves them into Ryan's room. As they prepare for bed, they talk about the deaths. It's three murders now. She even admits that she is now thankful Ryan has a gun. If the killer is tracking them, Ryan's intention is to make sure the killer is brought to justice or is the next casualty. Words are easy right now.

They lie next to each other in bed and talk for a while about the blessings in their life and their hopes for the future. They do not kiss or hug. They simply enjoy the extra security and warmth that sleeping close together in bed brings them. Yet, they both know that the sexual tension between them is high.

As they drift closer to sleep, Vanessa wonders if making love will happen tonight. If it does, she wants it to come naturally, and at the right time. She will not initiate it. If Ryan is ready, he must take the first step. If he does, she will enjoy it beyond imagination.

Ryan holds her tightly. The only thing on his mind right now is making passionate love to Vanessa. But he recognizes her vulnerability right now, and does not want to appear to take advantage of this emotional fragility, especially after the Aldo scene. He is content to simply try to sleep next to her. He hopes that love may happen sometime, but if it does, it must come naturally and at the right time.

Vanessa fantasizes about being intimate with Ryan for a few minutes but, eventually, fatigue wins out and she falls asleep.

Ryan kisses Vanessa on the head and watches her sleep for a few minutes until he also drifts off. Intimacy will have to wait.

His sleep is restless, with wild dreams of people and animals chasing him. He runs as fast as he can through ancient villages. He wakes multiple times to see Vanessa sleeping quietly, and then doses off. He knows she is safe lying next to him.

At 7:00 am, Ryan wakes up in the midst of a strange dream. He turns to see Vanessa. To his surprise, she is not in bed, or in the room. His alarms go off, until he sees the note on the desk. The note reads—I went downstairs to get coffee and breakfast. See you there.

He quickly puts on his running clothes, and heads down to the lobby. He sees her sitting alone drinking a cappuccino, in the corner of an elegant sunroom that serves as the hotel's breakfast room. Flowers and old vines surround her with a brightly colored Murano glass chandelier suspended from the ceiling to lighten the room.

Ryan gives her a big, good morning hug, and wanders over to the buffet line to find some coffee. He comes back with his cappuccino and sits down at the table. She looks more miserable than he'd expect for early morning. He tries to put on a positive face to perk her up. "You look so beautiful sitting there in this ornate breakfast room, sipping your coffee with the sun brightening your face."

"*Boun giorno,*" she says as if it was a complaint. "I could not stop thinking about Dr. Unico. Everywhere we go, we bring tragedy. We are *sfortuna,* bad luck, for everyone."

"We just need to get some exercise to boost our energy, right? Remember the *Rule of Challenges.*"

"So, we'll be killed on a run!" she says sarcastically with a look that could kill a rat. "Great idea, Ryan."

"We can't just sit in the hotel room all day. I want to see some of the countryside. And it's a beautiful morning. We need the energy. I'll make sure we're safe. I'll bring the gun."

"I'll kill you if we get killed, Ryan," she says seriously, and then laughs at the contradiction. "Oh, what the hell! We all die sometime. At least we will do it with high energy. Let's go."

They head back to their rooms and do some yoga stretching after Vanessa gets dressed in her running gear. Ryan tucks the gun securely in his waist pack and they head down to the street. They start off running down Viale Buoncammino. The old road gives them a broad view of the Gulf of Cagliari to their left with several majestic sailboats and cruise ships resting on the calm aqua sea of the bay. They pass by the busy Mercato di San Benedetto. The covered market is filled with people crowding the fish stalls to buy from the local fisherman after the early morning catch. It's just as busy at the adjacent open markets for meats, fresh fruits, and vegetables.

They run through the ancient Lion's Gate to the old city and pass by the ruins of the restored Roman Amphitheatre that hosted some of the most spectacular gladiator battles outside of Rome. They pass the fourteenth century prison and sanctuary that includes an ancient statue of the Blessed Virgin of Bonaria. They hear the bell ringing from the Elephant Tower of the fourteenth century church of Saint Lawrence.

The chimes remind Vanessa of her father's stories of the tower. She talks about the tower as they run. "The tower takes its name from the small, marble elephant on a ledge in one of its corners. The bell tolls for those who are condemned to death on their way to the gallows."

"I wish the bell tolled for bringing the killer to the gallows right now."

"That would bring us some peace. But I doubt that could happen with the *polizia* here," Vanessa complains. "They are about as corrupt as the Sardinia mafia."

Their run brings them beyond the borders of the city to look out over the vast wetlands and rocky marshes of the regional nature reserve, called the Molentargius Pound. They are startled to see more than a thousand pink flamingos standing and flying in and out of the marsh.

"The flamingos have chosen these wetlands for their nesting," Vanessa continues retelling childhood stories. "The wetlands are home to hundreds of other birds too. When I was a little girl, I loved to sit and watch them flit about."

"Look at the array of colors," Ryan says. "The guide said that it has hundreds of species of birds including purple gallinules, herons, stilt plovers, little agreets, mallards, snipes, coots, you name it. They all seem to have settled here."

They stop to drink some water and watch the birds. They find it easy to lose track of time here. They shake back into reality when they realize that Aldo is going to pick them up soon. They take off in a steady vigorous run. Ryan is impressed at Vanessa's athletic ability. She is able to keep up with his long strides, despite being considerably shorter.

As they run back to the hotel, the Messenger sits quietly in his rented Fiat, following their every step. He patiently waits to complete his mission. Their running did not allow him the opportunity he wanted. He will find the right time to bring down the beast that threatens our world.

Chapter 44. The Beach

SARDINIA, ITALY
SUNDAY MORNING

When they return to the hotel, Aldo has already arrived, and is impatiently waiting in the breakfast room. He is alone and eager to drive Vanessa and Ryan around the countryside before they meet with Sister Ambra. They apologize for making him wait, and quickly run up to get dressed for the meeting.

When they return from their rooms, Aldo incessantly thrusts his self-anointed, but ill-directed, male charm on Vanessa. She simply ignores him, knowing that any encouragement only heightens his pursuit. She will talk about boosting his energy later as they discuss the *Prophecy Scroll*.

Ryan takes a hands-off approach, knowing that with some men, it's best to stay on the sidelines and let them make a fool of themselves. Still, they both appreciate his kindness for taking them around Sardinia, and thus, earning a limited right to be attentive to Vanessa.

They drive out into the winding hillside roads on the north side of Sardinia towards the town of Oristano. It eventually brings them to the Cathedral of Oristano where Sister Ambra works when she's not on her farm. "This town has some of the earliest settlements on the island," Aldo explains. "It was founded by the Phoenicians, but was also settled by the Punics and the Romans. It is right on the coast, and provides a door to some beautiful beaches too."

They drive through the mountainous countryside and Aldo points out the enormous rocks that protect the diverse wildlife. They see a deer cross the road ahead and a fox that sits on the side of the road watching them drive by.

Aldo stops at the side of the road and points at the pair of chaffinches in a tree. "See right there. They have orange bellies, black and white wings, and a green rump. A delicate beauty, si? I have found the Sardinians to strike a nice balance between preserving the beauty of nature and maintaining their health and prosperity. It's all connected."

The road takes them back by the steep rocky coast near a secluded beach. "Here is where Francesca and I spend our weekends in the summer," Aldo explains. "Arutas is a beach to die for. It has crystal clear waters that lap gently along the sugar white sand that is mainly made of small quartz. It makes swimming in the sea a treat. It's also quite secluded with these privacy cliffs protecting it from the road. You'd like it Vanessa. It's perfect for nude bathing."

Vanessa rolls his eyes at Ryan, and Ryan smiles back.

"Let's stop for a moment and I can show it to you," Aldo continues. "We're not in a hurry. Si?

"You'll not ask me to strip off my clothes, will you?" Vanessa asks sarcastically.

"Not if you don't want to, but I will be disappointed," he smiles. "I'm just kidding. We have a few minutes. The quaint tourist town of Stintino and Orestano, where Sister Ambra works, is just ahead. While only a thousand people live here in the winter, it swells to many thousand during the heat of the summer. Today is Monday. There will be nobody here since most are working, and the tourists hit the beach in the afternoon."

They spend a few minutes walking along the beach in the warm sun of late morning. They watch the waves roll in and out along the tranquil bay, and they discuss the events of the past week.

Aldo begins to think beyond his attraction to Vanessa, and is astonished to hear about the details of the murders and especially about the death of Dr. Unico in Rome. He becomes more somber as he understands the seriousness of the situation they are in. He would not want to be in their shoes, and is surprised that they continue their mission. Maybe, it's better to be on a road trip than a sitting duck at Brisighella. He appreciates the opportunity to help them as long as it does not put himself at risk.

What they do not realize is that all three of them are at risk right now. The Messenger is wearing shorts, a white shirt, and a Sardinia cap that is fitting for a tourist's day at the beach. He is perched on the edge of the cliff directly above the beach, waiting for the opportunity to get a clear view of the trio as they walk along the shore.

He did not have the opportunity to kill her in Brisighella, but will not miss his chance today. He brought the long-range rifle, which he purchased outside of Rome for this occasion. His sharp shooter status from the military should do the rest. He waits patiently for his prey. He has an excellent view of the beach on other side of the small bay, and expects they will walk right into an ideal shooting view. The rocks and close parking on the dirt road behind him provide excellent cover for an easy escape after the shooting.

He sits quietly and considers the moment. The Messiah will be happy with the events of today. We will continue to seek out and extinguish all activities that are considered heretical and against the Manifesto. It is his mission. His only concern is that pesky physician friend of hers and their driver. Does he kill them also? If necessary, they will all be an unfortunate casualty of the cleansing process.

He sees the trio walking on the beach towards his post. He gets ready to fire from behind a boulder. There is nobody around. It is a long distance, but he will have a direct shot as they walk by. He takes aim, but finds they are moving more quickly than expected along the beach. He stabilizes himself, and moves the gun in the direction they are walking. He fires several quick shots, hoping that at least one bullet will strike the target.

Vanessa feels a sharp pain in her right shoulder. Another bullet hits at their feet, scattering sand in all directions.

Ryan feels a bullet whiz by the right side of his head. Another hits the rock and shattered pieces cut into Ryan's arm. He yells, "Shit! Get down now. Stay down! There's a shooter on the cliff above us. The killer must have followed us here. Get behind these rocks."

They immediately fall to the ground, and then, quickly scramble behind a rock formation next to the beach. They hear a couple of more bullets come from the cliff opposite to the beach. Dust and rocks go flying. They are pinned down behind the rocks and are not sure if they are out of sight of the shooter or not.

Vanessa panics. "This is a nightmare. We're dead meat. What are we going to do?"

"Aldo, call the *polizia!*" Ryan yells.

"I will, but we will be dead by the time they show up," Aldo shouts back. "They're so damn slow!"

"Ryan, get the gun out!" Vanessa demands. "Now, is the time we need it."

Ryan checks his pockets out of futility. "I'm sorry, but I left it in my bag," Ryan says with frustration. "It's in the car."

"*Porca vacca!*" Vanessa shakes her head. "*Merda!* What good is the gun there? *Testa di cazzo!*"

Ryan looks dumbfounded wondering what she said but assumes it is disparaging. He would say the same thing. The shooter fires several more shots just missing them while creating a cloud of dirt where the bullets strike.

"Who is this guy?" Aldo shouts. "He's not letting up. Will he eventually kill all of us? *Cazzo!* I'm not even part of the research. We must do something now!"

To the surprise of both Vanessa and Ryan, Aldo yells at them, "We have to get to him. Stay here. Throw some rocks. Make some noise. Whatever you do, don't come out from behind the rocks. I know the area. He's on the cliff on the other side of this bay. I'll crawl along that gully in the sand behind us, and circle around behind him on the cliffs. I'll sneak up behind the *bastardo* and throw him over the cliff."

Vanessa looks at him like he's crazy. Then, she remembers that the prominent virtue of those with high energy in the Body Realm, is courage. Perhaps, it's a suicide mission but she will appreciate any hero at this point.

Aldo finds the low point behind the wall of rocks, and crawls on his stomach for about fifty kilometers. He makes it to the wall and stays still and silent. He hears several more shots at Vanessa and Ryan, who are making noise by throwing rocks in the direction of the shooter.

Aldo follows the rock ledge, and slowly climbs up the steep and fragile sandstone cliffs. He knows that with one wrong placement of his foot, he will tumble down the cliff into the rocks below in direct view of the shooter. He would be doomed.

With slow and careful climbing, he is able to make it up to the face of the cliff, behind the rocks where the shooter is. He crosses behind the shooter and slowly traverses his way along the ridge. The man is still shooting, keeping Vanessa and Ryan pinned down. Aldo peaks over the edge of the rock. The shooter is lying down, his rifle to his shoulder with the barrel pointing out over the edge of the cliff. He recognizes that his best chance is to get as close he can before running and yelling at him. He hopes to surprise and confuse the shooter.

Aldo stealthily crawls forward behind the rocks. He waits a few seconds until the shooter is firing again. After the next shot is fired, Aldo stands up, runs as fast as he can toward the shooter, wielding a large piece of driftwood in his hand. He is screaming at the top of his lungs, "*Testa di cazzo! Vaffanculo! porca miseria!*"

The shooter turns around, startled to find a man running at him and yelling a string of Italian swear words like a drug-crazed maniac. The shooter tries to turn the gun around to shoot him, but Aldo jumps on his back before he has a chance to turn around.

Aldo uses the piece of wood to knock the shooter in the head and the gun out of his hand. The shooter is stunned long enough for Aldo to hit him again. Aldo kicks the gun to the edge of the cliff, but not far enough to fall over it.

The shooter quickly recovers and lunges at Aldo, hitting him in the stomach. Aldo staggers back from the blows. The shooter runs for the gun and grabs it. Aldo quickly jumps up, runs as fast as he can, and tackles him near the edge of the cliff. The shooter stumbles back towards the cliff as he is reloading the rifle. He gets back up, and Aldo hits him with another body blow.

The shooter staggers back towards the cliff, but maintains balance enough to aim his rifle directly at Aldo at close range. If he hits him, Aldo is dead.

Lying on his back in the dirt, Aldo kicks him in the knees, as hard as he can. The shooter stumbles back towards the edge of the cliff. He aims at Aldo, and shoots. The shot grazes Aldo's left leg.

The recoil pushes the shooter back. He grabs for anything to keep from falling.

Aldo stands up, runs towards him, and pushes him further towards the edge of the cliff.

The shooter trips on the rocks at the edge and starts to slide down the bank. He grabs for Aldo's legs but Aldo shakes him off and kicks at him further.

The shooter looses his balance and tumbles back. He continues to slide down the edge of the cliff, and with his arms flailing, he falls thirty meters to a pile of sand and rock at the bottom. He hits his head on a rock, knocking him unconscious. He lies still with his gun by his side.

Aldo looks over the edge of the cliff. He puts his right fist in the air and yells at him, "*Ciao, brutta facia!*" He then slowly climbs back down the embankment, opposite to side of the cliff where the shooter fell, and limps back to the beach where Vanessa and Ryan are waiting.

They are relieved to see Aldo walking towards them in the distance. As he arrives, they can see the pain from the bullet wound on his leg.

"What happened? Are you okay?" Vanessa asks.

"I'm okay and we are safe." He responds looking at both of them with a look of exasperation. He tells them about the fight with the shooter and how he pushed him off the cliff. "I left him unconscious at the bottom of the cliff opposite to this bay. How about you?"

They review the status of their injuries. They are relieved that none are serious. "I'm okay," Vanessa replies while Ryan attends to her shoulder. "A bullet grazed my shoulder. The bleeding has stopped."

"I'm fine too." Ryan responds. "Only abrasions from rock fragments that hit my arm. We are lucky to be alive. Is the shooter dead?"

Vanessa agrees and turns to examine the long laceration on Aldo's leg from the bullet. The bleeding has stopped and they conclude that it does not require suturing.

"You'll live. Thank you for your courage, Aldo." Vanessa looks sincerely at him. She gives him a hug but stops short of a kiss. "I suggest we get out of here."

Ryan disagrees. "We should wait for the *polizia*. Yes?"

"The *polizia* are on their way," Aldo replies. "I told them where I left the guy. They're slow but they will come," "The guy was big and strong. I don't want to be here if he regains consciousness. It's hard to get to the base of the cliff where he's fallen."

Vanessa lowers her head and wipes the tears from her eyes. "This is too much to handle. We need to get out of here as fast as we can. We have no way to restrain him. If he wakes up, we're dead."

Ryan reluctantly nods his head in agreement. They all walk back to the car leaving the *polizia* to pick up the killer.

Chapter 45. The Blessing of Prosperity

Vanessa, Ryan, and Aldo are silent in shock as they travel to meet with Sister Ambra in Oristano. They should be dead but for whatever forces are at play, they have survived. Aldo drives and is particularly somber about his altercation with the killer. Although he still cannot fathom why he put his own neck at risk, he has more understanding of the dilemma that the two travelers find themselves in. They quietly stare out the window as they pass through the picturesque green rolling pastures and rock outcrops of the countryside of Sardinia. Shepherds and their flocks of sheep and goats could be seen scattered about the countryside. The serenity of the countryside is in stark contrast to the dread they feel from almost being killed.

Vanessa, sitting in the back seat, acknowledges Aldo's quick and bold action, despite knowing that it provides him one more reason for him to continue his unwanted advances. "Aldo, that was courageous. You saved our lives. Were you able to ID the shooter?"

"Well, he didn't have a nametag on if that's what you mean?" He replies sarcastically still tense from the episode. "In the commotion, I didn't really get a good look at him. But, he looked like any other tourist. He was a young male, wearing shorts, a white shirt, and a Sardinian cap. He had a short beard and dark hair. Does any of that ring a bell with either of you?"

"No. It could be any number of people at the Terme," Vanessa says, frustrated.

"I didn't want to go down the steep embankment after him," Aldo replies. "It was inaccessible. I say that he hit his head quite hard. He may even be dead. The *polizia* will find him and arrest him. I can ID him once he's arrested. They have our number."

As they drive, Aldo's cell phone rings. It's the *polizia*. Aldo again explains the details behind the shooting and attempted murder. Ryan and Vanessa are silently watching Aldo as he listens to the *polizia* tell him what they found at the scene.

"Okay, please call us when you find him," Aldo replies. He gets off the phone and looks at Vanessa. "They can't find him. I told them right where to look. But nobody was there."

"This is the story of our lives right now," Vanessa tries to stifle tears. "We can't seem to get this guy off our backs."

"What did they say?" Ryan frowns and shakes his head angrily.

"They need time to investigate the area for evidence," Aldo replies. "They'll call us back when they find him."

Ryan swears, "Damn it! We should never have left the scene. We should have done something to keep an eye on him. We screwed up."

"He regained consciousness, Ryan!" Vanessa defends their decision. "He had the gun at the bottom of the cliff. If we stayed, we'd be dead now."

"Aldo, did you tell them to keep us posted about what they find?" Ryan asks. "If they can't find him, rest assured, he'll be back."

"And, then, we're screwed," Vanessa says quietly to herself.

"This is bad," Aldo says dejectedly, thinking about his own neck. "You need to get out of town. Let's hurry up and visit Sister Ambra. I can then take you to the ferry to get off this island. Stay ahead of him."

They finally arrive in Oristano, and walk up towards the St. Mary's Cathedral of Orestano. Their excitement in meeting Sister Ambra and seeing the next manuscript, the *Blessing of Prosperity*, has been dampened by the trauma of the shooting.

Aldo tells them a little of the history to distract them from the threat on their lives. They walk through the Piazza while Aldo points out the old Tower of St. Christophoros and the Cathedral beyond. "The Tower and Cathedral were originally erected in the thirteenth century and used for the burials of the Giudici and their families."

He points out the marble monument from the late eighteen hundreds that is dedicated to Eleonora of Arborea. "She was the most powerful of

a long line of Sardinian female judges," He continues. "They were called
giudicessa, of the fifteenth century. Women have a long history of being
strong headed here on the island. I also know that from personal experience,"
He laughs. "Sister Ambra is no exception."

"Let's see if we can find her home," Aldo suggests. "She is expecting us,
but we must make haste. Get in and get out."

They walk into the majestic church with its broad arches, tall stained
glass images, painted murals, and detailed woodwork. They see an old
woman sweeping up and arranging chairs around the church altar. She is
dressed in a loose white shirt, baggy pants with a tassel around her waist
for a belt, walking shoes, and a broad hat like many of the local farmers.
Ryan wonders if this old woman who looks like a peasant could possibly
be Sister Ambra,

"Is that her?" Vanessa asks.

"Si, that is Dr. Antonioni," Aldo reviews her credentials. "She may not
look the part of a scholar, or even a nun, but don't let her looks deceive you.
She is a rare breed among scholars. I come here often to talk to her about
my research. She is a rich source of knowledge on the relationship between
health and economics. She has an undergraduate degree in business from
the University of Roma and a PhD in economics from the University of
Vienna. Both are among the most prestigious business universities in the
world. She has traveled the world as an economic ambassador from the
Vatican, and has written several books on the social responsibilities of
corporations to promote the welfare of the people and its direct effect on the
prosperity of the company. Now, she enjoys a simple life in her homeland of
Sardinia, writing and farming."

"She's a farmer too?" Ryan states.

"Not only a farmer, but an organic farmer," he says proudly. "She's
working with the local Sardinians to avoid the trap that much of the world
has fallen into—the use of chemicals to protect but taint the crops. That
may be one of the reasons some cancers have increased around the world,
but not here."

The old nun sees them walk in. She walks briskly towards them with
a bright smile that shows her perfectly aligned white teeth to light up her
face and make her look twenty years younger. Aldo walks up to greet her
with a smile and kisses on both cheeks.

She speaks with excellent English, "Dr. Gaetti called me yesterday. She
said you'd be coming. She also told me about the murders. I'm sorry to hear

about Dr. Paolo. Dreadful. What is this world coming to? Anyway, welcome to Sardinia. I hope your stay has been enjoyable so far."

"Thank you, but we've already had a death scare on our way here," Vanessa shakes her hand gently and kisses her on both cheeks. "We were the target of a shooter while walking on the Autas beach. No serious injuries, but we were shocked back into reality after enjoying the tranquility of the Island. Aldo saved us. Unfortunately, the shooter got away."

"God has saved you," the sister says confidently to Aldo's dismay. "This has happened before. Si?"

"We were lucky in Brisighella and in Rome," Vanessa replies.

"Not luck, my dear," She states clearly. "I talked to Gabriela. You have great energy. The world needs you right now."

"I don't know about that," Vanessa looks up. "Aldo tells me that you hold the secrets to a long life of health and happiness. With a madman after us, those secrets could come in handy, particularly the long life part."

Sister Ambra laughs loudly, "They all want to know our secrets here. You have good reason to want to know. Ever since that pesky Blue Zones book came out, we've had a steady stream of tourists disturbing our tranquility in their search for the fountain of youth. I suppose you want me to tell you about the *Prophecy Scroll* too. Demands, demands," she continues to laugh.

"*Si, per favore*, Sister." Vanessa replies.

"*Viene qui*," she waves her arm and turns to walk with them down the center aisle of the pews towards the altar. "I completed the translation just last week. *Molto Interesante*. The document is surprisingly relevant today."

Ryan and Vanessa gaze at the Cathedral's large arches and impressive artistry from the work of hundred's of talented artisans.

"Would you be kind enough to share it with us?" Vanessa asks.

"I have no choice, do I? When the Pope orders something, we simply do it. You must have some friends in high places. He has taken a special interest in your work. Come in and sit a while. I've prepared some cappuccino and special treats for lunch. Do you have time, or is the killer still on your tail?"

"The killer is out there. We need to move quickly," Vanessa quickly replies.

"If he shows up here, we know how to take care of him," the old nun says with a serious look on her face. "The Guidici are very protective. I've already called them. They're watching us now. *Relassa!*"

"In that case, *grazie*. We'll stay," Vanessa smiles.

The old nun, with the elegant stride of a runway model, walks over to an old wooden table and chairs that are in an open room to the side of the altar. The large windows overlook the hillside towards the sea. The room is decorated with a set of old tapestries on the wall with scenes of the local countryside with fields of flowers, rock formations, marshes, and farm fields being worked by local farmers.

"Our lunch today is typical Sardinian. We have an old saying in Sardo, 'to know wealth you must know health.' Nothing is more important to your health and your prosperity than how well you eat, drink, sleep, and stay active."

The three are astonished to see the colorful spread of local foods. The nun walks over to the table and points out the various foods she had brought in for them, "Let me show you what we have here for you." She takes out a board of cut whole-grain breads and describes each one as she points them out. "The *pane carasau* is a thin circular pastry bread. Here, the *civraxiu*, is a hard bread with soft inside. The Sardinian's most common staple bread is this one. It's called *su coccoi*. Then, she shows them a variety of cheeses, meats, fruits and vegetables, all laid out on colorful ceramic plates.

Ryan can feel his stomach rumble as he looks at them.

Sister Ambra tilts her head toward the cheese, "These natural foods all have an wonderful energy about them that is graciously passed on to those who eat them." She picks up a piece of cheese and brings it up to Ryan's nose.

"Can you detect the scent?" She asks. "It's the fragrance of the distinctive Sardinian grass that the sheep and goats eat. It's all part of the cycle of life."

"Thank you, Sister," Vanessa says. "Your kindness is appreciated, but are you expecting a crowd? This is way too much food for just the four of us."

"In Sardinia," she explains. "It is better to have too much food than not enough. Eat up and boost your energy. The plates and utensils are over here."

They all fill up their beautifully colored ceramic plates with a meal that will energize them for the day.

"And don't forget to try our health elixir," the nun says.

"What's that?" Ryan asks.

"The drink of the Lord. It's not surprising that our Maker has provided us with wine that has high levels of flavonoids to help protect us from a whole host of illnesses."

"Also, thank you for protecting us while we are here," Vanessa says appreciatively, knowing that they must move along. "We need a little breathing room from the killer. Can you tell us about the manuscript, the *Blessing of Prosperity*, as we eat?"

"This Blessing manuscript, to my delight, is a gem. And, I might add, it is quite consistent with our way of life here on the island. You can read it for yourself. If you want to really understand it, you need to live here for a few months and see the good life in action."

"I'm in favor of that," Aldo adds.

Vanessa rolls her eyes towards Ryan as Ambra hands them a copy of the final translation of the *Blessing of Prosperity*. "Let me first tell you about prosperity in the eyes of these visionaries," Sister Ambra raises her eyes to look at their reactions. "Strange, that it doesn't mention money as the focus of prosperity."

There is a puzzled look on their faces.

"What does it talk about, then? Isn't money the foundation of prosperity and wealth?" Ryan asks.

"Our Island is mostly poor people. Not much money here. But we do know how to live a wealthy, prosperous life. The authors of this document defined prosperity in their own terms. To each of us, prosperity and success means different things. To some it means having money and material wealth, but to others it means having a productive and healthy lifestyle, and even others, a wonderful supportive family, or even a successful career. Prosperity is in the eyes of the beholder."

"So prosperity is not about wealth," Ryan repeats. "Most people would not agree. To them, wealth equates to money. It brings economic stability."

"Si. Don't confuse the ends with the means," the nun explains. "Prosperity is the end goal to achieve the life that one seeks, but your way of life is the means to getting there. It's easy to be distracted by material wealth since our world is driven by this."

"This is consistent with our research at the Terme," Vanessa adds. "We found participants were more energetic, productive, and prosperous when they maintained a healthy lifestyle."

"Now, a life of Blessings may, on occasion, lead to one of material wealth. Bless you if it does because it is more often due to luck than anything else. But if fortune rests on your shoulder, do not waste what you have. Be frugal with it because it can leave you as quickly as it comes."

"Are the core elements the same actions that bring energy into the Way of Life Realms?" Vanessa asks.

"So you know them. Let me read for you. . . And Behold, the *Blessing of Prosperity*. For those who want prosperity and success in the life that one seeks is through strength of light in the Realm of the *Way of Life*. To strengthen this Realm is to work hard and steady, to live within your means, to have good sleep and breath clean air, to be modest in eating and drinking, and to have food and water that rises directly from the natural springs and soils of the earth, for these will bring light to all Realms and bring prosperity, success, and a life of wealth."

"It also mentions the virtues and vices of this Blessing," Ambra continues. "You know those angels and demons that sit inside you telling you how to act. Aldo knows all about them."

Aldo smiles uncomfortably. Everybody knows about his exploits. He wrinkles his forehead thinking they should be praising him for his actions instead of being critical. Everybody has vices. His just happens to be flattering beautiful women.

She smiles at him and continues to read, "For strength of the spirit in this Realm will bring angels to you that are evident as virtues to others as you will be active and productive, show industry and generosity, and be modest and patient in actions, for this will show prosperity and success."

She looks up at the group to explain further, "These virtues are characteristics that most Sardinians have. As I said, we are not rich here, but we are industrious, modest, and patient. Most authorities believe these virtues lead us to our health and longevity, but I believe the reverse is true. It is our lifestyles that bring these virtues and our long life. As you know, many people live to be over one hundred years of age on the island. We laugh because nobody here pays attention to our ages. We really don't know if we live to be fifty or two hundred years. We just live our lives. Why count if every day is a blessing?"

"So true. The more you count the years," Vanessa agrees, "the closer you are to death. *Vero?* Just live now, not one or twenty years from now."

"What else do you find in your way of life that contributes to your longevity?" Ryan asks.

"We work hard every day, but we have balance and moderation," she answers. "We take time to sit down and celebrate eating and drinking every day. This promotes our energy in many Realms. We do it together and we talk. Sometimes, we fight. It is all the same. We have an old saying—We are here now, not before, not later."

Ryan and Vanessa smile at the sardonic humor. The nun is on a roll with her optimistic clichés about life. They wish they had brought a recorder.

"Life is to enjoy. This manuscript does not tell us something we don't already know. Here, we see these virtues in all the people because the energy spreads. We do not hurry and rush through our days. We smell the flowers every day. *Tanto bella*."

"What about other Realms? How do they fit in?" Vanessa asks.

"Needless to say, both the Mind and Body Realms are important to Prosperity."

"Sister Ambra, I'm a physician," Ryan says. "I talk about these things to my patients all of the time, but talking is a lot different than changing their lifestyle. Bad habits of processed food, disrupted sleep and lack of exercise are difficult to change. They become ingrained in our lifestyles. It's a challenge to make changes."

"You have an American author who understands people quite well," she says, "His name was Twain. I remember a quote he once said about his habit of overspending money. He said, 'habit is habit, and not to be flung out the window by any man, but coaxed downstairs a step at a time.' I love this quote. Changing attitudes and habits take time and repetition—every day. First you must learn why and how to make a change, and then you need to be reminded day after day. I like these new smart phones because they can send to you reminders every day. Apply the four 'Ls' in changing your lifestyle and in one month you will change."

"The four Ls?" Ryan asks.

"You know, a lazy loser who is lost and lamenting," The nun teases.
"No. They are—listen, learn, live, and love. It's simple and includes all the theories of behavioral change—social, cognitive, emotional, and behavioral theories."

"Interesting," Ryan thinks how he can use it with his patients. "It makes sense. The four 'Ls.' Listen, learn it, live it, and love it."

"What happens if you have a bad job? Some people get stuck in a job and cannot get out," Ryan asks. "I have some patients like that."

"It's not what you do for work, or how much money you make, but how you do your work," she quickly responds. "Whether you're a brick layer, a homemaker, or a candy store operator, you can enjoy your work if you have high energy and follow the Blessings."

"What about our overloaded work schedule?" Vanessa questions, "Many people are caught in a cycle of too much work and too little time to change?"

"Your work at the Terme shows this quite well. People need the freedom every day to maintain high energy in each Realm," she answers. "If you have every minute of every day planned out, you will miss the goodness that life brings. Life is not about getting *molti soldi*, much money, or maximizing production, or meeting others' needs. People need to make exercise, eating well, sleeping well and all the actions in the *seven Realms* part of their normal daily activities. Employers want their employees to be productive. Following the actions will do this. When employers realize this basic fact, I believe they will give employees the freedom to do so because it benefits everyone, and the bottom line, if that's what's most important. But many people realize that making money takes lots of time and effort, and ultimately brings you no direct energy, just material possessions."

"What do you mean by no direct energy?" Ryan asks.

"Money is important and is needed for the exchange of commodities and goods. Our whole economy is based on this. Thus, a good income is still helpful for the *Blessing of Prosperity* and allows a person to maintain a good quality of life with healthy food, daily freedoms, and material comforts such as a nice house to live in and reliable transportation. But money has no intrinsic energy associated with it. If it sits in the bank, it does nothing for your energy until you do something with it. For example, giving money to someone helps enhance the *People Realm*. Using funds to eat well boosts the *Way of Life Realm*, or paying for a college course to boost learning in the *Mind Realm*."

"But money is so critical to our quality of life. It makes things happen. Without funding, I could not do this research," Vanessa argues.

"Si. However, material wealth is primarily related to only one Realm, your Way of Life, and then only indirectly when you use it. It is independent of the other six Realms and, in fact, may neglect and diminish other Realms. Those people who spend all of their time focusing on making or spending money will ultimately feel weak and unfulfilled. They may not even recognize their low energy."

"At the Terme, we call them zombies. The walking dead," Vanessa smiles.

Sister Ambra laughs. "Good label because it can be so true. If they have wealth and low energy, they frequently use the wealth and power to control others and suck the needed energy right out of the people around them. Several social psychology studies compared people with and without wealth and showed that the wealthy are more apt to act with blatant self-interest at the expense of others than those who are not."

"I'm not surprised," Ryan agrees. "Self-interest has made them rich. They don't need to care about others."

"Some wealthy individuals recognize both the burden and the responsibility that can come with wealth," Ambra continues. "They act to use their money to boost their own energy and the energy of the people around them. They do great deeds, set up foundations, help the poor, and promote the arts. Their wealth also allows them time to cultivate a healthy lifestyle. Wealth can help them become great people with high energy but it is difficult. But you can achieve this without wealth also."

"We call them warriors because they spread positive energy everywhere they go," Vanessa says.

"Si. In the future, greed for money will be replaced by a stronger interest in strengthening our personal energy and the energy of those around us," Sister Ambra continues. "Personal energy will gradually become the driver for enlightened people of the world. And it will be a natural non-disruptive change in society, not dictated by greed, war, and power. It's already happening in some circles of the world."

"High energy is contagious and spreads," Vanessa adds.

"Si, this is why your work is so important, dear," Sister says emphatically looking directly at Vanessa. "I'm almost eighty, and I hope to live many more years. It's people like you that help me be optimistic about our future."

Vanessa and Ryan are surprised to hear her age since she looks no older than sixty. They are impressed with Ambra's deep understanding of the principles of the *Prophecy*, and her appreciation for their work at the Terme. They all pray that as time passes, their efforts to train warriors will spread to others enough to diminish the threat of the Plagues to our world. But, right now, they need to deal with their own immediate threat. They must leave the island soon to stay ahead of the Prophecy Killer.

Chapter 46. The Plague of Poverty

Sister Ambra detects the change in Vanessa's energy and her urgency to leave. Yet, the nun feels a need to finish the discussion on the *Blessing of Prosperity* before they apply it in their research. "Before you leave, you must understand the negative side to this Blessing. The plague of poverty," the nun says seriously. "When the spirit in this Realm is low within a group of people, the demons come out in force and bring on vices and the plagues to the people."

As much as Ryan and Vanessa feel compelled to leave and minimize the chance of their own demise, they need to learn everything they can from this insightful woman.

Vanessa replies, "Tell us about the plague in this Realm. We can stay a few more minutes."

"Then, I'll be brief." She walks over to a big old wooden cupboard and opens it up. She takes out several plates with desserts on it. "While I talk, you should eat. Here in Sardinia, we also have many healthy desserts using the almonds we grown here."

Aldo and Ryan's eyes light up as they look at the cakes before them.

"You must have some," Ambra insists. "We have *ciambelle* cake made with honey and orange peel, *copulettas* cake with meringue, and *amaretti suspirus* with macaroons."

The men immediately take a small serving of each one. Vanessa defers to feed her sweet tooth and her waist line.

"*Per favore, mangia!* Eat!" She states. "I will read about the Plague of Poverty and its vices from the Blessing manuscript. I hope you don't lose your appetite."

She pauses a moment to let them sit and eat *la dolci*. Then she reads, "Beware, for weakness of the spirit in this Realm will bring demons to live here and show vices to others. For, they are lazy and sloth, have gluttony and greed, and are selfish, excessive, and impatient. And lasting weakness of the spirit in this Realm among a third of the people will bring plagues of poverty and destitution, and people will beg for food and drink, and have no bed to lay and no refuge for comfort."

"We're already there," Vanessa responds cynically. "Greed and selfishness have taken over as the dominant motivator in our society. As a result, the separation of the rich and poor has increased dramatically. Poverty, destitution, and hunger are growing at an alarming rate in the world."

"You see it happening, too!" Sister Ambra exclaims. "Most people choose to ignore it. Yet, there is so much that can be done to change this. Let me explain how the collective energy in this Realm impacts society. Economic development of a society is a double-edged sword. Strong economic development will boost energy in the Way of Life Realm and help people of a country achieve the *Blessing of Prosperity*. This wealth can bring us food, housing, and material comforts.

"However, it can occur at the expense of losing collective energy in other Realms," Vanessa responds.

"You are correct," She replies. "Both the People and Nature Realms can be depleted. As a result, there are many social and environmental problems that can develop. There is an increase in poverty, social discrimination, crime, poor health, and other social ills. There is also an increase in pollution such as they have seen in China and destruction of natural resources such as the deforestation and the loss of fish in the oceans. Economic development should not be viewed as the primary goal of society, but rather the means to achieve all of the Blessings for all of the people in society and not just the wealthy. It is only the means to the end and not the end itself. But people lose sight of this in their efforts to make money. As I said before, the true currency in the world, whether you are rich or poor, is achieving high energy in each Realm. This is what will bring a good life to each of us."

"That may not so obvious to our leaders," Ryan says. "They see success mostly in terms of economic success, and the accumulation of money, not energy."

"Si. And those leaders tell us that there is a major economic crisis," she says. "This crisis has already laid siege to some of the world's biggest banks and pushed the global economy into a deep long lasting recession. Greed, graft and corruption are rampant. The public finances of governments have been ravaged, particularly, here in Europe. The leaders who have seen their tax revenues drop have brought severe austerity measures to balance the budget. They are supposed to represent and support the people, but they cater to those who control the wealth."

"Si. *Capito!*" Vanessa replies with disdain. "The governments are forced into doing this by their wealthy creditors. Those who want more wealth."

"Creditors are banks, and they focus only on their money, as their charter dictates," the nun replies. "But they forget about the people. As a result, governments have reduced their obligated payments to citizens who are dependent on the government for sustenance. Poverty among the elderly, retired, unemployed, and disabled has caused homelessness and alienation that is so rampant that it has lead to nearly a quarter of the world living in poverty and a third of all deaths being due to poverty. The governments are frozen in political gridlock, held hostage by the banks, the wealthy creditors, and the threat of economic depression. They refuse to cut expenses or increase taxes to pay bills because they fear it will stifle economic growth and be unpopular."

The old nun takes a deep breath in exasperation. "Unfortunately, it is the current way of our world, but it does not have to be our future. I believe mankind can evolve by embracing innovative solutions with this new definition of prosperity."

Vanessa stands up and looks out the window of the room to see if anyone is there. She turns back to Sister Ambra and shakes her head as she poses the obvious question. "But what can be done? Inertia is a huge challenge to overcome."

The nun smiles warmly. "Much can be done. First, individuals need to get into the act. They need to work on strengthening their individual and collective energy so that greed is not the focus of our lives but energy is. People need to determine where their priorities lie. A good life or making money? They are not mutually exclusive, but people need to set priorities. If enough people have sufficiently strong energy in each Realm, they will make wise decisions for themselves, and if they are leaders, for their group. The positive energy will then spread to others."

"The solutions are not easy. There are several strategies needed to deal with it. Poverty and hunger are non-partisan issues. By solving them, we can support both the rich and the poor, the liberals and the conservatives. Everybody wins when we take action to solve this problem now. Both the public and private sectors need to work together to achieve solutions. We can avoid the impending tidal wave of protests, and expand prosperity among the people of all nations. When we help each other, it can be done."

"Good luck with the politics on that," Ryan responds. "In our country, the national and state politics are so divided that they're worse than the most dysfunctional families. There is more dissatisfaction with our elected leaders than anytime in history."

"If we were to work on one issue right now, what would it be?" Vanessa asks.

"*Ei facile!* It's easy to say, but not easy to do," she says with enthusiasm. "We need to stop world hunger now. This goal is within reach in our generation, if we take action now."

"But what action?" Vanessa asks.

"We need to expand international humanitarian aid instead of military aid to all countries," she replies. "And we need to provide knowledge and teachers as well as funding for better distribution of the huge surplus of food that exists in the world. Did you that 1.2 billion tons or 50% of the worlds total food production gets thrown away—never eaten. What a waste. We simply need people to help each other. We need to teach people in developing countries how to farm locally and organically, and how to transport and distribute food efficiently."

The old nun lets the information sink in and then continues, "The starting point for change is to help people boost their energy in each Realm. Only when people have high energy will they not only see the problems but also the solutions. And they will be motivated to do what is necessary to solve these problems and prevent the Plagues. This is our primary mission."

Aldo checks the time and realizes that they have to leave now in order to catch the ferry. He nods at Vanessa, letting her know that it's time to go.

"Sister Ambra," Vanessa says. "You have been so kind to us, but we need to leave. Before we go, you still need to tell us your secrets to long and healthy life!" Vanessa smiles as she ask curiously, "Are you protecting them?"

Sister Ambra laughs. "Oh my dear, Vanessa. I've been talking too much. You already know the secrets of a long life. I know because I feel the strength of your energy. Most Sardinians share similar lifestyles. My mother and father were farmers and both lived to be over a hundred years. They lived the same way every day of their lives. They walked the roads and hills of Sardinia. Walking is better than the joint-pounding running of long distances and still improves our heart, muscles, bones, and metabolism. They ate simple cuisine at home with lots of beans, nuts, whole-grain breads and natural fruits and vegetables from our gardens. Every family grows something. When one family doesn't have it, another family will bring it over. They also foraged for fennel, asparagus, mushrooms, myrtle, and other foods that grow wild. They ate pecorino cheese made from grass-fed sheep and goat's milk both of which reduce inflammation. They never ate too much, just enough to fill them up. They were modest in eating and did not waste. They loved leftovers for the next meal or for those that needed a meal.

"We all like our strong family values and work hard to care for each family member. Our parents and grandparents passed on their love, financial help, wisdom, and traditions to help us achieve the same prosperity and success. We laugh a lot. We gather most days to talk at local markets and cafés. We tell stories, and watch the beautiful women and handsome men walk by. You will be our story tomorrow. We take time every day to say our prayers and meditate to seek inner peace and slow down the aging process. All of these are our secrets to a long life."

She laughs and then says, "But right now the secret for your long life is to get your butts out of here. You already have this knowledge. And it will bring you not only prosperity, but also long life. It is my pleasure to have you here. Where are you off to now?"

"We need to keep moving and stay a step ahead of the killer," Vanessa says. "And see that long life. I wish we could stay longer but we need to catch the next ferry to Civitavecchia and then the train to Pisa to retrieve the *Blessing of Love* from Father Fabio. It seems quite relevant right now."

"Ah, so you will meet with Father Fabio there?" Ambra asks.

"Why, yes. Do you know him?" Vanessa is surprised.

"Everybody knows Fabio, the movie star priest. He's an illuminating character. He's on the cover of *LiUomo Vogue*. The article is entitled 'The Psychology of Love.' You will enjoy him."

"Can't wait," Ryan says sarcastically.

"Vanessa, if you want to catch the ferry this afternoon, we must hurry," Aldo says with urgency.

They all thank Sister Ambra for the lunch and for providing a copy of the manuscript. They have lots to think about. The *Blessing of Prosperity* was quite different than they had imagined.

They each give her a hug and kiss, and then, return to Aldo's car. They go directly to the docks to catch the busy ferry, the Tirrenia, back to the mainland of Italy. They find it's not the same luxury tourist boat that brought them here. Many workers who commute for the weekend to help handle the busy tourist season are also boarding. They purchase tickets and arrive at the ramp to embark onto the large boat.

Vanessa thanks Aldo, "You have been kind to show us your island and introduce us to Francesca and Sister Ambra. And, si, you did save our lives. We are indebted to you. You seem so happy here and Francesca is a good woman. Keep her happy. I expect you'll be quite successful in your work and your love."

"Please stay in touch, Vanessa," Aldo says sadly. "And most importantly, *per favore*, stay safe. Nobody wants to lose you. The research needs you right now." Then, he leans over and says quietly in her ear, "Come back soon. I would love to work with you." He winks as he gives her a lingering kiss on each cheek.

Vanessa stands stiffly, and rolls her eyes. Some people never change.

Chapter 47. The Confrontation

The sun is approaching the horizon as they look out over the bay of Cagliari. Ryan and Vanessa board the large ferryboat without frills via the ramp, and head up the stairs to find two seats with a view from the upper deck. Aldo is still waiving as the boat pulls away.

Vanessa tries to relax by propping her feet up on the bench in front of them and slouching down. She closes her eyes and lets the warmth of the sun bask on her face. The cool breeze gently caresses her hair, as she thinks about her situation.

Vanessa, still feeling low energy from the day's events, needs to tell Ryan the obvious, and get it off her chest. "Ryan, it's hopeless. I'm dead. If the killer is so determined that he will follow me anywhere, then so be it. I need to just turn myself over to him. I don't want you to be in harms way any more. This is useless. If it's my destiny to die, I will accept it. This is the path that the Lord has chosen for me. You should leave me as soon as we arrive."

"I don't want to hear that, Vanessa," he looks at her with a face of stone. "Listen! There is no way I'm going to leave you at this point. LeGrand is on his tail. He's a professional. He knows what he's doing. He'll get his man. And if he doesn't then, damn it, I will!"

Despite the difficulties he's had since Sophia died, Ryan still has an inner determination and intensity that compels him to do what needs to be done. He's done this in med school, in his residency, in triathlons, and with

Sophia's and his father's deaths. When he gets knocked down, he gets up and pushes even harder. It's in his genes, his mindset, and his energy. The Italians call it *cativa*, guts.

Unfortunately, Vanessa reacts in the opposite direction. She has never dealt well with stress. She likes tranquility, calmness, and a life under control. She gets too empathetic and emotional under stress. She acts rashly without thinking through it. She feels the tension in her neck and arms and rubs her temples to alleviate her headache. She pleads, "Ryan, you're so damn stubborn. You're going get yourself injured or killed. I don't want this on my conscience, even if I'm dead. Don't you understand this? *Tu sei stupido?*"

"Well, if that's my destiny, then so be it," Ryan states emphatically. "I can handle myself. We have survived so far and we will continue to survive. This guy will go down."

Vanessa doesn't know what to say to convince him otherwise. She knows that she needs him right now but hates to admit it. "Are you sure?"

He looks out over the water and then turns to say to her with assurance, "Its okay, if he shows up, I can handle this."

Within a few minutes, a rowdy crowd of drunken construction workers startles them. The group stumbles their way across the deck, bumping into several anxious passengers. The young workers laugh at their own drunken escapades.

But their rudeness is threatening to others on the boat. The passengers' angry looks and whispers of disapproval ripple through the boat. The motley crew of drunken Italians, then, turns their behavior into fighting when one drunkard starts to pound on another. Most of the passengers leave the deck. Ryan and Vanessa stay.

Fists fly amidst the fury. Men stumble and fall over chairs and laughter ensues at their clumsiness. One inebriate nearly falls off the boat as he stumbles back from a blow to his face. Two others appear to be injured. Blood streams down their faces.

Finally, a fearful mother with a young girl in tow jumps to her feet. She surges across the deck swearing at the top of her lungs. Her arms are flailing and she hits one man enough to send him stumbling back. It leaves all of the drunken workers stunned and struggling to maintain their balance as they attempt to calm her.

Vanessa, acting with empathy, approaches an injured worker and introduces herself as a doctor. She asks if he needs help. The largest worker comes over and they strike up a conversation. Evidently, they had been laid off from jobs in Rome and arranged some work on a church in Sardinia. He explains that they are all friends and apologizes for having too much to drink, and too much rowdy fun. He said it's common after working twelve-hour shifts in the heat for five days. He apologizes for their rudeness and impaired judgment.

Vanessa patches up two minor injuries and the workers expressed their appreciation. The men stay on the deck, but settle down to sleep it off.

Ryan and Vanessa stand at the boat railing to watch the red-orange setting sun illuminating patchy clouds. It's a romantic scene that brings a brush of contentment to Ryan and Vanessa, despite their circumstances.

Vanessa decides to walk around the boat as they wait for the ship to speed across the sea to mainland of Italy. Ryan goes back to his seat and pulls out his book. As he reads, he feels a tap on his shoulder. He turns and is shocked to see a smiling Brian Johnson standing there with shorts, a checkered shirt, a white hat, and his bags in his hand.

Brian says to Ryan in a fresh upbeat tone, "Hello, Dr. Laughlin. Do you remember me from the Terme? Brian Johnson, from New York." He extends his hand to shake his.

Confused and shocked, Ryan immediately feels his heart pound at the loss of energy from seeing the person whom he thought had just tried to kill him. He weakly shakes his hand and is speechless.

Brian takes a seat. "Mind if I sit down? It's quite a coincidence that we're all on this ferry at the same time. Did you enjoy Sardinia?"

Ryan sits up and begins to realize that this is either a dream or he's in deep trouble. He takes a deep breath, looks for Vanessa, and says, "Ahhhh. Hello, Brian. What are you doing here?"

"As I mentioned Monday night, I've always wanted to see Italy," Brian answers. "I found out what I needed for my church group at the Terme, and then decided it was time to travel some before heading back to New York. How about you? You also seem to be seeing some of Italy. Sardinia is a beautiful island, isn't it?"

Ryan, wondering how best to respond, says honestly, "Yes, it is. We were visiting some scholars who are involved in health related research. Vanessa asked me to come with her."

Brian says with his typical cynical tone, "Well, how convenient it is for you to be sleeping with the boss. I heard about what happened to Dr. Nobili. I'm so sorry for the loss. What a tragedy. Do you think it could have been prevented?"

Ryan looks around for Vanessa and cannot find her. Although Johnson's comment could have been interpreted as showing concern, Ryan believes the statement was threatening and addresses it directly and honestly, "Brian, why did you do it? What do you want from us?"

Brian opens his eyes in surprise, "Do what? I wasn't even there. It was a sad situation."

"What do you want from us?" Ryan asks. "Where's Vanessa?

"I'm sorry," Brian responds. "I don't understand. I don't want anything. I thought I would just have a friendly conversation with an acquaintance from the Terme. And I don't know where Dr. Venetre is. Is she on the boat too?"

Ryan looks around, and with relief, sees Vanessa coming up the stairs. "Then, why did you try to run me over with your car on Tuesday outside of Brisighella. Why did you kill Dr. Nobili and Dr. Unico? Why did you shoot at us at the beach?"

"You must be mistaken," Brian says. "I didn't kill anyone. I didn't have a car at the Terme. And, I don't even own a gun much less know how to use one. Don't accuse me of things I didn't do!"

"Brian, let's not play games," Ryan says forcefully. "We know who you are and what you're planning to do. We've alerted the police. They are looking for you right now."

Vanessa sees Brian talking to Ryan and freezes in her tracks. She grabs a chair as she feels the blood drain from her head. Her breathing becomes quick and shallow. Her heart is pounding out of her chest. What is happening here? Why is Ryan talking to the killer?

She tries to gain composure but cannot. She walks up to them and says emotionally, "Why are you here, Mr. Johnson?"

"Hello, Dr. Venetre," Johnson says. "I was so surprised to find you both on this ferry. What a coincidence. I was just telling Ryan how much I enjoyed visiting Rome and Sardinia. He said you enjoyed it also. I was wondering if you were here."

Vanessa screams, "Get out of here! We've called the police."

Johnson responds, "Why the hostility? I've done nothing wrong. I'm simply a tourist enjoying my time in Italy."

Vanessa, in tears, yells at him, "You've killed Dr. Nobili and Dr. Unico! And now you plan to kill me. I'll not let that happen!"

Brian, with a serious look on his face, scans the area to see if anybody is watching this scene. Then, he says firmly but quietly, "Shhhh! You must be mistaken. I didn't do that. Do I look like a murderer to you? I've never hurt anyone. You must be mistaken."

Vanessa feels her emotions erupt as she raises her voice to the level that most people on the deck, including the Italian workers now can hear. They look in her direction, "*Tu se cattivo. Una testa di cazzo.* A murderer. I wish you were dead."

At that point, the large Italian worker steps over to see what all of the commotion is about and asks, "Doctor Venetre, is this man bothering you?"

Vanessa begins to scream hysterically, "Si. He's evil. He should be thrown off this ship immediately."

Brian stands up and grabs her, trying to shut her up. "Please be quiet. I don't want a scene just because I don't like your research. It's not personal. What's wrong with you? I didn't kill anyone."

The Italian man, still a bit drunk, reacts instinctively. He picks up Brian, holds him over his head, and throws him over the side of the ship into the sea. Then, he takes both of his bags and throws them overboard after him. Vanessa, in an act of contrition, takes a lifesaver ring from the side of the ship, and throws it in after him. She yells, "*Ciao brutta facia!* Do not return!"

Meanwhile, Ryan is shocked at what just happened. He's not sure what to do or say next. He asks Vanessa, "Tell me again, what does *brutta facia* mean?"

Vanessa looks at him intensely, "Ugly face!"

Ryan scratches his head, puzzled over what just happened. He tells her, "We better tell the skipper to have a rescue ship pick that ugly face out of the sea, and arrest him for the murder of Dr. Nobili and Dr. Unico."

She thanks the large Italian worker for his quick action to save them and asks him to talk to the skipper to arrange a rescue ship for Johnson. She sits down with a sense of relief and satisfaction that Johnson got what he deserved.

Ryan sits down next to her and says, "I just learned to not mess with a certain angry Italian woman."

She looks at him with a face of relief, and then simply holds him tight. It's been a long day.

Chapter 48. The Train

The ferry arrives in Civitavecchia at 3:30 pm. Vanessa and Ryan quickly disembark from the ferry and find their way to the station to wait for the train that will take them to Pisa. On their way, they stop at the Italian Coast Guard office to inquire about the status of Johnson. The gentleman behind the desk is dressed in dark pants, white shirt and tie, and a coast guard jacket. He is busy shuffling papers.

"Excusa me, per favore," Vanessa interrupts. "A gentleman fell overboard on the ferry from Cagliari this evening. His name is Brian Johnson. We would like to know what happened to him. Would you be able to call your colleagues in Cagliari to find out?"

The man responds politely. *"Si, un momento."* He comes back after five minutes and says, *"Signora,* a gentleman was picked up near the coast of Cagliari. He evidently fell overboard from the ferry. Is he a friend?"

"No friend," Vanessa responds. "We wanted to make sure he is in taken into custody. We believe he's a criminal who has committed murder. Did they say if he was arrested or not?"

"No, they did not say," he responds. "They said that he was an American tourist. I know nothing else right now. Check later to see if he is in custody. If you would like to call back, here is our number."

Vanessa takes his number and thanks the guard for checking. As they walk out, she says to Ryan, "I don't trust the coast guard. We need to get out of here quickly and call them back when we are on our way to Pisa. Given our luck, I would be surprised if they arrested him."

They walk the four blocks to the non-descript Civitavecchia train station. It's an easy walk, and they are more relaxed now that Johnson has been apprehended, or at least detained in Cagliari. They walk into the station and see few people waiting for trains. They go to the ticket window to buy their ticket. The agent tells them that the train to Pisa left an hour ago, and they must take a local train to Florence, and then switch trains to get to Pisa. The train leaves in twenty minutes and takes about two and a half hours to Florence with many stops along the way. Frustrated at the poor connection, they have no choice but to buy the ticket. They hurry to find track three and hop on the train to locate their reserve seats. They sit quietly and say nothing as they look out the window as the train pulls out from the station.

As they sit down, Vanessa holds onto his arm. Her energy is depleted now, and she knows it. She needs to do something about it. After a few seconds, she puts her head on his shoulder, and closes her eyes. As the fatigue sets in, she whispers, "I love you." She begins to breathe slowly and deeply. She repeats her phrase to calm her mind and emotions. She imagines herself surrounded by love, Ryan's love. It's a peaceful pleasurable feeling. She quickly transitions from meditation to sleep.

Ryan puts his seat back and closes his own eyes to let them both get some rest. He also needs more energy and takes a few slow deep breaths to quickly slide into a state of relaxation and focused awareness. He breathes slowly and deeply. The noises of the train riding over the tracks, the people in his car, and the wind blowing all become distant. The imagery that comes to his mind is affirming. He sees a warm blue glow surrounding the train and knows they are safe. After ten minutes, he slowly comes out of the meditation. He feels more refreshed and comfortable. His emotions calm down and his thoughts become clear.

He is amazed at how helpful the practice of meditation has been for him. It's a practice that keeps on giving back. He feels more connected to the people he cares about and to the world around him. His energy heightens. Like they said at the Terme, he feels like an enhanced Ryan each time. As Vanessa sleeps, Ryan stares out the window watching the countryside and the passing sights.

Suddenly, Vanessa jumps out of her sleep with an anguished look on her face.

Ryan, startled by her reaction, looks at her strangely and asks, "What happened? Nightmare?"

Her face is drawn and the soft smooth of her forehead is furrowed with alarm. "Si, sort of. I had a terrible feeling of death come over me as I was sleeping."

"They say if you die in a dream, you will have a long life," Ryan replies. "Seeing the bottom provides you with an understanding of the source of your energy. Didn't you tell me that?"

"I know, but that's not how I interpreted it. It was as if I was being prepared for the inevitable death that lies ahead."

Ryan disagrees. "Sometimes you can be wrong, Vanessa. You know your energy is depleted with the stress you're under. You're beginning to see the bottom. You're just worried. We need to call LeGrand. See if he has found out anything about Johnson. Knowing if he's on the trail to bring Johnson in will help."

"I suppose," she says reluctantly, also recognizing that negative information will make her even more worried and paranoid.

She dials the number and quickly hands the phone to Ryan. The phone rings once, twice, and three times with nobody picking up. It goes to the recording, "LeGrand here. Please leave a message and I will call you back."

"Mr. LeGrand," Ryan says curtly, "In case you are interested, we were lucky to have escaped Rome and Sardinia alive, and are now on a train to Florence and then Pisa. Someone killed Professor Unico at the Vatican, and shot a rifle at us outside of Cagliari. We survived, but did not stick around to get killed. We met Brian Johnson on the ferry, and he was thrown overboard by another passenger. We do not know where he is. Can you find out? Please call us when you have a chance."

The call reminds Vanessa to check on the status of Johnson again. She dials the number and gets the guard on the phone again. Ryan listens pensively while she talks to the guard, "*Grazie.* Call me when you hear something. *Si, prego di.*"

She hangs up and complains to Ryan, "They still don't know what his status is. He is being interrogated, but he was not able to confirm that they can hold him. He said to try again in a few minutes. I need a drink. Let's get some wine."

Ryan agrees and they walk back to the train's restaurant. They scan the room and see nobody suspicious. They both order a glass of the Montepulciano and down it quickly. They order another and reflect on the day's events.

"Vanessa, I still cannot believe you did that," Ryan says. "What were you thinking?"

"Did what?" She asks curiously.

"You know. Having Johnson thrown into the sea."

"I just wanted him out of my face and off the ship. I'll have to admit, I was a bit emotional, and didn't believe the big Italian would do what I asked. It was classic Italian machismo."

The wine begins to loosen them both up and they have another. They laugh as Ryan describes the scene. "The look on his face as he was falling into the sea was unbelievable. It said, 'What the fuck? Are you really doing this to me?' I'd say he met his match."

Vanessa, losing some of her inhibition, pulls him over to her chair and puts her arms around his neck. "Ryan, you're a special doctor. I like being taken care of by you." She kisses him slowly on the lips and laughs. "I'll never throw you overboard, *mio dolci*. But if I did, I'd jump in after you and save you."

"I don't need saving, my dear," Ryan says indignantly. "It's you who needs to be saved."

Vanessa gets defensive. "Well, I didn't see you throwing him overboard."

Ryan snaps back, "I don't throw people overboard. I was talking to him to find out what he was up to when you had the big brute throw him overboard. Now, we don't really know his intentions. Maybe, he's not the killer."

She yells, "We know what his intentions are. Wake up, Ryan! He was going to kill me! Right there! *Uccidere. Capice?* Talking is BS. Someone needed to take action. So, I did."

Ryan realizes that Vanessa is a bit drunk, but so is he. "You're right. Just pull out a damn gun and shoot him on the spot. Kill him before he kills us. Then, I get twenty years, maybe ten for good behavior, for murdering a damned tourist! I repeat. We don't know for sure if he's the killer. He denied everything."

"Ryan, do you have your head screwed on? Listen to the evidence, the Terme comments, the reception conversation, running you off the road, the picture from Julia, and now, he's in Rome and Sardinia. What are the chances? *Niente!* He's stalking us. Waiting for just the right moment, and bang! We're dead. Don't you get it, Ryan? He's the killer."

Ryan says nothing. He looks at the panic on Vanessa's face and realizes that it's best to not throw fuel on the fire. He sees her insecurity and need for some sense of being closer to resolution, to safety, even if it may be wrong. "Maybe, you're right," he agrees, placating her anxiety. "We may not know for sure if he's the killer, but we have to assume he is. Either way, he just got to see Sardinia and the Mediterranean Sea in a whole new way."

They both laugh at the image of Brian Johnson treading water in the sea next to his floating luggage.

"Aren't you worried that he's still out there?" Vanessa asks, looking at her empty glass of wine. "We didn't get confirmation that he's been arrested yet. We still may not be safe! Will this ever end?"

"Yes, I'm worried. We still have to be vigilant," Ryan says. Then, his vigilant nature and search for the truth gets the best of him, "We can't assume he is in custody or that Johnson is the killer. He still seemed like any other tourist to me on the Ferry."

"What do you mean like any other tourist?" Vanessa counters.

"Vanessa, he wasn't threatening me. Actually, he was acting kind of like a tourist visiting Sardinia. He was genuinely surprised to see us on the same boat."

"What do you mean? Are you questioning whether he is a monster or not?"

"No, the facts point to him. But it surprised me that he came up to me on the boat to talk. Why didn't he just kill both of us? Throw us both over. He looked, acted, and conversed like a simple tourist, a weird one, but still a tourist. Why would he have done that?"

"He's sneaky. He wanted to mess with our minds," she says with indignation. "Are you saying that we should not have thrown him overboard?"

"We can't look back," Ryan replies. "It is what it is. You didn't do it anyways. The big Italian guy did it. He was drunk and didn't know the situation. He wanted to throw somebody over the side, and it just happened to be Johnson because of your screaming. However, if Johnson is the killer, I worry that he gave some excuse to the coast guard that he fell overboard and now has been let free. Again, we didn't close the loop to make sure he was arrested. For what we know, he may still be out there. In either case, I expect he's fuming right now. We need to find out."

"You're right," Vanessa says with a sinking feeling. "I better call again."

She re-dials the Italian Coast Guard again and talks to the person she spoke to earlier. She takes a deep breath and bites her lip. Then, she says to the Guard,

"You're saying there was no way you could keep him under arrest? He's a dangerous homicidal criminal on the loose! What do you mean he's simply an American tourist with no criminal record and did nothing wrong here? He murdered at least three people! Isn't that enough?" She screams into the phone, "Well, you better investigate him further. This is crazy. *Pazzo!* Do your job, *per favore!*"

She hangs up and covers her face with her hands. She starts to cry. "He wasn't held. You were right. What if they are wrong and Johnson is still following us here?"

"If he still is the killer, he would be at least a day behind us," Ryan assumes. "Either way, we need to be cautious."

"The guard said they investigated him thoroughly," Vanessa says as she begins to settle down. "They checked his background, his passport, his family and found nothing. They said he's not Anton Trevick. I have a hard time believing that. He seemed so strange in Brisighella. He looked and acted the part."

"But I believe people are innocent until proven guilty," Ryan adds. "If he's not the person who killed Dr. Nobili, who is?"

"I don't trust the Italian *polizia*. I still believe it's him," she affirms. "There is nobody else at the Terme who would do this atrocious act."

"You have a point, but if it was someone at the Terme, who else could do this?" Ryan asks. "Wayne? Trent? Jack? It's definitely not Bob from Nebraska. What about someone from the other groups? Do any of them fit the bill?"

"I can think of a dozen men who have a distant resemblance to the picture of Trevick, but they all appeared to be sincere and hard working. Brian Johnson had the lowest energy and acted so strange. And he kept skipping out on the activities. They said that he's now headed back home to New York. *C'est la vie.*"

"Well, if he is not the killer, he'll remember this as a trip of a lifetime." Ryan laughs. "I feel bad for him. Let's try to forget about this episode. Whoever the killer is, let's hope he cannot track us to Pisa."

Vanessa puts her hands in her face again. "That's not so difficult if he knows where the manuscripts are. For God's sake, he killed Gene Unico."

The train slows down to make a stop at Florence's Campo Marte Station. The passengers stand up to get their things from the storage rack above the seats. Ryan and Vanessa need to change trains to the high-speed rail that goes on to Pisa.

Their arrival in Florence worries her. "Ryan, I'm calling LeGrand again." She dials the number and waits for each ring. No answer. This alarms her. "Damn it! Why won't he answer? I don't like it. He's supposed to be covering our back, but he doesn't even know where we are. Do you think he's been killed too? What should we do?"

"I doubt that he was killed. He wasn't in Rome or Sardinia to our knowledge. I was hoping that he would be watching us from a distance. Perhaps, he is or he's trailing the killer right now."

"Do you think so?" She says with a sense of relief.

"I don't know, but we need to get off this train. If we stay on the move, it is harder to follow us. The schedule says the Frecciarossa high-speed train to Pisa is at track five. We can't dawdle."

Vanessa knows in her mind what to do, but her emotions control her thoughts right now. "What if he's waiting for us at the station?"

"We'll cross that bridge if it happens," Ryan states. "Let's get our things. We need to move fast and be vigilant."

They stand up, get their luggage and drag it down to the exit door at the end of the car. They hop off with their luggage, quickly looking both ways. There are people everywhere in the station, busily finding their way. In this station, Ryan moves fast, encouraging Vanessa to follow closely.

They are hungry and need to eat before finding the connecting train to Florence's Campo Marte Station. They stop at a food kiosk and grab a *panini* with *proscuitto, formaggio,* and *pomodoro* and a bottled water for each. They hope this will settle their hunger, and their anxiety.

The trip between the Florence Santa Maria Novella Station and Florence's Campo Marte Station is about ten minutes. They walk between platforms, carefully watching the people around them. They do not see anyone who looks suspicious. They get on the connecting train and find a seat with no problem.

They have no time to settle in. Their train arrives at the commuter station quickly. They need to transfer to the train to Pisa, a couple of platforms down. They see the rush of the crowd getting off, and cannot watch everybody. They wish that LeGrand was here. It would help if they knew that he is watching. The Italian *polizia* are always there when you don't want them, but never there when you need them. They make the transition quickly and without incident. They settle into their seats for the hour ride to Pisa.

A passenger with a beard, brown raincoat and black brim hat pulled down over his eyes is already on board, watching Ryan and Vanessa enter the train to Pisa. He has no luggage, and appears to be a commuter. He watches them put their luggage on the rack above and take a seat from the car behind.

The Messenger considers how he will do it this time. He realizes they were lucky to escape with their lives in Brisighella, Rome, and Sardinia, but this time it will be the end. He will make sure of it. He would like them to be afraid, very afraid. After the train takes off, he realizes that they cannot escape this time. He is patiently planning his next act of retribution for their sins. He reads a newspaper and thinks about the surprise on their faces when they see him. It will be so apt, so timely—and so final.

Chapter 49. The Passenger

Ryan and Vanessa relax as the train slowly moves out of Florence's Campo Marte Station. They are relieved to have made the transition from one train to the next. Their car has few people in it—an older couple and a couple of late night commuters sitting up front. The train rambles on its way to Pisa, first through the urban landscape of Florence, and then through the rolling green hills of the Florence countryside.

They take a deep breath and settle into their seats at the back of the train. "Tell me more about Father Fabio," Ryan asks as he thinks about the meeting tomorrow.

"From what I heard from Gabriela, he is a devout, spiritual man," Vanessa explains. "After his famous movie career and his dedication to the priesthood, he completed a PhD in anthropology and religion at the Sapienza University of Rome. His thesis was on the practice of prayer and meditation in the world's religions. This is unusual for a Catholic priest. He traveled the world and learned to speak multiple languages, including Hebrew. Because of his language skills, he has been involved in the translation and interpretation of ancient biblical manuscripts and their implications for the twenty-first century."

"Interesting background," Ryan says. "Sounds like a good person to translate the *Blessing of Love*. Regardless, he will need a pretty broad view of religion to understand my relationship with the Church. Since Sophia died, I've had waning if not negligible interest."

"What do you mean?" She asks.

Ryan needs to be honest with her. "From my experience, sometimes the Church is lacking in what some say is spirituality. It seems more a social club or a way to reduce the guilt of the sins a person commits in their daily lives. Sins, from my perspective, which should not have been committed in the first place, if you care about people. Sometimes, I just don't get it."

"It's true," she says. "Religion can be divisive, corrupt, focused on money, and may not bring people closer to spirituality. Some religions actually fuel hate. It depends on the leaders—the clergy who sets the stage. I have met a few with very low energy who should never be allowed to counsel people on spiritual matters."

Ryan is surprised to find she understands his somewhat cynical view of religion.

Vanessa continues, "On the other hand, I believe religion in society is very important. By believing there is an infinite power beyond us, it can help us transcend our limited abilities, and free us to understand there is something bigger than ourselves. And it can provide a place to learn values, which may not be taught at home or school."

"But what happens if God is left out of religion?" Ryan counters.

"I suppose you're correct then," Vanessa replies. "Religion then becomes a social club, and its teachings are comprised of activities to facilitate a helpful social life, which to me is not such a bad role either. This will enhance energy in the People Realm, but we may lose our energy in the Spiritual Realm. Love dwindles and we fail to explore the deeper connections that may exist between us and the universe."

"Then, what happens when science leads us to discover things that we assumed were part of religion, like your research?" Ryan probes. "Does it now move religion into the realm of science? Does science replace religion? That, my sweet lady, is quite threatening to some people."

Vanessa looks out the window and thinks about their situation. "I still don't fully understand the reasons for the killings. Maybe, I just don't get the religious fanatics, but it seems more like a conspiracy than a nutcase here. The Manifesto is quite political. If so, who is behind it and what do they really want? That's what I want to know."

"If so, who could be behind it?" He questions.

"Those with money and power?" she speculates. "That's the source of much evil in the world. Perhaps, the killer has the support of a group of powerful elite. Maybe, the Terme project represents an effort to shift the power back from the one percent to the ninety-nine percent. Power mongers never let go of that which they believe is theirs. The *Prophecy* does give ordinary individuals more power and insight into their own lives and thus, power to control the direction of the world. I don't know. It's just speculation, but most wars are about power and money. The killer may use religion as his reason, but I bet it in the end, it will all come down to money, power, and greed."

Ryan says doubtfully, "That may be. But there are religious fanatics all over the world, and some would kill for their beliefs."

"History does repeat itself," she replies. "You know what they did to the witches during the medieval age, and in Salem, Massachusetts. They burned them at the stake."

"Now I know what those who were burned at the stake felt like," Ryan states with queasy feeling. He purposefully changes the subject and asks, "Where are we staying in Pisa?"

The train slows as they approach the Pisa station. The Messenger with the black brim hat needs to move now if he is to accomplish his mission. He has the needle and solution prepared. With a simple, sharp bump on the shoulder, he will be able to make a quick exit into the crowd at the station. His mission will be accomplished. He walks down the aisle, and sees them sitting together alone in the back.

Instead of taking action immediately, he decides he wants to play with their minds a bit. He sits in the empty seat across from Ryan and Vanessa, and listens in on their conversation. He knows that they may not recognize him at first, but eventually, they will. He wants them to be confused, and then afraid, very afraid.

Vanessa, sitting on the aisle, looks up from their conversation and takes notice of the familiar gentleman who is now sitting across the aisle listening to their conversation. She recognizes that it is Trent Reed, a participant at the Terme. She is startled and doesn't respond to Ryan's question. Why is he here? He should be back at the Terme finishing up his sessions. She turns to him, smiles, and says, "Trent! What are you doing here?"

Trent smiles at her. "Hello, Dr. Venetre. I'm traveling around Italy. It's such a coincidence to see you on this train. Where are going?"

Vanessa detects an attitude in his voice that she did not see at the Terme. Confusion fills her mind. It's too much of a coincidence. She cannot put it in perspective. "Did you enjoy your week at the Terme? We appreciate your participation. Where else have you visited? Are you going to Pisa?"

"I enjoyed the Terme greatly. It was productive, and helped me complete most of my mission. I've been to Rome and Sardinia, and now I'm stopping in Pisa. Nice places. Have you been there?"

Vanessa's confusion is gradually being replaced by concern.

Ryan observes the conversation and is dumbfounded and silent.

Vanessa says hesitantly, "Ah, si, both places. What mission are you talking about?"

Trent relishes her confusion. "I'm the Messenger. I'm simply delivering the message."

"What message might that be?"

"I noticed you are talking about science as the new religion. My message is that this will not happen!"

Both Vanessa's and Ryan's energies suddenly drop. They realize that they may be talking directly to the Prophecy killer. But how could that be? How could Trent Reed go undetected under their very noses? They are stunned. This cannot be true.

Vanessa probes further, "How will you keep that from happening?"

"I will simply stop it. Whatever it takes. Your physician friend stopped me in Sardinia, and that was unfortunate. The same mistake will not be made today."

Vanessa gets louder, so that the people sitting in the front of the car can hear it, "What do you want from us? Are you going to kill us in front of everyone? We did not do anything to you!"

"This is not personal, Dr. Venetre. You are doing the work of the Beast, and it must end. Both the Messiah and the Lord have commanded me to do so. It's my mission."

"Who are you? Who is this Messiah? You are so screwed up. Even the Pope supports us."

"I'm the Messenger, and the Messiah is Frank Kolb. We have both seen God, and the world knows of our Manifesto. With his wealth, he will convert the world into the vision of the Lord."

"You're wrong. He's wrong. The *Prophecy Scroll* contains the words of the Lord. You know it. You've been there. You've seen the benefits."

"There are no benefits. Measuring souls is the work of the devil, and it will take us down the path of destruction instead of righteousness. You are pretending to be God, and telling people how to live. It is written. You are the second Beast from the sea, with the tongue of a dragon who speaks for the first Beast of seven heads. You deceive the people. You take our spirits and send demons to live with us. You are evil. And for this, you must die. I'm sorry."

Trent reaches into his coat pocket and finds the syringe. While in his pocket, he removes the cap of the needle and readies it for a surprise injection. Vanessa turns to Ryan, hoping that he does something, anything right now.

Ryan still cannot fathom that Trent Reed is the killer, but he realizes that he must act now. He searches in his pack to find the leather cased Beretta. He does not want to make the same mistake as he did in Sardinia.

The other passengers are listening to the conversation, and are getting up to leave the car.

Trent stands up and moves towards Vanessa hiding the needle in his hand. Just a pinprick, he says to himself.

Then, to everyone's surprise, Francois LeGrand appears at the door of the train. He runs down the aisle with his gun pointed at Trent. "Sir, you are under arrest for the murder of Paolo Nobili."

While the Messenger is distracted, Vanessa leaps from her seat and pushes him away from her just missing the needle stick. She runs to the end of the aisle and into the next car leaving LeGrand and Ryan alone with the killer.

Ryan grabs Trent's arm forcefully and knocks the needle to the floor. He frantically searches his backpack for the gun. He finally finds it and nervously tries to pull it out of the leather case.

LeGrand approaches Trent slowly and cautiously with his gun pointed at him. He knows that Trent Reed, Anton Trevick, the Messenger, and the Prophecy killer are all the same people. He spent the morning on the phone talking to Steiner in St. Paul. He knows of his background in the military, his failures, his connection and funding from the Kolb Freedom Group. He has read the Manifesto and understands his clever chemical methods for the three killings. Until now, he was not sure that he had the right man. But Trevick has finally shown his colors.

The older couple in the front of the car sees LeGrand's gun and pulls the stop cord on the train. The train suddenly jerks to a stop. LeGrand is startled and thrown forward.

Trevick pulls out a stun gun from his coat, which he keeps with him for just this kind of situation, and hits LeGrand in the neck with it. LeGrand falls to the floor of the train. He drops his gun.

Ryan reacts and puts his hand on his gun and takes it out of his pack. With his hand shaking, he points it at Trent before he can pick up his needle and LeGrand's gun.

Trent, surprised that Ryan has a gun, doubts that he will use it. He cautiously turns his back on Ryan, and walks slowly toward the exit door.

"Stop or I will shoot!" Ryan calls out.

Trent continues to slowly walk towards the exit. He looks back at Ryan, who is frozen in fear with the gun still pointing at him. Trent walks out the door of the car and sees Vanessa standing in fear in the next car. He points at her, and says with his lips, "Tomorrow, you will die!"

Ryan, still standing in his seat, could not pull the trigger. Trent pushes the train door open and jumps off the train. Ryan snaps out of his shock and turns to watch Trevick through the window. He sees him running between buildings and out of sight. Ryan turns to LeGrand who is slowly regaining his strength and helps him up.

LeGrand sits in the seat Trevick had just occupied, and complains, "Damn it. We had him. That was Anton Trevick, alias Trent Reed. He will not get away. We will have the entire police force on top of him soon. We will not let him threaten you again."

Vanessa returns to her seat. She is so relieved to see LeGrand that she gives him a huge bear hug. They tell him about the Trent Reed they met at the Terme and the bizarre conversation on the train.

LeGrand tells them about Trevick's background and military training. It will not be easy, but they need all the evidence they can get to put him away for life. LeGrand explains that the Polizia di Pisa have been alerted. "We will be with you all night and tomorrow, but we need to stay in the background, in plain clothes, to avoid scaring him off."

"You mean we'll act as bait?" Ryan asks accusingly, "That's not very comforting."

"Trevick will not come into the open if the *polizia* are surrounding you."

"Isn't that the idea? Keeping him away from us," Vanessa says emphatically.

"Yes, but the main idea is to catch him and lock him up. You need to go about your day. Visit the churches and the monuments. Be visible and surrounded by tourists. Trevick will show up again somewhere. I guarantee it. As we say in French, *Il est fou*. He has a few loose screws."

"But what if he simply pulls out a gun again and tries to kill us from a distance?" Vanessa says with doubt in her voice. "He's already tried that once."

"We will follow you to your hotel tonight and tomorrow, we will have every building and window in the Piazza dei Miracoli watched. We will have your back."

"For some reason, I don't feel comforted by that," Vanessa replies cynically.

Regardless of their skepticism, they thank LeGrand for being there. He did save the day. He tells them not to lose their composure. He promises to get Trevick.

Ryan and Vanessa take a taxi to the Hotel Novecento, a cozy old hotel, strategically located in the centre of Pisa. It's not fancy but is within walking distance from the Leaning Tower, the Piazza, and the old town. They check into the only room available, but the question of romance is secondary to the simple priority of surviving. They get a nice room with a balcony overlooking the beautiful courtyard garden with the Piazza monuments in the distance. It has two antique four-poster single beds with highly ornate oak frames dating to the 16th century. The bed has solid gold covers and white sheets made of a satin mixture. Although tiny, the room is beautiful, and tranquil. The balcony sets the stage for staying calm and vigilant.

They both spend the evening in the room, quietly meditating to strengthen their energy. They throw in an ample amount of prayer for good measure. With Trevick's hate still permeating them, they know they desperately need love to fill their lives. They don't dare venture out onto the streets of Pisa, so instead they order from the hotel's pizzeria that delivers to the room. They are quiet and pensive as they eat. Trevick's words keep going through their minds. "Tomorrow, you will die."

"Ryan, I don't feel too secure about LeGrand's assurances," Vanessa ruminates. "Neither do I like the idea of being bait to bring Trevick out into the open. Trevick is unpredictable. He shows up in places and does things that they would never expect. He has killed three people already."

"I agree, but we need to catch him," Ryan says. "LeGrand promised to get his man."

"But Ryan, think about what the killer has done," she says. "He has poisoned in St. Paul, injected a toxin in Brisighella, and then the shooting in Sardinia. Trevick was an undercover military agent. He is clever and can masquerade as anybody. His methods are sophisticated. What will he think of next? Maybe, he'll bomb us all in Pisa. We just don't know."

"We're lucky to have survived to this point," Ryan sighs. "Or, maybe, as Sister Ambra pointed out, it is more than luck. Either way, we can't sit in our room all day. We need to meet with Father Fabio at the Cathedral tomorrow, and get back to Brisighella. You need to continue the next phase of the research with the additional Prophecy manuscripts. I need to go back to Minnesota. We have much work to do!"

"We need to survive first," Vanessa sighs. "I have to admit my enthusiasm for this research is waning. I simply want to live. I want to fall in love, get married, have a family, raise my kids and see them grow up. You know, live a life worth living, a good life. I can't do that if I'm dead."

Ryan laughs nervously at her directness. "I understand. Tomorrow will be a rough day. It'll be over soon. You will survive. I'll make sure of that. I love you. I loved you from the first day I met you. I want to be with you. That's why I'm here." He walks over and hugs her closely.

"You're sweet, Ryan," she pushes him away with a frustrated look and goes to find her nightgown in the luggage. "We have no time or energy for love right now. Come on. We need to focus on surviving. Why do men always bring up love at the worst time? I just can't think about that now." She puts her face in her hands and tears roll down. "I'm sorry, but this weekend has been too much for me. I cannot take being a target of a mad man, or even bait for the police. I'm a peaceful person. I don't even like suspenseful movies. My life has become a thriller, and I hate it."

She finds her nightgown and looks up at Ryan. "Well, tomorrow will come whether we want it to our not. Let's get some sleep. It's been a long day."

While Ryan is in the bathroom, Vanessa puts on her nightgown and gets under the covers in the single bed, away from the window.

Ryan returns and sits down on the other bed.

She looks at him and asks, "Why are you sleeping way over there?"

"Well, these beds are singles, and small at that. They don't quite fit two people, especially someone who is six foot three and solid."

"Don't do that," she pleads. "Please, come here by me. I need you close."

He stares up at the ceiling, gets up, and moves over to her bed. He lifts up the covers and slips under them. There is not enough room for both of them so half of his butt is hanging over the side of the bed. He holds her tightly, to prevent himself from falling out of the bed. Eventually, she falls asleep in his arms.

After few minutes, he moves back into the other bed. He keeps his backpack with the gun close to him. This time, he will use it if he needs to. His sleep is restless. He dreams of running as fast as he can down a forest path, being chased by something evil. He does not get caught before he wakes up.

Chapter 50. Pisa

The Messenger sits next to the quaint old lady on the bus driving to the Piazza Miracoli. He is proud of his authentic disguise as an older tourist with grey hair, grey mustache and beard, short brimmed hat, a tan shirt with dark dress pants, and comfortable black dress shoes. He has little resemblance to Anton Trevick, and has the good fortune to be invited to join a senior's tourist group at the hotel. He mixes well with the other patrons, and has befriended an older lady with white hair dressed in a colorful flowered pants suit. As part of this older tourist group, he expects that his plan to take care of Vanessa Venetre and end the research will go more smoothly today.

The old lady tells Trevick about her first trip to Italy. "It's been a marvelous trip so far. I never realized how beautiful Italy is."

"It certainly is," Trevick agrees. "Have you been to Rome yet?"

"Not on this trip. We're visiting Florence and Pisa today, and then Venice. I hope to come to Rome next year. Are you going on to Venice with us?"

"I hope to, if I'm welcome," Trevick lies. "I was just in Rome, and it was beautiful. The Coliseum is not to be missed."

She smiles with delight to have met such a nice gentleman. Since her husband passed away two years ago, she has met few older men who are as charming as this one. She turns to her female companions and smiles at them. They all know that finding good men at this age is difficult. How fortunate that he is alone on this trip. The other ladies are green with envy.

"My name if Rosemary Larsen from Wisconsin," she says.

"Glad to meet you, Rosemary. My name is Frederick Hague, from California."

"You'll like Venice," she continues. "I've read all about it. I want to take a gondola ride along the Grand Canal complete with a singing gondolier. So romantic! You should come with us."

Trevick looks around at the other women on the trip and smiles. How lucky he is to have found a benevolent senior ladies group to flock around him. He knows that they enjoy having him there and will keep him close. A single older man who, in his own estimation, is quite handsome and charming, among a group of older women is a rare breed. It is a better disguise than he had expected. They will not check every tourist group on the Piazza.

It's all planned. The needle and chemical is ready and will not be detected by any screening at the entry to the ancient buildings. When he follows her into the church to see the Father, she will not even know when it happens. It's just a quick sharp pain, hardly more than a pinprick. It worked so well with Nobili, and it will work well with her.

His mission will be accomplished, and then he will slip quietly away with his charming senior group. Clean and efficient. With the two leaders gone, the heretical research will end. He will discard his old passport with the name Trent Reed, and then return to the United States with his new name and passport for Frederick Hague. He can then move on to his next assignment as the Messenger. His message to humanity through his Manifesto will hit the news over the next weeks. He smiles to himself, happy that it's all working out as planned. Thank God for the Messiah and the Freedom Group.

Vanessa and Ryan hurry to make their 10 am appointment with Father Fabio at the Doumo, the Cathedral de Pisa. They leave the hotel at 9 am and walk over to the Piazza dei Miracoli, vigilantly watching the people they pass for anyone who may resemble Trevick. When they arrive at the Piazza, Ryan is astonished at its majestic beauty with the four monuments to the Church built a thousand years earlier. The Duomo Cathedral named after Santa Maria Assunta is their first destination to meet with Father Fabio. If they can fit it in, he would like to tour the other exquisite examples of medieval architecture including the leaning Campanile bell tower, the Baptistry and the Camposanto.

They stop at one of the vendors for a cappuccino and a brioche pastry. They sit for a few minutes at a small set of tables at the edge of the Piazza, trying to identify the *polizia* who are supposedly protecting them and watching for any sign of Trevick. There are several hundred people in the Piazza attending to their daily activities, but no uniformed *polizia* are apparent.

Tourists are arriving at the Piazza on buses from all over Italy. One of the buses contains an older tourist group. As the group walks out of the bus one at a time, the Messenger stays close to his new found friend, Rosemary Larsen. He walks carefully and slowly down the stairs of the bus, with a slight bend at the waist, a hitch in his step, and a cane. He wants his old age to show. He is helped by several of the women who are each in great touring shape. They walk across the Piazza dei Miracoli taking the obligatory photos of the Leaning Tower from a distance.

Trevick is careful to offer to take photographs, but not to be in any of them. The group first wants to see the majestic Duomo, with the adjacent medieval cathedral named for Santa Maria Assunta. The touring ladies are all excited. They open their tourist books and chat among themselves. It is about 9:30 am.

The Messenger appreciates the information Dr. Unico provided to him, though, unfortunately, it did lead to his demise. He knows that Father Fabio is translating the *Blessing of Love* at the Duomo, and will be visited by the two doctors soon. As he walks with his lady friends, he scans the Piazza to find his target. He is excited to see both Dr. Venetre and her troublesome physician friend sitting at a table, observing the scene. This is such convenient timing. Perhaps, it can happen right there in the Duomo for all the tourists to witness. They will be headed there any minute.

As Ryan and Vanessa sit observing the scene on the Piazza, they realize that it is almost impossible to pick out Trevick among the many people coming off the buses and milling about. However, they feel safer in the confines of the Duomo with Father Fabio accompanying them.

They walk to the Duomo and enter the massive intricately decorated bronze doors to see a young woman behind the information desk. She has red hair and dressed like a rainbow, with a blue fuzzy sweater, tight green pants, pink hard rim glasses, a red scarf, and a purple name tag with Brittany on it. She has a perky British look, and is working here as a summer intern.

"Excuse me," Vanessa asks the rainbow girl. "Do you know where we could find Father Brizi? I understand that he works here."

"Oh, si. You mean Fabio, the movie star priest?" The girl asks, "He's right over there." She points in the direction of a crowd of women. "His tours are always packed with women."

Ryan's curiosity perks up and he asks the girl, "Is this the real Fabio? The Italian body builder, model, spokesperson, and heart throb of romance novels for millions of women world-wide?"

"No, he's not that Fabio," the girl replies in a chatty tone. "But he might as well be. Our Fabio is just as handsome and charismatic. He's a heart-throb to the many women who come here to see our monuments. He is one of our biggest attractions. We call him the love priest. He starred in several Italian romance movies as a young man, but to the dismay of many, he's changed careers. He realized that there was too much waiting around in making movies and not enough helping others. He wants to be more than a pretty face. Funny, isn't it?"

"You know him well?" Ryan asks curiously, raising an eyebrow.

"All the ladies here know him. He's just such a hunk, that we all go gaga around him."

"But he's a priest!" Ryan comments as he raises his eye brows.

"Yes, the priesthood has taken him away from being a movie star," she says. "But he's still very sincere and sweet. It's hard not to like being around him. He also has a PhD in something and is quite popular with both tourists and church members. When he gives a sermon, there's not an open seat in the house."

"It's too bad for the ladies that he became a Priest," Vanessa says carefully studying the priest from a distance.

"Well, it doesn't really matter if he's a Priest or not," The girl says as a matter of fact.

"Why's that?" Ryan asks.

"He's one of the few priests who has acknowledged that he's gay," the girl says quietly under her breath.

Ryan raises his eyebrows. "I heard. He is pretty bold to admit it?"

"It really doesn't matter to anyone if he's gay," she explains. "He's a hunk either way. But Father Fabio wants to be honest with people. Nobody questions his faith or his motives. Anyway, he'll be done in a few minutes. Though, you may need to pull him away from the many ladies' questions."

Ryan and Vanessa sit down and watch the handsome, charismatic Father Fabio work the crowd. The tour group of mostly senior women with a few men has flocked about him. He is the epitome of attractiveness. He appears charming, cordial, and respectful.

Ryan and Vanessa fail to notice a man in the older group who is casually looking around the church for people he knows. The Messenger is patiently waiting for Fabio's tour with his group to end so that the doctors will come over and mix with them. If he can get close enough to her, a little needle stick amidst all of the commotion will hardly be noticed.

Fabio answers the older lady's final question and thanks the group for their kind attention. He sees Vanessa and Ryan standing behind the group and excuses himself. He walks through the group to greet them.

Trevick is ready to make his move, and walks with the group towards Vanessa. Suddenly, Rosemary grabs Trevick's arm and pulls him to the side. She wants him to continue with her group and says, "Come on, Fred. We don't want to miss the next tour."

She pulls him toward the exit, and his opportunity to complete his mission disappears quickly.

"Damn it," Trevick says to himself. He realizes there are disadvantages to being so charming. There will be other opportunities today. He may have to be a bit more disagreeable to his companions.

Chapter 51. The
Blessing of Love

Father Fabio approaches Vanessa and Ryan. Vanessa extends her hand to shake his. "Ciao, Father Brizi. I'm Dr. Vanessa Venetre. This is Dr. Ryan Laughlin."

He shakes her hand and then kisses both her cheeks. Even through the traditional priest robe, Fabio appears to be a large muscular man. He has a big smile with perfectly aligned white teeth. He says with a low masculine voice that has an immediate calming effect on anyone listening, "Si, si. Dr. Gaetti called me the other day. She said you would be coming. I'm sorry you had to wait. There is always great interest in my tours. I'm flattered by the attention. Welcome to our modest digs."

"Not so modest," Vanessa replies. "The Duomo is more beautiful each time I see it."

"I have a break right now. I assume you would like to know more about the *Blessing of Love* document. I've finished the translation and am preparing a concise interpretation of it. It's really quite interesting and relevant to our current times. Do you want to get some coffee at the local café and sit down for a few minutes to review it?"

"That would be nice. But I have to warn you," Vanessa looks at him directly.

"Warn me about what?" Fabio asks.

"I assume Gabriela has told you about the murderer of Dr. Nobili and Dr. Unico," Vanessa says with seriousness.

Fabio nods with a forlorn look on his face and only listens intently.

"They have not apprehended the killer yet. He intends to kill me today."

"How do you know this?" Fabio becomes even more somber.

"He told us this on the train," she says. "I'm afraid. . . very afraid. And we all may be in danger."

She looks at Ryan with her soft brown eyes. "I'm sorry I bring both of you this trouble today. How do you deal with this level of hate? I don't understand why he wants to do this. Why do people hate and kill others?"

"I want you to feel safe," Father Fabio states as a matter of fact. "Would you rather meet in my office behind the altar?"

"Yes, thank you, Father, for your understanding. I think that would be better."

As they walk to the side of the carved dark wood altar and the white marble pulpit with two beautifully carved angels suspending it in the air, he tries to distract her from the lurking danger. "Did anyone tell you about the artistry behind the altar and the pulpit?"

"Yes, while we were waiting. The rainbow girl at the info desk gave us a little tour," Vanessa says with an emerging smile, "We heard that this carved naked Hercules looks a lot like you."

"Brittany. I don't quite understand her infatuation. I must say she doesn't really know that, but she's a big fan of my movie days."

Vanessa laughs and looks at his deep dark eyes, surrounded by his handsomely chiseled and tanned face. "I understand."

He takes them back into his office. An ancient room with dark carved wood bookcases from floor to the ceiling. He invites them to sit down at the long thick wooden pedestal table in the center of the room. "Would you like some coffee or tea?"

Father Fabio gets up and walks over to the coffee stand. His muscled arms can be seen under his robe. He has spent significant time at the gym. He pours three cups of coffee, one for each of them, and serves them with some *Biscottini di Milano* cookies. "The plague of hate is growing in our world and we need to reverse it," he begins. "The foundation of all religions is to replace hate with love. This is my life's work. And the *Blessing of Love* fits right in. It makes sense, and I believe it will change the tide of hate if people implement it into their daily lives. You know there is a thin line between love and hate. Both can be inflamed by passion."

"What do you mean?" Ryan asks sipping his coffee.

"Passion will increase motivation, excitement, and energy in the Emotional Realm. But it can also cloud the spirit of love. In the Blessing, love is different than emotional energy."

"Tell us about the *Blessing of Love*," Vanessa asks. "What is love?"

"Oh, you go right for the jugular, with the mother lode of all questions," Fabio laughs. "Everybody wants to know this, and everyone has their own definition. What is it for you, Dr. Venetre?"

Vanessa squirms, not realizing that her question would bounce right back to her.

Ryan is all ears, paying close attention to what she says.

Vanessa clears her throat while tipping the coffee to her lips. She thinks before she says, "I don't know. It's about caring for another person more than yourself. It's about having and showing respect, kindness, and affection for others. There are lots of definitions. What is yours, Father Fabio?

"I believe it's an intimate state when one has deep affection and caring for others in our world," Fabio replies. "It's a state of inner faith of knowing that life is good, the world is a good place, and there are good people all around you. Love inspires you to make it better. Your turn, Ryan. How do you define it?"

Ryan put his hand on his chin and pauses to think about it. "It's not so simple. Love is about how you live it. It's about caring for others as well as yourself. I feel strongly that you cannot love others without loving yourself. It's about giving more than you receive. It's about being unconditional and permanent. What does the Blessing say?"

As Ryan talks, Vanessa sits at the opposite side of the table watching him, with affection in her eyes. She knows that he is a good man. Amidst all of this unpredictable trauma and fear, is it still possible to have room in her heart for love?

Fabio answers Ryan's question, "The Blessing states that the capacity to love is reflected by high energy in the Spiritual Realm. When you have love for another, there is a synergy of energy between two people. This is why there is such a thing as love at first sight. In love, it's not what you see on the outside, but what's inside that matters. Many people miss this point."

"We know from the *Seven Realms of Life* manuscript and our research that the Spiritual Realm is the most powerful of all Realms," Vanessa says.

"Si! When you boost energy in this Realm, your capacity to love, whether it be for yourself, the people around you, life in general, nature, God, and everything else in between is enhanced," Fabio says confidently. "In contrast, when you lose energy, love is diminished in many Realms, and hate can emerge."

"At the Terme, we boosted our spiritual energy through meditation and prayer," Ryan replies.

"The Blessing also reinforces the importance of these actions. Let me read from the translation." He stands up and turns to find the document in the old leather-bound folder on the book shelf behind him. He sorts through the folder and reads, "To strengthen this Realm is to learn to receive help through prayer, to be calm and seek insight through meditation, to understand the meaning of your life and your past, present, and future, to live a life that is merciful each day and you will find the *Blessing of Love.*"

"It's interesting in that it mentions both prayer and meditation," Ryan comments, "Do most religions distinguish between the two?"

"As Vanessa knows from her teachings at the Terme, they are different, but both are helpful," Fabio continues. "Most religions recognize both. Prayer is used to show appreciation and to ask for help and guidance from God, while meditation is opening up yourself to receive the help."

"But most people do not seem to practice both," Ryan questions.

"Most people know that when we need help, we pray. But it is not well known that in most religions, when you want insight you practice meditative prayer. In our church, it's called orison. When you practice orison, there is no worshiping, thanking, or asking for help, but rather calming yourself and seeing inside of you so that your life becomes clear and you become more receptive and open to achieving insight. It also becomes a source of spiritual energy and enhances your capacity to love."

"We do teach meditation, which I suppose is like orison, to our participants at the Terme," Vanessa responds. "It's presented in the *Seven Realms of Life* manuscript."

"As a priest, do you practice orison?" Ryan asks.

"Of course! How do you think I developed my charm?" Fabio laughs. "You think women flock around me because of my good looks? No, it's my spiritual energy. It's very attractive, especially to women."

Vanessa leans over to Ryan and says quietly, "Aldo is a good example of someone who needs an energy boost in his Spiritual Realm."

"Tell us what you do when you practice orison," Ryan asks.

"I see orison, or meditative prayer, as learning to achieve a deep and relaxed state of the mind, body, and emotions. You start by finding a quiet place with no distractions. The deepening process involves taking deep slow rhythmic breaths, an inner awareness, quieting of the mind, and focusing on a singular object or image. The object of focus can be anything, but usually it is repeated and consistent in daily practice. The object can be defined like a word, light, or warmth or it could even be an open concept such as the infinity, love, God, or spaciousness. Some people like to focus on body sensations such as breathing in and out or the tingling of their hands and feet as they relax. Others like to focus on a mantra, prayer, saying, or song going through their minds. You should enjoy the object of focus and become increasingly absorbed into it. As you meditate, your mind is gently brought back to the object of focus and insight just comes. Guided imagery such as seeing yourself in a pleasant place, a beautiful scene, the sky beyond, a hammock swaying, or a vision of God helps you stay focused. Many feel their body relaxing as they sink deeper into the chair. It may feel like you're floating, numb, tingling, or even twitching, almost like sleep. It's like you're in a dream world."

"Sounds the same as our approach at the Terme," Vanessa replies. "The research suggests that daily practice has a profound effect on health and well-being. You lower your risk of heart disease, have less muscle and joint pain, and fewer stomach and breathing problems. It's almost a panacea for many chronic problems."

"Yes, and it's easily learned and practiced," Fabio states enthusiastically.

"I agree, but doing it regularly is the key to learning it well."

Vanessa agrees, "Unfortunately, some people think it's silly to spend time out of our fast paced world to just sit there. They get bored."

"Obviously, these people don't know what they are doing," Fabio agrees. "Sitting is only the beginning." Fabio smiles and says, "A big motivator for many people is that it enhances your attractiveness to others. Meditation is literally a love machine. People love people with high energy in this Realm. That's why they call it the *Blessing of Love*."

Ryan and Vanessa look at each other and laugh realizing how he got his nickname, the love priest. They can feel his energy. He's just so charming and irresistible when he talks about love.

"What are you laughing about?" Father asks.

"Sorry, but we're laughing because we can feel it in you so clearly," Vanessa smiles. "Your energy in this Realm is irresistible. You're like a people magnet. We can listen all night long."

Fabio takes a deep breath. "It's true. I get this all the time, but I don't mind. My job is to teach," Fabio continues. "The Blessing also brings us many virtues and angels that are like honey to bees. These include having faith, clear beliefs, and inspiration to give and receive love from those around you. A person's beliefs are the foundations and primary motivators for our actions. What is held to be true on the inside will manifest itself on the outside. It will also banish the demons of doubt, darkness, and hate. It's much better than any drug. And it costs nothing but a little bit of time each day."

"That explains why meditation is not used too often," Ryan laughs. "Free often means worthless to some people."

"Meditation is catching on and becoming more common practice," Fabio continues. "Studies have shown that nearly ten percent of adults practiced meditation within the past year, and this is growing. It has also been a practice used in many ancient and primitive civilizations, including prehistoric times. Ancient tribes used repetitive, rhythmic chants to focus their attention and energy. When explorers came upon wild ceremonies in primitive cultures, they thought it was voodoo. Well, now, we realize that they were gaining insight and building community spirit through group meditation and love. They are smarter than we thought they were."

"Interesting!" Ryan counters. "I really never realized how these tribal ceremonies are often misinterpreted."

They sit at the table gazing at Fabio and listening carefully to his every word. They realize that his charm, expressive hands, and handsome animated face can keep the attention of those with even the shortest attention span.

Fabio loves to teach, and has so much to share. He continues, "It is also thought that the capacity for focused attention in meditation may have contributed to human biological evolution and intelligence. Meditation is powerful. It can be used for other things than love. For example, in my PhD thesis, I studied the control of pain using meditation and found it to be as powerful as a narcotic medication."

"I'm not familiar with this research. Tell us about it," Ryan says.

"I found that with only a few days of meditation, people with pain conditions found a decrease in pain that was equivalent to morphine. A brain scan showed that altered brain activity in the very same regions of the brain where painkillers work."

"It's like a powerful drug," Vanessa adds.

"Si!" Fabio states, "And because it has a direct link to all Realms, it can help achieve all of the Blessings including wisdom, happiness, peace, prosperity, health, beauty, and of course, love. It is the soul of man that first needs to be fed. It provides spiritual nourishment. You can become more effective in life only when your Spiritual Realm, and your love, is strong."

"So, how do all other Realms play into this one?" Ryan asks.

"Love drives all Realms, and all Realms drive love," he explains. "It's reciprocal. Think about it. The positive energy from helping others, from trust and honesty, from natural beauty, from being happy and healthy, from being prosperous, and from peace among men. They all can strengthen the Spiritual Realm, and come from the *Blessing of Love*. You can have beauty all around you, but without love of yourself and others, it is nothing. Love is at the top of a triangle with virtues such as faith, trust, beauty, and happiness as its foundations. In the People Realm, you must have a strong faith that the person of your affection loves you. You do not know for sure until this faith is replaced by trust as you see your mate show his or her love."

"How does sex play a role in this Realm?" Ryan asks as he avoids looking at Vanessa. At first, she smiles at Ryan, but then wrinkles her forehead in displeasure for him asking the question.

"Kudos to both of you," he laughs. "First, you ask the mother lode of all questions, and now, you ask the father lode. Sex brings together the synergistic energy from all Realms between two people. It's emotional, physical, nurturing, pleasurable, beautiful, and can make you happy and at peace. It's powerful, particularly, if a strong love in the Spiritual Realm brings two people together."

"What about the opposite?" Vanessa asks, "When hate replaces a lost love?"

"The *Prophecy* predicts that when spiritual energy is low, hate will grow. Let me read." He again takes the document off the table, and reads aloud, "Beware, for weakness of the spirit in this Realm will bring demons to live here with no faith and hope, to see only doubt and darkness, and to follow a path of hate for yourself and others. And lasting weakness of the spirit in this Realm among the people will bring Plagues of hate and violence without any hope and promise."

Father Fabio stops a moment before going on. "The problems of racism, discrimination, and hate crimes around the world are increasing, especially against minorities and women. Ultimately, this low energy in the population will lead to the same mentality among leaders, and result in conflict and war between groups and nations. There is much work to be done to diminish hate and replace it with love in the world."

"If we don't, we'll have a world full of zombies like Trevick," Vanessa laughs.

"Zombies?" Fabio asks.

"You know, from the movies. Zombies are the walking dead filled with hate and vices. They are low energy folks with no clue. How do we change their hate into love?" Vanessa asks, "Is this an impossible task?"

"Zombies!" He exclaims. "I can see the parallel. I like it. When zombies have enough energy to love themselves, they will have the capacity to love others. As Ryan said earlier, they come together, never separate. When a person needs more love energy, they must pray for help and meditate to receive it.

"You both ask a lot of tough questions," he smiles. "Is this a tribunal or just an inquisition?" He looks at them with those deep big brown eyes.

"I'm sorry. Our intensity is high today," Vanessa says apologetically, "We are grappling with the issues of hate and violence in our lives right now. It's hard to understand. We believe they are religiously motivated. Your insight into these issues will help us get through this situation. We can move on if you would like."

"I take a broad view of religion," Fabio replies. "Religion is not the same as spirituality. However, religion can be the cornerstone to achieving high spiritual energy, love, and peace in the world. The practice of a person's religion and faith can be so fulfilling that it often leads to a good life. However, I believe it is not essential for a good life."

He pauses and pulls out a book from the library. It's the Bible. "Most religious texts tell us that religion is fundamental set of beliefs and practices that are generally agreed upon by members of the church. Spirituality is the inner path that enables a person to discover themselves and their deepest values and meanings by which to live. Both can help understand a person's connection to God and how it applies to each Realm of their life, particularly love."

"What about people like Anton Trevick using religion as a vehicle for hate?" Ryan counters.

"In the case of Anton Trevick, and millions around the world, religion can be used as a political force to divide us and promote intolerance."

"And create conflict and hate in the process," Ryan replies.

"These are people, and not their religion taking the action," Fabio states clearly. "As you call them, they are zombies. Every religion teaches love, acceptance, and tolerance in their set of beliefs to achieve an inner path of enlightenment. They all have a strong faith in God, and a belief in a universal divine knowledge that is important for meaningful moral and ethical decisions and actions. Despite what individuals do in the name of religion, we need to respect all religions."

"What do we do when a guy like Trevick is pursuing us?" Vanessa complains. "Today, he said he'd kill us. And he is most likely looking for us right now. You talk about love, but we're pursued by a hateful zombie."

"You need to protect yourself and be safe. I wouldn't worry about love right now. Are the *polizia* watching you?"

"They're crawling all over this place," Ryan replies. "Francois LeGrand from Faenza is in charge of the case. He's in the Piazza right now."

"Then, you should be safe. He will be there when you need him. Unfortunately, you will most likely need to draw him out."

Vanessa looks at Fabio with a sense of inevitability in her eyes,

"I know. We are the dreaded bait. We don't like being the bait for hate. But if it must be done, we might as well get it over with."

"Yes. As much as we're reluctant to go, we must leave you now," Ryan says.

Vanessa agrees, "Yes, unfortunately. Thank you for your work on the *Blessing of Love* and your interpretation and wisdom. We now have six of the ten *Prophecy* manuscripts, and are excited to use them to expand our research. We hope that it will help change our destiny in every corner of the world and stop its slide into the pits of the Plagues. We hope to survive to see the results."

Fabio looks at them with sincerity and understanding. "I have faith. You will survive and blossom together. I see lots of love."

Then, he says with a laugh, "Remember, they call me the love priest for a reason. I know about these things." He laughs again and gives them both a big hug and kiss on the cheeks. "Take care, both of you. You're doing great work with your warriors, spreading positive energy and fighting to bring zombies back from the dead. I like the sound of that."

With the Blessing manuscript in hand, they leave the Duomo, but are not relieved to walk out into broad daylight. They know that the impending confrontation is ahead of them. But where, they have no clue.

"The gay love priest," Ryan smiles. "What a guy. I don't know quite what to say."

"Sometimes, there's nothing more to be said," Vanessa laughs, "we simply need to let it sink in. Are you ready to tour that infamous Leaning Tower of fear? Are you sure you want to do it? We can bail out and go back to our safe hotel room."

"No. We are here. Let's go for it," Ryan laughs. "I can always close my eyes."

Vanessa holds his arm tightly as they pensively walk across the Piazza looking for any sign of Trevick or LeGrand. They know that both are there somewhere. They can see a few regular *polizia* spread about the Piazza. Despite having LeGrand and the *polizia* of Pisa to cover them from all angles, Trevick's voice still resonates ominously through their minds. "You will die tomorrow."

Chapter 52. The Leaning Tower

The senior tour group, which the Messenger has leeched onto, slowly walks out of the Duomo into the bright lights of the morning. The group leaders decide where to go next, the famous Leaning Tower in front of them or the Baptistry next door.

The older-looking Trevick walks with them and stews at missing his opportunity to complete his mission in the Duomo because the old nag pulled him away. He realizes that Mrs. Larsen is quickly becoming a nuisance. He complains about his hip to his new friends, and tells them that he needs to sit and wait a spell on a chair at the outdoor café near the Tower. Mrs. Larsen, his newly found friend for life believes that she cannot let him wait alone. Heaven forbid! She must sit down right next to him until he feels better. Empathy and companionship heals all, she thinks.

As they sit down to rest, Trevick surveys the scene as the other ladies walk up and down the tourist venues along the road. Then, he sees the doctors walk out of the Duomo together. His timing is ideal. He watches them walk over to the ticket counter by the Tower, buy tickets, and then walk across the Piazza to stand in the line for the tower. He notices how careful the doctors scrutinize everybody around them. There are several young couples and older couples in line with them. He surveys the location of the *polizia*. He assumes there are *polizia* in hiding ready to pounce on him at a moment's notice.

As they stand in line, Ryan complains, "Damn it, Vanessa. I left my backpack in the Cathedral. Let me go get it. Just wait in line. I'll be right back."

"I guess," says Vanessa hesitantly as she studies the others in line with her.

"It'll just take a minute. I run fast." Ryan assures her.

Without considering the dire circumstances, Ryan leaves Vanessa alone and runs over to the Cathedral.

Trevick realizes this may be his best opportunity to complete his mission. He gets up and tells Rosemary that he is better now, and insists that they see the famous Tower right away. Rosemary consents and a couple of her women friends, who are standing near them, agree to accompany them to the top. As they walk over to the line, the ladies are surprised that the old man has so much pep in his step after just limping out of the Duomo. Love works, she thinks. They stand in the back of the line as it moves slowly into the tower. Trevick watches as Vanessa enters the door to the Bell Tower alone without her pesky physician friend.

As Vanessa is about to enter into the dark staircase, she looks out to see if Ryan is coming soon, and does not see him. She debates whether to wait or enter and follow the crowd up the stairs. She decides to just go ahead and let Ryan catch up.

Trevick and his female friends are talking as if he has been on their entire tour with them. As his position in the line gets closer to the entry, Trevick looks out to see if he can see the physician. He is pleased at his timing. He is nowhere to be seen. Big mistake. It may save his own life, but unfortunately, not that of his lover, Dr. Venetre.

The line continues to move until he is about to enter the building. He takes his sunglasses off and flashes a final look towards the Duomo.

Ryan is walking briskly out of the large doors of the Duomo with his backpack in hand, looking at the line for Vanessa. He does not see her. She must have gone up. He looks at the line for any signs of Trevick. For a brief moment, he sees an old man looking at him and about to enter the Tower. There is a familiarity in the eyes and jaw of the old man. He is not sure, but the old man does seem to resemble Trevick. But it can't be. He looks like an old man and is with a senior tour group. He's talking and laughing with the older group of ladies. One lady is holding his arm. They are having the grandest of times. It can't be. Ryan watches the old man enter the building. Right before he disappears from sight, the old man flashes a look at Ryan.

Suddenly, Ryan's heart beats faster and stronger as anxiety overtakes him. He is convinced that the old man is Trevick. "Damn it!" He yells out loud recognizing his mistake of leaving Vanessa alone, even for a few minutes. He begins to panic as he looks around to see if he can find LeGrand or the *polizia*, or anyone to help. He sees nobody. He knows they are watching so he waves his arms to alert them. Nobody seems to see him or react, so he has to take action himself.

He calms himself and rationalizes that he has to get to the top of the tower and find Vanessa as quickly as possible. He sprints towards the tower. The line has twenty people in it, and is moving slowly. He goes directly to front of the line. "*Escusame per favore, emergenza. Escusame,*" he says apologetically.

There is some grumbling among the others in line, but Ryan ignores it. If the old man is Trevick, Vanessa is in serious danger. He arrives at the entrance to the tower, and is suddenly frozen as he looks up the side of the tower. It is tall, thin, and leaning towards the old town. His fear of heights stops him in his tracks. He studies the climb in front of him.

People behind him are complaining, "What are you waiting for? Are you going or staying? Let's move it!"

He must go now. He closes his eyes and enters the tall narrow and awkward tower. He opens his eyes to find a dark tower, with little natural light along the staircase. Fear penetrates his mind as he looks at the steep, worn, and slippery marble steps. He is realizing his worst nightmare. Despite his gripping fear, he takes two steps at a time up the winding, unstable staircase in hopes of catching up with the old man.

He jumps past several groups as they complain about his hurrying, "What's the hurry, buddy. We're all waiting."

Ryan urgently replies, "*Escusame, per favore. Emergenza. Grazie.*"

He continues up the steps towards the old man, with fear in his heart. The steps are leaning to one side, causing a nauseating unsteadiness, as the building seems ready to fall on its side. He cannot go down for fear of leaving Vanessa to her death. But his fear of heights escalates with each step. He stays close to the inside wall. He climbs as quickly as possible, being careful not to slip on the marble steps. He looks out the small deep slit of a window, and sees the distant ground below. It makes his head spin with dizziness. He looks at his shoes, and one of the laces is untied. He cannot believe it, but he is reliving his recurring nightmare.

He backs off against the center of the circular staircase gasping for breath. He bends down to tie his shoe. He takes off up the stairs again. His heart is racing. He needs to catch up to the old man to see if it is Trevick. He takes two steps at time, but his fear is overwhelming. He keeps going up the staircase, but never seems to find the end. It seems to become narrower as he climbs higher. He is terrified and not thinking clearly. He notices his shoelace untied again. Damn it! He ignores it and continues to jump up the stairs.

Trevick hears the complaints of people below, as someone is rushing up the stairs and pushing past them. He looks behind and sees nobody, but he hears the footsteps and grumblings getting closer. He realizes that it is the doctor coming up the stairs. He must do something to stop him. He excuses himself from the ladies with the pretext of resting, and tells them to continue on. He steps into the shadows of a doorway. He has only one syringe so he has to stop the doctor some other way. He lifts his metal tipped cane.

Suddenly, as Ryan comes around a curve in the steps, he feels a sharp pain on his head, and then on his shoulder, and again on his head. The old man is striking him with his cane. He falls down on the steps. The people behind him gasp in horror as blood flows from multiple wounds on his head. The pain is unbearable. He works to avoid losing consciousness from the blows, and tries to protect his head.

The old man is yelling, "*Bruta, bruta. Al Ladro!* Thief!"

The people behind Ryan are shocked to see him lying there in a ball, his arms over his bloodied head, nearly unconscious. The old man quits hitting him, and turns to run up the stairs with more agility than any old man could ever have.

Despite his head injuries, Ryan sees the old man disappear around the winding steps. The old man surprisingly leaps up the stairs two at a time. Ryan is now convinced that it is Trevick and ignores the pain and dizziness. He gets up and staggers further up the stairs holding his head.

Some people step out of his way while others yell at him to leave the old man alone.

Ryan ignores the complaints and continues to chase him up the stairs. He passes the old ladies, and they look at him rudely, yelling at him to stop. Some men try to stop him, but he shakes them off. He points to the old man, and says, "*Uccisore.* Killer. Murderer. Stop hm." They become confused, and let him go.

Ryan cannot catch up to the fleet old man. He steps on his shoelace, and falls down, scraping his knee. Shit! He gets up again and keeps running, panic stricken.

Suddenly, he finds himself at the top of the staircase inside the belfry, just behind the old man. The old man looks back and Ryan recognizes that the old man is, in fact, Trevick in a clever disguise.

Trevick hits him several more times with the cane.

Ryan holds on to the railing and fends off the blows. Ryan looks around and does not see her on this level. He calls out, "Vanessa! He's here! Trevick is here!" She does not respond, and he realizes that she must be on the top balcony of the tower.

Ryan's heart is beating like a drum. He's gasping for air that doesn't come. He sees Trevick moving quickly around the belfry platform to the outside of the large cast iron bells. The breeze is strong in the belfry. Ryan avoids looking out over the rooftops of the old medieval town, and yells again to Vanessa. She does not respond. He is blinded by the bright sunlight coming through the opposite side of the Tower. He gets a glimpse of the old man through the housings of the bells, on the opposite side of the belfry, heading up to the balcony.

Trevick leaps up the final staircase looking for Vanessa at the top balcony. He knows this is the end of the line for her. She cannot go any higher. She will be there looking out over the old buildings of Pisa, not suspecting that it is here at the top of the tower that she will find her demise.

Ryan takes off across the platform of the belfry to catch him. He comes around the corner to see Trevick disappear onto the balcony at the top of the Tower.

Trevick sees Vanessa standing by the railing looking out over the town with seemingly not a care in the world. Trevick recognizes that this is the chance he has been waiting for—to hit her with the needle. If he is lucky, the quick action of the poison will lead to rapid convulsions. She will either fall off the edge of the Tower to her death or die from the poison on top of the tower. Either way, she will be out of the way, and his mission is complete. He can slip away unnoticed.

Ryan arrives at the top of the stairs right behind him and sees him running towards her. He yells again to Vanessa, "Vanessa! Get out of here. He's here. It's Trevick."

Vanessa is confused by Ryan's screams. The old man is walking briskly towards her. A panic freezes every part of her body and mind as he sees the old man's hand reaching out towards her as he approaches. She has nowhere to go on the small platform. She turns her back on the old man and runs to her left away from him.

Ryan runs at Trevick. Just as he extends his hand with the needle to puncture Vanessa's arm, Ryan tackles Trevick to the ground. The needle is knocked away as they struggle with each other.

Trevick is lying on the ground hitting Ryan with the cane yelling, *"Bruta! Aiutami! Bruta!"*

The scene on top of the Tower is one of confusion and pandemonium as the two men wrestle with each other on the deck. The old lady friends are screaming to stop it since they believe Ryan is assaulting the old man. They hit Ryan with their bags and several men pull him off of the old man.

Then, the old man surprises the ladies with a show of strength and agility. He jumps up from the ground, and hits Ryan on the head with the cane. Ryan falls to the floor, desperately trying to maintain consciousness. Trevick picks up the needle and runs towards Vanessa again.

With blood flowing down his face, Ryan quickly shakes off the pain and dizziness and runs after him. As the old man approaches Vanessa again, Ryan broadsides him with a lunging football block. They both crash against the short railing of the balcony, again, dislodging the needle from the Trevick's hand. Trevick loses his footing, and nearly falls over the railing.

Ryan unsuccessfully tries to push Trevick over the edge, but instead Trevick swings back to kick Ryan in the groin with enough force to knock his breath out. Ryan falls back against the railing, holding his gut. He hits his head on the top rail and falls to the ground, silent.

Vanessa is shocked by the sudden flurry of fighting between the two. She stands to the side not knowing what to do. With Ryan down, Trevick picks up the needle again, and heads toward Vanessa. He moves closer to Vanessa readying the syringe.

Vanessa sees the syringe in horror and realizes that the old man is Trevick. She gains her wits and quickly runs away from him around the small platform.

The blow to his head stuns Ryan. He tries to stand up in a daze. With the instincts of a boxer who is down, but not out, he quickly runs toward Trevick and lunges at him again. He hits Trevick as hard as he can with his shoulder, and knocks him towards the railing on the lower side of the leaning building. As Trevick stumbles backwards, Ryan jumps up and runs over to kick him with a huge blow to his legs.

Trevick tries to brace for the kick but loses his balance and falls over the top of the railing. He grabs the top of the wrought iron railing, but his grip is slippery from sweat. Trevick finds himself dangling over the top of Leaning Tower, looking at the ground eight stories below.

Ryan stands up and walks towards Trevick, tenuously hanging over the edge of the building, wondering whether he should help him or not. Before he can make a decision, Trevick's slippery hands fail him. He loses his grip and falls towards seven stories to the ground. When, he hits the ground, his body shudders, and he lies still as death.

Tourists on top of the tower watch over the edge and shaking their heads in shock, as they see the old man lying still on the ground below. The *Polizia* and LeGrand surround him. They pull off his hat and recognize that it is, in fact, Anton Trevick, the Prophecy killer, in disguise.

At the top of the tower, Ryan and Vanessa hold each other with an embrace that lasts into eternity. Ryan picks up the needle in a tissue to turn over to the *polizia* for evidence. Vanessa tells the people at the top of the tower who the old man was and they back off from the accusatory looks.

As the shock is still setting in, they walk slowly down the worn steps of the tower and work their way through the crowd to where the body lies. They find LeGrand and confirm the identity of Trevick. They tell him the story of the fight at the top. LeGrand apologizes for not recognizing Trevick's surprisingly simple, but clever, disguise. Ryan and Vanessa do not care. They are simply relieved that the ordeal is over and they are still alive.

Chapter 53. The Energy of Seven Realms

As dusk arrives, the noisy crowd around the scene is finally disseminating around the staked out crime scene. After the surrounding publicity, interrogations, and police activity, Vanessa and Ryan simply want to be alone and head back to the hotel. LeGrand indicates that he will be in touch. They still have many questions of which few will be answered with the death of Trevick. Was Trevick working alone? Was it a conspiracy with the Kolbs or another group? Are there still others who might threaten them? They simply need to trust the police in their investigations and, as hard as it is, try to move beyond this episode in their lives.

When they arrive at the hotel room, Ryan flops down on the bed in exhaustion. He laughs at the thought that this was planned to be a vacation. He is relieved to have this part of his vacation over. Vanessa sits down beside him and inspects his many cuts and bruises. She gets some warm water and a washcloth and carefully cleans and kisses each wound. She applies the bandages given to her by the front desk. She is surprised that he has no major injuries from the incident. They decide to head down for a quiet dinner at a small, centuries old restaurant, Il Vecchio Dado, recommended by the concierge. It is on a quiet back street of Pisa, hidden away from the crowds, perfect for their needs right now.

They are uncharacteristically quiet as they walk through the back streets under the dark moonless night to the restaurant. They ruminate about the scenario that just happened. The paramount but unspoken question on their minds is—what is next for the two?

Vanessa's dreamy look into Ryan's eyes tells one of a million stories that has been repeated in this ancient town over the centuries. She is in love with this man who saved her life. She cannot, and will not, forget these courageous actions from a near stranger. For God's sake, they met for the first time just a week ago. Only a very special man would have the surprising devotion to do such acts.

They have a quiet dinner, and then, stroll back to their hotel, holding hands and talking about what's next for them. She will introduce the two new *Blessings* manuscripts at the Terme, and he will apply this new knowledge to his patients in his clinic. They avoid talking about the obvious—their relationship. They are both exhausted yet choose to walk up the stairs to their roof top room to avoid meeting anyone. They are both in desperate need of sleep, but it is the last thing on their minds.

When they arrive, Ryan walks out onto the secluded balcony overlooking the courtyard garden with a distant view of the Piazza, while Vanessa gets ready to leave for the Terme in the morning. Ryan can see the top of the Duomo, the leaning bell tower, and the Baptistery in the distance illuminated brilliantly by the spotlights. The bustle of tourists roaming the streets of Pisa has slowed to a few laughing couples.

A thousand doubts fill Ryan's mind as he stares into the distance. The dark sky has gradually surrendered to the brilliance of the stars above. He thinks to himself, "I've walked from hell into heaven here but where do I go now? I don't know if this love will bring me anywhere. But here, right now under the lights of this heaven, I don't care. It is Vanessa whom I want to love. And, now, I want her love."

He stands motionless on the balcony watching her through the door. She slowly undresses and pulls the sheer satin nightgown over her long flowing dark hair and sensuous body. She is oblivious to his watchful eyes. It stirs a desire in him to kiss her passionately.

He becomes aroused, knowing that deep inside him, there is a carnal passion for her that he cannot stifle much longer. She is so full of life and energy from every Realm. She has high expectations, but is so direct and honest while at the same time nurturing and loving. He watches her every move as she carefully folds her clothes and places them in her luggage. She looks so emotionally drained from this week. He knows that she still clings to whatever fragile security she can find.

He hopes that his love can become her security right now. He is ready to make love to her and finally commit to this relationship. From the moment he first laid eyes on her walking into the Terme, he felt the sexual energy that comes into play long before any sexual relationship develops between two people. He has learned this past week that the greatest pleasure is not in the ultimate sexual act, but rather the increasing passion that comes from the energy of the seven Realms.

But if it's not mutual, it will not happen. He will not take advantage of her vulnerability and reduce her to being a receptive body that meets his animal desires for sexual pleasure. He will not submit to his own long-standing physical need if her desire and passion are not there.

He turns away from his voyeurism and looks back over the stunning view of the city. The conflicting thoughts about his relationship with her dominate his mind and create a hesitancy to pursue the passion he wants from her. He concludes that simply arriving to this night alive and well is a miracle in itself, and whether love comes along or not, so be it.

As Vanessa prepares to leave tomorrow, the fatigue of the week draws her closer to bed. She turns to watch Ryan stand on the balcony looking over the city. He looks so alone right now, and a thousand thoughts are circling through her mind. He is the brightest romantic encounter of her life to date, a dream come true. He is handsome, respectful, strong, loyal, and most importantly, kind. He has been there for her when she needed someone the most and saved her from her worst nightmare.

Any doubt that she has about making love to him has passed today. Right now, she craves holding him tightly, kissing him and enjoying the taste of him. It is time to break down her high walls of restraint and finally complete this dance between unlikely lovers. She may be damned for it, but she understands deep inside her that the time is now.

Vanessa walks out to the balcony to find Ryan staring out over the garden and the distant Piazza. She puts her arms around his waist from behind, and hugs him with all her strength. "What are you thinking about out here all alone? We need to celebrate your triumph today. You've saved my life. And overcome your biggest fear in doing so."

"What do you mean?" Ryan turns around to look her in the eyes.

"You overcame your fear of heights and climbed the Bell Tower to save me from the evil villain. I said I wouldn't ask you to do that, but you did it anyways. How can I ever repay you?"

"I wasn't completely responsible for it," He replies modestly. "Your wish at the Trevi Fountain simply came true. I was just a tool."

"I'm not sure if my wish has come true yet. I'm hoping that it will."

"What do you mean? Didn't you wish to be saved from this monster?"

"Not exactly."

"Are you kidding?" He says with surprise. "What else would you have wished for then?"

"I can't tell you. I don't want to jinx it."

It suddenly hits him that her wish was not to be saved, but rather to be loved by a man she loves. She knew then what he knows now. His eyes well up with hidden tears of emotion. He puts his arms around her and pulls her face close to his. As she closes her eyes, he kisses her with a passion that comes when the weight of the world has just lifted off of their shoulders. He looks down at her and says, "My wish was to have us saved from the killer, but my dream is to show you my love. May I?"

She opens her eyes and says, "Then, my wish has also come true. Noble hearts such as yours, Dr. Laughlin, are deserving of the deepest love a person has to offer. And you have mine."

They stand on the balcony under the vast array of stars in the moonless sky on this Italian summer night oblivious to the rest of world. They both understand that their hidden desire for each other has finally surfaced and this realization drives their passion higher.

As she kisses him back, the paradoxical effect of the dissipating fear arouses Vanessa's pent-up passion beyond expectations. Her legs feel weak as her wetness becomes palpable. She can feel the tingling moving down her arms and legs. Her heart is beating faster.

Ryan could kiss her sweet lips all night long, but he wants more. He wants to love her so desperately, so completely right now. He holds the small of her back as he begins to gently kiss her neck and moves onto the gentle rise of her breasts above her gown.

She bends her head back in excitement and her face blushes red. She feels the sensations down to her toes as her heart beats even stronger in anticipation.

He gently moves the straps of her gown off her shoulders and the gown falls to her waist to expose her naked breasts. He buries his head in her bosom as he delicately kisses the softness of her breasts. He slowly caresses the smooth skin surrounding her nipples with the tip of his tongue.

She feels his every touch as if a rush of passion shutters through her body. She holds his head tightly to her breasts to keep her knees from collapsing. She has waited so long for this. Whether unsuspecting voyeurs are peering heatedly at them or not, she cares not, and dares not leave him at this moment. She races to unbutton his shirt to expose his bare muscular chest and pulls it off his back and arms. Her hands grab at him to feel the strength and power of a well-conditioned athlete. The passion is accelerating.

He pushes her gown to the floor and she stands on the balcony in only her panties. He begins to kiss every corner of her naked body. He kneels down while she stands wrapping his head in her arms. He moves his gentle kisses down to the curves of her firm belly. Then, he pulls down her panties and kisses the moist flesh between her legs. The rush of ecstasy is beyond pleasure, and she can barely stand it anymore. She nearly faints, only to be swept up into his arms.

He lifts her up and carries her off the balcony to lay her gently on the bed.

Without hesitation, she sits up and grabs the belt of his pants and pulls him over to her naked body. She unleashes his belt and drops the zipper to expose his shorts. She pulls his pants to the floor and reaches inside his shorts to feel his pulsing erection. She pushes his shorts to his ankles to expose his naked muscular frame. He freezes in pleasure as she touches every part of his erotic hardness as it stands tall in front of her. She lays gentle kisses up and down it. Any inhibitions and restraint have now been thrown aside as their excitement grows exponentially.

She wants him inside her now, and she pulls him down on top of her. She wraps her arms and legs around him with their eyes connecting, but not seeing. Their skin against each other is warm and wet. He lies on top of her with his strong arms bracing himself above her. He gently kisses her forehead and then her nose. His kisses move down to her neck with the gentleness of a butterfly. He feels his hardness pressing firmly between her legs wanting to enter.

Her heart beats fast and strong as she feels all of his weight on top of her. She sighs in his ear and grips his shoulders. He reaches down to let his fingers trace the curves of her belly, her hips, and her soft hair. Then, he delicately opens the soft lips between her thighs and gently massages her point of passion. He feels the warm wetness inside and knows she is ready. He is gentle in touch and deliberate in his movements. He directs himself carefully inside her.

Her nails dig into his shoulders as she arches her back in anticipation. He cradles the small of her back with his strong right arm to bring her hips up to his. At the same time as their moist lips taste each other, his thrust brings them together to become one in love. She lets out a moan of pleasure as he penetrates deeper. The physical ecstasy grows with each movement. She enjoys every touch, every sound, and every scent of their lovemaking. The sensations are deeply satisfying and she wants it to continue forever.

She has no doubt in her mind and heart about this man and their love for each other. The blood swims in her veins, from her head to her fingertips as he presses his hardness over and over into her soft wetness. Her legs become tangled around him holding his body firmly into hers.

He thinks a lifetime of nights spent between her thighs would not be enough. He patiently waits, and then, continues his strong thrusts as she arches her hips. His anticipation is almost too much to bear after more than a year of not being intimate, and now, to be inside the woman who he adores. The pleasure is beyond his imagination. He has dreamed about making love to her for what seemed like eternity, but in reality, he cannot fathom that it has only been a week.

He continues the rhythmic movements in harmony with hers, and patiently waits until she is ready. The sensations have an intensity that takes them beyond the physical realm to reach a level of pleasure that they have never felt before. Then, when he cannot bear to hold on any longer, he releases his climax with an intensity that he had never achieved before. The peak of their energy explodes in the ultimate expression of their love.

As the pleasure of the climax slowly dissipates, they embrace each other with their legs and arms intertwined. They are both spent and exhausted. Without saying anything, Vanessa slowly falls asleep in his arms, bringing the experience into her dreams. As he holds her, Ryan lays awake for a few minutes thinking about her and his experiences in Italy before he drifts off. It has been a trip to die for. And it's only the beginning of an adventure with no end in sight. For the *Prophecy* will be told.

Chapter 54. The News

Cindy Miles stands in front the St. Paul Hotel at night, the lights shining brightly on her as she prepares to present a special newsbreak on the developing story of the murder of Dr. Jack Killian. Her voice is serious as she introduces herself, "This is Cindy Miles of National News reporting. There are exciting developments in the murder of Dr. Jack Killian, the renowned researcher from the National Institute of Health. Apparently, the chief suspect in the murder, Anton Trevick, is an employee of the Kolb brother's Freedom Group. He turned up in Pisa, Italy, where he fell from the top of the Leaning Tower of Pisa. Federico Famosa, in Pisa, has the story for us."

"Buon Giorno. Yesterday, the man in this picture, Anton Trevick, fell from the Leaning Tower of Pisa. A group of tourists visiting the Tower reported a struggle between two men at the top of the Tower. Here is an eyewitness account of the incident."

He puts the microphone in the face of an older woman, and asks her, "What just happened here?"

"Oh my! It was so upsetting. My name is Rosemary Larsen, from Wisconsin," she says. "A handsome single man from our group was running up the stairs to the top. Then, this other dreadful man came out of nowhere and started fighting with him. Then, he pushed our friend right over the edge. It was terrible. I hope the man is caught and goes to prison for a long time."

The camera then cuts to Federico holding a microphone in the face of Francois LeGrand. They are standing at the Piazza di Miraculo with the Leaning Tower in the background. "Francois LeGrand is the detective involved in the case. Detective, thank you for speaking with us. Who is Anton Trevick, and how did he fall off the Tower?"

"*Il tuo benvenuto, Senor Famosa*," LeGrand responds, "Anton Trevick is the chief suspect in the murder of three people, one in the United States, and two here in Italy. We have been tracking him all week. He's been quite elusive in escaping capture, but met his match here in Pisa. He was disguised as an older adult tourist in a group visiting the famous tower. He attempted to kill Dr. Vanessa Venetre, a physician and researcher here in Italy who is studying the *Dead Sea Scrolls*. If it were not for an American tourist's fast action, he most likely would have killed her, and perhaps, others. "

"Who was the tourist?" Famosa asks as the camera scans the spectators in front of the Leaning Tower of Pisa.

"I would rather not say at this moment to protect his privacy," LeGrand replies.

The video cuts back to Ms. Miles as she speaks to the camera. "Who is Anton Trevick, and what was he doing on top of the Leaning Tower? We now go to Detective John Steiner of the St. Paul Police to find out."

"Thank you, Cindy. With the help of Francois LeGrand in Italy, and an American tourist, the killer has been stopped. The exact motives of Trevick are unclear. We have a copy of his Manifesto, and it is similar to that of the Kolb funded Freedom Group where he worked. We have contacted the leaders of the Freedom Group, and they said they were just as surprised as everyone else. They reported that Mr. Trevick was a hard worker for the group, and never presented any trouble."

The camera comes back for a close up of Miles. "Evidently, he got carried away with the responsibilities of his job. We checked with Kolb Industries and their Freedom Group, and both have no comment on why they employed a murderer. Were they involved or not? We have yet to know."

She turns back to Steiner. "Who is the American tourist in Pisa who stopped this killer?"

The camera turns back to Steiner. "I'm sorry, but for reasons of confidentiality, we are not able to release his name. All I can say is that he acted courageously and wants to return to his normal life."

Chapter 55. The Return

PISA, ITALY
TUESDAY MORNING

Dawn is arriving too fast as Ryan slowly wakes up with Vanessa still asleep, snuggled in his arms. The sky is getting bright and the stars are burning out. He had a long and peaceful sleep with wonderful dreams of optimism, love, and hope. He watches her as she sleeps, and then kisses her gently and repeatedly on her head. What a remarkable woman. He knows that his love for her is blossoming.

Tears fill his eyes. He is staring at her perfection in his arms; so beautiful, so true. He wishes that somebody could slow it down. This morning has come too fast and this night will soon be a memory. This may be his last glance of his sleeping angel. Right now, he needs to hold her so close because when the daylight comes, he will have to go and leave her side. He will be on his own, again, alone in the world.

Vanessa slowly wakens to Ryan's affection and warmth, and she immediately feels her energy buoyed with relief and contentment, and then love. She holds on to him tightly and snuggles closer, kissing his neck gently. As Ryan's pleasant anticipation of another love session develops, she suddenly breaks free of his embrace and jumps up out of bed. She throws open the curtains to see the daylight of a glorious new day and a bright future.

"Why are you getting up?" Ryan protests. He turns to lay on his back with his arms folded behind his head. "It's much safer right here by my side."

"There's no need for safety anymore. You've already saved me, and of course, I saved you right back."

"Please refresh my memory," he asks inquisitively, smiling. "How exactly did you save me?"

"If I have to explain that to you, then perhaps, you were not saved," she answers.

"Oh, yes, that's right," he responds. "You've saved me, my dear, from a normal life of peace and quiet."

"No," she smiles. ". . .from a life of sorrow without romance and excitement."

"Or. . ." He raises his eyebrows. "From a life that came close to ending in pain, misery, and death."

"Well, if that's what you think, then perhaps you need a little more saving."

She walks over to the bed, jumps up on it, and sits right on top of him, holding his arms down. She looks at him with her bright eyes and a sly smile, and says, "Let me see. How should I start saving you again?"

She kisses his neck, and he laughs out loud. "Stop it. I'm ticklish there."

"I'm sorry, but you need more saving," She kisses him on his sides and on his belly, still holding his arms down. He tries to push her away, and laughs uncontrollably.

"That's even worse. Okay. Okay. I give up. You've saved me enough. Thank you."

"And I thank you, too, for saving me," She kisses him passionately on the lips.

"Don't worry. I'll save you anytime you want," He kisses her right back. They both laugh with relief, knowing that nobody is out there threatening them. Today is the first day of the rest of their lives, and they realize the future for them is open to so many possibilities.

Then, there is reality to contend to. They need to take the train back to Brisighella this morning, and have yet to do their packing. Ryan is somber, knowing he has to leave from Bologna to fly back to Minnesota this afternoon. Vanessa has already missed the Monday introduction for the next group of warriors, and does not want to miss all of today's session. She also wants to present the new manuscripts—the *Blessing of Prosperity* and the *Blessing of Love* to the staff and participants. They will all be excited.

Vanessa calls the staff at the Terme and tells them that she is on her way, and will arrive this afternoon. If she is lucky, she will arrive in time to say a few words to the new participants. She is sketchy about of the circumstances of the last few days. They will hear about the gory details soon enough, if not from her, then from the paparazzi who have flocked to Pisa and most likely follow her to Brisighella.

Ryan calls LeGrand to thank him for helping avoid all of the media hounds and to get an update on the status of the investigation. LeGrand tells them that it is not only his responsibility to brief the media about the whole story, but that he revels in the publicity. He considers the publicity an opportunity to leave his dismal life in Faenza, and even perhaps, move back to France to start over again.

They finish packing and quietly leave the hotel by taxi to make their way to the central train station. They feel fortunate to see no paparazzi as they board the train to Florence. They simply sit and relax on the train, and enjoy being with each other without much conversation. They relish the quiet activities of reading a book, looking out the window, and daydreaming about last night and their future lives as the train rolls along its tracks.

They quickly forget about the danger that has passed, and instead, think about all that has transpired in one long week, and about what their plans are for the future. The two of them do not bring up any plans to continue their relationship because they simple do not know what will happen. They recognize there are huge challenges ahead for both of them.

Vanessa needs to bring the new Blessings manuscripts back to the Terme and expand their research. It will be a challenge to fill Dr. Nobili's shoes, particularly in raising the funds to continue the controversial research. When she returns, she knows that there will be much sadness at the Terme, and it will be her job to recover the lost energy. But she is buoyed by the Pope's support of the research and the knowledge found in the new Blessings manuscripts. But what is most on her mind and in her heart is her growing love for Ryan.

Ryan, on the other hand, is looking at life quite differently than when he arrived. For one, he's in love and will return to Italy at the nearest opportunity. He is also excited about bringing the knowledge of the *Prophecy Scroll* back to his clinic and his patients. He sees the knowledge will be transformative and believes he will be at the horizon of an entirely new approach to health care that puts the *Seven Realms of Life* at the center. He wants to be at the crest of the wave as a warrior of the *seven Realms*. This goal is only trumped by his desire to be with Vanessa.

They arrive at the Florence station glad that the paparazzi have yet to catch up with them. They know LeGrand held his press conference by now and everyone in the news world will be trying to find Dr. Venetre to get the scoop directly from her. The door of the train opens, and they step out with their luggage. They are relieved to be alone together with nobody in sight. They grab two *paninis* with prosciutto and apple juice at a food kiosk, and casually walk to the Brisighella platform eating and laughing at their good fortune in staying anonymous.

As they turn to head down the platform, they are surprised to see a large crowd of people standing by the train as it waits to leave for Brisighella. It puzzles them that on a Tuesday morning, there are so many passengers to board the small train to a little known medieval town. Then, one member of the crowd yells out, "There she is! She's coming this way."

The crowd of over thirty reporters storms down the platform like a tidal wave of people rushing towards them. Vanessa freezes, with no clue of how to react.

The crowd surrounds her and starts a barrage of questions, "What did it feel like to be pursued by a mass murderer?" "How did you escape the shooting in Sardinia?" "Why was Trevick after you? Did you oppose his Manifesto?" "Did you know about the Freedom Group?" "Tell us about the research? Why is it so controversial?"

Vanessa has little experience with the news media. Paolo had always dealt with them, while she worked with the staff and participants. She looks at Ryan, realizing that she has to say something. She cannot deny being Dr. Venetre. Her pictures are all over the Internet, news, and the television.

Ryan turns to Vanessa and says, "Vanessa, let me handle this. Pretend that I'm your publicist."

She looks at him dumbfounded, trying to figure out what he's going to say, other than the long complicated truth. He raises his hand and the media frenzy dies down. Microphones are thrust into Ryan's face. He takes control of the conversation. He talks fast and definitively, with a look of excitement and passion in his eyes. Nobody among the media can get a word in edgewise. They don't even know who he is.

"As each of you realize, Dr. Venetre has been through a nightmare this weekend. She spurned the grim reaper when she was saved by the gallant efforts of Detective Francois LeGrand, the hero of the hour. You need to talk to him about the details of his heroic deeds. Dr. Venetre is excited to tell her story. Hers is a bold story about idealist researchers at the Roman Terme of Brisighella, led by the late Dr. Paolo Nobili. Their research breaks new ground in studying the essence of life, the human spirit, in applying ancient knowledge from the last of the *Dead Sea Scrolls*. It's a story of hate and violence, of courage in the face of darkness, of everlasting faith in the power of the human spirit, and of a dedicated love. It is a great story that you will not want to miss. Unfortunately, right now, you must excuse us, since we need to catch a train. Rest assured, the story will be told. Ciao!"

With that, he takes Vanessa's arm, and their luggage, and quickly walks through the crowd to get on the train.

The paparazzi stand stunned at what they just heard. They know this could be the story of a lifetime—and they just let the two walk away.

Finally, a woman reporter yells to them as they step up into the train, "You're the American tourist who saved her. What's your name? Don't worry, we will find you. You're right. It's too good a story to let you go. Rest assured, we will find you."

As they find their seats, Vanessa is puzzled. She looks at Ryan and asks, "What was that all about? Spurned the grim reaper? A bold story of idealist researchers? Courage in the face of darkness? Dedicated love? Where did you get all of that? It only fuels their pursuit. Haven't we been chased enough already?"

"I was simply allowing us to make a gracious exit while making you into a great story. Face it. You and your Terme research is a wonderful story. And you could use a little publicity and a little money to continue this project. I just brought you millions."

Vanessa rolls her eyes. Ryan looks out the window and waves to the media. Although she may not recognize it now, she will be quite indebted to Ryan. They both know that the paparazzi will be back, and she will be quite prepared when that happens.

For both of them, returning to a normal life may not be as easy as simply returning home. The final train of their journey leaves the station and heads back to Brisighella. During the two-hour ride to Brisighella, they are quiet and pensive. Vanessa is preparing to return to her life at the Terme, a life that was normal less than a week ago. Now, her life has been dramatically altered by the loss of Paolo Nobili, the two new Blessing manuscripts, the publicity that the incident will bring, and most importantly, her blossoming love for Ryan.

Although she is excited about these developments, her mind quickly moves on to Ryan. She wants to continue the relationship with him more than anything else right now. She will miss so many things about this man when he leaves—his kindness and gentle touch, the security she feels when he is near, his cynical sense of humor, and his desire to please. But mostly, she will miss his love.

But there are so many obstacles, and the demons of doubt are creeping in. Will the love become stronger when they are away from each other or will it dwindle simply from being thousands of miles apart? When Ryan leaves to return to Minnesota, when will he come back? How will their love be sustained? How much of the love was a product of the fear and need for help, security, and safety? These demons of doubt make a long-term relationship with him a near impossible challenge. Thus, she feels vulnerable and has vowed never to be in that situation again. Yet, here she is set up for pain and hurt again.

She repeats to herself, "What am I doing? Where am I going?" She cannot and will not repress her strong feelings for him. He has all of the qualities that she dreams about in a man and she wants to be with him. She prays that something will work out. She must have faith that the energy that brought them together will help them to stay together. Everything is different, but nothing has changed.

Ryan is happy to be done with this vacation adventure, and to have survived it. He will to return to Minnesota later today and resume his busy life of patient care, biking, and caring for his busy mother. He will stop by and see Julia in Boston on his way back to Minnesota. He does not know what will happen to his relationships with Vanessa, or Julia, for that matter. He wants to get to know Julia better also. After all, she is responsible for initiating his salvation.

Right now, there is nothing he wants to do more than spend time with Vanessa without the demons of fear haunting them. He loves everything about her. Her charm and intelligence, her honesty and idealism, and, of course, her beauty and love. But he also recognizes that there are many walls to climb. He knew the limits of this trip when he left for Italy, but had no idea the drama that would befall him.

For a man who refused to be vulnerable again, how could he have anticipated meeting Vanessa, fall in love, and put his life in danger to save her? And how can he leave Vanessa here alone? But how can he not? How can a long-term distant relationship be sustained? Does he want to return to his comfortable, but suffering, life? It's a life that even he admits could not go on as usual.

He is just like Vanessa with his demons of doubt casting a broad net. Vanessa lives in Italy, and he lives in Minneapolis. They both have all consuming jobs. Both are still fragile from previous losses. Both are idealists looking for a relationship they may not exist.

He realizes that he has many more mountains to climb. Some will be impossible to scale so he will turn around and head back down. Others will not interest him so he will take a different route around them. But the most satisfying mountains to climb for Ryan have always been those that motivate him to pedal the hardest to reach the pinnacle and, then, discover something, which is truly special. He knows that Vanessa is worth the climb. Right now, he is pumping as hard as he can but knows that he has only just begun the journey. Nothing is different, but everything has changed.

Acknowledgments

The author wishes to thank many people who have helped make this book a reality. First and foremost, this story is dedicated to my patients, whom I have had the blessing of helping. I thank my family for their support in allowing me to take time away from them to complete this book. I thank my wife, Delia Dall'Arancio, for much of the insight into the Blessings, the characters, and the Italian people and places used in the story. I appreciate the direction of the staff at iUniverse, and especially, Sarah Disbrow, for her excellent guidance in producing a quality book. I also appreciate the talents of Kelsey King, for her creativity and illustrations, and Ricki Walters, for her skill and commitment to fine editing. I also thank those who have guided me in the content and style of the book including Connie Brothers, Mary Bennett, Randy Anderson, Thomas and Desiree Fricton, Josiah and Jennifer Fricton, Regina Fricton, Vincent Fricton, Thomas Doyle, Jerry Steiner, Betsy and Ed Hasselman, Matthew Monsein, Andy Nelson, James and Lisa Hawthorne, Joseph Barber, Mary Pepping, Dan Satorius, and a special thanks to Susie Farquharson for her editing and steady stream of positive encouragement. Finally, I also thank all of those who have provided me with comments about the book during its development—you are too many to mention by name. You know who you are, and I thank you.

The Last Scroll
manuscript translations

THE SEVEN BEASTS

Blessed is he that readeth, and they that hear the words of this prophesy, for he will have salvation. Behold, the beast with a leopard body and seven heads of the lion with ten horns on each head and the feet of the bear came from the depths of the seas, the bottomless pit, when light from the angels in the Realms of Life was weak. And the Beast brought demons upon mankind and seven plagues to destroy a third of the world and its people.

When people learned the wisdom of the Seven Realms of Life, the Blessings came forth and the people cast away the demons and spite the beast to thrust him back to the bottomless pit and peace returned. And it is said, the beast with seven heads and ten horns will come again one thousand years after the first millennium when light from the angels in the Realms is weak. And with him, the seven Plagues will again come forth.

And seven angels are sent to the earth and they are given seven trumpets to warn of the coming beast with seven heads and ten horns. And the seven angels, with the seven trumpets, prepared themselves to sound.

And the first trumpet sounded and it fell upon the Realm of the Mind, and it is revealed, a third of the people will have ignorance of the ways of the world and speak of ideas that are dishonest and strike down the common good. They rise to become the leaders of the world and gain power through greed, force, and dishonesty.

And the second trumpet sounded and fell upon the Realm of the Body, and it is revealed a third of people have affliction with heavy heart, thick blood, slow healing, and poor breath, and early death will come.

And the third trumpet sounded and it fell upon the Realm of Emotion, and it is revealed a third of people will feel despair and poor in spirit, and be drunk with wine, and lay down their tools, and have sadness that overcomes.

And the fourth trumpet sounded, and it fell upon the Realm of the Way of Life, and it is revealed that a third of people will have poverty, and beg for food and drink, with no bed to lay, and no refuge for comfort, and death will come to the children and the frail.

And the fifth trumpet sounded and it fell upon the Realm of Nature and it is revealed that the earth will be dry, and the rivers and seas are made bitter, animals and plants will die and a third of people have drought and no water, their tongues are parched with thirst, and famine will bring hunger upon them, and death will come.

And the sixth trumpet sounded, and it fell upon the Realm of the Spirit, and it is revealed a third of people feel hate and vengeance towards their brother and forsake them for reasons unknown, and bring wrath and violence against them.

And the seventh trumpet sounded and it fell upon the Realm of the People, and it is revealed that a third of all people will bring war against their neighbors, and through fear and greed, they raise arms against each other and bring swords to the hand of man, and they will hunt and kill one another. For a third of the world will die and the good life will then be gone for the beast has arrived.

And the people of the world do not heed the Angels and the trumpets of warning. They act against the Realms of Life and bring evil to their brothers. Then, the beast with its seven heads and ten horns, and feet of the bear comes from the depths of the seas, the bottomless pit, to bring back the demons to the people and plagues on mankind.

And a second Beast comes with the body of a lamb and the tongue of a dragon. He speaks for the first beast and tells the people about his heaven. For he comes to Earth in full view of man and brings promises of wealth and power when they live in his place. But the Beast is given power to rule but deceives the people of the earth.

And the Beast takes their light and sends his demons with their eyes of fire and deceiving spirit to act as false servants of righteousness and live in the people.

And they bring the seven plagues upon the people and they have ignorance, afflictions, despair, poverty, drought, hate, and war.

THE SEVEN REALMS OF LIFE

Behold, an angel descends down to Earth and brings the seven Realms of Life for which the light of the stars resides. And with each Realm lie the Rules of the Blessings and the secrets to the seven Blessings of Life. Those people who seek salvation in the Realms of Life and follow the truth of the Blessings will escape the carnage of the plagues. They will come out of fear and hiding and resolve to take up the Blessings of Life to bring light into the Realms.

And when a third of the people take up these Blessings in their lives, the Beast and its demons are cast back into the bottomless pit, to be shut up again, and set a seal upon him, so that they deceive the nations no more, and he shall be tormented day and night for one thousand years.

And the Blessings of Life will flourish on Earth, the light of the stars will fill the Realms again, and the plagues will end. For, the good life returns to the people and we will have peace for the next one thousand years.

So behold the seven Realms of Life, for every man hath Realms of strength for which they live in and Realms of weakness, for which they learn more.

When light from the angel shines in the Realm of the Mind, it will bring the Blessing of Wisdom and insight into the past, the present, and the future by understanding of the knowledge of man and the ways of the world by reading, studying, listening, and learning of the truth each day, and by being honest to yourself and others.

When light from the angel shines on the Realm of the Body, it will bring the Blessing of Health to the flesh and take away affliction and crippling by being active, walking, running, stretching, and using the body well each day.

When light from the angel shines in the Realm of Emotion, it will bring the Blessing of Happiness and a life of contentment that lifts you to the heavens by bringing the creative spirit with smiles and laughter, music and art, sport and games to your life each day.

When the light shines in the Realm of the Spiritual, it will bring the Blessing of Love for yourself and those around you by learning to seek help through prayer, to be calm and seek insight through meditation, to understand the meaning of your life and see your past and future and to live a life that is merciful each day.

When light from the angel shines in the Realm of the Way of Life, it will bring the Blessing of Prosperity and success in life by working hard and steady, by having good sleep and breathing clean air, by being modest in eating and drinking the purity of nature's food and water, for these will bring light to all Realms.

When light from the angel shines in the Realm of Nature, it will bring the Blessing of Beauty and abundance will come by living in and being part of the harmony with the earth its land, seas, and skies, and by being organized, clean, and not wasteful and taking care of that which surrounds you.

When light from the angel shines in the Realm of the People, it will bring the Blessing of Peace and a life of harmony and goodness by sharing and helping others, being generous and giving of yourself, and supporting those around you and the communities you live in.

THE RULES OF THE BLESSINGS

And when the people seek salvation in the Realms of Life and follow the truth of the Blessings, and take shelter in nature, for they will escape the carnage.

And the people will come out of hiding and resolve to take up the Blessings of Life. They will embrace their angels, discard their demons, and become skillful in their actions and virtuous in their being. For when each of the Blessings of Life flourish on Earth, the light of the stars will fill each Realm, the good life will come back to the people, and we will have peace again.

For he who walketh in the midst of the seven golden candlesticks will see clearly the seven Rules of the Blessings. For the journey to the divine involves each of the Blessings of Health, Wisdom, Peace, Happiness, Prosperity, Beauty, and Love. For those who achieve the Blessings will have the secret to a good life. For these Rules are revealed to bring understanding and light from the stars and help those who resolve to take up a life of the Blessings.

For those who know the Rule of Doing can take actions that bring strength into a Realm and shun actions that weaken a Realm. For light will be brought into each Realm by actions from each of the Blessings and the demons will be banished.

For those who know the Rule of Being will see virtues in those with angels from the strength of light in a Realm and vices in those with demons from weakness of light in the Realms.

For those who know the *Rule of Keys* will know how to bring strength into a Realm by bringing light in from its neighboring key Realms.

For those who know the Rule of Balance will know that to have equal strength in all Realms will bring more fullness and goodness to life.

For those who know the Rule of Moderation will take care to not bring too much strength of light into one Realm for this can weaken other Realms.

For those who know the Rule of Gatherings will understand the light of one person will spread to strengthen or weaken the light of those people around him. For when a third of the people bring positive light together in a gathering, their light will show brightest in changing the gathering for the better.

For those who know the Rule of Challenges will understand that when challenged by problems or others who take away the light from your Realms, you will have no strength when you respond by taking light from your Realms, you will have more strength to respond when you bring more light into your Realms, and you will have the most strength to respond when you bring light into the Realms of all people who gather with you.

When people understand the Rules of Blessings, the Blessings flourish on Earth, And when people are virtuous in life with strength of the light in all Realms, then peace will reign on earth and banish the Beast to the depths of the Earth for a thousand years. And nations will not lift swords against other nations and the good life of Blessings will return to the people of earth.

The Blessing of Health

And Behold, the Blessing of Health. For those who want health and to be well is through strength of light in the Realm of the Body. To strengthen this Realm is to be active, to walk, to run, to stretch, to use the body well.

For strength of the spirit in this Realm will bring angels to you that are evident as virtues to others as you show strength of the flesh, be regular and routine in health, be steady and resolute, and show courage and boldness.

Beware, for weakness of the spirit in this Realm will bring demons to live here and show as vices to others with weakness and fat of the flesh, be unsteady and cowardly with no control, and have sickness that comes easily.

And lasting weakness of the spirit in this Realm among the people will bring plagues of afflictions, pain, and sickness of the flesh.

And the Keys to bring more light into this Realm is through the Way of Life and the Nature Realms. For those who are modest in eating and drinking, to have pure food and water that rises directly from the natural springs and soils of the earth, to breath clean air, to work steady, have good sleep, are organized and clean, to take care of and waste not the abundance that you have, for the spirit flows freely from these realms into the body and strengthens in health and wellness.

THE BLESSING OF PROSPERITY

And Behold, the Blessing of Prosperity. For those who want prosperity and success in the life that one seeks is through strength of light in the Realm of the Way of Life. To strengthen this Realm is to work hard and steady, to live within your means, to have good sleep and breath clean air, to be modest in eating and drinking, and to have food and water that rises directly from the natural springs and soils of the earth, for these will bring light to all Realms and bring prosperity, success, and a life of wealth.

For strength of the spirit in this Realm will bring angels to you that are evident as virtues to others as you will be active and productive, show industry and generosity, and be modest and patient in actions, for this will show prosperity and success.

Beware, for weakness of the spirit in this Realm will bring demons to live here and show vices to others. For, they are lazy and sloth, have gluttony and greed, and are selfish, excessive, and impatient. And lasting weakness of the spirit in this Realm among a third of the people will bring plagues of poverty and destitution, and people will beg for food and drink, and have no bed to lay and no refuge for comfort.

And the Keys to bring more light into this Realm is through the Body and the Mind Realms. For those who are active, and walk, run, stretch, and those who study, listen, learn, and understand the written word and the ways of the world, the spirit flows freely from these realms into the Way of Life and strengthens you in prosperity.

The Blessing of Love

And Behold, the Blessing of Love. For those who want to receive love and to share love with others is through strength of light in the Realm of the Spirit. To strengthen this Realm is to learn to seek help through prayer, to be calm and seek insight through meditation, to understand the meaning of your life and your past, present, and future, to live a life that is merciful each day and you will find the Blessing of Love.

For strength of the spirit in this Realm will bring angels to you that are evident as virtues to others as having strong faith and beliefs, having hope and promise, be inspiring to help others see the light of the heavens, and follow a path of love for yourself and others. Beware, for weakness of the spirit in this Realm will bring demons to live here with no faith and hope, to see only doubt and darkness, and to follow a path of hate for yourself and others.

And lasting weakness of the spirit in this Realm among a third of the people will bring plagues of hate and violence without any hope and promise.

And the Keys to bring spirit to this Realm is through all other Realms. The Realm of Nature with natural beauty, care, and harmony with the natural world, the Realm of the People to share and help others, to be generous and give of yourself, and to support those around you, the Realm of the Way of Life by working hard and steady, by having good sleep and breathing clean air, by being modest in eating and drinking the purity of nature's food and water, the Realm of Emotions to be creative, to sing out with joy, to have fun with games and sport, and smile and laugh with the enjoyment of each day, the Realm of the Body by being active, exercising daily, and living a life of health, the Realm of Nature to live in harmony with the natural world, to be organized and clean, and to enhance beauty of that which surrounds you, to be part of nature and waste not, and the Realm of the Mind to listen and learn, to understand the written word, and the ways of the world. The spirit flows freely from all these realms into the Spiritual Realm and strengthens you in love of yourself and others.

Questions for discussion groups

1. Dr. Killian asks the audience how they define a good life. What are your ingredients for a good life? What barriers do you have to accomplishing them?

2. Dr. Killian presents evidence that seven Plagues, representing each Realm of our lives, are spreading around the world? Do you see any evidence of these plagues happening around you? How can you change them? Does an individual have the power to change them? What responsibilities do we have to do so?

3. Understanding the human spirit is the basis behind most religions. Yet, we know little about the human spirit. In *The Last Scroll*, they measure the human spirit with sophisticated technology. What is the human spirit and how does it manifest itself? How do you know whether your spirit is high or low? Positive or negative?

4. The *Prophecy Scroll* presents seven Realms of a person's life— the mind, body, emotions, spirit, way of life, people and natural environment around you. Do you see these different Realms in your life? What actions do you take to boost your energy in each Realm? What activities or people deplete your energy in each Realm?

5. The *Rule of Balance* suggests that it is important to understand and have balance in all Realms of your life. How important is balance in these Realms in your life? What are your strong Realms? What are your weak Realms? What activities do you do to strengthen each one? In what ways do you lose energy in each Realm?

6. The *Rule of Being* suggests that vices and virtues are demons and angels in your life, and reflects whether there is high or low energy in each Realm of a person's life. Do you see angels and demons in any people around you? What are your vices and virtues? How can you rid yourself of demons and show virtues and positive energy to others?

7. The *Rule of Moderation* suggests that you can bring too much energy into a Realm. Do you have any Realms that are excessive and may create problems in other Realms? How can you find moderation, and will it help your life?

8. The *Rule of Gatherings* suggests that when people are together in a group, they will strengthen or weaken a Realm more than when people act alone. Do you find this in the groups that you belong to such as your family, neighborhood, religious, or work group? How can you bring positive energy to the group to make them more successful and productive?

9. The *Rule of Challenges* suggests that when other people and situations drain your energy, there are different ways to react—you may take energy from other Realms, you may realize the challenge and bring in more energy, or you can help all people who gather with you to have energy. How do you respond to challenges? How could you bring in more energy to the situation? How will people around you respond to this strategy?

10. Dr. Venetre talks about the *Blessing of Health*. What strategies does she present to enhance health? What do you do in your life to prevent illness and enjoy health? What factors lead to the growing increase in chronic illness?

11. Sister Ambra talks about the *Blessing of Prosperity*. What do you do in your life to achieve prosperity and a happy productive life? How does money influence this positively or negatively? How can you maintain a happy balance between work and play? How can you prevent the plague of poverty and hunger among so many in the world?

12. Father Fabio talks about the *Blessing of Love* and that each person has their own definition. How do you define love in your life? How can you work to enhance love of yourself and those you care about? How can you prevent the plague of hate and anger among a growing number of people in the world?

OTHER BOOKS BY THIS AUTHOR...

Look for *The Seven Beasts*, the second book in *The Last Scroll* Trilogy, to be published later in 2013.

CPSIA information can be obtained at www.ICGtesting.com
Printed in the USA
LVOW06s0332280915

455978LV00001B/66/P